F. G. Cottam

Brodmaw Bay

First published in Great Britain in 2011 by Hodder & Stoughton
An Hachette UK company

First published in paperback in 2012

1

A CIP catalogue record for this title is available from the British Library

ISBN 978 0 340 98101 6

Typeset in Sabon MT by Hewertext UK Ltd, Edinburgh

Printed and bound by CPI Group (UK) Ltd, Croydon, CR0 4YY

Hodder & Stoughton policy is to use papers that are natural, renewable and recyclable products and made from wood grown in sustainable forests. The logging and manufacturing processes are expected to conform to the environmental regulations of the country of origin.

Hodder & Stoughton Ltd
338 Euston Road
London NW1 3BH

www.hodder.co.uk

For my sister, Sharon, with love and pride

After five novels and five years, acknowledgement for their unfailing encouragement and support is well overdue to some of the splendid people who work for Hodder and Stoughton. I would like to express my lasting gratitude in particular to Carolyn Caughey, Francine Toon and Eleni Fostiropoulos. To the three of you, sincere thanks.

Chapter One

James Greer sat on a modular plastic chair in the crowded A&E department of the hospital and tried the technique of visualisation to escape the panic threatening to submerge him. He pressed the pads of the thumb and forefinger of his right hand gently together. He closed his eyes. He drew in a deep breath. He pictured a shoreline in early, gentle English light. Emerald waves tumbled on to sand at the edge of the sea, smoothing out with rhythmic, dissipating force.

The sand was exposed, yellow and compacted, hissing in odd fissures and pockets on the retreat of the water, leaving behind translucent bits of shell and trailing wisps of kelp. He exhaled, at a blessed and deliberate remove, suddenly, from the chaos around him. It had worked. He was alert to the tug of his sleeve or the mention of his name over the public address system. But he was away from it, in the mental refuge of a place that meant calm and release. He even sensed he could smell the salt scent of a coastal morning.

He had learned this coping exercise two years earlier. He had been obliged to give a series of presentations. James had always suffered a secret terror of public speaking. As the moment approached, he would succumb to an attack of nerves. He would stammer and shake. So he had sought the help of a hypnotherapist.

Two sessions had been enough. He had not actually been hypnotised at either. Instead, he had been advised to deal with the onset of panic by picturing in his mind a place that symbolised calm and happiness to him. He supposed the business with his hand was meant to help with focus. He didn't over-analyse the whole procedure. It had succeeded. He had paid his fee and left the hypnotherapist's consulting room relieved and grateful for the ploy that put an end to the sweaty helplessness that the pressure of public performance had always inflicted upon him.

It was not fear of facing an audience that forced him to visualise now. It was an ordeal much more grave and testing. It was panic over the plight of his son. The call from the police station in Peckham had come an hour earlier. Jack had been mugged aboard a bus on the way home from school for his mobile phone. The level of violence used had been out of all proportion to the prize involved, his father had been told. The ambulance had delivered Jack to the hospital unconscious. Three assailants had beaten him senseless.

They had taken his wallet, too, which had delayed the process of identification. An alert constable had found a name tag on his shirt when they had stripped him at the hospital. He was concussed and the socket of his right eye was fractured. He was in theatre now, having the damage to his brain assessed. It was why his father was sitting in A&E, dreaming of a beach and breathing sonorously with his eyes clenched tightly shut. There were tears trapped under the lids of his eyes. But James knew that if he gave in to the loss of composure they signalled, he would not be of any practical use at all to his injured son.

Their Bermondsey townhouse was at the centre of London's latest fashionable district. James could lunch each day at Borough Market. His wife's steel and granite studio was on the south side of Blackfriars Bridge, with a panoramic view of the river through its tinted glass windows. They were handy for the Tate Modern and the Globe Theatre and Hay's Wharf and he was only a scenic fifteen-minute stroll north to where most of his clients were based in Clerkenwell. But schools were difficult in inner London and Jack's was in Peckham and he had been assaulted and robbed on the bus journey home by what the police were saying were members of a Somali street gang housed in one of the area's sink estates.

Jack tried not to think about the price his son had just paid for maintaining the family's metropolitan cool. He thought instead of his imaginary beach, with its emerald waves and wan English sunlight and the sand glimmering wetly under the light's gentle spread. He thought of that, amid the sprained and cut and drunk and overdosed, among the toxic casualties of a typical early evening in an inner-London hospital.

He was there for two hours before a staff nurse summoned him to see the consultant. James shook his hand, thinking him young for a neurosurgeon, observing that there was none of his son's blood on the spotless white coat the doctor wore. Maybe that was a good sign. Or maybe he had just changed out of one drenched to the elbows in gore and dropped it into a laundry bin. He smiled but the smile was tight, unreadable. The specialist might be miffed at having missed a dinner party. He might be on the brink of the delivery of tragic news.

'Sit down, Mr Greer.'

'I'll stand for what you have to tell me.'

'Very well, then. Your son will make a full physical recovery. He is severely concussed, but there is no cranial or arterial damage; no fractures to the skull, no blood clots causing any pressure to have to attempt the tricky procedure of relieving. He is young and healthy and the physical trauma will repair itself fairly rapidly. The damage to his eye socket will cause him a few weeks of pain and discomfort. But there is no evidence of nerve damage. His sight will be unimpaired. He retains his full capacity for facial expression. There will be no paralysis or permanent scarring.'

'You mean there will be no physical scarring.'

'Your son was very lucky.'

'Was he?'

The doctor was studying something on a clipboard. 'Jack was hit repeatedly about the head with a blunt instrument. Probably a tyre iron, the police think. Knives are the preferred choice of weapon among London's feral youths. In the circumstances, I'd say he's extremely lucky.'

It was all relative, James was thinking, who was thinking no longer about a beach. His thoughts were landlocked now and consigned to a sunless interior. 'How long will he have to remain here?'

'He'll be here at least a few days, under observation, as a precautionary measure. The police will wish to take a statement. As the victim of a violent crime he also qualifies for counselling, which over the coming weeks, after a trauma such as this, he will almost certainly need.'

'The hospital provides that?'

The doctor smiled his thin smile again. He tapped his clipboard with a pen. 'Of course we do, Mr Greer,' he said. 'We're a front-line resource.'

James nodded. 'May I see my son, now?'

'You may. I can't predict this with absolute certainty, but it will be at least a few hours before he comes round, probably about breakfast time tomorrow. He will be sore and thirsty and I should think very happy and relieved to see you.'

James looked at his watch. It was just after eight o'clock in the evening. He needed to call Lily. His wife was at home, fighting a mother's natural instinct to be at the bedside of her injured son, because right now their eight-year-old daughter Olivia, frantic at her brother's plight, needed a parent's care and consolation. He would make the call. The news was positive. It was all relative, as he had just conceded to himself. Relatively speaking, the duty of phoning home would be a happy one. Then he would endure the night vigil of waiting for Jack to regain consciousness.

After delivering the glad tidings to his wife, James sat at his son's bedside in the private room for which his credit card had paid. The monitoring equipment to which Jack was attached by various tubes and wires beeped discreetly every now and then. Time passed until outside, beyond the hospital buildings and its grounds, he began to hear the idling lorries and the raucous cries of the porters unloading them at the neighbouring market. Air brakes hissed, carts and trolleys clattered, laughter erupted at swapped banter. As Jack slept his oblivious, healing sleep, his father was reminded that the city in which they lived never slept at all.

There was no practical point to his being there until Jack awoke. But he was a father who very much loved his son and the situation here was way beyond the practicalities. He would not have chosen to be anywhere else. Pads of cotton wool were blood-soaked under wound lint covering Jack's head, entirely concealing his features. His chest rose and fell with his breathing and his father put a hand there gently just to feel the proof of the life in him. It was an hour before he sought any diversion beyond sitting and gazing at his son's bandaged head and face. When he did, he saw that there was a shelf of books and heaped magazines mounted to the left of the door.

The light was low in the room, but he had become accustomed to it and could see perfectly well. He got up and walked across and looked at the spines of the books. None of their titles or authors really took his fancy. He needed diversion but did not have the concentration for a plot and the books were mostly thrillers and espionage stories and romances. Only one volume intrigued him, took his eye, so he levered out the book and took it back to his chair to look at it.

It was a children's story and as soon as he glanced at the cover of the book, James was aware that Lily had been responsible for its artwork. His wife's style of illustration was vivid, atmospheric and, to him, instantly recognisable.

The front cover showed a village rising above a curved inlet as it would be viewed, or imagined, looking landward from the sea. The cottages of the village were clustered cosily under the ascent of a grassy hill contoured with deep green tussocks. The dwellings, picturesque and mostly whitewashed, rose above a sea wall. The beach was covered in orange shingle and the intense tones of the picture and its long shadows suggested sunset. To the left of the panorama, a small flotilla of fishing smacks sat at anchor. The picture was detailed and authentic-looking but James thought it much too unspoiled and charming to have been taken from life. The title of the book, lettered in gold over the deep blue sky above the summit of the sheltering hill, was *Brodmaw Bay*.

The calendar provided what slight plot the story possessed. It followed the seasons from autumn through to summer and the bay was pictured by his wife in all its varied and entrancing moods. It was a tribute, he thought, to the fertility of Lily's imagination, as well as her decorative skill. Brodmaw Bay had not just charm but character. He was distracted, looking up every now and then from the images on the pages to watch and listen to Jack's breathing, making sure for himself, despite the battery of hi-tech monitors, that his son was not slipping elusively away from the short life he had enjoyed.

The author of the book was credited, but he could find his wife's name nowhere between the covers or on the fly-leaf either. It had been published by Chubbly & Cruff, a house he had never heard of, and the year of publication was given as 1993. Lily had still been at college. She must have done it for rent money in the period when she'd been struggling along on a tiny grant and the tips from Covent Garden waitressing shifts.

How things had changed, he thought. Now, she was one of the most sought-after illustrators of children's books working anywhere in the world. Characters she had copy-righted were animated on children's DVDs. They appeared in comics and on the backs of cereal packets and it all ticked along very lucratively.

Brodmaw Bay was an atmospheric place, with its slate roofs and lobster pots and steep cobbled lanes. There was a chandlery and a boatbuilder's yard and a butcher's shop with partridges and hares hanging from hooks above the display of sausages and choice cuts of lamb and beef in the window. There was a pub with a wooden sign and welcoming yellow light in the darkness behind its mullioned glass. The place was all of a piece, James thought, an idealised bit of Little England, quaint and folkloric, from a time easy to feel nostalgic for that had never really occurred.

Only one image jarred in this portrait of an idyllic coastal village. A church was pictured on one page towards the back of the book. It was seen from the perspective of a gate leading to its porch and in the foreground there were graves to either side of the short path to the church door. The season was winter. Snow sat in white slabs topping the headstones of the graves and sagged in ripples on the roof of the porch. The headstones had mostly surrendered to some instability of the earth and were canted at angles that seemed sinister. Moss and lichen had crawled across their inscriptions. They did not look as still as James thought gravestones should. The church spire was crooked too, a casualty of the subsidence that had shifted the graves, but the effect on it was slyer, more subtle. The church had about it the sunken character of faith undermined.

He saw that the windows of the church were smashed, the small panes between their lead lattices, each and every one of them, broken. The damage looked deliberate and vindictive. Then he noticed that the door in the porch hung slightly open, an iron hasp twisted where he supposed a padlock had been forced, a hint of darkness where it opened inward, to the right of the doorframe.

Studying this scene, James shook his head. The whole image was out of sympathy with the rest of the illustrations, weirdly out of kilter with the mood of starry-skied, lantern-lit cosiness conjured by the other pictures in the book. He thought its inclusion a misjudgement, on the part of his wife and on the part also of whoever had overseen the editing. But its inclusion suggested something intriguing. It hinted that Brodmaw Bay, far from being a townscape of his wife's imagination, was somewhere real she had simply documented with her palette and brush.

Jack groaned then in his sleep. He coughed and the cough was wet-sounding and his father rose and waited with dread for blood to bubble and well from his mouth. He continued to wait. He thought about saying a prayer. Instead, he just watched, tense, with his own breath poised. But no blood came. He realised that the book about Brodmaw Bay was still in the grip of one hand. He thought the location sounded Cornish. It had resided in the Cornwall of his clever wife's dreams in her student days. Either that or she had actually been there. He must ask her about it. He walked over to the shelf and put back the book.

Towards dawn his bedside vigil was interrupted. A nurse came into the room and measured Jack's pulse and took his temperature and made sure that the drip providing him with fluid was functioning properly and the bag supplying the saline solution still adequately full. She told James that it would be at least another few hours before his son stirred. It would be about lunchtime before the sedative wore off sufficiently. She smiled, he supposed to relieve the look of worry his face wore. She said that Jack's heart rate was slow and steady and his pulse strong. James nodded. The nurse patted his shoulder and left. He thought the contact probably a breach of protocol. It was comforting and he was grateful for it.

Light was entering the room, through its single tall window, from a courtyard space beyond the glass. It was June and dawn broke early in London in June. The room was in an old part of the hospital. The floor was black and white tiles of marble scored and faded with feet and polishing. There were still pipes on the wall, painted over, that must have fed the gas lamps that once provided the room's illumination. James decided he would go and get something to eat. Somewhere would be open. There would be a café, one of those old places with Formica-topped tables and steam from a tea urn and buoyant London banter. He needed a break, a change of scene. He needed to get some perspective on what had happened to his son and its implications.

He walked out in the early summer air to cobbles and bronze street bollards and iron railings topping old walls and the peal of a summoning bell from a church probably the work of Wren or Hawksmoor in the aftermath of the Great Fire in the time of Charles II and his Restoration. He could smell the cool drift on the wind of the Thames. This was an old part of London and the city wore its history in this vicinity in every lane and almost every building. Once it had charmed him. Once it had beguiled him.

It had gone further than that, hadn't it, he thought, sitting down to his fortifying mug of café tea. London in his younger life had been his vindication. The fact that he had prospered there and bought a home and found a wife and raised a family there and established a professional reputation had been the proof of him. He had arrived as a raw and provincial northerner and London had tested and challenged and then opened its welcoming and generous embrace to him.

He had believed the Johnsonian adage about the man who was tired of London being tired of life. But he did not believe it any more. The older you got, the more abrasive London became. Or perhaps it was just that the older you got, the less tolerance you had for London's unchanging abrasiveness. As you matured and your values and responsibilities became inevitably different, aspects of the capital revealed themselves that were less and less easy to tolerate.

And the place was changing. The demographic was altering. The *Guardian* was James Greer's newspaper of choice. But he had eyes in his head.

Turkish drug gangs fought turf wars in Finsbury Park.

Muslim kids from Pakistan had beaten up a Shoreditch vicar because they were affronted by a church they claimed should have been transformed into a mosque. It didn't matter to them that the church had been consecrated in the eighteenth century. Their own faith had been set in stone much earlier than that. Now a group of Somali youths, schooled in the medieval ghetto values of Mogadishu, had beaten his son almost to death in Peckham for the sake of a mobile phone with a street worth of perhaps ten pounds.

It was called white flight, wasn't it, the middle-class escape from this sort of urban pressure? That was the contemptuous name given it by the lofty liberal commentators who still set the tone in James Greer's newspaper of choice. But he didn't care. He really didn't, not any more. He had tolerated the alternative for long enough. What had happened to Jack had been both a punishment and a warning. London had been very good to him and even more lavishly generous to Lillian. But they had changed. They had become vulnerable. And the city in which they had both lived the bulk of their adult lives had changed too. If they were not to risk becoming its victims, the casualties of its changed character and increasing hazards, they should exercise the luxury of the choice their prosperity had given them and simply leave.

He was down to the leaves of his tea. It was one of those places where the beverage was poured from the sort of steel communal pot they would have used in cafés just like this one seventy years ago in the London Blitz. He was seated on a tall stool at a narrow counter that ran the length of the window. Behind him he could hear market porters and cabbies and hospital orderlies debating the previous evening's middleweight title fight. He could smell bacon frying and the pungent tartness of brown sauce smeared on warm plates. Outside, through the steamy glass, he could see the flagstones of the pavement glazed by the strengthening sun. Directly outside was a cast-iron lamp post, thickly painted in a municipal black and carrying a crest cast in Victorian times.

James Greer liked his Dickens and his Peter Ackroyd and he thought he knew what they were feeling when they celebrated London in their prose reveries. He shared the sentiment. He loved Gabriel's Wharf and Hampstead Heath and the river at low tide at Chelsea Reach and the Tate Modern and the hung game and pewter light of Borough Market at Christmas time when the stalls smelled of mulled wine and freshly baked bread and biscuits spiced with cinnamon. But he could carry all of these things with him in his memory. It was time to leave. It was time for the sake of the kids, for the sake of all of them. The adventure of resettlement would be exactly what Jack would need to help with his recovery from the trauma of attack and injury.

His son would not make it back to school for what remained of his term, even if they elected to stay. It would soon be the summer holidays and the best time possible as far as schools were concerned to make the break. Children were adaptable. Both Jack and Olivia had good friends they would certainly miss. But they had their social networking sites so the loss would not turn to grief. And he did not think that Jack would miss the running gauntlet of his daily bus ride to the Peckham badlands.

When he thought about it, he did not honestly know how Lillian might react to his insistence that they uproot and leave. She had shared his sofa-born dreams of escape to somewhere at the seaside. They even subscribed to *Coast* magazine and had often spun verbal fantasies together about a wave-lapped refuge from their daily lives in Ventnor or Whitstable. But he did not know everything about his wife. In some ways she was unpredictable and in some ways unreadable.

After fifteen years together, Lillian was still capable of surprising him. It was, he supposed, one of the reasons why he retained the fascination with her he had held at the outset, when they had first met. It was an attribute that had helped keep their relationship fresh despite the mundanities of shared parenthood.

He thought that she might miss Starbucks and the gym. She was a pretty solitary individual socially. More accurately, they were rather self-contained and insular as a couple. He did not think she would particularly miss the people loosely regarded as her friends. What was certain was that as an illustrator, she was even better placed professionally than he was to live wherever they chose. The only question was whether he would be able to persuade her to do it.

He could not insist on the change. He was not the dominant partner. They were not really quite equals in their relationship. She earned more than he did. By any measure she was the more successful of the two of them. He might be able to persuade her to try a different sort of life and after what had happened to Jack he thought that she would certainly consider it seriously. But he could not dictate such radical and wholesale change in the pattern of their lives.

He looked at the leaves drying now in the bottom of his mug. The mug was a white, ceramic item and the leaves a green so dark they looked black. They formed a pattern that was dense and unreadable. But then James Greer did not believe the future could be read in tea leaves or crystal balls or tarot cards or anything else. You determined your fate for yourself. You created your own destiny and you did it out of determination, ambition and force of will.

He thought of his unconscious son and it occurred to him that fate was decided most by need. His was compelling. Theirs was compelling. Their need for change was urgent. It was escape, of course. He was honest enough with himself to admit that. But it was something else, too. It was opportunity. It would not just be an adventure for Jack, but for the four of them.

A police officer was standing at Jack's bedside when he returned to the hospital room. He was immaculately uniformed, bareheaded, around six feet tall, about thirty years of age and black. He introduced himself as Detective Sergeant Alec McCabe. They shook hands. McCabe looked him directly in the eye. They probably stressed the importance of eye contact on the courses they all did these days. The policeman had a firm handshake, but then he was powerfully built. James thought about all the articles he had read over recent years about institutional racism in the Metropolitan Police. He wondered what rank McCabe would have achieved by now if he had been white.

'They've left your son in a dreadful state. I'm very sorry, sir.'

'Will you catch them?'

'Catching them will be the easy part. Charging them will be a formality. Bringing a successful prosecution might be more difficult.'

James gestured at his son. 'Why would it be? There's no shortage of evidence of assault. It might even be a case of attempted murder.'

McCabe nodded. 'I don't wish to sound cynical, sir. But for some elements of the legal profession, recent human rights legislation has turned defending the sort of offenders who did this into a very lucrative industry. Bringing a prosecution will not be straightforward. Technically, your son's assailants were boys. Even if they're proven guilty at trial, even if the jury agrees, a custodial sentence isn't guaranteed. They might even be on bail or parole or serving out community orders or under probationary supervision already. They're feral. This will not be a first offence.'

'Welcome to London in the twenty-first century,' James said.

McCabe looked at the boy in the bed and raised an eyebrow. 'You agree with me?'

'I was born in Brixton, Mr Greer. I was raised just off Coldharbour Lane. I got out as soon as I could. I live with my wife and daughter in Kent. The commute's a slog, costly in time and in money. But for my family, it's worth it.'

'Feral, Detective Sergeant,' James said. 'I've heard that description used twice now. What exactly does it mean?'

'These youths are wild. They are literally untamed. It means that they never plan a crime and they never consider the consequences. Notions such as ownership and personal integrity are completely alien to them. They regard anything they want as theirs by right. They act without compunction. There was CCTV on the bus where the attack was carried out. The whole event will likely have been filmed. The cameras are supposed to be a deterrent. Nothing deters them, though.'

'Can the film be used at the trial?'

'If it doesn't appear in public prior to the trial and thus pose a potential threat to judicial fairness. If footage appears on YouTube or if stills are used in newspapers pre-trial, it won't be allowed as evidence.'

James bit his lip and looked at the floor.

'This gang will be known to our community officers on

the ground in Peckham. But only locking them up in a barred cell with a locked steel door can really inhibit their behaviour. You can't modify it. They have no understanding of or respect for the values we live by.'

'For fuck's sake, McCabe, why are they even here?'

The policeman shrugged. 'They're refugees from a war zone. They'll likely have been granted asylum. They have their human rights.'

'Then they have an obligation to behave like human beings.'

McCabe smiled and glanced at the boy in the bed. 'I couldn't agree with you more,' he said. 'And I will do everything I can to catch them and ensure that they are convicted.'

'And subsequently deported?'

'A conviction and a custodial is the very best you can hope for. The defence will argue that it breaches their human rights to send them back to the place that brutalised them in the first place and made them into what they are. I've dealt with several cases like this. The Home Secretary will say otherwise in a *Newsnight* soundbite, but he is lying when he does. There is no chance at all of repatriation.'

'But your cases generally go to trial? Please tell me you have a good conviction rate.'

'I do. I have an excellent conviction rate. I believe in what I do for a living and I'm good at it, sir.'

When DS McCabe had gone, James took out his laptop and did a search for Chubbly and Cruff. More accurately, he did a search for Chubbly & Cruff, because that ampersand seemed so much a part of the character of that particular publishing house. He remembered that the 1980s had been the age of the ampersand in marketing all those bogus heritage brands so popular then. Chubbly & Cruff sounded exactly like one of them, though the book on the shelf in the hospital room had been published in 1993.

There was absolutely nothing on the publisher when he did his internet search. Nor was there anything on the title Lillian had illustrated for them. James concluded that Chubbly & Cruff had been a short-lived project, probably the still-born brainchild of some marketeer in bright red braces and spectacles with oversize frames in matching colour. He glanced at Jack, who was still sleeping deeply. And he did a search for Brodmaw Bay itself. Here, he had immediate success. The little port was real. It was located on the southerly coast of Cornwall. Recent photographs showed it to be entirely unspoiled.

There was a fairly recent piece about the place, a sort of essay or meditation written by a man called Richard Penmarrick. It had been carried in a couple of the Sunday newspaper supplements and travel sections in the autumn of 2008 and appeared also, slightly annotated, in an issue of *Reader's Digest*. Penmarrick was a local man, the piece implied of some standing in the Brodmaw community. His essay took the form of a tribute to the unchanging values of the place. James read it. When he had finished he glanced from his laptop screen to the bed and the still shape of his sleeping son. Then he read it again, more carefully.

I write these words from the desk of my library. The library is sited on the first floor at the front of my house and the house itself is sited on the rising ground to the rear of the Cornish coastal village of Brodmaw Bay. It is early morning. The window of my library runs the length of the room. Through it, I can see the boats returning with their nets hauled and their holds, I hope, full of freshly caught fish. The lead vessels lie low in the water, an encouraging sign.

I can hear the clatter of beer kegs on the cobbles as the draymen unload outside the cellar of the high street pub. A milkman on his rounds is whistling and the tune carries cleanly through the salt air. Above me, the gulls are gathering in the sky with familiar shrieks. The hoardings are coming off the shop fronts and I can see a string of pennants testing the breeze, fluttering as they rise on the flagpole above the chandlery. There is the hammering of nails into the teak planks of a hull in Billy Jasper's seafront yard.

I've been pondering on the subject of tradition. The old traditions are dying out. In some places they have been revived for the sake of profit from tourism and exist as cheap parodies of what they once signified. Elsewhere, though, there is a general and persistent pattern of decline of custom and ritual that is perhaps inevitable, as populations, once isolated, succumb to the migratory shifts that seem so much a part of the way life is lived in our transient time.

There are exceptions to this new rule, of course. The bonfire parades come to mind, celebrated every November in the Sussex town of Lewes. Lewes lies only seven miles across the Downs from its garish modern neighbour, Brighton. But spend a Bonfire Night in Lewes and look at the faces in the torchlight processions and watch the nonchalant way even the children trail their burning cargos and parade their flaming torches through the streets. You are in an ancient English town. The mood and atmosphere are unmistakable and unique. You could not be anywhere else in the world at any other moment. Why would you wish to be?

So it is each April 30 in Brodmaw. Walpurgis Eve is a pagan celebration with its origins stretching murkily back to at least the eighth century. It might have begun in the Scandinavian countries much earlier than that. But it has been a tradition in Brodmaw for as long as surviving archives record and as far as local folk memory is able to recall. Mention of it was made by an irate cleric in the years immediately prior to the Norman Conquest. This pompous prior considered the public ritual an affront to the Almighty.

It might be said that in the intervening millennium nothing very much has changed. The established Church still frowns upon what it sees as the mischievous antics of the Walpurgis Eve pagans. In the ancient parts of Europe, the priests and ministers see the glow of the fires from their porches and shake their pious heads. Perhaps they see it as sacrilegious. Perhaps they simply resent the competition.

For my part, since the Brodmaw event is hosted on my land, I take a very different view. I see our April ritual as the innocent celebration of seasonal change. We light our great pyres and sing our cherished songs and dance the self-same steps as our forefathers did. There is comfort in familiarity and joy at the return of light and warmth to our little corner of the world. And when I look at my costumed neighbours, at their flushed faces as they recite with me in unison the words that greet our dawn, I am reminded of who and where I am. And I am pleased and fulfilled and rightly and completely unashamed.

Identity is a precious attribute, increasingly threatened by the promiscuous values of modern life. But I am a Brodmaw man, a Cornishman and an Englishman and proud. I would not lightly surrender the unique and ancient traditions that have helped shape me.

I am obliged at this point to confront the paradox of political correctness. In pleading the case for local custom, it seems in our intolerant times that any resident of any small town risks accusations of insularity. This is particularly true of a local landowner, such as I am guilty of being. But Brodmaw is an inclusive place. Visitors have always been warmly welcomed. Fresh blood is lifeblood, after all.

In championing tradition, I am not adopting the fortress mentality of the regional bigot. I am simply doing what it is in my power to do to preserve that which I most value. In a country criss-crossed by motorways and studded by the totemic masts of mobile phone networks, you might think the Little England of Chesterton and Brooke and Belloc and Housman gone for ever. But we still have it here in Brodmaw Bay, unsullied and somehow magical.

Some might disparage the very name and notion of Little England. But I do not. I cherish it. And I will do all in my power to preserve my piece of it.

James thought that Richard Penmarrick could only have written this article in response to some critical attack. Its tone was an uneasy mix of defensiveness and defiance. He did not really, personally, have an opinion on paganism. He had seen the druids at the summer solstice on the evening news at Stonehenge. The footage tended to raise a smile. He knew the old faith survived in the ancient parts of Britain marked by such enigmatic features as burial mounds and standing stones. Those features were found mostly in the western counties of England. Nowhere was more westerly than Cornwall.

He had been to the bonfire celebration in Lewes. His brother had lived there for a time. He had thought it entertaining and sinister in equal measure. But the Lewes event had its origin in Christian religious conflict and Protestant martyrdom. However bizarrely, it commemorated historic fact. By contrast, Walpurgis Eve was a black magical celebration, wasn't it? Penmarrick's comparison was at the least disingenuous. He was comparing chalk and cheese.

What was really magical about the piece he had just read

for the second time was what James thought for its author would be the throwaway section, the second paragraph, where he had painted a careless picture of the port summoned from its slumber in the early morning. For James, that paragraph offered the promise of something serene and idyllic, a coastal refuge where the future would seem bright and beautiful at the dawn of each new day.

The place described in that paragraph sounded many miles and a hundred years away from the volatile ethnic stew of contemporary London and the threat of violence on its streets to which his precious son had fallen savage victim.

In the bed, as though aware of his father's thoughts and the violent emotion prompting them, Jack stirred for the first time. James looked for the spreading bloodstain of the haemorrhage he dreaded, but the bandage remained unmarked. He saw that there was sunlight through the window in a splash on Jack's face and wondered if it was bothering the boy. He went and closed the blind over the window, without taking his eyes off his son. Gloom enveloped the room.

There was a sound from Jack's throat. It was the first audible sign of life and James tensed and approached the bed and, in the grey absence of light, took his son's limp hand in his and squeezed it. His own fingers and palm were gripped in return with a strength that surprised him. The sound, a sort of cough, emanated again from his son's throat. It did not sound like Jack. It sounded deep and somehow gleeful and a note sounded by someone far older than his adolescent son.

His body had started to shake. The bed was on wheels. James could hear them scrape back and forth in minute but rapid progress on the parquet beneath them. The sound came out of Jack again. James used his free hand to press the bell above the bed that would summon a nurse. He feared that his son was fitting. The neurosurgeon had not mentioned the hazard of a brain seizure. He might choke on his tongue. He might suffer heart failure. A noise rumbled and barked deep within Jack, further down than his voice box, from in his chest. Words emerged from his mouth. His grip on his father's hand tightened.

'Gresh,' he said, 'flood.'

A nurse bustled into the room.

'Gresh flood.'

The nurse bent over her patient from the other side of the bed, checked that his air passages were clear and then moved the position of his head on the pillow and raised his free arm to take his pulse.

'Gresh flood,' Jack said. He tried to raise his head from the pillow. His grip on his father's hand was briefly strong enough to inflict real pain. Then it weakened. The head sank back down. The bed stopped shaking on its wheels. His breathing became regular once again.

'He is fine,' the nurse said.

'What was that?'

'It was a dream, perhaps, but he is all right now and should awaken before long.' She looked around in the gloomy light. With the high ceiling and painted-over pipes of its obsolete gas supply, it looked a grim sickroom.

'Open the blinds,' the nurse said, 'and he will probably come around.' She poured a fresh glass of water from the carafe on the night stand next to the bed.

'His eyes are bandaged.'

'The sun is shining strongly outside. He will sense the brightness and warmth. They will bring him back to consciousness reassured.'

James nodded, reminded that nursing was more a vocation than it was a job. He walked across and opened the blind and sunshine spilled into the room. Jack stirred. His head shifted towards the light and he moaned softly in what his father recognised as his real voice.

'Fresh blood' had been the phrase he had uttered in that gleeful-sounding earlier growl. He had been trying to say, 'Fresh blood.' Jack had moments before read the phrase in Richard Penmarrick's Brodmaw Bay eulogy. It must have been a form of telepathy, thought James, who did not believe in coincidence. He did not really believe in telepathy either, but was fairly certain of the two words Jack had been trying to articulate. He must have communicated them to his unconscious son. In the context of the article it had seemed an innocuous phrase. In isolation, in the presence of his bandaged, wounded child, the form of words was sinister and repulsive.

Jack came around slowly. The nurse gave him a drink of water and then left them to their privacy, promising to return in a little while with soup. James looked at her objectively, noticing her in physical detail beyond the uniform and her busy efficiency, for the first time, as she glanced at him before leaving. She was slight and blonde and pretty, drawn and a bit pale with tiredness, blue-eyed, her hair restrained by clips. Of course she was tired, he thought, as she smiled briefly at him and left. She was no more than twenty-two or twenty-three and she was manning a front-line resource.

James sat and held his son's hands in both of his on the blanket of the bed. 'Do you remember what happened, Jack?'

'Dad? Where am I?'

'You're in a hospital bed.'

'Where's Mum?'

'She's at home, with Olivia.'

Jack nodded. 'I remember all of it. Well, I remember it all up to the point where they beat me unconscious. I must have a hard head, Dad. It took a lot of blows.'

'The doctor says you're going to be okay, son. You'll make a full recovery, he's confident of that.'

'I tried to fight back. But there were three of them and one of them had a tyre iron. It isn't like in a film, where they queue up and Jet Lee or Jason Statham or somebody takes them on one at a time. In real life, they all come at you at once.'

'Did no one on the bus try to help?'

James smiled. 'Get real. This was Peckham High Street, Dad. Peckham's a place where heroes are thin on the ground.'

James nodded, which was pointless because his son's eyes were bandaged and therefore blind. He felt relief and shame, both emotions very strong in him and struggling for ascendancy. He thought that shame was winning. He should have been a better father than to put his son at risk. He would never do anything so irresponsible again. He would protect his children as a father should who was deserving of the name. He would get his family out of the war zone London had become. He was resolved.

'I'd like to see Mum.'

'You won't be seeing anything for a while, Jack.'

'You know what I mean.'

'I'll call her.'

Lillian brought Olivia with her. She had established over the phone that Jack was a fit sight for his sister to see.

'There's no blood, just bandages,' James said. 'She'll be relieved, I think. He isn't slurring his words or anything, Lily. The trauma seems to be entirely physical.'

'Time will tell where that's concerned,' Lillian said. 'But it sounds as though it's better to bring her than not.'

They burst into the room less than an hour after the summoning call, a beautiful woman and her equally beautiful daughter, both possessed of a careless glamour their ordeal of concern over Jack had done nothing to diminish. They looked stylish and prosperous and a little fraught. And then they looked dismayed at the quantity of gauze wrapping the head and concealing the features of the prone figure on the bed.

Jack sensed the presence of his mother immediately and managed to sit up as James got out of the way and she sat and hugged him hard, holding his damaged head against her chest, the tears leaving her eyes so forcefully with sorrow that they dribbled down her cheeks. Olivia had started crying too. She turned to her father for comfort and he put his arms around her and her face, hot and damp now, not composed and beautiful, sought refuge and consolation against his chest.

There was a clock on the wall of the hospital room. It was an old-fashioned item with a ridged case fashioned from black Bakelite. It was an electric clock, not battery-powered, the movement fed by a current that sent the second hand coursing smoothly in its circular progress rather than jerking around the face by the second.

James Greer looked at the clock, quietly recording time, as it must have for decades. And he thought about how unbearable that moment and the moments to follow it would have been had his son not survived the attack that had put him in the hospital.

Time would heal. The old cliché would vindicate itself now. But if Jack had died, time instead would goad and torture and stretch forward bleak and interminable. Where there was sadness and relief in their togetherness in that room, there would have been only loss and desolation and he did not think they would have survived it, the three of them, intact. It would have broken what remained of their family. The grief would have sundered them. He was certain of it.

About fifteen minutes after the arrival of his mother and sister, Jack fell asleep again. James was not surprised at this. The attack had taken its physical toll. His body was tired. He had eaten a soporific bowl of broth only a few minutes before their arrival. And the emotion of the moment, intensely felt, would have fatigued him further. He had a long way to go to recover his strength, despite the surgeon's upbeat prognosis. But it was sleep and not unconsciousness he had lapsed into and sound sleep was a healer in itself.

James asked Olivia to stay with Jack. She nodded and smiled. Her expression told him it was a duty she was pleased to be charged with. She would text them should her brother stir in their absence. He took his wife across the cobbled courtyard of the hospital and out through its historic gateway. It was late afternoon now but the traffic was heavy, as it always was. They crossed the road and found a coffee shop and sat where it was quiet, at the rear.

Lillian smiled at her husband over her cappuccino. 'I could do with something stronger,' she said.

'It could have been worse.'

She sipped. 'Infinitely so,' she said.

'Do you blame me?'

'Not in the slightest. Do you blame yourself?'

As the parent with the stronger academic background, James had carried the deciding vote in choosing their children's schools. There had been some debate about private education. They had opted against it on the principle that real life had to be lived in public. Education was the preparation for it. 'Yes,' he said. 'I do. I think it is entirely my fault.'

She had put down her cup. He reached for his wife's hands across the table. She returned his grip with gentle force. 'I want us to get out, Lily.'

'We've endured a nightmare, so you want us to pursue a dream. That's very you, James. Let me guess: Ventnor? Whitstable? It's always some idyllic coastal location you fantasise about.'

'There's no reason we couldn't do it, Lily. And every reason now that we should.'

'No reason other than the disruption to four lives, two of them only half-formed. And there's Jack's rehabilitation. That will take months.'

'Weeks, the surgeon said. There could be no better rehab than resettlement, somewhere beautiful and safe.'

'Where do you have in mind, James?'

'Somewhere you once knew pretty well. I'm thinking about Brodmaw Bay.'

'I don't know it.'

'You do.'

'I don't tell lies. And I can assure you I've never heard of Brodmaw Bay in my life,' Lillian said.

Chapter Two

Jack was allowed home after five nights in hospital. By that time the bandages had been unwrapped from his eyes and the swelling had lessened. He was given what he called his Phantom mask to wear to protect his damaged eye socket. He liked it because he'd seen some famous footballers wearing the contraption in matches on television, after suffering similar injuries. But he had no intention of wearing his. He did not plan to risk further damage until well after his facial bones had knitted strongly. The mask would be nothing more than a souvenir.

After a week, he was interviewed, in the presence of his parents, by Detective Sergeant McCabe. By then three Somali youths had been arrested and charged with aggravated assault and robbery with violence. They had been bailed. A trial date was yet to be set. The weapon had been found and from that had been recovered the DNA of both Jack and one of his alleged assailants. There may have been no heroes on Peckham High Street that afternoon, but there had been two fellow bus passengers prepared to come forward and make detailed witness statements.

Then there was the CCTV evidence. This was not only admissible but also quite damning, DS McCabe told the Greer family. The case was not exactly cut and dried, because no case ever was. But it was very strong. Despite it, the perpetrators had indicated that they would enter a not guilty plea. He was obliged to caution Jack that defence counsel would likely call him to the stand for cross-examination. It would bring the event vividly back to the present. It would be an ordeal for him.

'Are you comfortable with that, Jack?'

'I want them punished, Alec.'

The detective had insisted that Jack address him by his Christian name. They had bonded very quickly over a shared allegiance to a particular football club. James Greer took no interest whatsoever in the game. But Jack was a talented player and, like DS McCabe, a passionate supporter of Chelsea FC. They had waxed nostalgic about the great days under the management of the Portuguese maestro José Mourinho, the self-elected Special One. They had swapped eulogies about the world-class midfielder, Frank Lampard. This had all quietly amused James, who calculated that when the Special One had left Chelsea, his son had only been about eight years old.

Even at that age, though, his birthday present had been a replica kit. He'd won a Southwark-wide, borough-run keepy-uppy competition held for under-tens that year. Now a couple of London clubs were sending scouts to watch the games he played for South London Boys. Or they had been, before the attack and his injury. He had the off-season, the whole of the summer to recover. He would recover of course, but, if his father had his way, Jack had played his last youth match for any team based in the capital.

They were in the sitting room of their handsome Bermondsey house. James had seen McCabe raise an appreciative eyebrow when he'd shown him in. He had inventoried the wall-mounted Bang and Olufsen plasma widescreen and the Naim audio components stacked in their steel and granite rack. He had catalogued the artwork, carefully accrued and proudly hung by Lillian. You could not live like this on a detective sergeant's remuneration. Not if you were honest, you couldn't, and James thought DS McCabe probably as straight as they came. He had accepted a cup of coffee and James had gone and made it and he sat with the mug rested in his hand on his knee.

Lillian said to him, 'Would it jeopardise the chances of a prosecution if Jack refused to take the stand?'

'I'm not going to refuse to take the stand, Mum,' Jack said. 'I want them punished. I want to help to put them away.'

'It would be far better if he were prepared to testify,' McCabe said to Lillian. 'He's clearly attacked in the CCTV footage. The attack is sudden and unprovoked. But before he's hit with the tyre iron and subdued, for the first half minute of the fight, Jack is actually getting the better of it. It would be much more damning if he could talk the jury through the film. He could stress the fact that they were total strangers to him. That's more effective coming from him under oath. Your son has an engaging personality. He's a very sympathetic character.'

And you want them nailed, James thought. You're a copper for reasons that go a long way beyond the uniform and the pension provision. He wondered what sort of childhood McCabe had endured. He looked more than capable of taking care of himself now. He looked well capable of taking care of anyone else, come to that. But he had been small and vulnerable once. He'd said he had a daughter. Should he go on to have a son James thought the boy would be very fortunate in having him for a father.

To his mother, Jack said, 'I don't need the kid gloves treatment, Mum. I'm not traumatised.'

'You were violated.'

'No, I wasn't. I was beaten up. I got my head bashed in by a gang of scumbag thieves who robbed my wallet and mobile. What was in the wallet? A five pound Virgin top-up voucher and my Oyster card, that's what. They could have killed me for that. They didn't care. I want them locked up and the key thrown away.'

McCabe stood. He put down his empty coffee cup on the low table in front of where he'd sat as he rose. He tugged his tunic absently straight and looked from Lillian to James and said, 'With respect, the lad has a point.'

'We'll be the judge of that,' James said. But he said it for Lillian's benefit. He actually felt proud of Jack's mental strength and decisiveness. He had never thought of himself as decisive and it was a quality he could easily admire in his son. Of course, Jack had inherited it from his mother.

That evening James went on to the Bookfinder website and sourced a copy of the illustrated Brodmaw Bay volume published in 1993 by Chubbly & Cruff. A shop in Hay-on-Wye had a copy they claimed was in pristine condition priced at thirty-five pounds and James ordered it with a feeling of relief. He had begun to think that it did not actually exist, that it was a figment of an imagination heightened by the awful anxiety of waiting for his son to return to consciousness and cogent life in the hospital room.

He did not really allow himself to believe in the book's existence until two days later, when a large heavy envelope lined with bubble-wrap arrived in the post, bearing the logo of the shop he had sourced it from on its gummed flap. He opened the envelope straight away, in the kitchen. The kitchen had a glass wall for which they had sought and been granted planning permission seven years earlier, shortly after moving in, a couple of years before the dwellings in their street had acquired their current lofty status in the property market.

Their glass kitchen wall seemed more and more an act of vandalism or even desecration to James. But it did allow in a lot of light and in the bright morning he was able to sit at their breakfast bar and examine the book in a way he had not been able to, distracted, a week earlier in Jack's hospital room.

In the chrome and glass and stone of the Greers' bright kitchen, the painted images of the little port looked more mysterious and folkloric than they had viewed at the hospital. Light brooded and coalesced in some of the illustrations, as though they depicted a scene at dawn or dusk. There was a flushed look to the cobbles and slates on the roofs. The ruined church looked darkly sinister, the smashed stained glass of its windows, portals of black mystery. The pub and the butcher's shop, though, had only increased in their charm and the vista of the village from the sea was utterly enchanting.

It was still only six in the morning. The post arrived early and James was an early riser. Lillian would wake with her alarm call at seven and Olivia would stir half an hour after that. It was a school day. Jack was still a couple of weeks away from his potential return to school. Potential only, because his father had determined that he was never going back there.

James put the coffee pot on, his eyes on the book on the polished grain of the kitchen counter. Its images had reminded him that Cornwall was probably the English county richest in folklore and legend and myth. It had been the only Celtic kingdom in ancient England, hadn't it? It had been isolated. He did not know enough about Cornwall. He would have to do some research into the history of the place.

He was more convinced than ever that his wife had illustrated the book. It was her work, vivid, clever and unmistakable. It had that spellbinding charm and originality that had made her so successful. The details in the illustrations had a charm independent of his wife's style. But the way they had been portrayed added to their allure. Her touch with a brush was seductive, beguiling. It had a dreamlike quality that had made her fortune. He had not calculated it to the pound, but they both knew that she earned substantially more than he did.

Theoretically, they were peers in their relationship and they ran their family as a democracy. But Lillian's professional success and the relative wealth it had brought meant that important choices could not be made if she felt any reluctance over them. He was allowed the illusion of equality, but decisions were never reached without her assent, which meant that, in reality, she made them. There was a name for this. He remembered it from his own school history lessons. It was called benevolent despotism. That was harsh, he thought, hearing the feathery thump of his wife's feet descending the stairs, because Lillian was not really by temperament at all despotic. But it was accurate. It was the truth.

She came into the kitchen, tousled and lovely, her dark blonde hair tangled around her head and shoulders, her breasts pushing against the taut sheen of her satin dressing gown. She rested a hip against the counter and picked up the book and hefted and opened it and the colour drained from her face.

'Jesus,' she said.

'You can see what I mean.'

'It's unbelievable.'

'Except that you're holding it in your hands.'

'I can't believe it.'

'I think you're going to have to, Lily.'

'Jesus,' she said again.

Her eyes rose from the page she was studying to meet his. She had pale blue eyes and they were startling in the bright light of the morning kitchen, because her pupils had narrowed to nothing with the shock of what she had just seen. 'It's like some uncanny forgery,' she said. 'I mean, these are my pictures, James. This is my work. But I swear to God I have no recollection of this job whatsoever. I would take an oath on a Bible that I have never been to this place.'

'You don't believe in God.'

'No more than I believe in magic or predestination. Or re-incarnation, come to that.' She had turned to the frontispiece.

'It was published in 1993,' James said.

'Then the illustration must have been done the previous year. I was in my second year on the graphics course at St Martin's.'

'I know.'

She snapped the book shut and put it on to the counter. She exhaled a long, steadying breath through her mouth.

'On the plus side, you did a beautiful job, Lily.'

'Evidently it's a beautiful place. At least, it was then.'

'It still is. It's completely unspoiled.'

'I'm going to have to examine my old diaries. This is a mystery I need to solve for my own sake, if I can solve it, of course. It's funny because I'm not an amnesiac and I don't recall having had a breakdown at college. Maybe I was just hypnotised into completing this commission.'

'You believe in hypnosis?'

'It worked for you.'

James didn't say anything. That had been hypnotherapy.

Lillian nodded at the book. 'So that's it then,' she said. 'That's your white-flight destination of choice.'

'It isn't as simple as white flight.'

'Yes it is.'

'London is more dangerous and volatile than it was when you were a St Martin's graphics student. It's become a far more hazardous place. I don't think I like it very much any more.'

'And immigration is to blame for that?'

'I don't want to get into the politics of it, Lillian. I just know that we're not going to encounter the sort of people who attacked Jack if we relocate to the Cornish coast.'

'Had it escaped your attention that the police officer determined to bring those boys to justice is a black man?'

'I'm not a racist, Lily.'

'I should bloody well hope not. Your biggest contract last year came from an Asian entrepreneur. You've got Muslim clients. You'd be some kind of bloody hypocrite if you were racist.'

James did not reply.

'What about Jack's football? He might be good enough to turn professional. He's not going to get competitive games if we relocate to the West Country.'

'It's going to be some months before Jack is medically fit to head a football. It's going to be longer before he's going to be able to risk a clash of heads challenging for a high ball. He's just thirteen. When the time comes I'll drive him to trials. When he's selected to play for a team I'll drive him to games.'

It was Lillian's turn to remain silent.

'It's a dream we've harboured for ever, Lily. We can go on dreaming about it until the day when we need to install one of those stair contraptions just to get us up to bed. Or we can do something about it while we've got the drive and energy and the kids are still young enough to appreciate the adventure.'

Again, Lillian said nothing. She sipped the coffee her husband had poured her.

'One thing's for sure,' James said. 'My son has caught a bus to a school in the south London badlands for the last time in his life.'

'Our son,' Lillian said. 'He's our son, not just yours.' She put a hand on the cover of the book. Above them, they could hear their daughter leave her bedroom for the bathroom, heavy-footed, thumping like the eight-year-old she was. 'Maybe you should go and take a look at the place, James.'

'I might come back and paint a rosy picture.'

'I've already painted a number of those,' Lillian said. 'I just can't remember having done so. Anyway, you won't do that. There's too much at stake.' She smiled. 'I trust you.' She drained her coffee and went off upstairs to dress.

He knew that she would look at her old diaries to rediscover what she had been doing in the eighteen months or so prior to the publication of the book. Lillian was a well-organised and punctilious person and not at all the type just to forget about such a substantial professional accomplishment as the Brodmaw illustrations represented, even if she had done them for pin money as an impoverished student. They had both been hard up back then, when they had first met. And much as he loved his children and appreciated his family life, it was difficult for James to look back on the period of their courtship without an intense feeling of nostalgia flooding through him.

It was not that he was exactly unhappy now. It was just that he was a different person and so was his wife. Then, they had been carefree and independent and making life up as they went along and the world had seemed infinite with exciting possibilities. Nothing replicated that intensity of feeling now. He had tried to compensate by indulging in expensive toys like the watch on his wrist and the Jag he rarely drove parked in an underground garage half a mile away. Expensive hobbies didn't do it, either. They had given up on their wine cellar after the delivery of the first few cases. The most recent remained on the basement floor, half-heartedly unpacked. The bottles hadn't even made it to their designated rack.

Perhaps they would end up relocating to Brodmaw Bay. And perhaps the abrupt drama of that massive change in their manner of living would restore to them some of the old feelings they had shared at the outset of their lives together. He was optimistic that it would.

He was relieved that Lillian had sanctioned his exploratory trip without too much debate. He was glad too she had not read the Richard Penmarrick article he had discovered on the internet. He hoped, when he pondered on it, that she would never now read it. The more he thought about the piece, the stranger its tone of injured defiance seemed to be. And the values it championed were not exactly those espoused by Lillian, were they? He smiled to himself. He thought that if Oswald Mosley had penned something from beyond his Blackshirt grave for the English Tourist Board, it might read like Penmarrick's championing of his unspoiled West Country hamlet by the sea.

It was a Friday. Lillian would drop Olivia off at school. Her school was only a couple of blocks away but the roads were always hostile with traffic. Walking on summer mornings was an ordeal of exhaust fumes and impatient pelican crossings. Riding a bike was simply too dangerous. There were too many lorries with too many blind spots on the stop-start rat run of a route. Anyway, the school was on the way to Lillian's studio.

Later, since it looked already like being a fine day, James had decided he would take Jack out. They would do something gentle, maybe just stroll in the fresh air along the river westward as far as Gabriel's Wharf and back. But Jack was a teenager now and slept like one and since sleep was recuperative, James would let him sleep until at least mid-morning. He would make breakfast for Lily and Olivia. Then he intended to settle down to a couple of hours of research on Cornwall generally and the area specifically in which he increasingly looked forward to the romantic adventure of relocating.

He had never been there. He had never travelled further in that direction than north Devon. Until seeing the Brodmaw book, his impression of Cornwall had been lazily accrued from newspapers and television. He knew vaguely from television about Padstow and its seafood restaurants run by the celebrity chef Rick Stein. He knew from newspaper stories about the little resort of Rock, blighted each summer by hordes of delinquent hoorays from the sixth forms of English public schools. He had heard dimly of the Poldark novels and the hit series on television they had inspired in the 1970s. He had never read them and he never would. Period fiction wasn't his thing at all.

When he really thought about it, he remembered that

there had been an artistic colony in the port of St Ives in the mid-twentieth century. He thought they had been abstract colourists, but wouldn't have bet on it without asking Lillian, who would certainly know. His impression was that Cornwall had thrived on tin mines and fishing and then gone into serious economic decline. It had prospered in more recent years as a tourist playground. There were surfing and kite and windsurfing and the proximity of the Gulf Stream made the sea warm enough for sharks. There were great whites, if you believed the stories in the *Sun*. There was the Eden Project, which he thought was something to do with ecology. The entrepreneur Peter de Savary had built a theme park at Land's End.

He thought that at the remoter spots there would still be morris men and much folk tradition. There would be standing stones and corn dollies and ancient burial sites; the Richard Penmarrick article had promised as much. And there was all the Arthurian stuff, the Tintagel-based legends of Avalon and Camelot and the Lady of the Lake. Excalibur, if you were of a fanciful turn of mind, lay waiting to be rediscovered, buried in Cornish silt. When it was found it would summon the Round Table knights from their slumber. The legend insisted that they would rescue England from peril.

It was James Greer's private and strengthening opinion that it was all a bit late in the day for the rescuing of England from peril. At least, that was, for the major cities. The task had become way too intractable for a band of chivalric warriors attired in rusty armour. Peril was kept at bay by complex alarm systems and private security guards and heavy locks and cautious habits such as not going out on foot in Southwark after dark if you were a woman.

He kissed his wife and daughter goodbye at their front door. He bolted the door behind them. He went upstairs and checked briefly on his sleeping son, baffled as he always was at the variety and pungency of smells an adolescent boy's bedroom could generate despite a fairly strict insistence on domestic hygiene. He picked up the Brodmaw book from where Lillian had left it on the kitchen counter and took it into his study, where he switched on his laptop and began a bit of preliminary research.

His study was on the ground floor of the house and looked out on their tiny back garden through the single window he faced at his desk. It was a quiet room. They had installed double-glazing to insulate them against the constant traffic hum and the daily barrage of noise from construction sites. Most days he could hear a pneumatic drill or a pile driver hammering away somewhere in the locality and the double-glazing could not combat the deep vibration from passing lorries so heavily laden they made the road outside rumble. But quiet in central London was always a quality measured in relative terms.

The area was in the latter stages of that transition converting it from its light industrial and mercantile past to its heavily residential present. It was a pattern pursued everywhere in close proximity to the river. It had begun in earnest in Bermondsey a decade earlier, when the old Hartley's Jam Factory a block away from the Greers' house had been cleverly transformed into apartments. The process had been accelerated by the rumour, ridiculous in retrospect, that the American film star Robert de Niro had put a deposit down on one of them.

Their house was no sort of a conversion, beyond the glass wall they had erected in the kitchen. It had been built originally in the mid-eighteenth century by a merchant who had traded profitably in tobacco and cloth and slaves. The garden too was original. Somewhere at the back of it, overgrown by a tangle of thorn bushes and ivy, was a water fountain that had long since ceased to function. In the stone above its perforated bronze bowl, the date of its manufacture was engraved as 1743.

The garden was verdant. In every one of the eight years they had lived in the property, the spring and summer in their garden had surprised James with its sheer abundance and richness of foliage. Laurel bushes were a deep green at the garden's rear, behind the trunks of two small silver birches. On the ground, the grass grew in velvety, uncut clumps. In the morning and evening, there was the loud and piercing chorus of songbirds. James had read that cats had done in recent years for most of London's bird population. He thought that Bermondsey must be a district happily short of cats.

They had never done anything to their garden but look out at it. It had always been too small for the children to play in given that there was a spacious grassy square, enclosed by railings and a locked gate, less than a block away that their freehold had given them residents' access to. That was where Jack had learned to kick a ball and Olivia, on the gravel path at its perimeter, to ride a two-wheeler bike without falling off. James thought that if it came to selling the house, he would probably have to pay someone to tame the little tangle of wild seclusion that provided the view through his study window. He thought that would be a shame.

Cornwall was a place apart. That was the point repeatedly made in whatever he read about the county and from whatever source it came. The Cornish had always been a people apart. Until well into the eighteenth century, there had been a language barrier. Old Cornish was a Celtic tongue similar in structure and grammar to Breton and Welsh. Nobody spoke it any more. But the language had been symptomatic of the willing isolation of the place.

Bound on three sides by the sea and on the fourth by the Tamar, long before it became a county, Cornwall was a domain easily defended. This was held to be the principal reason it had first attracted settlers in prehistoric times. Traces of these people were still very evident in dolmens and quoits, great stone circles and avenues that dated from about five thousand years ago.

The Celts crossed from mainland Europe from about 500 BC on. They brought their folkloric tales of gods and giants, demons and fairies and witches and their blood-chilling curses with them. Paganism persisted after the coming of Christianity in habits and symbols that had more to do with the old religion than the new. Holy wells were said to be able to cure disease and promote fertility. Sacred stones were invested with the same miraculous powers.

Two Cornish features fostered myth through the centuries, even after a railway bridge was built across the Tamar in 1859 in a feat of engineering that diminished the isolation of the region at a stroke. The first was the sheer quantity of coastline. Seafarers, sailors and fishermen, are deeply superstitious. They engendered and fostered their own legends. The second was the austere wastes of moorland. The moors bred dark stories of their own and they too stubbornly endured.

'Tin mines, trawler men and ancient magic,' James said to himself, reminded that Cornwall was the mythic home of Merlin, greatest and most famous of English magicians. It was notorious for smugglers and wreckers too. It was the setting for Daphne du Maurier's fictional masterpiece, *Rebecca*. In more recent times, its reputation had owed more, though, to seafood, surf and a sunny sort of hedonism that seemed very twenty-first century in its youthful orientation.

Then there was the Eden Project. James was unenthusiastic about that. He was a sceptic about global warming and the apparent reasons for it. He thought that wind turbines were a con, monuments to energy inefficiency that were built to cash in on subsidies and simply blighted the land. The industry built on environmentalism was inspired by science that was not just unproven but flawed. Like multiculturalism, another myth, it was sustained and perpetuated only by those who profited from it. He didn't bother reading about the Eden Project. It would only have raised his blood pressure and worsened his mood.

Physically, Brodmaw Bay lay on the southern side of Cornwall, between Veryan and Mevagissey. It was about twelve miles from Truro and the same distance from Castle Dore. Leafing through the book containing Lillian's illustrations, studying their detail, James thought that only the remoteness of the place could have kept it so unspoiled. The A303 was a venerable and often tortuous route to the south-western tip of England and there was no alternative road. That put Brodmaw Bay about four hours at best from London by car. Had the place been nearer, it would by now have gone the spoiled, affluent, weekend way of many of the more picturesque seaside settlements of Suffolk and Sussex and most of Devon.

He paused at the picture of the church. He switched on his desk lamp. It had grown overcast outside and gloomy within. He glanced up briefly and saw the fat raindrops of a summer shower hitting the panes. He looked at the illustration again, at the weirdly canted graves and the smashed windows of the church itself and its crooked spire and stove-in door and the pitch blackness beyond it.

The picture was suggestive of a furtive sort of violence. The church doorway seemed to pose an uneasy threat. It looked as though some dark and loathsome secret lurked within that was the opposite of what it should have been in such a building. Old churches in his experience were characterised by a kind of serenity; as though the spirituality of faith elevated them from the hurly-burly of a sometimes harmful world. They were redolent of peace and dignity. This one did not look like that. It looked like it sheltered something that squatted and snarled among its rotting, gloomy pews.

James heard a snicker of something like laughter then from beyond the window before him. He thought that the sound was impossible. The double-glazing would have prevented him from hearing so deliberately sly and secretive an utterance. But he looked up anyway, at the dark green of the bushes beyond the matt trunks of the silver birches in the grey light, dripping.

He could see a face. The eyes stared back at him through baleful yellow pupils set in skin as coarse and featureless as sacking. And he thought that the sound he had heard was doubly impossible. There was no nose and no mouth to the unblinking visage. There was nothing out of which sound could have escaped. There were just the eyes, surprised and surprising and watching him intently from a place of concealment in the hedge at the back of the garden.

James blinked, deliberately, looking away when he opened his eyes again, before looking back. The face was still there. But the expression had changed, somehow. The eyes had narrowed. They looked provoked and angry.

The face was only a couple of feet off the ground. Either it belonged to a child, or its owner was crouching down in an effort to hide. James did not know which of these possibilities was the more disturbing. He thought that the woven texture of the skin might be an effect caused by the rain on the glass. But he could not understand how the bleared pane could be depriving the sackcloth face so completely of its nose and its mouth. He had decided it was an optical illusion, a simple trick of light and shrubbery when, just as he had a moment before, the apparition blinked.

James stood and backed out of the room. He thought that he had to do something. He was not a confrontational man and he was not physically formidable. But his son had only recently been very badly hurt in an assault. He was not in the frame of mind to tolerate an intruder. He had not been entirely able to make sense of the face he had seen in the shrubs but it belonged to someone and they were not welcome; and his son was asleep and vulnerable under his duvet in his bedroom upstairs.

James stepped into the kitchen and took the carving knife from the block on the kitchen counter. Their kitchen knives were German, bone-handled, expensive and extremely sharp. He would take one further look through the study window. And then he would unbolt the back door and confront this strange and unwelcome visitor and he would do so lethally armed.

There was nobody there. He rubbed at the pane, at the slight film of condensation that had settled over it during his earlier examination of the book. The face had gone. He went outside anyway. The rain had stopped. The sky had cleared. The garden smelled sweet and pungent with damp grass and leaves drying already in the sunshine. There were no footprints, no sign of shrubs trampled or petals torn among the clusters of wild flowers blossoming. At the exact spot, he thought there was an odour, very faint under the strong garden scents. It was the snuffed candle harshness of burning wax, mingled with a sour hint of something he thought might be sulphur. Then a breeze soughed through the wet foliage and it was gone.

He went back inside. He bolted the door and replaced the knife in the block, thinking that anger at what had happened to Jack had influenced his behaviour, made him aggressive. The reasonable thing to have done was to have remained secure behind the locked back door and calmly dialled the police. That was what he would have done before the assault. The assault had made him angry and filled him with a desire for retribution. It had stirred the vigilante in him. It was quite surprising, because he had not suspected for a moment prior to this that there was any vigilante in him to stir.

He switched on the study radio, seeking the consolation of familiar sound, aware even as he did so that he was already humming a melody, aware that his doing so was both a nervous reflex and a way of deflecting his thoughts away from the disturbing ugliness of the apparition he had imagined he had seen squatting among the shrubs, observing him. He was shaken. He shivered as he pressed the button and song emerged from the radio's speaker to deliver to the moment something mundane and recognisable.

Except that it was the same tune, wasn't it? He had been absently humming a Sandy Denny song called 'The Sea' and when he switched on the radio she was there, on the station he was tuned to, unmistakable, singing it. Surely that was just his fraught imagination? Coincidence didn't stretch that far. He had been humming something else. He must have been.

James loved folk music. Sandy Denny was one of his favourite singers and it was one of her best songs. But he could not listen to it, now. It sounded shrill and discordant, almost hysterically loud and intrusive in the confines of that small room. He switched the radio back off.

He was about to sit down again, before the open book and that image of the violated winter church, when he heard his son cry out from above.

Jack was lying on his stomach with his head in his pillow and his duvet shrugged down across his hips when James entered his room.

'Sorry.'

James looked at his son's broad back, at the fast-developing musculature of a young athlete, wondering, as he often did, how something born so small and precious had got so big and so very beautiful in so short a span of time. Blink and you miss it, the cliché about the growing up of your children ran. But then clichés were only derided as such because they were so true.

He went and sat on the bed. 'You okay?'

'Sorry, Dad, it was just a bad dream.'

James put his hand on the back of Jack's head and ruffled his hair. 'Want to share it?'

Jack groaned. 'It was way beyond weird, Dad. I was at a church service. There was incense and there were candles. And the congregation was scarecrows.'

James swallowed. 'Burlap sacks for faces?'

'I don't know what burlap is. They were scarecrows, though. And they weren't the cheerful sort. Not the type to travel the yellow brick road with Dorothy, that's for sure.'

James laughed. The laughter was forced, but it was the reassuring response his son would have expected and so he felt it tactful to provide it. Olivia had gone through a *Wizard of Oz* phase the previous autumn that had lasted for months. And so Jack had unwillingly endured the DVD to the point where he could probably have recited the entire film by heart.

'Fancy a cup of tea?'

'I'll have a mug, Dad, if you're making it.'

Jack was of the belief that only people of northern extraction could make tea properly. His father's flat vowels might have embarrassed him on occasion, but the tea was adequate compensation. James thought the scarecrows in the church were of the same vaguely telepathic nature as his son's words when he was coming back to consciousness in the hospital. The brain was an infinitely complex organism. Jack's had somehow tuned in to the same frequency as his father's, now, twice. It was not something that would persist. The healing process would narrow and discipline what entered his son's mind.

More worrying was the spectre in the garden that had triggered Jack's nightmare. James could not really rationalise that and, a rational man, it bothered him that he could not.

'Fancy a bite to eat in Borough Market?'

'It'll be way too crowded, Dad. We won't be able to move for tourists and celebrity chefs.'

James nodded. This was true. Aldo Zilli and Jamie Oliver and their entourages were always trailing flamboyantly through the rows of stalls. And over the past decade, the market had steadily become a tourist attraction to rival Covent Garden. 'We could do the *Belfast*.'

Jack groaned into his pillow. 'We've been doing the *Belfast* since I was six. I practically feel I served aboard her. Like I was maybe press-ganged.'

'Wrong era.'

'I know. But you know what I mean.'

'You used to like the engine room.'

'I used to like Club Penguin. I used to collect Pokémon cards. Go back far enough and I probably liked Thomas the Tank Engine.'

'You did. Whenever we caught a train, you used to ask me its name.'

'I hope you told me they didn't have names and not to be ridiculous.'

'Nope. I used to make a name up.'

'So fostering a pathetic illusion and deliberately stunting my mental development.'

'Yep.' I'd tell you the train was called Philip or Catherine and your little face would light up. And now you have Megan Fox in a bikini as the screen saver on your desktop and it's all happened in the blink of an eye. 'I'll go and make you that mug of tea.'

They didn't do anything, in the end. They just ambled along the river in the sunshine. Jack was healing with the speed of youth. The discolouration around his eye socket was fast fading and the swelling had all but gone down. He wore his sunglasses because he had an adolescent self-consciousness about disfigurement but by any objective measure he was a very handsome boy and his father was relieved to see, when he scrutinised the damage in the sunlight, that the surgeon had been telling the truth. The attack would leave no physical damage at all.

'What are you thinking?'

'I'm wondering when I'll be going back to school.'

'Looking forward to it?'

Jack stopped. They had just emerged from the pedestrian tunnel under the south side of Blackfriars Bridge. Sunlight glazed the footpath under their feet and shimmered on the glass of the city buildings teeming unevenly on the other side of the river. Wakes glittered in the water cut by bright, cleaving boats. The vista was familiar and beautiful. James thought that a boy of Jack's age would very likely miss all this and find somewhere remote and rural crushingly dull.

'I'm dreading it to be honest, Dad.'

'Why? You're not telling me you're bullied at school?'

'Can we find somewhere to sit?'

They found a bench facing the water. They had seclusion, amid the indifferent foreign visitors and lunchtime runners along the embankment. 'There's a pecking order, Dad. There's a sort of hierarchy.'

'Are there gangs?'

'Yes. There are gangs.'

'Are you in a gang?'

'Don't be silly. The gangs are all black and Asian. I get left alone, though. I have status because of my football. My being so good at football gives me respect.'

'For Christ's sake.'

'It's just the way it is, Dad. You have to live with it.'

'So the black gangs are at the top of things? They rule the roost?'

'No. They don't. The toughest kids in the school are Irish. They come from a travellers' site. They're wild, lethal. None of the gangs would take them on.'

'So they're a gang then, surely?'

'They're all related. They're not a gang. They're more a family.'

'Why, specifically, do you dread going back?'

Jack was silent for a long moment. Then he said, 'I've had time to think about it. School shouldn't be somewhere where you live on your wits just to avoid physical harm. It shouldn't be somewhere where the teachers are dissed just for wearing clothes bought from Marks and Spencer. It should be somewhere you can learn stuff that interests you without everyone calling you a suck-arse or a geek.'

'Is that why you don't try at your lessons? God knows you're bright enough.'

'Pretty much. It doesn't pay to stand out from the crowd. There are subjects I like but if I was to show that I like them I'd live to regret it.'

'In what way?'

'It just isn't clever to be clever in a place where it's cool to be thick.'

'What would happen if you did show some enthusiasm?'

'I'd be a joke. I'd risk a slap.'

'We're thinking of getting out, Jack. Your mum and I have talked it through. We're thinking of moving a long way away, to somewhere on the coast, starting over, starting afresh.'

Jack turned to look at his father. He took off his sunglasses. 'Have you any idea how long you've been saying that for, Dad? You and Mum have been moving to the coast for as long as I can remember. You've been discussing it since the dawn of time. Except that we never actually go, barring a fortnight in the summer holidays.'

'I'm going to look at a place called Brodmaw Bay next week. It's in Cornwall. If it fits the bill, your mum and I would like to give it a try. How would that sit with you?'

'I just hope you are serious. I'd go tomorrow, if I could. Blimey, if I could, I'd go today.'

They had lunch in a pizzeria at Gabriel's Wharf. They walked on to the south side of Lambeth Bridge. There, at the café on the small pier tucked into the side of the bridge, James drank a cappuccino and bought an ice-cream sundae for Jack, reminded of what a complex age thirteen was. It was an age when you lusted after pretty actresses and still spent your pocket money on sweets. It was turbulent and contradictory.

Jack had made his school sound as brutal and hierarchical in some of its bleaker characteristics as a top-security prison, let alone a place of learning. Prisons were there to house criminals and his son was innocent of any crime. School was supposed not to punish but to educate. It was a complication he did not need in his young life. The stress of it was making him unhappy. Getting him out and away was the right thing to do.

'Your football might suffer, if we move. The competition, the leagues, they won't be so strong in the south-west.'

Jack just shrugged. He spooned ice cream into his mouth.

'Don't you care?'

'In the squad, at South London Boys, we're told that we have to want it more than anything, or we won't make the grade. And then we're told by the very same coaches that we shouldn't let it rule our lives, because any of us could pick up an injury that could ruin our chances and because almost nobody makes it through to the top level anyway. If I'm good enough, I'm good enough, Dad. I can't play at all till Christmas, the surgeon said so.'

'You've had a change in attitude.'

'Not really. I think I've got the ability. You know that police officer who came round?'

'Detective Sergeant McCabe.'

'We got talking when you were making the coffee. He was an amateur boxer. He represented England. He was undefeated as a middleweight. I asked him why he didn't turn pro. He said he got the offers, but that he wanted to make a difference, so he became a policeman.'

'I don't see your point, Jack.'

'I think I'm good enough to go all the way. I think that one day I'll play in the Premiership. But if I don't, it won't be the end of the world. I'll do something else.'

'You could be a police officer. Like DS McCabe.'

'Don't you think that's cool? Wanting to make a difference?'

'I think it's very commendable,' James said.

They discussed going to the Imperial War Museum a couple of blocks away, but Jack had been there recently with his school and was unenthusiastic. He had tired, too, his father thought. The walk in the sunshine had tired him. He was recovering from his beating but was nowhere near at full strength yet, despite the cosmetic evidence.

They went and looked at Captain Bligh's grave in the churchyard of St Mary at Lambeth, just across the road, almost opposite the café. Bligh had been buried a hero after the feat of navigation that got him and his few loyal crewmen to safety during a prodigious voyage in an open boat. That was before the family of the mutineer Fletcher Christian began the propaganda campaign that successfully besmirched his reputation.

James explained all this to Jack, who walked around the handsome stone tomb and read the inscription carved there without comment.

'Won't you miss all this?'

'What? Some old guy's grave?'

'Not just that, all this history on your doorstep.'

Jack shrugged. 'I'm sure this place in Cornwall will have a history.'

James held his arms wide. 'All this, I mean, the river, everything, the whole spectacle of London.'

'You sound like a tour guide, Dad.'

'Won't you miss it?'

Jack smiled. 'Why would I miss a river, when we're going to live by the sea?'

That night, the Greers went out for a family dinner. James and Lillian told Olivia about the possibility of the move. Like Jack, she must have heard it all before, her father thought, as he described some of the charms of Cornwall. But eight was a vastly less cynical age than thirteen. She seemed intrigued and excited by the scheme.

'Your dad's going to take a look, before we commit to anything,' her mother cautioned.

She nodded enthusiastically, her eyes wide above a broad smile. James thought the dark romance of the west of England was probably appealing to the latent Goth tendencies his daughter's wardrobe and reading matter had hinted at. She was an imaginative girl. She was also very much at the centre of her own drama. She probably wouldn't miss her friends as much as he had feared she might. In what he knew of her evolving social life, she led rather than followed. She was not as hostile to her school as Jack was to his. She had not been given reason to be. Nor, though, was she attached to school as emotionally as some children became.

Children were ruthless and elitist in an instinctive way caring adults learned to temper. That was the essence of maturity. But at their ages, among their peers, what mattered about Jack and Olivia was that they were good-looking and skilled communicators and that they each wore fashionable clothes and owned an impressive hoard of cool stuff. They were kids who scored on all counts. And they would be a novelty, wouldn't they? They would make friends easily. They would have children's amenability to change. They would probably relocate more painlessly than their parents would.

Olivia turned in as soon as they got back from the restaurant and Jack followed her half an hour later. He had been determined to demonstrate his rank by going to bed later than his younger sister, but by the way he trudged up the stairs, would be asleep the second he closed his eyes.

James took a drink into the study. He looked out of the window. It was never completely dark in central London. There was always some ambient light and with the interior light switched off, he could see the hedges and shrubs at the back of the garden shift and shiver in the night breeze. Lillian followed him in there, reaching her arms around him, resting her head on his shoulder, kissing his ear. He looked from the garden to his desk and the book she had illustrated still open on it, at the picture of the looted church.

'This move could be the making of us, Lily.'

'I hope so, darling. You haven't been happy for a long time.'

'And you've thought about leaving me. You have only stayed for the sake of the kids.'

'Not entirely. I still love you. But you don't love yourself. You don't even like yourself much, James. It makes you hard work, sometimes.'

He nodded at the book on the desk. 'Have you remembered doing that?'

She laughed softly into his ear. 'The butcher, the baker

and the candlestick maker,' she said. 'No. I haven't. It's very curious. I'm going to have to investigate, see if I underwent any treatment for amnesia in my second year at art school. When do you plan to go? I'll be very happy to take next week off, if you like.'

'No pressing deadlines?'

'I'm on top of things.'

'You're always on top of things.'

'It will be good to have a few days at home, give Jack some motherly TLC. I'm becoming excited about this scheme of yours, darling. We might finally do it, this time.'

His eyes were taken by some momentary movement beyond the window, in the shrubs. But it was surely only the bolt into flight of a small bird or more likely a bat. He put his hands over Lillian's, which were linked by their fingers around his waist. Her skin was smooth and cool and the touch of her never failed to bring the stir of arousal. Repeating himself, aware he was, he said, 'It really could be the making of us.'

Chapter Three

It was the Monday before he got the chance really to investigate thoroughly the history of Brodmaw Bay. After dropping Olivia at school, Lillian returned as she had promised she would, to give Jack the motherly TLC she really needed no excuse to lavish on her son. They were an affectionate family, naturally and uninhibitedly demonstrative in their affections for one another. Sometimes, when they watched television together, it looked to James like Jack was welded to his mother. James thought it wonderful. He was just sorry that adolescent self-consciousness would probably, fairly shortly, inhibit his son's tactile nature. And when it did so, where his parents were concerned, it would likely do so for ever. It was a shame.

Lillian's return gave James the time to lock himself away in the study and learn about the idyllic settlement beside the sea on the way to capturing their hearts and futures. He planned to drive to Cornwall early the following morning. He would take the family car, their beaten-up old Saab, rather than the Jaguar. The Jag would likely add another ten grand to the speculative value of any property he viewed in the mind of the seller, should he spot somewhere they might like to make an offer for on his trip. He knew enough about the traditional shrewdness with which Cornish folk dealt with outsiders, to guard against that sort of opportunistic profiteering as best he could.

Fewer than four hundred people lived in Brodmaw Bay. It

had grown over the years. At the time the Domesday Book had been compiled, it had been a coastal hamlet of sixty souls. So it had not grown that greatly in the nine hundred-odd years since then. Topography determined its physical size. The land rose steeply behind it and its harbour sat at the centre of a claw-shaped breakwater hewn from the coastline by nature. To either side of it, the land receded sharply, isolating the area that could actually be built upon.

Then there was its economy. It survived on what its fishing fleet brought in. The prosperity or poverty of the town was determined entirely by the weight and character of what was landed in the nets. There was no land worthy of cultivation in the area. Thin soil and salt saw to that. There had never been a tin mine in the vicinity worth working. Everything, ultimately, depended upon the catch.

There was some patronage and had been down the centuries. The Penmarrick family were local and very wealthy. The wealth was long established, but its source was obscure. It could not be fish, James concluded, wryly. Crabs and lobsters would always have fetched a fair price at the market towns inland. But not profit on that scale. It seemed to be dynastic wealth. But the Penmarricks held no baronial title bestowed in Norman times by a grateful king. It was a bit of a mystery where the money came from.

He thought that perhaps it originated in tin deposits or land owned elsewhere. It could have been generated abroad at some time in Britain's imperial past. Maybe a distant Penmarrick ancestor had been a successful mercenary in the pay of the Crown during the century of war with the French in medieval times. Or there was piracy, which had brought immense rewards from about the fourteenth century on. It did not greatly matter. Richard Penmarrick was rich and generous and rightly popular. That was what counted. In Brodmaw Bay, his was a powerful and very influential voice.

The only really unusual thing about the history of this Cornish fishing village was its association with witchcraft. The first trials had come in the aftermath of the Black Death, in the fourteenth century. But they had been followed by a further, even harsher incidence of persecution inflicted by one of the Witchfinder Generals in Cromwellian times. His name had been Jacob Ratch. There were some etchings of the executions, women in the black habits they had been ordered to wear for their interrogations.

The images were grim and pitiful. James thought that the witchfinder must have been very enterprising in his accusations and questioning to find quite so many servants of Satan in such an isolated spot. Either that or the informers who had summoned him had been particularly spiteful and convincing.

Beyond the left claw of the Brodmaw breakwater, there was a shore beneath a cliff. This shore was strewn with boulders. The legend was that these rocks were the litter left by careless giants from a game of quoits played in ancient times. In the witch trials, suspects had been chained to them at low tide. Cromwell's man had argued that any woman who survived this ordeal was guilty. The innocent, drowned, would blamelessly ascend to paradise. A total of twenty-eight women drowned chained to the rocks. By the time he read this, James already assumed that Jacob Ratch had probably been clinically insane.

There was a circular plain where the rising land finally flattened to a plateau to the rear of Brodmaw Bay, overlooking it. This grassy circle was marked out by a series of ancient standing stones. There were twenty-one of them and they were evenly placed and dated from the Neolithic period.

Nobody knew their exact significance. But they had fostered their own legend over the centuries.

The stones were said to be the remains of a druidic temple dedicated to the summoning of the Singers under the Sea. There were no images of the Singers. But James did not very much like the idea of them. To hear their chorus was to suffer their curse. It delivered madness and death. He could not imagine why even the most self-aggrandising druid would wish to summon them. It sounded a very dangerous party piece. He wondered if the women chained to the rocks on the shore accused of witchcraft had heard their song with the incoming tide.

Brodmaw Bay had been home to two illustrious sons. One had been an early nineteenth-century prizefighter called Gregory Abraham. After beating all comers in Cornwall, he had beaten the Devon and Somerset champions too. He had boxed a champion from Ireland at a sporting club on the Strand. They had fought one another to a standstill over seventy-five rounds. His fame growing, Abraham had boxed an exhibition with Lord Byron, an enthusiastic amateur pugilist. He had retired, prosperous, to run a tavern in his home village.

Then there had been Adam Gleason, a soldier-poet in the Great War who had been killed in 1916. His one volume of verse was still on the West Country A-level curriculum. James thought that Gleason fitted the flower of youth stereotype of Western Front sacrifice very neatly. He had been brave, good-looking and only twenty-nine years old when he met his death on a night patrol in no-man's-land.

Abraham's tavern was still open, a pub now renowned for its seafood and run by one of Gregory's direct descendants. A marble statue of the bare-fisted battler stood outside it, his bare torso mighty above his britches, his hands raised in a guard. It had been built after his death, the money to pay for it raised by generous public subscription.

Not far from the pub there was a high street monument to the Great War dead and, beside it, a bust of Adam Gleason on a plinth. A plaque was screwed to the plinth and into its brass face had been engraved a stanza from one of his sonnets.

In the photograph of this commemorative sculpture James found, fresh flowers sat in a bronze vase before it. They seemed symbolic of a place that cared for its own and its heritage; a place that was confident in its identity, a settlement guided by tradition and continuity in which such contemporary blights as vandalism and graffiti simply did not exist.

Nowhere was perfect. From Brigadoon to Balamory, the perfect place to live was no more than a seductive fiction. But Brodmaw Bay was picturesque of itself and occupied a quite beautiful piece of coastline. It seemed genuinely unspoiled. It was quiet and prosperous. It fitted perfectly their family dream of living somewhere serene and lovely at the edge of the sea. Over the next couple of days, he would discover whether it was also welcoming.

After spending the morning researching Brodmaw, James had lunch with his wife and son. Then he spent an hour invoicing clients and dealing with admin generally, before leaving the house for the fifteen-minute stroll to go and pick up Olivia from school.

It was a hot day. Pollution lay in a shimmer from the road surface to the height of the roofs of the cars gridlocked on the route. Monday traffic throbbing at an angry standstill was so much a part of Bermondsey life he barely gave it a thought, usually. But in the heat he could taste the exhaust fumes, inhaling them as he knew his daughter would have to on the walk back home. He thought of clean sea air and a salt breeze teasing the tresses of Olivia's lovely auburn hair. It seemed a seductive alternative to their present reality.

Lillian Greer had made the decision to end the affair the moment she had entered the hospital room with her daughter and seen the expression on James's face as he looked down at their stricken son. She had known at that second that her family was the most precious thing in the world to her and the thing above all else in the world she would fight most desperately to preserve.

She knew that she had come very close to throwing it all away. She had been recklessly indiscreet with a man she could not count upon to behave predictably. Robert was capable, in rejection, of knocking on the door of their home and pleading his case in front of her husband. He was young and headstrong and completely selfish. The youth had seemed a quality attractive at the outset: vital and flattering. But he was too immature to accept the rebuff gracefully. He would plead for another chance. And when it was not given, could easily respond to the fact of defeat with self-destructive spite.

That was why she had agreed to give serious consideration to the Brodmaw Bay proposal so readily. In a more sedate frame of mind she might have taken issue with the Little Englander reaction the assault on Jack had provoked in James. But this was not the time to be philosophical and she was in no position to claim any kind of moral high ground when it came to principles or politics.

She had betrayed her husband and by extension her children too. She wanted to flee the problem, in Robert, she had inflicted upon herself. She wanted to escape to a fresh start somewhere that wasn't characterised by claustrophobia and deceit and guilt. She thought that the Cornish coast would do very well. It was beautiful and, even better, it was remote. It removed her physically not just from the threat of Robert's exposure of her adultery, but from the temptation of his company.

She thought about this while she was not lavishing TLC on Jack because he had dozed off on the sofa next to her, halfway through something entertainingly puerile on his favourite television channel. The channel was called Dave. It had been new to her until today. She thought its output a bit pathetic, but not unendurable. It was mostly a very male cocktail of slapstick and testosterone.

Ads for personal injury solicitors and lenders offering unsecured loans between the programmes were a strong clue as to the channel's intended demographic. But Jack was only a child and had a very good reason for occupying his temporary couch potato role. His resting head had slid on to her lap. She twisted a lock of his hair between her fingers as his father researched a potential new life in the study behind them and she pondered on the affair from which she had yet formally to extricate herself.

She had met Robert three months earlier. He was a successful children's author. They had an agent in common. He had written the first of a proposed series of books about a solitary, slightly scary young girl who secretly – and sometimes not so secretly – possessed telekinetic powers. In the first story the heroine, a twelve-year-old Irish girl, lived with her parents in the county town of Ennis in Clare in the first decade of the twentieth century. In the second book, she would relocate, in domestic service, to Edwardian Dublin.

The third book proposed to take her, still in the service of her wealthy employers, to New York.

Lillian had not known much about Robert O'Brien as an author but she had read the manuscript of the first story and thought it would be a very enjoyable project to illustrate. She had been told that he was thirty, eight years younger than she was. This had not been an issue either way. If anything, she was the more successful name in children's fiction. She had not known anything about him at their first meeting because, beyond the obvious, she had not needed to.

He came to her studio. He arrived on a motorcycle and when he took off his helmet, a dark mane of hair tumbled about his head and shoulders. He was half-Irish, with a Spanish mother, and the most exotically beautiful man she could ever remember having met.

She had never been unfaithful to James before. And she had not lied, in telling him that she loved him. But he had been difficult over the past couple of years. She thought that he suffered from depression. It was not so bad that it debilitated him totally. It was not so bad that he was forced to seek medical help. But there was this air of melancholy about him most of the time. And she had come to think it contagious. It afflicted her and it afflicted the children too. She had not realised the extent of the damage it had done to their relationship, how far they had drifted apart because of it, until Robert rode with his dark good looks and humorous dynamism into a life he made her suddenly aware had become more solitary than it should have.

In retrospect, she wished she had considered matters dispassionately at the outset. Had she thought it through, she would not have committed the betrayal. Had she calmly inventoried what she stood to gain from the affair against what it stood to cost her, she would not have gone to bed with Robert. Desire, mingled with a sort of loneliness, had combined to make the temptation strong. But it had not been irresistible and in surrendering to it she had let herself down.

Had she thought about it, she would not have become involved with someone so volatile and needy. The problem was, though, that she had not started the affair thinking about how she would end it. She had started it intrigued, aroused and somewhat intoxicated by the flattering attentions of a beautiful man.

Robert's flaws only manifested themselves once you were intimate with him. They were partly instinctive, but partly also, she thought, a consequence of things having come so easily to him. He had actually qualified as a doctor. But he had never practised medicine. His first children's story had been accepted for publication when he was still a student at the School of Medicine at Edinburgh. He had found a popular following straight away. His stories had inspired two successful television series and a feature film that had been a box-office sleeper hit in America.

When a man achieved this sort of success, without much effort, before getting out of his twenties, Lillian discovered in Robert that it did two things. It made him feel he had attributes out of the ordinary. And it led him to believe that he deserved to be treated as someone special. All her instinct and experience with him told her that he was a man who would have difficulty taking no for an answer, because in his adult life rejection was something he had simply never experienced.

Lillian stroked her sleeping son's head on her lap and twisted his hair into silky ringlets between her fingers, wondering how Jack would react to exposure to his mother's sexual betrayal of his father. He loved his dad. Both of the children did. James was a kind and attentive and generous father. He was generous in the way a child most valued in a parent: not with money to buy capricious gifts but with his time and his attention. She thought this sort of generosity not all that common in fathers simply because they were men. Men competed. Most competed to such an extent it left little time for anything else. James chose not to compete. He had all the time in the world for fatherhood.

Adulteress was an archaic word, seldom used. But it had a brute honesty about it she thought her son might find it hard to comprehend and difficult, once he did so, to forgive. James might forgive her. She thought that he probably would. The children never would. She had to think of a way of extricating herself from Robert without any of them finding out about her involvement.

James waited outside the school gate feeling slightly guilty. He nodded to a couple of familiar parental faces to whom he could not have put names or occupations. If all went according to plan, Olivia would be leaving St Paul's at the start of the summer holidays for a new life in Cornwall. She would be leaving an excellent educational establishment when she did so. But it was one with which he had never properly engaged. He had never joined the school parents' committee. He had never helped with the theatre programme they ran. He had never even helped out as a volunteer on a stall at the Christmas and summer fêtes held to raise funds for books for the school library or a new bicycle shed.

It was not that he was apathetic about his daughter's education, he reflected. Both he and Lillian always attended the parents' evenings and any theatrical production that Olivia was actually in. It was just that neither he nor his wife really had any appetite for community involvement. They were wrapped up in their own lives. They were rather insular as people and as a family.

Where he was concerned as an individual, James thought this probably an extension of the antipathy he had felt towards team sports in his own childhood. He had not been interested in football or rugby or cricket. He had been a strong swimmer and had represented the school and the county at crawl and freestyle. But swimming was an individual sport. You were isolated by your lane and you swam against the stopwatch, even in the relay events. He had never really understood the team ethos. Team spirit was something he had never experienced, let alone enjoyed. He was not by inclination a joiner-in.

He thought Lillian's lack of interaction with Olivia's school even more straightforward to explain. She was a loving and devoted mother but obliged to ration her time. Professional success meant a great deal to her both financially and in terms of her self-esteem. To sustain it, she naturally had to put in the hours.

The children were trailing out now across the playground from the single-storey main entrance in twos and threes. There was no sign of Olivia yet. This was unusual, he thought, looking at his watch, because she was characteristically out of school as soon as the bell sounded to maximise what leisure time she had between completing homework and eating dinner and going to bed. But it was not a cause for concern. Security at the school was vigilant.

He saw Olivia's form mistress, Mrs Chale, scanning the waiting parents beyond the gate and railings, looking, he realised with surprise, for him. She spotted him and came striding over and gestured for him to breach the normal protocol and enter the school grounds through the gate.

'Is anything the matter?' It was a stupid question. Of course something was the matter.

'Olivia is absolutely fine,' she said, 'there's no problem whatsoever. She is with her class teacher Miss Davenport and we can collect her together in a moment. But there is something Jenny Davenport thinks that you should look at first. And I agree with her.'

Mrs Chale led him along a corridor. They passed the music and pottery rooms. The corridor was lined with shelves and display cases. Papier-mâché and pottery constructions were bright and gaudy tribute to the industry of the kids being educated by the school. They came to the art room. Sunshine slanted through the bank of windows on its west-facing wall. Paint had dried vividly in recent splashes on the parquet floor. The teacher walked to the desk at the front of the room and picked up a folder from it and slipped out a sheet of cartridge paper on which something had been painted.

'Olivia finished this about forty-five minutes ago.'

It was a seascape. The water was turquoise and eerily calm. Olivia had inherited her mother's ability to paint and draw and what James held between his hands did not look like the work of a girl of eight. At the centre of the painting, a rock rose from the still water. The height of the tide made it semi-circular in shape and gulls wheeled in the empty sky above it, giving it scale against the picture's general emptiness.

Reaching out of the water, against the rock, a pair of human arms was visible from just below the elbow. They were bare. And they were not really reaching, were they, James acknowledged in his mind. They hung, because they bore the weight of a body submerged beneath the water and because the hands from which they extended had been hammered through their palms to the rock by two great and bloodied iron spikes.

'Our principal concern was to make sure that none of the other children should see it,' Mrs Chale said. 'It would distress a child.'

'Did they?'

'No.'

'It would distress an adult,' James said.

'I'm sorry to have to confront you with it in this way.'

'Has she ever done anything like this before?'

'That was the question I was about to ask you. Has she?'

'Never,' James said. 'I mean, she paints and draws all the time. Her mother is an illustrator.'

'I know. We have any number of examples of her mother's work in our library. None of it looks like this. I used to teach Jack, when he was a pupil here in year five. He would be what, thirteen now?'

'Jack's internet and games access is carefully monitored, Mrs Chale. I can assure you he has not exposed his sister to anything that looks like this.'

Mrs Chale took the picture from his hands and put it back in the folder and gave the folder to him. 'This is something you might wish to address,' she said. 'I don't really expect any repetition, because Olivia is a sweet-natured and intelligent child and not generally given, in our experience, to producing dark or violent images. Perhaps she was merely illustrating a nightmare.'

James nodded.

'If there is any repetition, it will become a matter of pastoral concern,' Mrs Chale said.

James looked her in the eye. 'There won't be any repetition,' he said. 'I'll address it with her. Her mother and I will talk to her.'

'Thank you.'

She took him to pick up his daughter. Olivia sat at her desk, her satchel and lunchbox clutched impatiently on her lap between both hands, her legs swinging under the chair because they were not yet long enough to reach the ground. She wore black leather T-bar sandals over white ankle socks. She wore the striped pinafore and purple cardigan and straw boater of her summer uniform. Her face broke into a broad grin when she saw her dad. She slid from the chair and ran to him.

He did not mention the painting to Olivia on the way home. He knew, or thought he knew, what had inspired it. Both of his children had picked up on his discoveries about Brodmaw Bay the way someone tuning a radio might be surprised by a strong and totally unexpected signal. Jack had heard a phrase James had read but never consciously uttered. Olivia had painted something he had pictured just for a moment in his mind.

The gruesome image must have entered his daughter's head more or less at the moment he was reading about the atrocities carried out in the name of Cromwellian justice by the mad witchfinder Jacob Ratch.

'What lessons did you have this afternoon, darling?'

'We have double art after lunch on Monday.'

'What did you paint?'

She walked silently along the pavement beside him, her hand in his. 'It couldn't have been very good, Daddy,' she said, 'because I can't even remember what it was.'

'Don't worry about it,' he said.

They came to a junction with a newsagent's shop on one

corner. A gang of hoodies on mountain and BMX bikes loitered outside, one with an American bulldog or pit bull at his feet. The dog was not on a lead. Of course it wasn't, its job was to intimidate. Its owner probably didn't even possess a lead.

James thought the boys probably about fourteen years old. They should have been at school. But what truant officer would have the nerve to approach them? A Metropolitan Police patrol car was parked on the kerb on the other side of the road from the hoodies. They were monitoring, he supposed, racking up their salaries safe behind the locked doors of their vehicle in their stab vests with their cans of pepper spray and their radios to call for back-up if things got out of hand.

Maybe the hoodies had drugs to trade. Almost certainly they had knives. But the dog was a useful deterrent and the libertarian pressure groups had anyway made stop-and-search something officers like the ones in the car had to justify with reams of time-consuming paperwork. The pit bull indulged a growl, from low in its chest, as he passed by the boys with his daughter. One of them hawked and spat on the pavement, very deliberately.

Three blocks from the school, James took the folder tucked under his arm and tore it and its contents into four and put the pieces in a street litter bin. Olivia did not even ask him what it was he was discarding. He was confident she would not produce so ghoulish an image again. He had done his reading on Brodmaw's sometimes sinister past. He would not dwell on it. The future was the subject occupying his mind and it was bright and optimistic and did not involve dabbling in magic and the bloody retribution doing so had summoned in past centuries.

He was much more troubled by Jack's scarecrow dream.

This was because the thing he had seen lurking at the rear of the garden had somehow inspired it. And the thing he had seen had seemed not just real but malevolent. Was it really safe to travel hundreds of miles to the remote west of England, leaving his family undefended, after seeing that?

He forced himself to think about it rationally. He had gone outside to confront the apparition, gripping his vigilante blade. And there had been nothing there. He had looked for physical evidence and found none. Beyond a vague odour, there had been nothing suspicious in the garden at all. Yet if someone had come or gone back over the wall, there would have been wet footprints. If someone had really crouched in the shrubs, there would have been bruised grass and trampled flowers and their fallen petals.

There had been no physical sign of intrusion because he had imagined it. His lurid reading about Celtic pagan myth and ancient ritual in Cornwall had provoked his imagination into seeing something fanciful. Lillian was far less suggestible to such nonsense than he was. She would keep the back door securely locked, as she always did. The security light would be operating and the alarm would be switched on. At the first hint of any danger to their little urban fortress, she would dial 999. She was a sensible woman. She already had the number of the local nick on speed dial on her mobile.

Later that evening, he did mention the picture Olivia had painted to his wife. He had promised her teacher he would and he endeavoured to keep his promises. He did so because he valued the trust between them. He knew that when his dissatisfaction with his own achievements and character made him low, he could be uncommunicative and sometimes even remote. But he thought of Lillian as his best friend and would never have lied to or deceived her.

'I wish you had kept it.'

'It was not a pretty sight.'

'What do you think provoked it?'

James told her. When he had done so he said, 'Do you think that far-fetched?'

She was silent for a long moment. Then she said, 'It's all relative. In isolated terms, yes, it is far-fetched. But neither of us much believes in coincidence.'

'No.'

'She is not of a morbid or ghoulish disposition.'

'No.'

'And it is not so far-fetched as my illustrating an entire children's story book and eighteen years later having not the slightest recollection of having done so.'

'Have you given any more thought to that?'

'Jack was still in the middle of his afternoon nap when you went to fetch Olivia. So I took the opportunity to go up into the loft and look at my old diary for 1992. There is a six-week blank. I was very punctilious in those days about keeping my diary. But from the beginning of April until the middle of May of that year, I did not write a single entry.'

James thought about this. Lillian's father had died five years earlier. If she had endured some kind of breakdown in the blank period, he would have been the best person to ask about the specifics. Her mother was alive and physically robust. But she was gripped by dementia. She remembered her daughter's young childhood with perfect clarity. But the Lillian of early adulthood was someone she was now only able to recall vaguely. 'Do you think it sinister?' he said.

Lillian shook her head. 'No, I don't. The only sinister aspect to it is that picture of the ruined church I painted. I can't imagine why I included something as sombre as that image in a book clearly intended for children of a fairly young age. The fact that I can't remember doing it isn't sinister. It's just bloody odd and slightly infuriating. You'd think I'd at least remember getting the fee, banking the cheque.'

'Maybe you were told to include the image of the church. Maybe it was one of the stipulations when you were offered the commission.'

'Maybe it was. But I wish I could remember whether it was or it wasn't. Not to mention who it was did the commissioning.'

James pondered for a moment on the blank diary period. Four of the six weeks would have been Easter vacation, plenty of time for Lillian to have travelled to Cornwall to paint her vistas from life. Two of those weeks would have been term-time though and her old tutors were very much alive. He concluded in his mind that if she had been behaving oddly, they would certainly have noticed. And they would remember. Was it worth pursuing? After eighteen years, it was not a mystery in urgent need of solving.

'It might all come back to you while I'm away,' he said.

'What time will you leave?'

'I'll leave as soon as it gets light.'

'How long will you stay?'

'I'll come back on Friday. Two full days should be enough to decide whether it's a fit place for us to live.'

'Are you excited?'

'Yes. It's exciting, don't you think?'

'I do,' Lillian said.

James got out of bed quietly the following morning, able to do so without waking Lillian. She slept on and for a moment he stood by the bed and looked at her, just for the pleasure of being able to do so. It was a privilege, he thought, as much as it was a pleasure. He had never been guilty of the marital crime of taking his lovely wife for granted.

Once he was beyond London, he relaxed and allowed himself to think about the implications of the trip. His being at the wheel of the car on the way to his planned destination was a consequence of his own decisiveness. The assault on Jack had been more than just a catalyst. But he was the one insisting the event required a fundamental shift in how and where they lived their lives. He could not remember having been so decisive in years. Planning and taking action had brought changes to his mentality and mood. He felt confident, buoyant with optimism and exhilarated.

Brodmaw might be the heaven he hoped for and it might not. But if Brodmaw didn't fit the bill, somewhere else would. And James would make it his mission to find that place. He was determined on the change. He was intent on finding somewhere his family would be safe and happy; somewhere their relative prosperity and willingness to live honourably and with integrity would be rewarded with a better quality of life.

James thought that his real professional talent was not for Steve Jobs-type software innovation, but for creating computer games. He had almost completed a game of his invention he still thought could be a global hit if he ironed out its remaining glitches. He had set it to one side shortly after Jack's birth, when Lillian had not been earning, time had been short and economic necessity had quite reasonably prevailed.

In the decade-plus since then, computer memory, software and graphics cards had improved beyond all measure. The technology had caught up with his original games concept. He thought that if he invested between three and six months to fine-tune what he already had, he could sell his game as a complete package. It would easily adapt to the most popular desktop platforms. A hand-held version was also feasible.

Best of all, his game had the sort of architecture, time-frame, density of plot and appealing central characters that had Hollywood film studios thinking franchise. He was almost forty. He was neither delusional, nor in the grip of a midlife crisis. It was just that the second chapter of his professional life could hold the promise of vastly more fulfilment and reward than the first chapter had. He felt that the family's relocation could give him the impetus to realise that promise.

He could imagine presenting his game to the CEO of a major industry name. He could imagine doing it before a sceptical board of directors. He would present with confidence and panache. He believed that his game was a winner.

He would not be troubled by the anxiety that had sometimes hampered his past efforts at public speaking. He would not need the diversionary tricks the hypnotherapist had taught him. There would be no nerves to conquer. His ordeal of waiting in the hospital for his son to return intact to consciousness had cured him of anxiety. More accurately, the experience had been a harsh lesson in teaching him just when anxiety was actually justified.

Jack knew that it could not be his dad his mum was calling darling on the phone. His dad was at the wheel of the Saab, driving to the Cornish coast. His dad had a word for people who used their mobiles while driving. Regardless of their gender, the word was arseholes. He very seldom swore, but spotting the arseholes always made him do it. His dad never made or took a call at the wheel and his destination was a drive of four hours. Therefore, it definitely wasn't him she was speaking to.

It didn't sound like a business call. Anyway, she didn't make those from home. She made them from the studio. And she didn't make them on the landline. She made them on her BlackBerry. She was trying to keep her voice down. Probably she didn't want to wake up Olivia. She would assume he was asleep too and, ordinarily, he would have been.

A dream had woken him. It had been an unpleasant and scary dream and when he had looked at his bedside clock it had read 6.55. The phone had rung only a minute later. And his mum had been up. She had taken the call at the extension on the kitchen wall. The kitchen echo was carrying her whispering voice up the stairs to where he lay.

It definitely wasn't his dad. His dad could have been on the hard shoulder having broken down. Or he could be at a truck stop. You took an A road west, so it would be a truck stop, not motorway services. He could have pulled in and parked up at one of those. But his mother's tone of voice told him it wasn't his dad she was speaking to. She sounded like she didn't want to be speaking to the person at the other end of the line at all.

She was saying no, over and over again. But she wasn't saying it in the way she said it to him. Jack thought it much easier to get around his dad than it was his mum. Even his dozy sis, Olivia, had long tumbled to the fact that Dad was by far the softer touch when it came to their parents. When his mum said no to Jack, she used her 'No means no' voice. It didn't really invite much argument. She wasn't using that voice on the phone now, though. It was a voice new to him. He thought that she sounded a bit frightened and he had never in his life known his mum to be scared of anything.

The call ended. Jack closed his eyes and tried to get back to sleep. It seemed unlikely in the aftermath of her whispering from the kitchen that his mum had really been scared by the caller. She was cool and calm and quite tough. She was cool in the sense of the word that made him pretty thrilled to be her son, at least most of the time. But she was cool too in the way people were who didn't panic in a crisis. She drove fast and she liked the white-knuckle rides at the fair. She had told him once that she had never been afraid of the dark and he believed her.

It was not dark now. The light was coming through the blind against Jack's window like it did in a movie towards the end when the game was really up for the vampires. The sunshine was already strong, red against his closed eyelids. But in the aftermath of his dream, it was not all that much of a comfort. He had been among the scarecrow congregation at the ruined church. They had been reciting some lines that rhymed in a raspy straw chorus. Then they had gone quiet as though waiting for something. Then they had started to smoulder and burn and screech in terror and pain.

There was a faint knock at his door. He opened his eyes. He thought that his mum must have somehow sensed he was awake and made him a cup of tea. His mum's tea wasn't the epic brew his dad was capable of making, but it wasn't at all bad. He sat up in bed.

'Jack?'

It wasn't his mum. It was just his numpty sister, Olivia.

'Can I come in?'

He sighed. 'I suppose so.'

The door opened and Olivia came into his room, careful to weave a way through the games and DVDs and consoles and remotes littering the floor without damaging anything;

careful not to collide with the model aircraft and spaceships hanging on strings from the ceiling.

'What do you want?'

'Can I get into your bed? Can I get in for a cuddle?'

Jack sighed again. He aimed for exasperation, but the noise he exhaled was half-hearted. He was actually quite glad and relieved for the company after the dream he had endured. 'I suppose so.'

She got into bed with him and she held him and he returned her embrace. He noticed she was paler than usual and shivering inside her pyjamas. Obviously, just by being born, she had completely ruined his life. But deep down, he loved her very much despite this.

'You okay, Livs?'

'I went into Mum and Dad's room first. But Dad's gone away and Mum wasn't there.'

'It's all right, Livs. She's downstairs. Why are you shivering? Are you cold?'

'I had this horrid dream, Jack.'

'That makes two of us.'

'I didn't know you had nightmares.'

'I don't usually. Maybe my bang on the head is to blame.'

'Shall I kiss it better?'

Jack laughed. He was very glad Olivia had knocked on his bedroom door. 'Bit late for that,' he said. He kissed her forehead. 'Tell me about your dream.'

'Way too weird,' she said. It was a phrase she had learned from her brother and it made him smile, hearing and knowing it.

As Jack comforted his sister, in the kitchen below, their mother reflected on just how badly her conversation with Robert had gone before he had terminated it by angrily hanging up.

The injury to Jack had interrupted her routine. Her time was never entirely her own, but she had less leeway than usual because his recovery was the priority and both she and James were doing everything necessary to accommodate that.

She had not told Robert about the assault on her son. It had seemed an intimacy too far. Given that she had slept with him, this was probably sanctimonious and certainly contradictory. But telling him would have felt wrong, an invitation to somewhere in her life and heart he had simply never been welcome. Besides, she had made up her mind, hadn't she? Or her mind had been made up for her. The threat to the integrity of her family inflicted by the attack on Jack had made her decide to end her involvement with Robert at that moment in the hospital room.

Since that moment, Robert had existed only in the past tense for her. But he had not known it when he had rung her half an hour earlier.

He had not risen early. That was not his style and he had, of course, no children of his own whose timetable he was obliged to accommodate. Instead, he had been up all night. He had been drinking and brooding and for all she knew doing a few lines of coke to give his thought processes the illusion of clarity. Paranoia had prompted the call. He suspected her of neglecting him because someone competing for her attentions had roused her libido and claimed her heart.

Libido had not entered into it. Heart had, though. Robert had been right about that. And he had known she was no longer interested as soon as she had begun to respond to his plaintive imploring and his silly accusations and the puerile insults that had followed. He had said something cutting about the imperfections childbirth had inflicted upon her body. He could have said nothing that would have done more harm to his own hopeless cause. She was proud of being a mother and proud too of looking like one.

Threats had followed the insults. And they had alarmed her. She thought it ironic that a man who made his living writing children's books could be victim to such personal immaturity. But she did not have time to indulge in irony. Instead, she had found herself pleading with him to stay silent, to say and do nothing that would embarrass and expose her and jeopardise her family life.

Feigning indifference would have been a better tactic. But she was not a poker player. The call had taken her by surprise. And anyway, she knew with dismay and the bitterest regret that Robert was not someone she could ever have really trusted to keep his word. He lived like the indulged adult infant he was. He took what he wanted. When the toy he coveted lay behind the window of a closed shop, he was the sort who smashed the glass and took it anyway. Just the desire for something signified ownership.

Upstairs her children, in their shared warmth, lay drowsing together on the verge of sleep. 'Tell me your dream, Livs,' Jack said.

'It was night time,' Olivia said. 'And I was on a beach. And the sea was singing.'

Chapter Four

Robert O'Brien did not want to let himself off so lightly as to blame his performance on the phone either on the booze or the coke. Fatigue had also played a part, but he was not at all in the mood to mitigate his own offence. He had initiated the call. Then he had handled the call very badly on every single count. He had suspected that Lillian was, for whatever reason, having doubts about their affair. But instead of trying to discover the reason for those doubts, he had harangued and insulted and finally threatened her.

Her interpretation would be that he had revealed his true colours and they were all of an unattractive hue. She would come to that conclusion because for her, their affair was a casual diversion; no more than a bit of sexual adventure with a good-looking and slightly younger man. Ending it exacted no emotional cost. It was something she could take or leave and the time had come to bid him and their relationship farewell.

It could not be more different for him, he thought. The sex was good with Lillian; the sex was, in fact, the best he had ever had. But the reason for that was that he loved her, body and soul. It was because of the desperate depth of that love that he had lost control and spoken so spitefully to her during his call. She wanted to end it. He simply could not bear the thought that he had shared her willing company for the last time.

Aware that it was the classic response of everyone who did what he just had, but unable to help himself doing it nonetheless, he found he was wishing with all his heart that he could turn back time and make the call again. Better still, he could not make the call at all until he had slept on his suspicions and was rested and sober. Sober, he would not have made that vindictive remark about her body signalling the ordeal of childbirth in its flaws.

He closed his eyes. He groaned. He still had the phone in the grip of his hand. He was not just weak and stupid, he was unforgivably cruel. Lillian's body was the more attractive for its curves and creases. They were features particular to her. The toned, anonymous, air-brushed perfection of a lap dancer's physique did not do it for him. He had been there and tried that. When he had seen Lillian naked for the first time he had been beguiled precisely because she was so subtly imperfect and sweetly self-conscious and utterly unique. In her pale-eyed, honey-haired, fecund beauty, she was completely irresistible.

Robert paced the marble floor of his sitting room. His Queenhithe penthouse had a commanding view of the Thames. He loved London. Every time he looked at the view from his balcony, it brought home his success with a fresh thrill of vindication. But he did not feel like looking at the view just at that moment. Across the river, a mile to the south-east, the woman he frankly adored was in her Bermondsey home thinking, at best, dismissive thoughts of him. Contemptuous was probably nearer the truth. He should take a sleeping pill and awaken in a few hours free of the fog of the booze and the febrile jitter of the coke; free of the tiredness of a night devoid of rest.

He did not think it could be the husband. She had

mentioned him vaguely. He had sounded dull and inconsequential to Robert; a talent-free man devoid of charisma who had hit the jackpot with his wife and then squandered his winnings. He hadn't just sounded dull, actually. He had sounded terminally dull. Some problem with anxiety had sounded the most interesting aspect to his character. He was some kind of software design hotshot and this flaw had hampered his ability to present to potential clients and handicapped his progress in his career.

Creativity was not a very democratic attribute. You possessed it or you didn't. But Robert did not feel lucky in possessing his own talent. He had exploited it, working bloody hard. He was consistent and prolific. If he had not earned his talent, that was all right, because no one did. It was a gift. He felt, though, that he had justified the gift he had been given. And he felt that achievement made him special, singling him out, apart from the rest.

The press release version of his life sold him as the Celtic product of picturesque Ennis in far-flung County Clare. It was a portrait misty with soft-water rain that dwelt on standing stones, peat-warmed cottages, the vastness of the Burren and the gaunt magnificence of the Cliffs of Moher. Had there been a soundtrack to it, Enya would have provided it. Or it would have been the Cranberries when they were still largely wistful and acoustic, before their antsy singer changed their sound.

The reality was a council house on a miserable estate, an absentee father and a mother who regretted bitterly leaving rural Spain as a teenager for a man she quickly stopped loving. His early years had been bleak and lonely. It had not been a childhood for dwelling on nostalgically. It had been the sort you escaped. His talent had given him the means to escape it and his industry had done the rest, but he was intelligent enough to know that you never truly escaped your origins because what happened to you when you were very young shaped your character for the rest of your life.

The Seasick Steve album he had listened to the previous evening summed it up very well for Robert. Its title was *I Started Out With Nothing and I've Still Got Most of it Left*. He knew how that felt. He had started out with nothing. He had grown up deprived of possessions and self-worth and parental affection.

Now he had lots of things. He had a state-of-the-art laptop and a growing collection of expensive wristwatches and his Queenhithe penthouse and the Harley Davidson motorcycle in the basement garage below. He was proud of the oil painting over the marble fire surround on his sitting room wall. It was of modest size. But the signature in its bottom right-hand corner was Peter Doig's. He had a thriving investment portfolio and money in the bank and the respect of his peers.

All of this was important to him. He had constructed himself, piece by punctilious piece. And overall, he was pleased with what he had fashioned. He wouldn't be thirty-one for another month. He was the third bestselling children's author in Britain and the fourth most borrowed from the nation's lending libraries. His books had been translated into fourteen languages and he had a development deal on the new series with a major Hollywood studio.

He still had the common touch. That very afternoon, he was scheduled to give a talk to the sixth-formers of a large north London comprehensive. The subject was creative writing. He would read passages from one of his own novels aimed at the young adult market. It would hit the spot. It always did. Afterwards, he would inspire them with some off-the-cuff observations about how many enjoyable ways there were to translate aspects of the world into words on the page.

He was a natural with kids. He liked them and they responded positively to him. He had been looking forward to meeting Jack and Olivia, Lillian's two children; the two reasons, he thought, with something like self-loathing, that her body bore those tell-tale signs of motherhood he had just goaded her about.

He groaned and threw the phone at his sofa. It bounced off the buttoned leather and skittered on to the floor. He caught sight of his reflection in the mirror hung artfully on the wall opposite the balcony to backlight anyone who looked in it. He looked tanned, composed and compellingly handsome. It was a Dorian Gray illusion. He felt soiled and tormented. He looked at the costly ticking bauble that kept the time on his wrist. It was seven-thirty. If he took a sleeping pill now, he would be groggy at the school later and would under-perform.

Robert trudged to his bathroom to get a Valium from the cabinet there. The cabinet had a mirrored door but he managed to open it without undergoing the ordeal of seeing himself for the second time in less than a minute just by glancing instead at the tiled wall. He swallowed the pill and drank a pint of water, standing over his kitchen sink. The kitchen gleamed. In the early light, everything did. He was dehydrated and his mouth tasted drily of stale booze. There was darkness here, he thought, but all of it lay within.

He took off his clothes and discarded them on his bedroom floor. He lay down naked and buried his face in the pillow. He would sleep till noon. The alcohol and narcotic effects would have worn off by then. The injury to his heart would only have become more raw and unbearable.

He did not really know what to do. He had never been in this predicament before. The emotional stakes had never been so high. He would awaken later sober enough to see the situation he was in with greater clarity and calm. All he was sure of, as sleep gratefully claimed him, was that he would not give up on her. The prize was too great. He would never do that. He would never give up. He knew above all else that Lillian was worth fighting for.

The road reached towards the village of Brodmaw along a series of acute hairpins in woodland so dense James realised it was the reason why the route had been invisible in Lillian's painted view from the sea. He had to put on his headlamps to pick out the way. The trees were ancient and deciduous. He could smell the bark and bittersweet, full summer leaf scent of them through his open driver's window. Then he was out of the twilit tunnel they formed and in front of a painted iron sign bearing the name of his destination.

There was no hotel in Brodmaw. He had booked a room at the pub opened with the proceeds of his ring career by the prizefighter Gregory Abraham. He had memorised the way there. His sat-nav had packed up about twelve miles back, just beyond the outskirts of Truro. But he reckoned the village too small a place to get lost in.

His first thought on seeing the narrow streets and alleyways through the Saab windscreen was that Brodmaw was characterised in a weird way by absence. It wasn't that there were few people about, or that the traffic seemed very light, though both those observations would have been fair ones. It was that James saw nothing that signalled generic trade.

Driving along the high street he did not see a Starbucks or a McDonald's or a Subway. There was a shop that sold cards but it wasn't a Clinton. There was a bookshop, but it wasn't a Waterstones and there was a bakery but it did not say Greggs in bold lettering above the door.

He supposed that the small population and consequent lack of trade would put off the big retail franchises. But he thought there might have been a recognisable off-licence, given what thirsty folk fishermen were reputed to be. There wasn't a bank or even a cash machine, at least not on the high street, there wasn't. There were shops with bright frontages, glass gleaming as though freshly cleaned and awnings gaily striped. But they were all independents. He was reminded of Lillian's jokey remark about the butcher, the baker and the candlestick maker and wondered whether his wife hadn't lived here in a former life. He was walking from the small car park to the rear of the pub with his overnight bag in his hand when he realised that he had not even seen the familiar red livery of a post or telephone box.

He took a moment to examine the Portland stone statue of Gregory Abraham, on its plinth outside the Leeward Tavern.

'He didn't really look like that,' a voice from behind him said.

James turned. The man facing him was about six feet four and broad-shouldered and had the coarse, reddened complexion of a lot of exposure to the sun and the salt air. He looked about forty years old, older at first glance because his hair and beard were a grey becoming prematurely white. Between his arms, he held a basket of fresh loaves. James could smell their freshness and see the flour powdered on their crusts. The man bent and put the basket on the cobbles and dusted his palms and said, 'You'll be Mr Greer.'

'And you'll be related to the fellow on the plinth.'

'Charlie Abraham.' They shook hands. The landlord smiled. He had a broad smile and bright eyes, somewhere between grey and green, sea-coloured, thought James, who warmed to this fellow immediately.

They went inside. The Leeward was low-ceilinged and lamp-lit, dark after the sunshine outside, but more atmospheric, James thought, than gloomy. There was a lunch menu done in chalk on a blackboard on the wall behind the bar. There were horse brasses and odd bits of nauticalia mounted and shelved. There was music, but it was not the sea shanty he would have expected on his experience of the village so far. It was Fleetwood Mac. It was Stevie Nicks, warbling her histrionic way through 'Sarah'.

The music was coming from an old cassette player on a shelf under the optics. Charlie Abraham went behind the bar and turned it down. 'Always had a soft spot for Stevie,' he said. 'Can I offer you a drink, after your journey? The first one is on the house. There's tea, there's a pot of coffee fresh on, or since you must have been up since the crack of dawn, you're most welcome to a glass of beer, if that's your preference.'

James thought it astonishing. The landlord of the Leeward spoke in a dialect that sounded as if it might have travelled intact from the eighteenth century. He was no expert on idiom or semantics, but thought that this was exactly the way the man celebrated on the plinth outside would have sounded. He accepted a cup of coffee and Charlie Abraham poured one for each of them and they sat down at a table under the big curved window overlooking the bay on the far side of the pub from the bar.

'Beautiful view,' James said. The ocean glittered, boundless, under sunlight. The compliment was redundant.

'It's fair all right, Mr Greer.'

'Please call me James.'

'Then it's Charlie to you.'

'What did you mean, Charlie, when you said your ancestor didn't resemble the likeness outside? Did the sculptor not know his business?'

'Oh aye, he knew his business. His job was to render something formidable in stone. But prizefighters were agile, crafty men. No one built like the stone fellow outside could fight seventy rounds. He couldn't go seven, carrying all that muscle. Old Greg had as much guile as strength. He was a wrestling champion, before he turned pugilist. He taught Lord Byron some of his ring craft.'

'I'd heard they boxed an exhibition.'

'More than that, old Greg coached him. They became friends and corresponded. Byron was always very concerned about his weight. I've got the letters his lordship sent along with a poem his lordship wrote in honour of the Brodmaw Battler.'

James absorbed what he'd just been told. 'Where are these papers?'

'They're in my safe.'

'Have you had them valued? Do you know what they are worth?'

Charlie smiled down at the table and blinked and then raised his head and looked at James squarely. 'I know what they are worth to me,' he said. 'That's the only value with which I concern myself. When the time comes, I will pass the papers on to Victoria, my eldest child. She can have the cache valued, should she wish to do so.'

But she won't, the look on the landlord's face said. To do so would never occur to her as it never has to me.

When he had put his bag in his room, James reflected on this. He was in a place where little ever changed. Tradition endured. Family was fixed and distant ancestry was viewed with an intimacy untouched by the remoteness of calendar years. It was a way of thinking that guaranteed identity and brought security. There was the solid comfort of continuity.

Charlie Abraham had not had the Byron correspondence valued because he would never have dreamed of selling it, regardless of the market price. He would not even have regarded it as his property to sell, James realised. He was only taking care of the cache for the next generation of Abrahams to treasure and take rightful pride in.

His bag on the bed, James unpacked what few items he had brought with him on the trip. It amounted really to a couple of T-shirts and a change of underwear. He was only going to be here for two full days. He felt very positive, very optimistic about his first impressions. He represented business, obviously, so it was in the man's interest to be polite. But the pub landlord had seemed to him much more open and friendly than the Cornish, with their reputation for a surly sort of insularity, were often held to be.

He went back down and decided he would fuel his afternoon on an early lunch. Charlie told him that the kitchen opened at twelve. It was now almost ten. He would walk through Brodmaw and climb the hill and look at the standing stones on their plateau above the village.

'So it's a sightseeing trip you're on,' Charlie said.

'No, it isn't. Something recently happened to my son that made me think my family might be better living out of London.'

'You will have heard the saying about the man who's tired of London.'

'I will have heard it, yes. I used to believe it, too. But I don't any more.'

'You're on a property scouting expedition, then.'

'I suppose I am. Are newcomers welcome here, Charlie?'

The landlord smiled his open smile. 'We can always use fresh blood,' he said.

James passed fewer people in the streets on the upward walk inland than he would have expected to. He did not see any children, assuming they were all at school. Not much chance of truants slipping through the net in a place like this. And he suspected that tolerance of loitering gangs of hooded youths would be extremely low. There was no litter. There was no graffiti. Everyone he passed gave him a nod of acknowledgement and some of them even smiled. He did not see so much as a cigarette butt besmirching the street gutters.

Brodmaw Bay was real enough. It was vivid and authentic in its sights and smells and sounds. It was not an idyllic illusion on a Hollywood back-lot. There was no twee, theme-park fraudulence to it. It was rooted and real. It was there in the clack of the cobbles under his feet and the sturdy whitewashed walls of terraced cottages. It was there in the viscous, rainbow glitter of the scales in sunlight on the hake and haddock on the fishmonger's iced slab. It was there in the whistle of a window cleaner and the sour wince of sherbet from the confectioner's open door and the pained gait on the pavement of an old man made arthritic, James supposed, by drenched winters chasing the shoals at sea. You could not have made it up or imagined it, but it was a dream nevertheless in its bright, provincial perfection. To him, it all seemed absolutely right.

It was a higher, steeper climb than he'd thought to get to

the plateau and the standing stones. His stamina and wind were pretty good. Swimming had become a habit in his school days when he competed at the sport. In adulthood, it had become a discipline. He swam about five miles a week, using the Olympic-size pool at Crystal Palace.

But the climb to the stone circle was uneven and arduous, up a narrow path once the village was behind him, beaten by generations of human feet. There were stretches of bare rock where winter rains had scoured the land. In other sections there were the surface roots of trees. Almost at the top he turned to look at the settlement laid out beneath him, breathing hard, thinking that this walk, as a daily constitutional, would make the whole family fitter in weeks.

Then he was there. The grass was short here, stunted by exposure to the wind, or grazed by sheep perhaps. The stones were rough columns of granite, each about eight feet high. They stood solid, still, enigmatic; as they had for around four thousand years. Perhaps longer, he thought, approaching and examining the nearest of them. He had recently read that Stonehenge was much older than the palaeontologists had originally thought. The theories had needed to be revised.

They would only ever be theories, James believed. After such a vast chasm of time, the secrets had perished along with the people and the faith that had inspired these austere and wondrous monuments.

He ran a hand across the rough surface of one of the stones. Rain and wind had pitted it where once a hand-held axe had made its facets smooth. How much would it weigh, he wondered, twenty tons? From where had these stones been quarried? How on earth had they been dragged to this solitary height?

He resumed his circular walk and smiled to himself. Futile

as it was, you could not but wonder why the place had been accomplished. It was human nature to seek the answer to mysteries so physically strange and provocative in their stature and their enduring silence. The silence of the stone circle seemed deliberate and stoical, though you could not in all logic endow masonry with characteristics that were essentially human.

Was this a holy place? He shivered. There was a brisk breeze in the high exposure of the plateau. He looked out over the land at the water, at the distant frets of white foam topping the waves where the sea became remoter and less calm. Actually, he thought the stone circle just the opposite: it was an unholy place, he was suddenly sure. It had been a place of worship, but the gods honoured had been dark. It had been a place not just of ritual, but of sacrifice.

He smiled again. This time the effort was harder. He did not know what had brought these sinister insights into his mind. His knowledge of ancient history was scant and though he had touched the stones in passing them, he thought the idea of psychic sensitivity the stuff of charlatans.

He saw someone, then. It was not a figure summoned by psychic power, he did not think. It was not a scrawny Bronze Age man, carrying a spear and covered in woad. It was a little girl. She was dressed in the pleated pinafore and short jacket and straw hat of a school uniform. The uniform did not look like it had been restyled since Edwardian times. But the little girl was not an apparition. The detail was too human. She held her hat in place in the breeze with the flat of one hand and the breeze made the grey cloth of her skirt shiver against her shins.

She was watching him. She was on the other side of the circle from where he stood. She was too far away for him to see her eyes but he was sure she was watching him. There was no one else there to see. Her face was very pale. They all wore high-factor sun barrier these days, didn't they? He waved, but she did not respond. She watched him for a moment longer and then turned and descended the hill out of sight.

He did not want to follow the girl. He had thought her too young to be on her own. It was probably perfectly safe here, but she was of a vulnerable age, no older, he had thought, than nine or ten at most. If he went back now, he might be seen and thought by others to be following her.

He had told Charlie Abraham of his intended destination, but you still had to be very careful and cautious these days about children who weren't your own. She had not seemed in any distress, quite the opposite. He was the only stranger she was likely to encounter. He would give her ten minutes to get well clear before taking the path back to the bay.

He was hungry now. In fact, he was ravenous. He sat down, at a spot equidistant between two of the stones, not really wishing to sit any closer to either of them, breathing in the pure sea air, chewing a sweet grass stem and enjoying the view until he thought his caution over the schoolgirl need delay him in returning to the village and the pub no longer.

It was just before one by the time he got back and ordered his lunch. He was thirsty and ordered a pint of shandy at the bar. A man of about his own age stood to his right at the bar, sipping from a half of Guinness. He was dressed in a well-cut charcoal suit with a floral shirt unbuttoned halfway down his chest and his blond hair was tousled and worn shoulder-length. A pair of sunglasses had been pushed up into his hair in a way James thought either a bit rock star or a bit girlish, depending on your prejudices. Glancing down he saw heeled boots that looked like they were made from snakeskin. When the man reached for his drink, his extended arm revealed a silver bangle. Rock star, James thought. Jack would probably be able to tell me who.

The man put down his glass and licked the white residue of stout from his top lip and swallowed. He turned and extended a hand. 'Richard Penmarrick,' he said.

'James Greer.'

'I know. Charlie told me.'

'I thought you would be older.'

'I wasn't aware my fame had spread to London.'

'I read the article you wrote, about tradition. The one where you spoke about the importance of maintaining customs.'

Penmarrick smiled slightly and glanced up at the ceiling and back. 'You mean the article in which I climbed aboard my high horse and cantered off dressed as Oswald Mosley.'

James laughed.

'Waving Excalibur as I went,' Penmarrack said, 'on a quest to find some morris men.'

'I particularly liked the second paragraph,' James said. 'It was very elegiac. It seemed written from the heart.'

'I suppose the description of the village was written from the heart. Most of it, though, was written from the spleen. Our less than esteemed Member of Parliament had just suggested that traditions with pagan origins should be banned. He said they were seditious and no different from terrorism. It was headline-seeking nonsense, but it provoked me into a reply. But it couldn't have just been the article that brought you here. Charlie said you're looking to buy a place.'

'I saw some pictures of Brodmaw in a book written for children. I suppose I fell for its picture-book charms.'

Penmarrick's eyes were brown and shrewd despite the

self-deprecation of his humour. 'Charm is largely a question of perspective. The village looks no less picturesque from the deck of a fishing boat returning to harbour with empty nets. But in those circumstances it probably seems entirely lacking, charm-wise.'

James paused before replying. Then he said, 'My wife and I are pretty much self-sufficient, financially. If we did come to live here, we'd be bringing something and taking nothing away.'

'Your children might be bored, here.'

'Like most middle-class kids housed in central London, my children live under siege. They have active cyber-lives. But when they're not using their computers, when they venture outside the front door, they have to be chaperoned. This place would be a playground for them by comparison.'

Penmarrick didn't respond to this.

'Are there vacant properties available?'

'If you are as affluent as you suggest, there could be one or two that might be suitable.'

'We live fairly modestly. Are newcomers welcome?'

Penmarrick smiled. 'I'll give you the same answer Charlie Abraham probably gave you. We always need fresh blood. And you must call me Richard, Mr Greer.'

'I will, only if you call me James.'

'There's a courier at the door, Mum.'

It was noon on Wednesday. James had been gone for only one full night. He had not called. He had said that mobile reception might be patchy in the far south-west. It was not a big deal. He was due back on the Friday. She was glad he was not there. She had not called a courier and she had not expected a delivery to her home. She knew someone who rode a Harley Davidson and wore motorcycle leathers and thought, incredulous at Robert's nerve, that Jack's mistake was in the circumstances perfectly understandable.

He held a bouquet of flowers between his leather biker gloves. It was a cover of sorts; publishers and television producers sometimes sent her flowers or bottles of champagne. It would do for Jack. But had James been at home, if James had opened the door, Lillian thought that her husband would have suspected something not right straight away. The bike was too extravagant and far too clean and Robert did not have the necessary air of scruffy nonchalance. He looked exotic and desperate and not at all like someone paid to deliver things.

'You must be mad to come here.' Her voice was a whisper, though Jack had retreated, indifferent, to his room.

'What happened to your son?'

He had noticed the bruising. He was a writer and observant but you did not need to be. It was impossible to miss. 'He was beaten up and robbed. Go away.'

Robert smiled. He made no effort to move. 'James isn't here, is he? Olivia is at school. It's just you and Jack.'

She wished she had never shared the names of her family members with this man. His casual use of them seemed more than intrusive. It seemed somehow almost sacrilegious. She did not think that he was deliberately provoking her, but that was the effect when the names of her children came out of his mouth. 'Go away.'

'You're prepared to discard me, just like that.'

Thankfully, so far, he had kept his voice down. He must be aware, she thought, of the people passing behind him on the street. And Jack might be indifferent a floor above, but he was not deaf. 'I explained on the phone. I cannot jeopardise my family for the sake of a fling. Find someone more suitable. Seek out someone your own age. God knows, Robert, you are eligible enough. They'll be queuing around the block.'

'I want you.'

'That's impossible.'

'It didn't used to be.'

'Robert!' She whispered his name fiercely. 'You sound like a child. Stop it. Please go away.'

'It's too late. You're an addiction, Lillian. I crave you like a drug. I can't stop now and if you are honest with yourself, you will admit that you feel the same way and have since the very start. We answer a compulsion in one another. Together, we fulfil a need. It's fate. You and I were meant.'

'Stop it.'

Jack listened to this exchange from the turn on the landing of the stairs. His skin had pricked with shock at what he was hearing. There was a buzz in his ears through which the whispered words carried like radio interference. His skin had covered in coarse goose flesh. His mouth had gone completely dry. He rubbed his arms, shivering. His mum was going to bed with the man in the bike leathers. He thought that he might be in shock. This was much worse than the way he had felt when he had been bashed up and robbed on the bus. It was much worse than how he had felt, coming around in the hospital. At least then Dad had been at his side.

'Mum,' he said to himself. He shaped the word with his lips but no sound came out. There were tears in his eyes, running down his cheeks. In a moment he would have to sniff and they would hear him. He began to climb the stairs, to creep away, aware of which steps would betray him with a creak if he stood on a particular point in their width. He did not need to listen to any more of the conversation at the door. He had learned all he wanted to know. He had learned much more than he wanted to and the knowledge was awful.

He thought that he knew the man from somewhere. He was called Robert. Jack sat on his bed with his head in his hands. He sniffed up the snot that had blocked his nose when the tears had come. He felt such an overwhelming sadness at the thing he had just discovered lost that he did not know what to do. His mum was not the person he had thought she was and his dad had been deceived. He frowned and reached for a book from the shelf above the bed where he put them once they were read. He took a volume from four stacked side by side, all with the same motif printed on their spines.

He looked at the author's picture on the back of the book and there was the man in the bike leathers carrying the flowers he had a few minutes earlier opened the door to.

He had looked familiar because he was. He was Robert O'Brien. He had written the Casey Shoals series. Jack had read them all the previous autumn, five books in a fortnight about the boy given a secret formula by his scientist father that ruthless aliens were pursuing him to steal.

The formula was for the Strength Serum. Instead of meekly handing it over, Casey secretly concocted and drank the stuff and so gained the power to defy his alien enemies. Jack had enjoyed the Casey Shoals books. They had spoken to him in a voice he knew. Truth be told, he had devoured them. He would have gone so far as to say that O'Brien was one of his favourite authors.

He groaned. Their family had been about to begin a new life. His dad was away looking at a fantastic place at the seaside they had thought about moving to. They had been about to embark on the family adventure of a completely new life on the coast with all sorts of new sights to explore and activities to enjoy. He had been about to escape that desperate shit-hole of a school. What would happen to them now? He threw the book at the wall and lay down on the bed and put his pillow over his head half wanting the world to end, half thinking that it already had.

At the front door, Robert put down the bouquet. His motorcycle was behind him on the short path of their railed front garden. His helmet hung by its chin piece from one handlebar. The machine ticked, the big engine cooling, the whole of it gleaming with a showroom finish. He stood in his leathers, the jacket halfway unzipped, a St Christopher medal hanging from a thin silver chain against his tanned upper chest, his long hair luxuriantly splayed across his shoulders and the look of a puppy beaten and neglected by a cold mistress in his eyes.

Lillian did not think that she was cruel. She thought that she had been stupid and deceitful and dreaded the price she increasingly suspected she would be forced to pay for that deceit. It wasn't just her, of course. They would all pay a price; the three innocents whose happiness she had jeopardised, the three people she loved most in the world, would pay it just as painfully as she would. But it would be exacted from them undeservedly.

'Go away, Robert,' she said. 'Just go away.'

He turned. He started to walk towards his bike. Then quietly, but audibly, he said, 'It isn't over.'

'Yes, it fucking well is.'

'Never,' he said. 'Not as long as I live and breathe.'

At Richard's graciously made invitation, James Greer dined that evening at the Penmarrick house. It occupied a forest clearing above and slightly to the north-west of the village itself. It was about a quarter of a mile from the one road leading to and from Brodmaw; secluded, Tudor in architectural style and with a view through its south-facing leaded windows of woodland descending to the crashing surf of the coastline and beyond, under a vast sky, the boundless sea.

Outside those windows was a roughly flagged area much too large and venerable to have been described as a patio. And it was there that James stood, at a quarter to seven, with a large single malt whisky in his hand, swirling his drink, chinking the half-melted cubes of ice chilling it, pondering on whether every visitor to Brodmaw was treated with the same distinction he was enjoying. It seemed highly unlikely.

He had been introduced to Richard's wife a few minutes earlier, on his arrival. She was in the kitchen now. Elizabeth Penmarrick was tall and dark and slender and very beautiful in a long-haired, Liberty-print-dress kind of way that made James think of female film stars and pop singers from the 1970s. There was a dreamy grace about her that made her seem slightly from another time. It could not be the drink that gave him this impression, he knew, since the whisky he sipped at was his first. It was elusive but there, like the vague quality of rock star dishevelment her husband possessed.

Perhaps they were in for a joss-stick-scented night of dipping over the fondue pot to a soundtrack on the stereo provided by the Seekers and Joni Mitchell. Then as midnight approached, Richard would put on Hendrix or the Doors and reach for his bongos as Elizabeth put the jewelled cocaine box on the coffee table. So much, he mused, for the sacred values of Little England.

Smiling to himself, he turned to address Richard, who was staring out over the empty sea. He said, 'I was crass enough to comment on the view from the picture window of the

Leeward. Charlie Abraham was diplomatic about it. But words fail a vista like that miserably. And yours is even more spectacularly beautiful.'

'One never tires of it,' Richard said. 'The familiarity never dulls the impact.'

'Your family have always lived here?'

'Primogeniture, James. It's the feudal rule or custom by means of which the oldest male heir inherits. I have a somewhat disgruntled younger brother. But this house has always been in the ownership of my family, yes.'

'When was it built?'

'Henry the serial monogamist was on the throne of England. Thankfully he never came here. He might have liked the house and he tended to appropriate that which he took a shine to.'

James said, 'Like he did Hampton Court.'

'You're a history enthusiast?'

'Research has made me one. I've been working for years on the prototype of a computer game set in medieval Europe.'

'What's the point of the game?'

'Survival is the objective, essentially. You have to survive religious pogroms, plague, martial conflict, court intrigue, all the usual stuff.'

'No witchcraft?'

'I've kind of avoided witchcraft. Once you get into torture and drowning and burning at the stake, you're into graphic horror. I want to encompass the teen market, where the game will provide a learning experience.'

'Teaching by stealth?'

'I just think games are better if they increase the knowledge and promote the curiosity of the player.'

'Spoken like a true father.'

'Well, I am one. So guilty as charged.'

Richard turned to face him. 'You must wonder why I invited you here, knowing nothing about you.'

'I had wondered that, yes.'

'I'm a father too. Our daughter, Megan, is away on a school trip this week. She is eleven and artistically inclined. She is a huge fan of Lillian Greer's illustrative work. Lillian Greer is your wife.'

'How did you know that?'

'When Charlie Abraham described the guest looking to buy a residential property in the locality, I recognised the name and description from that piece published last autumn in the *Telegraph* magazine.'

James remembered the piece. Essentially it had been a profile of Lillian. It had coincided with the launch on DVD of an animated series that had done well broadcast on the BBC. They had debated whether it was ethical to include their children in the article. But it had not been much of a debate; it would have been odd for Lillian to have discussed her family life, while deliberately neglecting to mention 50 per cent of the family that life concerned.

The kids had anyway been thrilled to read about themselves and see themselves in the family portrait the photographer from the *Telegraph* took. They thought their mum was famous. To a modest extent, James had to admit that they were right. He was as proud of her achievements as they were. Her public profile, the fact of it, was an inevitable consequence of her success. But he thought Richard Penmarrick the possessor of a very good memory to have made the connection.

'Great,' he said ruefully. 'I'm invited to dinner by the lord of the manor because I'm married to Lillian Greer.'

Richard took a step forward and reached out and squeezed his shoulder. 'Not at all,' he said with a chuckle. 'We're delighted to have your company and should our little community fit the bill, we'll be delighted to welcome the Greer family in its entirety.'

'Because you can always use fresh blood,' James said.

'You're learning,' said his host. 'Shall we go in?'

The fondue set was conspicuous by its absence at the dinner table. The Penmarricks dined somewhat formally. There was no 1970s-type running buffet to complement Elizabeth's personal style. There was a long oak table with candelabra and heaped bowls of decorative fruit and silver cutlery set on starched white cloth. They ate lobster tart for an appetiser and the main course was venison served with vegetables they had grown in their own plot. The vegetables were rather fibrous and lacked sweetness and James fancied he could taste in their wilted quality the damage done the soil here by the salt. But the venison was excellent, strong and succulent and served with a garnish of pine nuts and liquorice sauce.

There was music and it was from the 1970s. It was the English folk-rock band Fairport Convention, their late singer Sandy Denny interpreting laments and sea shanties in her uncannily perfect voice. The volume was turned low and between tracks, in pauses in the conversation, James could hear the crash of the surf on the rocks far below, carried on the southerly wind. His last exposure to the singer's voice had been that brief snatch of song on the study radio in Bermondsey and had seemed eerily wrong. Here, it seemed entirely fitting.

He would have put Elizabeth Penmarrick at about thirty-five. That would have made her a toddler at the time of

Sandy Denny's death. Perhaps the music was her husband's choice, though he thought Richard could be at most only a decade older than his wife. They were very relaxed company, despite the splendour of their table and the austere grandeur of their house.

Richard said, 'Have you seen any properties you like?'

James had not, in truth, been greatly spoiled for choice. He had not been able to liaise with an estate agent prior to arrival because none had represented properties in the area. He had seen two unoccupied houses he had liked. At least, he had liked them from the outside. He had been able to establish with Charlie Abraham that they were available to buy. But both were owned by the same local trust. He had arranged to meet a representative of the trust the following morning to see the interiors of the properties and ascertain their price. Again, this had been done using Charlie Abraham as an intermediary. He explained all this to his hosts.

'I'll show you around those two properties myself,' Richard said. 'I think you will like the house on Topper's Reach. It has commanding views of the bay.'

'You're a part of this trust?'

Elizabeth laughed.

'I'm the principal trustee,' Richard said.

'I'd kind of assumed it was the National Trust,' James said.

Richard said, 'It is entirely local. My grandfather established it in the 1930s. During that low decade a modernist architect came here, demolished a short terrace of cottages and built a granite and glass monstrosity. My father saw it as his seigniorial duty to stop anything like that being possible again. He set aside a fund to purchase any private properties coming on to the market. And he set up the trust.'

James wondered again what the source of the Penmarrick fortune might have been. He said, 'I've seen no modernist monstrosity.'

'It was fire-damaged beyond repair and had to be demolished,' Richard said, 'about a year after its construction was completed.'

'I presume with the offending architect inside?'

'Sadly, no, he was up in London at the time, involved in some professional act of civic desecration.'

Ancestral portraits decorated the dining room walls. And there were the heads of deer with splendid spreads of antlers mounted on shield-shaped slabs of wood. James assumed those predatory subjects of the portraits on the walls had been responsible for turning these unfortunate beasts into trophies. After a chase across Bodmin Moor, perhaps, their shrill horns orchestrating the hunters' bloodlust as they galloped after their prey through a Cornish mist.

Sandy Denny was singing 'Who Knows Where the Time Goes?'. It was her own composition, probably her sad and wistful masterpiece. Elizabeth was listening to the song seated on the other side of the table from where James sat, the light going now as the sun descended through the windows of the room looking out over the sea, her hair a russet halo in the last of it.

As if aware of his scrutiny she glanced up at him and smiled. 'Do you like folk music, James?' It was the first time she had addressed him by his name.

'I do,' he said truthfully. 'I like the older stuff like this and June Tabor. I also like the newer singers such as Kate Rusby and Kathryn Tickell and Cara Dillon.'

'All women, I can't help noticing,' Richard said.

In his breast pocket, James's mobile, set on silent, began

to vibrate. He looked at the number calling. It was Jack's. 'Please excuse me,' he said.

'Of course,' the Penmarricks said in unison.

In the high vaulted vestibule beyond the dining room, the west-facing windows were decorated by stained glass. In the orange strength of the descending sun, mirrored against the polished wood of the walls, the effect was kaleidoscopic and spectacular. In his anxiety over his son, James barely noticed it.

'Jack? What's wrong?'

'Nothing,' Jack said. He sniffed. 'I love you, Dad. That's all. I love you.'

'What's happened? Is it the injury? Christ, you're not bleeding?'

'No.'

Jack was crying. James was torn between relief that the patchy reception here had allowed the call to come through at all and worry at the substance of it.

'Is your mum there?'

'She's downstairs.'

'If something is wrong, Jack, speak to your mum. Please. If anything is wrong, just tell her.'

'Nothing is wrong, Dad. I just want you to know that I love you.' Something hitched in his throat. To his father, it sounded like grief.

'I love you too, son. Promise me nothing is wrong?'

There was a silence. Then, 'I promise.'

When James re-entered the Penmarricks' dining room, coffee had been served and the Fairports had been replaced by Julie Fowlis. James recognised the song as one from her first album, *Mar a Tha Mo Chridhe*. The title in translation was *As My Heart Is*. Probably because the singer was from the Western Isles and sang in Gaelic, he was reminded of the standing stones on the plateau above them that he had gone to look at the previous day. Seriously concerned about his own son, he was reminded of the girl he had seen up there alone. She could not have been more than ten years old.

'Do you like this album, James?' The question came from Elizabeth Penmarrick. The ice seemed to have been broken between them by the unexpected warmth of a shared and fairly esoteric taste in music.

'It reminds me that I visited your circle of standing stones yesterday. I saw a little girl up there, in school uniform in school time, quite alone.'

Richard had just poured coffee for James. He paused for a beat with the pot still poised in his hands. 'Are you sure? We only have two schools in Brodmaw and both are vigilantly supervised. How old would you say this girl was?'

'I'd guess between eight and ten.'

'Not possible,' Elizabeth said emphatically, 'not alone. All the children know their way around the village environs. This is a small locality. But she would not have been permitted to be there alone.'

'I didn't imagine her,' James said. 'She was wearing a grey pleated pinafore and straw hat. It had a hatband the same purple as the short jacket and ankle-length socks she had on.'

Elizabeth stood with a backwards shriek of chair legs on waxed parquet. She ran more than walked towards the door to the vestibule. 'I need some air,' she said into her own wake.

'You've just described an eight-year-old girl wearing the uniform of St Anselm's Primary School,' Richard said, sipping coffee.

'Well,' James said, 'there you go.'

Richard looked at him coolly over the rim of his cup. 'St Anselm's closed its doors for the last time in 1961,' he said.

Olivia Greer could hear Jack crying in his bedroom through the wall that divided it from hers. Her bedside clock told her that it was shortly after ten. That was very late, to her, with the next day a school day. She was supposed to be asleep by eight thirty except on Friday and Saturday nights when she went to bed at nine and on holiday when sometimes she stayed up outrageously late. That was her mum's description. 'You shouldn't be up, Livs,' her mum would say, looking at her watch in a foreign restaurant or on a foreign street. 'It's outrageously late.'

She would have liked to go and comfort Jack in the way that he always comforted her when she fell over and grazed a knee or banged her elbow or, most recently, when she had been upset by a bad dream. She loved her brother and the sound of his sobs was itself upsetting. It was shocking, too. Jack was brave and did not often cry. She could not remember the last time she had heard him do so. She wanted very much to go and climb into his bed and cuddle him and say the kind things that would make him feel better. But she did not dare.

She did not dare move or even properly open her eyes. Her eyes were not open. Neither, though, were they quite shut. They were open only to the sly point she opened them to when she cheated at hide and seek and secretly watched the person trying to find a hiding place through blurry lashes.

She was secretly watching now. She was secretly watching the girl standing in shadow to the left of her bedroom door, watching her. The girl was very still and pale and dressed in a school uniform from a school Olivia did not think was local to where she lived. She recognised all of those, knew by sight their colours and crests. This girl's uniform was not one of them. In the murk of her room, through the curtain of her lashes, she was pretty sure of that.

Olivia was not exactly frightened. The girl by the door did not look fierce or unfriendly. She did not look at all like someone intent on harming her. There was the question, though, of who she was. There was the question too of how she had got there.

Olivia had heard of having imaginary friends. She had never had an imaginary friend of her own. Perhaps that was what the girl watching her from beside the door was. But she thought it best to be cautious and pretend to be asleep. She did not really see how a friend could be termed imaginary if you could see them well enough to describe them. It kind of did away with the need for an imagination.

Had she imagined a friend, she thought she would have imagined someone really exotic and strange. She would have dreamed up a friend who dressed like Pocahontas or wore a suit of armour or had wings like an angel. At the very least, she would have Rapunzel-length hair. This girl just had a straw hat with a purple band. The only unusual thing about her was that her feet, in their leather shoes, did not seem quite to rest on the floor.

She thought that maybe she was just dreaming the girl. It was best to think that, quite comforting, really. The problem with it was Jack's sobs coming through the wall. Olivia sometimes had quite convincing dreams and the bad dreams were the most convincing of all. But the sobbing from Jack's room was a detail she could neither ignore nor consign to a dream. It was a detail too far. She knew in her heavy heart that her brother's sorrow was real.

Eventually, her eyes really did close. The tiny muscles around them grew tired from squinting and she relaxed them and the rest of her relaxed too and she fell asleep. When something woke her, something that felt vaguely like a breath of breeze, the figure by the door had gone and she was alone in the room. She was glad. She felt relieved. And she was glad that the sorrowful noise from her brother's room had stopped and the house was silent. She thought that it must by then be what grown-ups called the small hours. The world seemed very still. She descended into peaceful slumber for the remainder of the night.

Chapter Five

Jack did not feel like making his usual home alone joke the morning after calling his dad in Cornwall. He was tired, for one thing, and too irritable as a consequence to want to joke around. Plus the joke had been going on for a year, ever since his parents had first started to trust him in the house on his own for short periods. It was getting stale. There was the fact that his mum was only going to be the fifteen or twenty minutes it took to ferry Olivia to school. It was not a period of absence worth remarking on, was it? And finally there was the feeling that joking around with his mum was not something he really had the heart for. He was far too angry with her to bother.

She paused at the kitchen door with Olivia, waiting for him to say it as he stirred his cornflakes and milk into mush. But he did not say it. Instead he looked at his mum trying to see her not as his mum but as Robert O'Brien might. She was dressed in jeans and a white shirt and a short black jacket made of thin leather that was very soft to the touch. She was slim, quite tall and smelled of Jo Malone perfume. She had lovely hair and sparkling eyes and a very nice smile if she was pleased with you.

She jangled her car keys, impatient for the joke that would not come. Jack thought that his mum was glamorous. That was the word. She was pretty, but there was more to her than prettiness. She had this confident, successful thing going on and she was stylish too. She was glamorous, his mum, there was no doubt about it. And he was disgusted with her.

Actually, what he felt was worse than disgust. The word to describe what he felt was one he understood the meaning of but had never had a context for in his own life, not even when that gang had beaten and robbed him on that bus; not even when he had seen his own face in the mirror for the first time after the damage the tyre iron had done to it. What Jack felt, stirring the breakfast mush in his bowl, was the feeling of dismay.

'Do yourself a favour,' his mum said, 'say goodbye to Mr Grumpy.' He did not respond. She reached for an apricot from the fruit bowl on the surface next to her and made as though to throw it at him. He did not react. He was not willing to be playful. 'Suit yourself,' she said. She dropped the apricot back into the bowl and turned with Olivia and left.

After she had gone he went to his room and switched on his computer and googled Robert O'Brien. He was a pretty famous guy. He was pictured quite a lot astride the motorcycle he had parked outside their house the previous day. It seemed to be sort of his trademark. There were some pictures of him windsurfing with sunglasses on and his long hair gathered in a ponytail. He was in good shape, athletically built. He looked very fit and also very vain.

He did not much look like a writer. But then what did writers look like? They did not look much like William Shakespeare or Charles Dickens any more. Robert O'Brien wrote mostly children's stories. Chris Ryan wrote stories for kids; Jack had read a couple of them, and he didn't look like a writer at all. He looked like a Special Forces soldier who had killed people, which is what he was and exactly what he had done.

Appearances were deceptive. Jack's friends described his dad as a computer geek. On paper that was what he was, too. He was a software designer. But Jack could not imagine anyone less geeky than his dad. His dad was a brilliant driver. He could fix anything from a car engine to a hi-fi amplifier. He could swim two lengths of an Olympic pool holding his breath underwater. After a row with the builders, he had fitted their kitchen himself, cutting and smoothing and polishing the granite with power tools he'd got from a hire shop. He had no interest at all in sport. But that did not make his dad a geek.

Jack groaned and switched off his computer. He heard the front door open and then close behind his returning mum. What was she playing at, going to bed with a tosser with a ponytail? On paper, Robert O'Brien was an impressive sort of bloke. He was good-looking and successful. But he had sounded like a creep, wheedling yesterday at the door. And his mum was married and was deceiving his dad and acting like her own children didn't matter to her. They were supposed to be going off to enjoy a new life together but they weren't even really together as a family, were they? Was O'Brien going to tag along? Would he turf up on his Harley in his sunglasses and his ponytail? They were going to live at the seaside. He'd enjoy the windsurfing, wouldn't he?

Jack descended the stairs, thumping down them on feet as heavy as his heart. He wandered aimlessly into the kitchen. His mum was there, thumbing someone a text on her crack-berry. She did that thing with her head, the gesture familiar throughout his whole life to her son, that shook the hair away from her face and out of her eyes. For the first time in his life, he wished that he did not love her so much.

'What do you fancy doing today?'

'Don't know. Don't care.'

'Livs is going to a friend's for tea. That gives us until early evening. I think we should take the train to Kingston and then catch a boat to Hampton Court. It's a lovely day. We can have a picnic on the river and you will get plenty of fresh air to help mend that bruised brain of yours.'

'My brain isn't bruised. And I don't feel like going out.' His mum had grown up in Kingston. His dad sometimes made jokes about her being a posh Surrey girl. His dad was from a place called Moss Side in Manchester that apparently was the opposite of posh. Jack had been to Hampton Court before, but he had been about five and could not remember anything about it. Part of it was supposed to be haunted, but he could not remember by whose ghost. Probably there was more than one ghost, like at Hogwarts.

'We'll have a lovely time,' his mum said brightly.

Jack looked from her to the fruit in the bowl, the substance of her earlier, playful threat. He saw that most of the pieces were bruising slightly, neglected without his dad here to help eat them.

'What's wrong with you?'

'Nothing is wrong with me.'

They walked to the London Bridge underground entrance on Borough High Street and took a Jubilee Line train to Waterloo. They caught a fast train to Surbiton and walked along the Mall and Portsmouth Road to the top of Queen's Promenade and their first view of the river, the ancient island of Raven's Ait right in front of them and then to their left as they ambled along the sweep of the promenade to the Riverside Café. Parr's boats ran to Hampton Court Bridge from a landing stage more or less outside the café. Lillian Greer ordered a cappuccino for herself and a Pepsi for Jack and they sat on brightly painted metal chairs at a round metal table in the sunshine next to the water.

There were geese and ducks and swans swimming on the placid river and the odd cruiser or narrow boat chugged picturesquely by. The narrow boats had lots of decorative paintwork and polished brass fittings that gleamed. Some had plants flowering in lines of pots along the tops of their cabins. One was black with coach paint and gold, scrolled embellishments.

'Pimp my barge,' Jack said.

'Would you like something to eat? Maybe a tuna melt?'

'I'm not hungry.'

It had been obvious to Jack from the moment they got off the train at Surbiton Station that this was all very familiar territory to his mum. It was all a part of her early life, the part she had lived before he was born, when she was a child and then a young girl before going to college in London and meeting his dad. It was a mystery to him, this part of her life. But that was okay. It was a mystery she was perfectly entitled to.

They were both silent for a while. The café proprietor bustled around, greeting regular customers and whistling. He was really good at whistling, the way window cleaners and greengrocers were in old films on the telly, Jack thought.

Eventually his mum said, 'How much did you hear?'

'All of it.'

'I see.'

'I don't, Mum. I don't see at all. I thought we were a family. I thought we were locked on.' His eyes filled with tears and his voice was choked off by a rising sob. Locked on: it was one of his phrases. He knew what it meant. He knew that his mum did too.

'If you listened to everything, you know that I have ended it.'

'You should never have begun it.'

She did not reply to that immediately. She sipped coffee and then looked across the river to the far bank. There was a towpath there of orange clay, visible between still trees in full leaf. Even through the blur of tears, it was a very pretty view. His mum had a little moustache of milk foam on her top lip from sipping her coffee. It was completely unlike her to be careless of such things. She became aware of it and wiped it off quickly with the back of her hand. She said, 'Nobody is perfect, Jack. Neither your father nor I would ever claim to be that. People make mistakes. Both your parents have made plenty of mistakes. It's part of being human.'

'I googled him when you were dropping Livs to school. He's a complete twat.'

'I have made a mistake. It was a bad mistake I regret very deeply. I wish I had not made it but I did. I would ask you to think very carefully about how you use the knowledge you have gained about the mistake I made. And I would prefer it if you did not use that sort of language.'

'He is, though. He's a total twat.'

'Yes,' his mum said, smiling a smile complicated because there was no pleasure at all in it. 'I rather suspect he is. But that does not excuse the use of bad language from a thirteen-year-old for whom I am responsible.'

The house on Topper's Reach was a short climb through the village from the Leeward Arms. Richard Penmarrick turned up just as he had said he would at eight o'clock and breakfasted at the pub with James. They ate smoked mackerel fillets served on freshly baked bread and washed down their food with Charlie Abraham's excellent and invigorating coffee.

The previous evening had ended at about midnight, fairly soberly. He had not driven to the Penmarrick house for dinner and he had not driven back. He had actually thought about walking back through the summer darkness but his host had insisted that this was not a good idea. He had not been specific as to why. Instead, James had been diverted into a relaxed conversation about Lillian's art by Elizabeth Penmarrick and then Charlie Abraham had arrived at the wheel of an old Land-Rover and ferried him back to the pub and his room.

On the stroll to the Reach, Richard asked James about his liking for folk music. He seemed genuinely interested that a man who designed computer software for a living could have fallen for a genre so rustic and arcane.

James had never really analysed the reason for his partiality to the music he liked. He pondered on it for a moment. Then he said, 'When you listen to Kate Rusby sing 'The Recruited Collier', you are transported instantly to the distant, pastoral England of the war against Bonaparte. The same is true of listening to Sandy Denny singing 'On the Banks of the Nile'. She takes you back and you feel the grief and loss and hear the clamour of battle. This music makes a visceral connection with me. I think it does so actually on a genetic level. It feels familiar and intimate and right. It stirs my emotions. If you are English, this is our soul music.'

Richard had stopped walking to hear this. He began again. He said, 'What does Lillian think of it?'

'She thinks I'm melancholy by nature. She thinks I listen to the music that enables me to wallow easiest in the sadness with which I'm most comfortable.'

Richard laughed. 'I'm with her,' he said. 'I like soul music, James. But my idea of soul is Marvin Gaye and the Isley Brothers.'

'You'll get on all right with my wife, then. She likes Curtis Mayfield and Sly and the Family Stone.'

'Elizabeth sings.'

'Really?'

'If you are lucky, you might hear her sing tonight at the Leeward. There's a bit of a do on at the pub. My wife is shy by nature, timid concerning public performance but if she can be persuaded, you are in for a treat. She has a truly lovely voice. Either way, there will be acoustic music, a bit of dancing and an opportunity to see some of the more colourful local characters hereabouts.'

'Morris men?'

'Inevitably.'

'You're kidding me.'

'Why would I kid you? You're not in Bermondsey now, my friend. And we're here.'

James looked up. He was obliged to. The house on Topper's Reach was tall. It was also physically isolated, occupying a walled plot approached by a narrow lane that divided into two even narrower lanes that flanked either side of the property.

The house itself looked more Tuscan than indigenous. It was three storeys high, constructed from a reddish stone and roofed in yellow tiles. It looked a little austere in the shade of the sun above the hills ascending behind it. It faced west and in the afternoon, James realised, would be bathed in light. The windows wore closed wooden shutters. They were painted green and had weathered to a matt paleness in the sunshine and the salt air. The wall around the property was about six feet high and right before where they stood was a high ornamental metal gate secured by a padlocked chain. James thought it all very handsome.

'It might be a bit grand for us,' he said.

'And it might not,' Richard said. 'It might actually be a steal. Obviously it's beyond the means and probably, if we're honest, also the needs of the average Brodmaw native. And Brodmaw is beyond the reach of affluent weekenders from London. In the language of property dealing, this house is a bit of a difficult sell. That said, if you commit to living here, it might be exactly what you require.' He took a substantial key from his pocket. 'Let's go in.'

The house inside was large and airy and bright and very empty. The rooms were generously proportioned and the fittings and fixtures modern but tactfully chosen, not a vulgar contrast with the fabric or character of the building. The specification was discreet but high. Both of the bathrooms were tiled in a dark green marble and in the kitchen a newly fitted Aga gleamed. James ran a knuckle along one smooth wall and it came away white with plaster dust.

'The refurbishment has been done recently,' he said.

Richard shrugged. 'The salt air is unforgiving. Properties are well maintained or go into decline very quickly. It's just a question of looking after one's investments.'

It was odd to hear the language of an estate agent coming out of the mouth of a man with what James thought of as Penmarrick's slightly debauched, rock'n'roll air. But he had to admit to himself that Topper's Reach was very handsomely appointed. It was better than that, he thought, it was perfect.

'Who lived here?'

'Well, a few people have, over the years. The house has

been here for better than a century, after all. It was built in Edwardian times. Its first resident was Adam Gleason, our ardent hero of the Western Front.'

James thought Richard's tone, for the first time, slightly sarcastic. But he let it go.

'Gleason lived here with his young wife and baby daughter. Of course the daughter never really got to know her father. He was cut down by the beastly Hun, hit by a volley of rifle fire in no-man's-land when she was about four years old. Still, I suppose she had the poetry to console her.'

'Shouldn't there be a plaque on the wall?'

'Probably there should. And if we got more tourists than we do, undoubtedly there would be. That said, Gleason has his high street monument. And he is on the county's A-level English curriculum. It's consolation enough.'

James looked around the spacious room they were in. Its walls were smooth and white. The oak boards of the wooden floor smelled recently oiled. Light bathed them in two lambent beams through a pair of large east-facing windows. They were mirrored by two facing west and he walked across to one of these and looked out at the view. The elevation made it unobstructed. Sea and sky stretched out before him to infinity. This would be their sitting room. They would be happy here. Better, they would be safe and therefore carefree.

'Lillian will have to see it,' he said.

'Of course she will.'

'And you have not yet told me the asking price.'

'There is that to discuss.'

'But speaking for myself, Richard, I do not see how it could be bettered.'

* * *

Lillian Greer barely kept it together on what she already knew was the most abject day of her life. What made it so awful was that it could easily be only the precursor to a period even more bleak and despairing. She could lose her family. Even that wasn't the worst of it: the truth was she could have cost herself her family. Losing something was a passive and often blameless misfortune. She had been neither passive nor blameless in what she had done. At the very least of it, if nothing further occurred as a consequence of her actions, she had robbed her son of his innocence. She had disillusioned him.

Everything was recognisable and all of it was alien. She toured Hampton Court Palace with Jack, familiar with every room, every avenue of the ornamental gardens and each blind turn of the famous maze. Her surroundings were entirely faithful to her memory of them. How could it be otherwise in a place so rich in history it was almost sacred to those trusted to care for it? It was she who was different. She had been a confident girl and had grown into a confident woman. Now she was unsure of herself. She did not feel remotely in control of her own destiny. She thought the only thing that could have been worse was discovering one of her children had a serious illness with an uncertain prognosis.

Her recent vigil shared with Olivia, waiting for word from James at the hospital about Jack's condition after the attack, had given her a brief preview of how that might feel. She had not enjoyed it. She had taken what comfort she could at the time in the knowledge that his father was at her son's bedside and that nobody loved him more or could take better care of his parental needs.

They ate outside at the Tiltyard Café. Birds were tame and even bold, picking scraps from tables recently vacated and yet to have their debris cleared. Children climbed trees on the landscaped green beyond the flagged area where the tables were set. Sunlight bathed them. Jack toyed with a beef and veal pie made to a recipe five hundred years old and served with French fries. Lillian pushed a salad through the oil and vinegar making a streaked, rainbow pattern on the white surface of her plate.

Knights strapped into full armour had mounted their priceless war horses and jousted for sport on this very ground centuries earlier. They had done so on summer days such as this. They would have smelled the same smells of cut grass and fresh June blooms from their saddles. Time passed. It was life's great and enduring truism. Time passed. Lillian wondered if it also forgave.

She bought Jack an ice cream from the hut on the south side of Hampton Court Bridge and they walked along the towpath for a while. They walked in silence. Jack at least ate his ice cream and the chocolate flake stuck into it. They left the human traffic behind them as they progressed along the towpath and their surroundings became quieter and more remote. The odd boat idled through the somnolent water. Lazy wakes rippled against the bank they walked along. Jack stopped when he saw a bird standing in the shallow water a few feet from the bank, watching them.

'What's that?'

'It's a heron,' Lillian said.

'It's huge.'

'They are huge.' And they were also a symbol of bad luck. She tried to remember why. Then she did. It was because they searched out shallow water. They signalled to your enemies where the river could be forded and your defences thereby breached.

Alarmed by them, the heron took flight. 'Blimey,' Jack said, awed, his mother supposed, by its wingspan.

'Will you tell your father?'

'No.'

'Why won't you?'

'It isn't my place to do so, Mum. Will you tell him?'

'Yes. I will. Secrets are corrosive. That means they eat away at you.'

'I know what corrosive means.'

'I will have to tell him.'

'It will break his heart.'

'I know. I know it will.'

They paused there on the towpath at the riverside in silence for a moment. To her right, over the ragged border of treetops, Lillian could see the gilded spires of the palace glittering golden in the sun. She remembered how she had felt walking its rooms and corridors and the gloomy labyrinth of its Tudor kitchen complex an hour earlier. It had all felt familiar and yet alien; as though she wore someone else's skin and perception.

Suddenly she understood how she might have forgotten the Brodmaw Bay illustrations she had apparently done almost two decades earlier. She had thought, in her complacent way, that her mind was a citadel made impregnable by mental strength and confidence. She no longer thought that was so. She now thought it quite possible that back then she had endured some kind of breakdown. It seemed to her entirely plausible, in this new mood of vulnerability, made humble.

'I love you, Mum,' Jack said.

The mask had slipped. The humility and doubt and sorrow had shown on her face and her son had seen it. He came to her and put his arms around her and they held each other and she was aware of the surprising size and strength of him.

'It will all be all right,' he said.

'We'll go away,' she said. She kissed him and stroked his cheek. 'We'll make a fresh start somewhere new by the sea and we'll be locked on, Jack, all of us, I promise you.'

During his medical training Robert O'Brien had always scored highly in any test measuring diagnostic skills. He was pretty confident, therefore, that he knew exactly what was wrong with him. Many modern ailments were both a consequence and a reflection of the complexity of the modern world. No species was so adaptable to change as the human being had proven to be. But the pace of change was so fast that it inevitably took its toll on individuals from time to time.

He was necessarily honest with himself and admitted that a part of it was cocaine psychosis. He had been introduced to a very good dealer six months earlier at a Soho reception held by a film producer contact. This bloke's stuff had not been trodden all over. It was Bolivian product and about 80 per cent pure. Ever since this introduction, his consumption had steadily risen. By any standards, he had been caning the stuff.

Part of it was the trauma caused by Lillian's recent behaviour. He had invested a lot in that woman emotionally. The relationship had been clandestine, which was not ideal. But apart from that, it had been as satisfying as any he had ever enjoyed. It had been close to perfect and he had looked forward to having her entirely to himself once she divorced the tedious loser she had got herself hitched to in the long-ago time before her worldly success.

Now she wanted out. Or apparently, she wanted out. Robert did not entirely believe it. He thought that she might be playing some game of womanly politics, engaged in a double bluff to test the strength of his commitment. But whatever the motive and whatever the truth, her behaviour had shocked and upset him to his core.

The third influential factor was exhaustion, caused by overwork and no doubt exacerbated by the coke, which he had been guilty of using not just for pleasure but to combat tiredness. Hollywood loved a franchise. The major studios did not want to invest in a single, one-off movie. They wanted what the Harry Potter series had done and the Narnia films had signally failed to. They wanted the cost of building two or three sets and assembling an ensemble cast they could use repeatedly. They wanted the solid box-office return projections they could make for each sequel on the basis of the previous instalment in the series.

They loved the character of Kate Riordan, his spunky County Clare serving girl with the secret, telekinetic gift. They loved her underdog ethnicity and the Cinderella quality of her lowly social status. But they craved more stories and he had been under enormous pressure to produce plots that were cinematic enough to please them. He had been working very long hours, for many weeks, with a great deal at stake, always with the worry that one morning he might wake up and switch on his laptop and poise over the keyboard with the ideas and the words that followed them simply refusing to come.

Writer's block happened. It had happened to writers he knew. Their fertile minds and vivid imaginations had suddenly dried up. As one of them had said to him at a children's fiction conference, *I rubbed its polished side one day and the genie had vacated the lamp. Didn't leave a note, Robert, never even paused to say goodbye.* It could happen to anyone. He dreaded that fate, suddenly and randomly afflicting him.

Drug abuse, emotional trauma and exhaustion had combined to affect his mind. They had not affected his judgement, he did not think. And he thought that his behaviour, most of the time, was still rational and therefore normal. Turning up at Lillian's house with the flowers the previous day had been rash. But it had not exactly been the insane act of a stalker, had it? It had been spontaneous and driven by honest passion. And anyway, he had got away with it. The boy had taken him for a courier. Lillian had acted indignant, but in retrospect he thought had to have been secretly flattered by the extravagance of the bouquet.

He knew the causes of the hallucinations he was suffering. He even knew their inspiration. But rationalising them did not guarantee putting an end to them and the latest, the one last night, had really frightened him.

He had seen the little girl first in the wing mirror of his motorbike. She had been standing on the pavement behind him in sunshine in her purple and grey school uniform and he had registered how pale her face had looked. He saw her again, standing over the road, preternaturally pale and still, he thought, as he waited for Lillian to answer the door to him outside that handsome Bermondsey townhouse.

He had thought little if anything of this, until seeing her the previous night, standing at the end of his bed, when her curious scrutiny or perhaps the coldness she delivered to the room awoke him in the small hours. She had worn a frown across her wan features. Her stare had been intent. And there had been something poised and hostile about her posture that had chilled him, as he lay there, to the bone. Had she spoken, had words emerged from her mouth, he thought he might have screamed.

Robert recalled this, sitting outside a Soho café, drinking a double espresso at a pavement table as people paraded by and taxis and delivery vans levered their laborious way along the too-narrow street. He resolved to lay off the coke. He resolved to do what he could to work shorter hours and less intently than he had over recent weeks. He would get more sleep. He wondered if he should take up racket ball or squash. Competitive sport, when it was physically arduous, could provide stress relief and he would need the endorphins, weaning himself off the marching powder and the buoyant hit it provided.

His emotional state was a trickier problem to tackle but the face-to-face meeting with the flowers had left him feeling more optimistic than the phone call dumping him had. Anyway, he believed in the old Irish saying that a faint heart never won a fair maiden.

He knew what the source of the apparition was. His own creativity had inspired her, hadn't it? He was in a sense to blame for her. She was Kate Riordan, wasn't she? He had not pictured her in his mind looking quite so pale and had not knowingly resolved that quaint and pretty school uniform she wore. But the subconscious was a strange imperative and it did not do to examine it in detail too intense. You rubbed the lamp, as his poor past acquaintance and rival had said. You hoped the genie responded. You did not lift the lamp lid to see exactly how he lived.

It was ironic, to be scared of his own creation. But the hallucinations were a serious warning that he had to get a grip. He had to make some fairly profound lifestyle changes and he had to make them right away. Most importantly, he had to resolve the situation with Lillian. He needed to know exactly where he stood. He deserved to know exactly where he stood. He was prepared to accommodate her children, if that was what it took. Perhaps that was the cause of her concern, now that things had become so serious between them. Perhaps it had become a case, for her, of where do we go from here?

Almost certainly that was it. And it was not a problem at all, because he would be happy to provide her with all the assurance she needed. He was totally in love, totally committed, totally confident that they could and would be blissfully happy together.

He had sat alone outside the café. But when he looked up, through the ripple of heat shimmer at his reflection in a showroom window over the road, he saw that he shared his zinc table with a little girl, fleeting in purple and grey, blonde under the straw hat, swinging her legs back and forth playfully under her chair, staring intently at him and then concealed by a passing van and then when the van had passed, no longer there at all.

After his viewing with Richard Penmarrick of the house on Topper's Reach, James thanked him and they parted with a handshake. Then he went to a high street tea room where he drank a cup of coffee and looked at the photographs he had taken of the property on his mobile phone. They did not do it justice. He had seen some lovely photo essays in *Coast* magazine of houses occupying similar locations. But he thought the charms of the place he had just toured singular and potent and perhaps even unique.

The asking price was four hundred thousand pounds. It

was not possible, Richard had told him, to buy the freehold. The four hundred grand was the price of a ninety-nine-year lease. James did some calculations on the back of an envelope at his café table. They owned their Bermondsey house outright. They would qualify for tax relief on a mortgage on the second property. It would not be quite true to say that the deal would finance itself. But they could certainly afford to move without selling up. Anyway, they could rent the Bermondsey house for twice what the monthly mortgage payments on Topper's Reach would likely be.

He tried to send Lillian the pictures, but could not get a signal on his phone. He went back to the Leeward and retrieved his shorts and a towel from his room intent on a swim in the sea. The weather was fine, the water relatively calm and he had already established from Charlie Abraham the limits of the bathing-friendly area of the beach. There were no treacherous undertows or strong currents. The area was marked by bright orange buoys.

James swam in the sea for an hour. He had no fear of deep water or of the predatory monsters with fins the tabloid press insisted lurked ready to eat Cornish bathers. He was imaginative only when he chose to be, in the creation and development of his epic game. He was not by nature fanciful. The fact of his having seen a schoolgirl two days before in the livery of a school that had closed fifty years ago was more than intriguing, it was bloody odd. Penmarrick's revelation about St Anselm's had chilled him the previous evening, when it had made the hair bristle on his forearms and his skin prickle momentarily with cold.

There was a plausible explanation. There had to be, because the girl had been real. The sight of the little apparition troubled him. But the explanation would not likely be made more forthcoming by dwelling on the mystery. He could not and would not forget about it. The pragmatic thing to do, though, was to put it to the back of his mind.

When he got back to the beach and the pile of clothing and other stuff he had left above the high-water mark, he had a strong phone signal and had received a call. There was no message but the number was that of DS McCabe's mobile. James dried himself and dressed and then called him.

'Not good news I'm afraid, Mr Greer.'

'I'm a big boy, Detective Sergeant.'

'A conviction is looking less and less likely. The perpetrators were a fifteen-year-old ringleader and his cousins who were twins of thirteen. The fifteen-year-old is the one using the tyre iron in the CCTV footage we've got. There is legitimate doubt about his fitness to stand trial.'

'Go on.'

'He was involuntarily incarcerated in a Kent mental institution after being given a psychiatric assessment by the immigration service. His mother engaged a civil rights lawyer from Canterbury who ended up getting him out. He's been in and out of various psychiatric facilities ever since. Lewisham had him put in one after an assault on a teaching assistant at the special school he was attending there. The family were housed by Southwark, whose social services subsequently engineered his release. Are you keeping up?'

'More or less I am. I can see where this is going. It's multi-agency involvement. It will be argued that his problems were ignored, that he was a victim of official incompetence and neglect.'

'He was involved with eight separate agencies. That's become nine if you count us. Ten if you include his legal aid defence.'

'How many trained and qualified and salaried individuals are we talking about?'

'I would estimate between twenty and thirty. He's at the sharp end of a growing industry.'

James nodded, licking rime from his salty upper lip. He was thinking about council and social services jobs that were really sinecures and the pension provision that went with them. He was thinking of his taxes paying for all this and justice never being delivered as a rightful consequence of the damage done to his innocent son.

'What does she do for a living, the perpetrator's mother?'

McCabe said, 'Don't make me laugh.'

'His father?'

'His father was killed in Mogadishu in a firefight four years ago. He earned his living as a warlord.'

'What do you think the chances are of it coming to court?'

'The odds have dropped to about sixty–forty against. I'm sorry, Mr Greer.'

'Thanks for trying.'

'It's my job.'

'It's eleven, by the way.'

'Come again?'

'The number of agencies involved is eleven. A hospital surgeon and his theatre team were involved in patching up my boy. He hasn't needed the treatment for psychological trauma they offered to provide, but it is there if required. The case notes have been compiled and a psychiatric counsellor briefed. The NHS makes it eleven.'

'You're right. I stand corrected.'

James looked out over the glittering sea. 'How does it make you feel, all this stuff you have to deal with, Detective Sergeant?'

'Where this case is concerned? Like somebody drowning,' McCabe said.

The weather was on the turn by the time the evening's festivities began at the pub. The wind had changed and the atmosphere had grown heavy and humid and the sky had become the cloud-dense colour of impending rain. The troupe of morris men performed their enigmatic ritual on the cobbled square outside the pub, under the stony gaze and bare-knuckled guard of Gregory Abraham, the old prizefighter.

They danced to the music of an accordion and a fiddle, expertly clashing the sticks they carried, weaving in and out of clusters in their white costumes and black top hats, bright with tied ribbons and pinned rosettes and slung baldricks, bell pads jingling at their knees and their iron-shod boots ringing on the ground.

For one dance they carried handkerchiefs and for another swords that looked like naval sabres from Nelson's time. Perhaps they were, thought James, who watched the spectacle drinking a glass of ale and wondering what its origin was. The fact was that nobody really knew. All sorts of theories existed about the origins of morris and mummery rites but they had been established without their creation being properly chronicled. They were folk traditions, peasant in origin, and their mysteries defied scholarship as a consequence.

The tempo of the music was sufficiently rapid for dance and there was a definite enough rhythm to it, but there was also something plangent about the sound. Perhaps it was the instruments, James thought. The accordion had its avuncular wheeze and was redolent of sea shanties. Stringed instruments had a way of engaging the emotions though and the violin possessed a dark tonality. The effect of the two instruments combined was curiously wistful, melancholy almost. It sounded very Celtic. It could have been music shaped by a tradition that existed nowhere else on earth.

There was something about the costume and choreography that very quickly made a company of the dancers, so that it became impossible to view them really as individuals. They possessed a collective character. They were a skipping, clattering, jingling pageant. They also had about them, in their separateness and insularity, something slightly ominous. Some of the dances seemed warlike.

Fat raindrops began to fall in what soon became a persistent downpour just as the dancing finished. The morris men hurried inside the pub, their thirst fully justified by their exertions. James went into the pub in their wake and was standing at the bar ordering a fresh drink when the Penmarricks arrived and greeted him like an old friend. Curiously, on only his second full day in the village, it was almost what he felt.

Elizabeth Penmarrick seemed to have totally overcome her shyness of the previous evening. Her smile was broad and relaxed and she kissed him on the cheek in saying hello. He thought that tonight she looked like an advert for Laura Ashley from the pages of a Sunday supplement published in about 1975. Her husband was dressed like one of those louche former public schoolboys who managed rock bands in the same decade. He bought them a drink and the three of them toasted one another silently.

'I'm going to introduce you to a few people,' Richard said, looking around. The interior of the pub was atmospheric with lantern light and Charlie Abraham had lit a log fire in the large grate of the saloon bar. It was June and not cold, but the flames added to the cheery mood of togetherness and warmth as the rain lashed and the wind whipped up in strength around the building.

'Before I do that, though, I want to show you something.'

James followed him through the throng to the big picture window overlooking the bay, thinking that the Leeward did excellent business. Then again it was a special night, some sort of celebration of something. He would have to remember to ask the Penmarricks precisely what.

Beyond the window, beneath louring cloud, the sea boiled with elemental fury. It was green and glimmered and its white spume appeared yellowy in spires and peaks and the troughs of the sea were dark, lurching chasms. And it all stretched, this anarchic, watery violence, to a dim horizon.

'I hope that glass is thick,' James said, awed.

Beside him, Richard chuckled. 'It is. But a storm such as this is a reminder that we live at the mercy of the world. Our lives are grace and favour existences. At least, they are while nature rules us.'

'Let's hope she goes on doing so benevolently,' James said.

'Nature's benevolence is a relative thing,' Richard said. 'It would not seem benevolent tonight if you were out there in a boat.'

'But we are not. We're in here, in comfort and warmth.'

'And conviviality,' Richard said, putting a hand on his shoulder. 'And we are behind our goodly landlord's glass and Charlie Abraham is risk averse and I can assure you that the glass is very thick indeed.'

'So we can stand here and enjoy the view.'

'Only at the risk of neglecting my wife,' Richard said.

James looked back across the bar. Elizabeth Penmarrick did not look terribly neglected. She was standing at the centre of a group of people and looked deeply engaged in conversation with them.

'Come,' Richard said. 'There are several people you should meet.'

The butcher, the baker and the candlestick maker. That had been Lillian's phrase about the people she would have expected to populate the Brodmaw Bay of her Chubbly & Cruff book illustrations. He was reminded of it as Richard guided him back to the group. But in truth, none of them looked like tradesmen and when he was introduced to them, none of them was.

Philip Teal was the headmaster of the village secondary school. He looked reassuringly tweedy and wore a grey goatee beard and James estimated was in his late thirties, though he contrived to look older. His school, the Mount, was a co-educational secondary and the one, all being well, Jack would attend. He told James to consult the Ofsted report online if he had any doubts concerning the resources or academic merit of a school in so small a settlement as Brodmaw. Then, with an enthusiasm James thought charming as well as contagious, he talked about the after-school activities the school ran and promoted.

Martin Sharp owned the chandlery. James was frank with him about his own almost complete lack of sailing knowledge or skills. Martin said that the children should be encouraged to learn to sail because the benefits of doing so were considerable in terms of building confidence and independence.

'And they will enjoy it,' he said, 'and so will you.' Then he cautioned James to consult him before buying a boat from anyone in the locality. 'I'll secure you the friends and family discount,' he said with a wink. Physically, Martin reminded

James of a front-row rugby forward. He was warm and friendly, but possessed a stolid power in his thick neck and the broad shoulders above his massive chest.

Angela Heart was the principal of the primary school Olivia would attend. James did not think that she looked very much at all like an educator. She was svelte and stylish in a black pencil skirt and a matching black jacket and crimson lipstick. There was a femme fatale quality to her that seemed somewhat at odds with mixing poster paint and setting homework assignments. She was in her early forties, a few years older than he was, James supposed and the sort of woman he thought most men would be intrigued by. He put the apparent clash between her appearance and occupation down to male prejudice. But he found her green, appraising eyes totally alluring.

The last person he was formally introduced to in the Leeward that evening was Ben Tamworth, owner of the principal building firm in the region. In fact, Richard said, it was the only building firm in the region.

'Ben will take proper care of all your requirements, should you want or need anything done to Topper's Reach. That's assuming of course that you and Lillian take the decision to live there.'

'I'll give you a competitive rate on any work you put my way, James.'

James thought this unlikely. Richard had just told him Ben enjoyed a local monopoly. But he did not challenge or contradict what Ben had said. The blue eyes in the builder's broad, tanned, freckled face looked entirely honest. He did not wish to alienate the man whose workforce might be called out to do emergency repairs on his roof in weather like that currently raging outside. As if to remind him of the fact, there was a volley of thunder then that sang and whined through the pub rafters and made the polished glasses crowning the bar shiver on their shelves.

The butcher, the baker and the candlestick maker. Later, reminiscing about that evening in the Leeward, James would ponder not on who he had, but on who he had not met. Various people were pointed out to him. There was the boatbuilder, Billy Jasper, florid over a pint among the rest of the morris troupe. There was Michael Carney, a local poet and an authority on the short life and poignant times of Adam Gleason. There was the pharmacist, Rachel Flood, and Bella Worth who edited the *Brodmaw Clarion*.

All the leading lights of the little coastal community seemed to be in the Leeward that night, packing Charlie Abraham's pub to its oak rafters with boozy conviviality. The good cheer was almost palpable. The pub that evening was the village itself in gossipy, backslapping, flirtatious, chummy microcosm. And there was no man of the cloth present. There was not a dog collar anywhere to signal the vicar or priest whose job it would be to minister to the spiritual needs of the village and its inhabitants. This did not strike James as odd or unusual at the time. He was far too busy enjoying himself. Later, he thought of it as an omission so glaring he wondered how he could have missed it. But by then, it was far too late.

At about ten o'clock, sensing a lull in the storm in the lengthening pauses between thunder peals, he decided to brave the weather outside for a breath of fresh air before the singing began. The smell of salt was strong in the darkness and the washed cobbles black under a streaked sky still sullen and threatening. The storm had only paused to gather itself for a fresh assault, he thought.

He wondered what it would be like, then, to exist alone, in isolation. He was away from his wife and children for the first time he could remember. What if he could never go back to them? What if they did not exist and this place and the people here comprised the whole of his future? It was an odd, distressing, dislocating thought. His family, for James, were the whole of him. Without them, he would be the one to cease to exist. The charm of Brodmaw was intrinsic to the place. It was honest and unspoiled and picturesque. But its allure for him was entirely as a refuge for the three precious people who made up his personal world.

He was not alone though, was he? He was not even alone in the storm lull outside the pub. Someone was there, watching him. He looked and saw that it was Angela Heart. Her black clothing and black hair when she'd had her back to him must have concealed her in the surrounding darkness. But she was facing him now, pale-complexioned and crimson-mouthed and smoking a cigarette, standing next to the plinth on which Gregory Abraham maintained his granite guard.

Just for something to say, to allay the awkwardness of the moment, he said, 'Do you think the storm is over?'

She pulled on her cigarette. When she had exhaled, up towards the sky, her jaw taut and the skin of her exposed throat startlingly white, she lowered her head and smiled at him and said, 'I think the storm has only just begun.'

It was something of a contrast to a traditional night of song in a Bermondsey pub, James thought, when the music began. He was more familiar with the London knees-up, complete with pearly kings and queens and jouncing piano keys. There was always something very contrived about those events, a stagey air of knowing self-parody that made them seem bogus to someone from the north of England like him. After a few pints he'd find himself half expecting Dick van Dyke to take to the stage, dressed as a chimney sweep. London was like that, always peddling its own myth, striving to live up to the stereotype. The music in the Leeward that evening, by contrast, could not have been more authentic.

The wind and rain howling and hammering at the exterior of the pub increased the feeling of intimacy shared by those sheltering inside. The interior light was so dim that the major source of illumination seemed to be the fire, flickering as pockets of resin in the logs were found by the heat and flared into life. The thunder continued to boom sporadically above. Ale was an amber glitter in the glasses drinkers raised. Faces were shiny in the firelight and rapt with expectation as the first performer took to the small raised stage and coughed to clear his throat and began, in a strong tenor voice, to sing.

Sitting with Richard and Elizabeth Penmarrick, the three of them sharing a table, it struck James that the songs sung and the instruments that accompanied them combined to make sounds that would have seemed familiar to the pugilist celebrated on the plinth on the cobbles outside. There were eternal verities: truths common to every man and woman, subjects like love, loss, sacrifice, grief and joy that resonated in the human heart through and in spite of the passage of years. And these songs celebrated them in a way that was not so much traditional as timeless.

Billy Jasper sang a selection of sea shanties, finishing up with 'The Wild Goose'. Ben Tamworth sang 'The Sleepless Sailor'. Philip Teal sang George Butterworth's setting to music of 'Is My Team Ploughing?' from *A Shropshire Lad* in a high tenor voice so affecting that it silenced the pub entirely for a few seconds before earning a fierce and sustained ovation. Michael Carney recited a poem. Rachel Flood sang the Scottish lament 'Annan Waters'.

The stage cleared after the pharmacist had finished her sorrowful Highland song about a lover drowned on the way to meet his sweetheart and James had a heretical moment when he thought that perhaps Angela Heart, Brodmaw Bay's answer to Marlene Dietrich, might get up and growl her sultry way through 'Stormy Weather'. But of course that did not happen. Instead, Elizabeth Penmarrick stirred in the chair to his left and smiled across him at her husband and rose and, to loud clapping from what seemed every pair of hands in the pub, took to the stage.

She strapped on a guitar and tuned it, saying quietly that she was going to sing a Sandy Denny song. This announcement provoked a further ripple of applause. Either the population of the bay contained a disproportionate number of folkies, or they had heard her sing the song before. James assumed the latter. Elizabeth looked beautiful on the stage, lit by a single lamp and dabs of ochre from the declining fire. She looked calm and self-possessed and as comfortable in the scrutiny of an audience as anyone he had ever seen on a stage.

She strummed the opening chords of the song and he recognised it as 'The Sea'. Then she began to sing. Her voice was a contralto with no trace of sibilance or vibrato in it at all. It was a pure instrument. And it was a powerful surge-tide of sung emotion, thrilling, engulfing, almost overwhelming in the force and feeling with which it delivered words and melody.

'She's unbelievable,' he said to Richard, when the song had finished and the applause had finally subsided sufficiently for him to be able to be heard. 'She's a force of nature.'

Richard smiled. He raised his eyebrows and nodded at

the stage signalling that his wife had not quite finished performing yet.

Elizabeth sang 'John Barbury'. She sang it without accompaniment. Where she had sung 'The Sea' with a sort of powerful grandeur, she sang this lovely, wistful song with a delicacy that was almost heartbreaking. James sneaked a look round. By the final verses it seemed like half the audience were sniffing and dabbing at moist eyes with hankies.

Her interpretation of the song was precise and lovely and unbearably poignant. He struggled not to shed a tear and James was not a demonstrative man where emotions were concerned. He had simply never heard timbre or phrasing like that this woman possessed. The sung words shaped by her lovely mouth emerged into the room and left her audience spellbound. He felt as she finished that nothing of him had been left unaffected by her voice. It had stirred him to his core. It had flayed his heart. His very soul had been shaken just listening to it.

She slipped off the stage and sat down and took a sip from her drink. She cast her eyes down at the floor. The shyness had come upon her again. All around her people were on their feet, roaring and stamping and clapping wildly in celebration of a gift so profound that to James it seemed more than merely human. He had not over the course of the evening drunk more than three or four beers, but he wondered in the intoxication of the moment if he had not just heard the singing of an angel.

Chapter Six

After the concert had concluded and the last drinks had been downed and the farewells said and the pub doors finally closed and locked, James knew that the sensible thing to do was to go to bed. He had the drive back to London the following day and it could not be done in less than four hours even in ideal road conditions. The weather forecast was good, but it took only one breakdown or collision on the eastbound carriageway of the A303 to cause substantial delay on that journey.

He did not go to bed. He remembered his phone conversation with the detective sergeant on the beach after his swim in the afternoon. Its detail and implications returned to him and brought with them anger and frustration he knew he had no way of resolving.

There was such a thing as natural justice. At least in theory, there was. But to a crime victim such as his son, it seemed destined to remain an abstract concept. There was little likelihood of any justice for Jack, natural or otherwise. Nobody was likely to be called to account. James was honest enough with himself to admit that what he really wanted was probably better described as retribution rather than justice. He wasn't going to get that either, was he?

Perhaps it was a situation in which it was best simply to count his family's blessings. If you believed the tabloid newspapers, gangs of feral youths on Britain's council estates had respectable and industrious residents living in siege conditions. Emasculated police forces and impotent courts could do nothing to ease their predicament. These residents could not afford to escape the problems besetting them and blighting their lives.

He and his family could and were going to. Plus, he had stumbled by pure good fortune on a place that would enable them to live securely and even idyllically in a lovely location where the residents were apparently prepared to welcome them with a degree of spontaneous warmth as sincere as it was surprising.

He did not go to bed. He drank with Charlie Abraham from a bottle of brandy the landlord cracked before the dying embers of the fire. The label of the bottle was obscured by dust and very faded. But from the depth and complexity of the flavour when he sipped it, James suspected that it was an old and valuable vintage. He was flattered at the compliment. He was further flattered when Charlie asked if he would like to see the cache of letters sent to his ancestor by the poet pugilist Lord Byron.

The letters were written in his lordship's admirably legible hand. They were informal in tone, witty and confidential and obviously genuine. They alluded a lot to the poet's constant battle with his weight. Gregory had given him tips on the best exercise regimes for controlling it and it seemed to have been working and he was obviously grateful. There was quite a lot about boxing technique and James was reminded that Byron had been combative by nature, a soldier as well as a poet, a warrior determined to liberate Greece in a war of independence.

'Did he ever come here?'

'Yes, on two occasions. He stayed in the room I've given you.'

'It was a hell of a way to come on a horse.'

'Robust times, James. Robust men suited to those times. They thought nothing of it.'

'It must give you such a sense of security, of belonging, being able to trace your ancestry back through the centuries in the one location. It's becoming rarer, the way the world is now. People are so much more rootless. They're not anchored in the same way.'

Charlie shifted his weight and his chair creaked under him. He replenished their drinks from the bottle between them on the table and looked at the greying embers of the fire. 'It isn't all Arcadian delight, James. Communities like this one have bad as well as good about them. You saw the good tonight.'

'I certainly did. I heard an angel singing.'

Charlie smiled. 'Or a siren,' he said.

'It was wonderful. It was unearthly, magical.'

'You want to be careful how you apply those terms.'

'What do you mean?'

'This is the west of England. There's bad as well as good magic and there're those as still practise it. You are an awfully long way from London, James. This is an ancient and remote corner of England. Not all of its traditions would look appealing held up to the light. And yet there are those who revel in them.'

'Are you trying to warn me off?'

'I told you, fresh blood is welcome here. That's the truth. But you want to come here with your eyes open if you do come.'

James considered what he was being told. And he considered its source. He did not want to be rude. He thought that Charlie Abraham spoke sincerely and out of concern rather than contempt or hostility towards a stranger. 'You believe in magic, Charlie? You actually believe in the supernatural?'

'I understand you've seen a ghost of your own.'

James did not know what Charlie meant. Then he did. 'The little girl I saw up at the stone circle the day before yesterday? I'm sure there is an explanation for her.'

'I'm sure there is,' Charlie said. 'My fear is it is not one you would easily countenance.'

James drained his glass. 'I'm tired,' he said. 'I should go to bed.' He nodded at the letters, carefully rolled now and put back in the cardboard sleeve that protected them. 'Thank you for showing me those. They are fascinating.'

His anger over what DS McCabe had told him had gone, replaced by sympathy for the predicament faced by that dogged and principled police officer. McCabe had confided in Jack that he had joined the force to make a difference. He was prevented from doing so, probably on a daily basis, confronted by injustice at every turn. Jack would get over his physical injuries. James would get over his indignation at what had happened to his son. McCabe would go on being defeated by a self-serving and opportunistic industry that profited from championing the guilty.

He fumbled his phone out of his shirt pocket as he undressed. He had become quite drunk, he realised, on the brandy. Fatigue had played its part. Swimming in the sea was much more strenuous than swimming in a pool and he had subsequently stayed up, in the end, very late. He saw that someone had attempted to call him and recognised the number of the media rights agent he had engaged to help him market his computer game. Perhaps the fellow had positive news.

Dropping off to sleep, he thought about the landlord's

words of caution. They did not concern him. Not in the slightest, they didn't. He'd take the Green Man and a witch's curse and corn dollies and the Beast of Bodmin any day over what the Greer family were in the process of leaving behind.

It was playtime when Olivia Greer noticed her non-imaginary friend. She was outside the school railings over by the main gate. She was just standing there in her purple and grey uniform, her blonde hair falling in braids to either side of her straw hat. It was a bright morning and the sun on the brim of the hat cast her face into shadow. Olivia could not see what expression her face wore and she stood there perfectly still. But she wanted Olivia to go over and talk to her. She looked somehow nervous, like someone who has made a decision they are not at all sure about. Her fists were clenched. Olivia went over slowly, thinking that if she ran, the girl might change her mind and turn and flee.

Olivia was pretty sure by now that the girl was a ghost. She had never seen anyone else wearing that uniform. She did not think the girl could have got into her bedroom in the normal way, by walking through the front door and up the stairs, without her mum or brother noticing. She did not think any of the other children in the playground could see the girl. In fact, she was sure they could not. The girl was here for her. This realisation did not frighten Olivia. It just made her all the more curious.

'Hello.'

'Hi.'

'My name is Madeleine.'

'That's a lovely name.'

'You are kind to say so.'

'My name is Olivia.'

'I know.'

'You are a ghost, aren't you?'

'You must not be afraid.'

'I'm not. But when people are alive, their eyes are coloured. Yours are blank.'

'Once they were blue, like yours.'

'When you were alive?'

'Yes, Olivia. They were blue when I was alive.'

Olivia nodded. There were some things she did not need to be told. There were some things she just knew. She knew that had she met this girl in the normal way, they would have been friends. They might have been best friends who kept one another's secrets and never argued and lent one another their most precious things. She knew that the girl had died at the age she was now. She had never grown up. And she knew that Madeleine had been killed. Her death had been deliberate. Olivia knew that her daddy would have called Madeleine's death a crime. She had been murdered.

'You are clever, Olivia. I think you are much cleverer than I was.'

'We shall never know.'

'You must be brave, also. You must listen carefully and remember to do what I ask you to.'

Olivia wasn't afraid. But there were things about Madeleine that were scary, even in the sunshine, even though she gave her compliments and was nice. Her blank eyes were scary but her voice was scary too. There was a sort of echo to it as though it had come a long way, through a tunnel maybe, to be heard. And her mouth was dark. When she opened it, there was nothing to see beyond the shape of her lips but blackness. And the blackness seemed deep. It reached a lot further than the root of a living person's tongue.

Smart from a distance, the uniform she wore was worn and musty close to, its colours faded and drab and the fabric threadbare. The straw of her hat was so thinly woven in places it showed the dusty yellow of her hair. And her clenched fists were not exactly still. She did not move them. But something maggoty moved them anyway, writhing under their skin.

She's doing her best, Olivia understood suddenly. Being here is a struggle for her but she is doing her very best because she wants to help me somehow. She is here only because I am in danger and the fact that she has managed to come at all means the danger must be very great.

'Gosh, you really are clever.'

'Not as clever as you, Madeleine, you can read my thoughts.'

The ghost in front of Olivia nodded. 'You will be moving quite soon to live somewhere new. I think you know something about this already.'

'Am I in danger if I go?'

'There is no question of if. You are going. Some things are meant and you are meant to go. I am going to tell you about something you must look for and find when you get there. I do not know exactly where it is. But there will be clues and you are sharp enough to follow them. Follow the clues. Find the thing hidden. Show it to your father.'

'What is this thing?'

The ghost called Madeleine seemed to hesitate. For the second time, Olivia sensed her nervousness, as though she was unsure about what she was doing. Yet the effort involved in her coming at all had been enormous. Olivia was aware of that, too.

Madeleine told her what the hidden thing was.

Olivia nodded. Then she said, 'Was your death a painful one?'

Madeleine nodded back. 'My death was sad and horrid,' she said. Then she turned and in the bright sunlight, as Olivia watched, she withered away and was gone.

James slept later than he would have ordinarily. He awoke only at eight fifteen. During his last Leeward Arms breakfast, he decided that he would go and look at the ruined church of Lillian's illustration before his departure. Partly he resolved to do this because he did not think it could look anything like as sinister in life as she had depicted it upon the page. Partly it was because he had slept on Charlie Abraham's veiled warning and decided, having done so, not to ignore it completely.

If there were dark and malevolent aspects to Brodmaw Bay they were better confronted before his family's arrival. He did not really think there were. He was not much of a believer in anything irrational. But he thought he ought to take a look, just to be able to say later that he had done so. And he could think of nothing more menacing about the place than his wife's painting of the stark ruin that had once been a place of worship.

Over breakfast, he rang his agent. And he was delivered the intriguing news that a games company based in Colorado was expressing considerable interest in finally formatting his prototype and bringing it into production on a global scale.

'You'll have to go and see them, James.'

'I will, of course, though to be honest, Lee, this is not the best time.'

'This could be a life-changer, Jimmy. They call a meeting, I book you a flight. They're a start-up outfit, but with pedigree running right through the senior staff. We're talking software aristocracy with Silicon Valley lineage. These guys are very seriously capitalised. They're perfect for you. Okay?'

'Okay.'

He walked to the church. He got there at ten thirty, at the exact time that his daughter was walking across a Bermondsey schoolyard to converse with a pale and threadbare apparition who had once been a little girl called Madeleine Gleason.

The gravestones of the churchyard beyond the gate were canted at odd angles, just as they had been in Lillian's picture. In that, the churchyard had been snowy. It was summer now. Shadows were deep in the low sunlight. The angles of the granite and marble headstones suggested subsidence, which was a grim thought given the number and age of the graves. A resting place for the dead should not suffer such upheaval, James thought, lifting the latch on the gate and stepping on to the gravel path beyond.

The path was slick in places with patches of moss. They were still damp from the dew of the night. Tall surrounding trees, in full leaf, meant that the graveyard lay in gloomy shadow. This lack of light seemed to have leached the colour out of the wild grass and weeds erupting between the graves. The vegetation had a pale, anaemic character.

Its broken door on its twisted hinges gave the church itself a violated look. Beyond the door was only blackness. James had expected beams of light penetrating through those gaps where the roof had been stripped for reclaimed slates or lead with a high scrap value. But it seemed that the roof of the church was intact.

He found himself not really wanting to go inside. Doing so meant twisting on his hands and knees, squirming under the angle of the smashed, obstructing door. His instinct was to stay on his feet with his arms free to protect himself.

His senses insisted this was a hostile, dangerous place. His skin had begun to crawl with the swing of the gate as soon as he released the latch and set foot on the churchyard path. He could feel raised goose bumps coarsening his skin and his breathing had become shallow as his heart rate grew more rapid.

It was very quiet. There was no sound of birdsong. He looked around. It was very still there, too. There was no breeze at all. It was as though, on its abandoned plot, this place existed entirely separate to the rest of the locality. Nothing connected it. No one came here, James realised, the thought defeating, abject almost. It was a place of faith exiled and distress ignored. Prayers went unanswered and the ground writhed slyly in rejection of the dead.

He smiled to himself and rapped a tattoo on the oak solidity of the canted door, as if the resultant smart to his knuckles could distract him from the strange thoughts beginning to occupy his mind. He was at the entrance to a deconsecrated church. It was a derelict building, nothing more or less than that, bricks and mortar, stained glass and empty pews, flowers dead in petrified tribute, hymns for ever unsung.

He was doing it again. It was ridiculous. He stooped and scrambled in under the door and saw the seated spectres in their pews and almost screamed before his eyes adjusted to the absence of light and he made sense of what he was looking at; a sight that, actually, made no sense to him at all.

Burlap sacks had been placed on the benches in their rows. They were each bound by wound loops of ancient twine and sagged with age. He gained the aisle and walked along it towards the high altar, the sacks to the right and left of him, slumped and silent, stored and forgotten.

Was this some act of rustic sacrilege? It was very strange

and obscure if it was. He did not think it could be. He reached for one of the sacks. Its top had been sewn neatly shut in the manner of an old-fashioned mail bag. The substance of the bag itself was coarse and strong. Time had not made the fabric weak. Then again, he did not know how much time had elapsed since this strange cargo had been stored. He lifted and hefted the bag. Its contents slipped as he did so, heavy and inert. It landed with a muffled clatter when he put it back down again. He dusted his hands together.

He kept on walking towards the high altar. He counted the sacks as he did so. There were nineteen of them. The altarpiece was marble. There was a tabernacle at its centre, bronze and greenish with mould. It had a double door, modelled, James thought, probably on the entrance to some biblical temple of which he should have heard but had not. He was agnostic, hardly a scholar of comparative religions. Lillian shared his lack of faith. They had not even had their children baptised.

He opened the tabernacle doors, which parted with a creak. He did so with the sensation that eyes studied him from behind but knew that this was his imagination. There was no living thing in the church besides him. Foul air escaped in a salty stench of tidal rot as the bronze doors parted. The tabernacle was substantial, about two feet high and when he opened the doors, about the same depth. It was not empty. Within its gloomy interior lay a large sea crab.

The crab was black and its claws huge and bony and it had been there for a long time and James thought that its lurking presence there was sacrilege. This creature had not died drowning in air, netted and beached. The violent manner of its death was still visible in the iron spike protruding from its back. If its presence there was a joke, it was a spiteful and possibly blasphemous joke. James did know that Christianity in its early years had possessed many metaphors to do with fish. The Disciples, most of them, had been fishermen. Jesus Christ had been described in one of the Gospels as a fisher of men.

As he studied the old crustacean monster, noticing the barnacles on its ridged back and claws now that his eyes were fully adjusted to the gloom, he heard a noise behind him he knew was real rather than imagined. It was the clack of a heel in silence on a tiled church floor.

James turned, slowly. Angela Heart stood halfway down the aisle staring at him over folded arms. Her expression was severe and for a moment he felt absurdly as a child might, doing something naughty, caught red-handed in the act.

'Why are you here?'

'Why aren't you at school?'

'Inset day. This is a dangerous structure. It has lain derelict for years. It must be more than half a century since it was last surveyed. You should not be here.'

'How did you know I was?'

'You passed my cottage on the route. I was drinking a cup of coffee and enjoying the view of my roses through my front window. On foot, you could have had only one destination in mind. It seemed pretty improbable. I was fairly incredulous to be honest, but I knew I hadn't imagined you. When you had not returned after five minutes, I came to look for you. I did so out of concern, James. This place is not safe.'

He nodded. He thought her phraseology odd. It was the structure that was unsafe, rather than the place. Teachers were usually more pedantic in their linguistic precision. On the other hand, Angela Heart was not your typical teacher.

He had felt a physical thrill just now when she had used his Christian name.

She had not had time to change, surely, before following him to the church. It meant that she had been enjoying her coffee and her roses dressed as she was now, in a short black dress that showed her cleavage under a loop of black pearls and with her mouth shaped in crimson lipstick. The solitary clue to the impromptu nature of her errand was that her hair had only been carelessly brushed. Strands of it hung free on her cheeks, softening her features and making her look more youthful than she had the previous evening, especially now that she had dropped her hands to her sides and was smiling.

'Listen to me. I sound like I'm telling you off.'

'Are you going to make me go and stand in the corner?'

She looked around and pushed one of the stray strands of hair away with a thumb. 'Neither of us should be in here. Come on, James.'

They were at the churchyard gate before he said, 'What's in the sacks?'

'Bones,' she said.

'Not human bones?'

'Really, how would I know what's in the sacks? They look like they've been there for decades. They're probably full of debris from an attempt to clean up the place, between the wars, back before the bay gave up on organised religion. You should really be asking Michael Carney about this. He's our local historian.' She closed the gate latch carefully behind them. 'If I invited you back to my cottage for a cup of coffee, would you feel completely scandalised?'

James looked at his watch. He would set off at about one in the afternoon, the time when he judged traffic would be at its lightest, back in London to beat the rush hour. It was just after eleven o'clock. 'I'd feel flattered and delighted,' he said, which was only the truth.

They drank their coffee in her back garden. There was ivy on the ancient walls that formed its boundary. There was the smell of herbs and sweet grass and blossoming flowers. Birds sang from the branches of a sycamore tree. She studied him with her green eyes. In sunlight, after the gloom of the church interior, they were startling, almost mesmeric.

'I like men like you.'

'Oh? What's likeable about men like me?'

'You like women. In fact you are fascinated by women. It makes you attentive and charming and a bit flirtatious, but not in a patronising way.'

'You think I'm a flirt?'

'You do nothing to conceal the fact that you find me attractive. But you love your wife very deeply, James. When you talked about your family last night, the passion was plain to see in your face. It was ardent in the tone of your voice. You would never be unfaithful to her.'

'No. I would not.'

'I like that about you too.'

'Then we should get on.'

She smiled. 'But not *too* well. People might talk.'

'I've never met a teacher who talks like you.'

Angela lit a cigarette. She said, 'Many teachers draw no real line of demarcation between the children they teach and their parents. They speak to the parent as they might to a bright but sometimes tricky pupil. I've never done that. I have a mode of behaviour and a dress code and a rather correct and didactic persona I use in the classroom. I don't bring it home or use it after hours because to do so would be a bore and make me a slave to my occupation.'

And teaching was an occupation for her, James knew. It was not a vocation and she was not in the business of pretending it was. She was too honest, with herself and other people for that.

'What keeps you in the bay?'

She smiled again. 'Why would I leave?'

'You are clever and stylish and beautiful. I would have thought you'd have left years ago.'

'I did leave, James. I came back.'

'Why?'

'I don't mind telling you, but it is a complicated story and we don't have time for it now. You have a journey ahead of you.'

Lillian decided that she would tell James about her affair with Robert O'Brien as soon as the children had both gone to bed. She did not trust Robert. He was neither mature nor predictable and he was completely unused to failure and rejection. She thought it quite likely that he would compromise and expose her over the coming days and weeks. And living with that possibility would be a prolonged agony she was not prepared to tolerate.

She believed anyway what she had told Jack on the Thames towpath at Hampton Court. Secrecy was corrosive. She did not know whether her relationship with James, and therefore their family life, would survive intact her confession of betrayal. She did know that she could not live a lie. She had to tell the truth and then try to salvage what was salvageable once she knew the extent of the damage she had inflicted. She had to tell the truth as the first step in regaining the trust and respect of her son.

Love was a funny commodity. Lillian would have

sacrificed her life willingly for either of her children. She loved them profoundly, above anyone, above anything. She knew that they loved her unconditionally. Jack loved her despite the betrayal he had found out about. Sons tended to love their mothers. And until the catastrophic error of judgement with Robert O'Brien, she had been a good mother; an affectionate, unselfish provider who tried to teach her children right from wrong and good from bad through example.

The love an adult individual felt for their partner was a less certain, more negotiable commodity. There was still much that she loved about James. But she had meant it when she had said to him it was difficult to love someone who did not have any love for themselves. James felt that he was a failure in some important ways. What he saw as his defeat in the cut and thrust of the commercial world had made him melancholy. Perhaps he was even depressed.

His defeated mood had distanced him, at least in her mind. She could not have precisely identified the moment at which they had ceased to be soul mates. She thought that it had happened, though, in the months prior to Jack's assault. James had become moody and preoccupied and less easy to communicate with. He had not wanted to inflict his company upon her, she realised now, because he had not had sufficient self-regard to consider himself a worthwhile companion.

There was something quite noble about his reason for distancing himself. But the effect had been to distance her and that had been damaging to their relationship. They had become careful and tactful and deliberate around one another, where before there had been only spontaneity. They had grown apart. At least to her mind they had. They had started to behave around one another with a sort of formality that was alien to real intimacy. She had become isolated and she realised now, in retrospect, rather lonely.

She catalogued his attributes in her mind. He was loyal and faithful. He was sober and gentle and kind. He was selfless and patient and always had time for the children and was forever encouraging and trying to stimulate and inspire them. He was clever and physically courageous. She could not remember ever having seen him afraid. He was a bit of a flirt, but that was because he was good-looking and well put together and women responded to him positively. He was always encouraging her, was always genuinely thrilled by her achievements. He was a man who loved his wife.

How would he respond to her confession?

Her thoughts were interrupted by laughter from the sitting room. She was in the kitchen, making tea for the dashing DS sharing a sofa and some choice football anecdotes with Jack. She thought Alec McCabe less inhibited than he had been when James had been around. Maybe it was just a case of the second visit being one he was making to someone he had got to know a bit. It was obvious Jack liked him and the feeling seemed to be mutual. They had a rapport.

She looked at her watch. When she had made the tea, she would have to go and fetch Olivia from school. Clichés become clichés because their aptness earns them constant repetition, she mused, with an ironic little smile to herself. The cliché she had in mind, as she stirred sugar into McCabe's tea, was the one insisting that there is no rest for the wicked.

On their return, Olivia scampered up the stairs to her room, saying that she had something important to write in the journal she kept. Lillian made her daughter a snack and took it up to her. Then she went in to the sitting room for her formal chat with the police officer. He had rung that morning asking to talk to both the crime victim and a parent. Sensing that the boring, grown-up stuff was about to commence, Jack excused himself. He would nap for an hour. He was sleeping for less time in the afternoons as his strength recovered. But he still needed a little siesta each day if he didn't want the evening to bring a headache with it.

'He plays centre back, doesn't he?'

'He played centre back. How much relish he will have for aerial challenges when he's healed is yet to be determined.'

'He seems a resilient lad. And he's young, has youth on his side.'

'Maybe he can play on the wing,' Lillian said. 'Wingers provide the crosses, don't they? They aren't required to get on the end of them.'

'Sounds like you know a bit about football.'

'For a woman, you mean?'

'No. I mean what I say, Mrs Greer. It sounds as though you know something about the game.'

'I'm sorry. The sarcasm wasn't called for. When your son is a footballing prodigy, you do sort of learn about it.'

'By osmosis, you mean?'

'I wish by osmosis. If I had a pound for every time I've cheered him on from a rainy touchline . . .'

'You'd have a lot of pounds.'

'Quite. Does your daughter play a sport? She can hardly follow you into the ring.'

'Jack told you about that?'

'My husband told me. Jack told him.'

'These days, Dora could very well follow me into the ring, actually. It's an equal opportunities sport. But her passion is ballet, thank God.'

Lillian looked at the floor.

'I know what you are thinking. You are wondering how many black prima ballerinas there are and I can tell you, they're as rare as hen's teeth. But my wife is white and my daughter mulatto and quite strikingly beautiful.'

'Do you think my husband a racist bigot?'

'No, Mrs Greer, I don't. I think your husband is an empiricist. He doesn't have much time for righteous ideology. He judges the world on how he sees it.'

'You sound as though you approve.'

'I grew up watching news bulletins in which they constantly banged on about the black community. It's so ubiquitous a notion, people don't really question it. To understand just how bogus it is, consider the white community.'

'There isn't one.'

'No, there isn't. It's an absurd concept.'

'Why did you want to see me, Detective Sergeant?'

'I spoke to your husband yesterday afternoon. He sounded as though he was on a beach.'

'He probably was.'

'After I spoke to him, I had a call from the social services department dealing with Jack's three alleged assailants. They're all having the same dream, apparently.'

'That's nice and cosy for them.'

'One of them has mental health issues. The other two, the twins who are his cousins, are apparently well balanced mentally.'

'Well balanced, when they're prepared to beat someone half to death for a mobile phone?'

'Everything is relative, Mrs Greer.'

'What's the substance of the dream?'

'A little girl appears in it and threatens them.'

'I cannot see what possible relevance that has to us.'

'The little girl is white. And she is quite emphatic on the reason for the threat. She is very specific about what happened to Jack.'

'The poor darlings, my heart bleeds for them.'

'Sarcasm seems to be your default mode.'

Lillian bit her lip. 'I'm sorry, Detective Sergeant. It isn't usually. I'm under a bit of strain. I have a domestic issue. Actually it's truer to say that we have a domestic issue, my husband and me. It will have to be resolved after he gets back, tonight.'

McCabe sipped tea. It was his turn to look at the floor. 'They do say honesty is the best policy,' he said.

'You are very perceptive.'

'Not always a blessing.'

'Why do we need to know? About the dreams these boys claim to be having, I mean?'

'If the case comes to trial, I don't want you surprised by any tack their defence counsel might take.'

'We've got no influence over their dreams, for God's sake.'

'But they think you have, apparently. They think they're the victims of witchcraft.'

James got back to London in a buoyant mood. He did not honestly think that his trip to Brodmaw Bay could have gone any better. He had been warmly welcomed. The place was every bit as unspoiled and authentic as it had promised to be in Lillian's book illustrations. Topper's Reach was the perfect property to fashion into a wonderful home for the four of them. He had checked out the schools quickly in his room on his laptop while he did his bit of packing before departure and discovered that Philip Teal had been telling only the truth the previous evening in the Leeward. The Schools

Inspectorate had picked out both the Mount and St Paul's Primary for particular praise.

He had been obliged to pull into a lay-by to answer his mobile on the return drive to hear more positive news. Lee Marsden, his media agent, had just received a preliminary offer for his game from the people in Colorado. They had outlined a global sales strategy and come up with a provisional bid offer that was more money than James had earned in his entire professional career. There were also generous points on net profit percentage from retail sales down the line.

'They are anxious to fix some face time, Jimmy.'

James did not like being called Jimmy. In the circumstances, he was prepared to tolerate it though. 'Speak English to me, Lee.'

'They want to meet you in person. They have ideas for multiple platform integration and brand extension and package visuals they want to put in front of you.'

'Shouldn't it be me making the pitch?'

'We're way beyond the need to pitch. They're sold, brother. They're totally sold.'

After this short conversation, James took a moment to think about what the news he had just heard might mean for his future and that of his family. He sat at the wheel at the roadside with the engine switched off and his mobile on the seat beside him and gave in to the temptation to speculate on what it would be like, finally to achieve the success he had striven for during a stop-start career marked mostly by mediocrity, anticlimax and disappointment.

His children would be proud of him. They would take pride in his achievement and they would enjoy its material consequences in lives that would be financially secure.

Their peers would buy and play his game. They would queue to see the movies spun off from it. They would covet and then own the action figures based on characters he had created. His success would be tangible. And success bred success. The money would give him the time to create something even better.

It would change the dynamic of his relationship with his wife. She had always earned more than he had and that fact had to some extent inevitably shaped the way that they lived. Prior to his trip to Brodmaw, she had made every major decision affecting their lives together. Now it would be different. They would be equals. She would have more respect for him and, crucially, he would have a great deal more respect for himself.

It was tempting to credit Brodmaw itself with this sudden change in his fortunes and its potential effect on his status. It was just a coincidence of course that he had been there when the Colorado breakthrough came. But it did not really feel like one. What it actually felt like, to James, was that in finally making the decision to do something about their long-held fantasy of relocation, he had somehow qualified his family for an altogether improved fate. It was said that you made your own luck. He felt the strong conviction that an idyllic little village on the southern coast of Cornwall was going to be a lucky place for them indeed. It had started already and they hadn't even moved there yet.

He looked up. His mind cleared itself of speculation and his eyes focused on what lay beyond the windscreen. In the distance, on the parched plain to the left of where the road gently descended, he could see Stonehenge. In a humbler mood, the sight of the great megalithic enigma would have chastised him, making him feel trivial and his ambitions shallow. The indifferent might of the sea could do that to him, or the vaulting arches of an old cathedral. But he was not in a humble mood. In fact, he felt exultant.

The children were ecstatic to see him. He told them about his adventures in the west. He showed them the pictures he had taken of Topper's Reach on his phone and described the stone circle above the village and said that he had been swimming in the sea and that soon they would all be doing that. They seemed interested. They even seemed interested in his description of Lord Byron's letters sent to the old bare-knuckle boxing champion. But he thought Lillian subdued. He wondered if she was having second thoughts about the whole matter of moving before she had even seen their intended destination.

If she was, he was confident he could bring her round. All she had to do was to agree to a short visit without any commitment at all. He thought that as soon as she saw the bay from the plateau above it, she would be sold. She would remember the quaint details, all of them intact, that she had made the subject of those lovely student illustrations in the book. The house would seduce her. Dinner followed by a summer night of music at the Leeward would charm her completely. He knew his wife. The bay would prove irresistible to her if she just gave it a chance over one sunny weekend.

Jack went to bed at nine thirty. When he did so, Lillian was in the sitting room and James in the study, talking to Lee Marsden on the phone about Colorado. It occurred to James as he completed the call that the time difference between the two countries meant the Americans were just becoming animated about business when the British were readying themselves for a late drink in the pub, or for an early night in bed. He did not mind. The inconvenience was a small price to pay. He walked back into the sitting room, resuming the story he had been telling Lillian about Elizabeth Penmarrick's concert performance of the previous evening.

'. . . it's just unbelievable that someone can turn a lungful of air into the sounds that were emerging from her mouth. I promise you, Lily, to believe it, you'd have to witness it in the flesh.'

'Who was that on the phone?'

'Lee. Lee Marsden called. There's interest in the game, from America.'

'That's nice.'

'It sounds very promising.'

'There's something I need to tell you.'

'It's a Colorado-based boutique tech company with deep pockets.'

'There's something I need to tell you, James.'

And something in the tone of her voice made him look directly into his wife's face. And he knew. He did not want to know, but James knew anyway. A whole variety of small details that had not seemed quite right suddenly resolved themselves into a clear picture. He sat down. He sat down heavily, his legs weakened suddenly, his body an impossible weight to sustain, feeling as hopeless and weak and overwhelmed as the realisation of his wife's deceit had just rendered him. He tried to remember how to breathe and a sob broke out of him. He put his hand to his eyes and began to descend in his mind into some dark abyss and to weep with grief for his marriage.

'I'm sorry,' she said. She took a step towards where he sat.

He held out a hand to stop her. He was hurt beyond endurance. Only one person in the world could comfort him. And he craved her comfort, but it was impossible, because she was the person inflicting this unbearable pain.

'I'm going out,' he said, levering himself to his feet, his legs still unsteady and his vision blurred by tears.

'Will you come back?' Her self-possession failed her on the question, her voice cracking with emotion and something that sounded not far removed from fear. 'Will you?'

'Of course I will,' he said. 'This is my home.' He paused. 'Oh, Lily,' he said. And then he turned and went to walk out of the house, swiftly, because he could not bear the thought of her seeing her husband reduced to what she had made of him.

She caught him before he got to their door. She held him in her arms. He was aware of the familiar touch and scent and warmth of her, qualities all different now, like wealth he had once possessed, debased.

'Please, James,' she said. 'Please, please listen to me. I made a mistake and I am sorry. I need to tell you about it and you need to listen to me. This is about more than the two of us. You need to be mature about this, for the sake of the two people upstairs. They can't be mature because they are children. You are their father and they rely upon you.'

'That's a very nice speech.'

'Don't point-score, James. You've got all the points. I'm disgusted with myself, if you want to know the truth. The high ground is all yours. But we have to talk. We have to.'

They went into the study. It was the quietest room in the house, the room from which they would not be heard by one of their children lying woken by the human commotion at the door. Olivia, at eight, probably slept soundly and untroubled. But Jack, at thirteen, was easier stirred and upset already because he knew about his mother's infidelity.

James looked out of the window, at where he thought he had seen that watching apparition a week ago. It was fully dark now. He thought that nothing would ever frighten him again after this. Nothing could possibly hurt him more than the mundane catastrophe of his wife's betrayal.

'Jack knows, James.'

'You ended it because Jack found out?'

'No. Jack found out because I ended it.'

'Do I know your lover?'

'You might have heard of him. His name is Robert O'Brien.'

'O'Brien the writer?'

'Yes.'

'Jesus. Jack reads his books.'

'I don't expect he will be reading any more of them. I don't expect my son will ever forgive me.'

'He's our son, Lily. They're our children. It's our family. Don't speak as though I was dead.'

'I've ended it. It's over. If you can find it in your heart to live with what I've done I want nothing more than this shot at a new life that's had you so focused and energised. You came back this afternoon filled with confidence and optimism and when I saw you I realised how much and for how long I have missed those qualities in you. I have made a dreadful mistake. But it was a mistake and I want to move on from it. I don't want to lose you, James. I don't want our family fragmented and destroyed. We can move on, literally. But you have to give me the chance if that's to happen.'

James thought about this. Then he said, 'Tell me everything, Lily. Tell me what you did with him and tell me why you did it. Tell me all of it. Leave nothing out.'

He was not masochistic by nature. He did not relish

hearing the detail. He was not sadistic either and did not want to punish his wife through the humiliation of making her relive her marital crime.

He suspected, under the shock and pain that had been his first, reeling reaction to her adultery, that he had provoked it. He thought that it would be easier to forgive if she confirmed this. His withdrawal into despondency had made her lonely and probably bored. He had not driven her into O'Brien's arms, but he had failed her in the matter of love. Over the past year or so, he had not cherished his wife.

What Lillian said to him confirmed this. She did not try to exonerate herself. She did not try to shift blame and evade moral responsibility. But she was almost brutally honest about their growing apart and the reasons for it and as she spoke he found himself nodding with recognition and regret and even in the end with sympathy.

Lillian was not a high-maintenance woman in the WAG tradition of ski holidays at smart resorts and trophy cars and the frequent sprinklings of gifts from Bond Street. She was successful and admired and affluent in her own right. But she had her needs and he had failed to meet them and she had strayed.

'Will you forgive me?'

'I will only if you will forgive me,' he said.

'James, I'm so sorry to have hurt you like this.'

'Don't cry.' He managed a laugh. 'If you cry, I'll feel even worse.'

She reached for him and held his head in her arms against her chest and kissed him.

He said, 'Do you really think we have a chance?'

Upstairs, the children slept, peacefully, their daughter unaware of the not quite imaginary friend, frayed and vigilant at the end of her bed. Outside the study window, if anything crouched silently and watched, the darkness was too full and the people behind the glass far too absorbed with one another to notice it.

'I think we have every chance,' Lillian Greer said firmly.

And so it was she omitted to tell James about the curious conversation with the teacher at the school who had supervised that morning's playtime. Olivia had conducted a one-sided conversation, over by the school gate, through the railings with someone who wasn't there. The teacher had thought it both odd and uncharacteristic and had said that they would monitor her to see if there was any repetition. Preoccupied by her impending confrontation with her husband, Lillian was distracted, listening to this. And then she forgot about it. In the circumstances, her failure to mention it to James was surely understandable.

Chapter Seven

Jack spoke to his mum about the affair three days after his dad's return. It was the Monday and Lillian's TLC commitment to her son had not noticeably wavered. There was work he knew she could have been doing because there was always work for her to do. Her stuff seemed to him to be wanted everywhere.

He thought that she could spare him the time because she was well organised and kept on top of her deadlines. She never did anything at the last minute, as he was apt to do with his homework assignments. That was how she was able to do it. The fact that she wanted to do it he knew was down to the fact that she loved him.

His dad had gone off to an afternoon meeting. There was to be a conference call in the afternoon in his agent's office concerning the game. It seemed to Jack that he had been hearing about the game all his life; certainly for as long as he could remember. His dad had even let him play a version of it on his Xbox 360 and he had given it a solid nine out of ten. His dad had smiled and said when he ironed out the kinks it would merit a perfect score. Jack believed him.

They were in the kitchen. His mum was filling the dishwasher with the plates and glasses and cutlery from their lunch. She was trying to feed him up because he had lost weight in the period since the attack on the bus. But Jack knew that the scales did not tell the whole story. He had lost muscle mass. Muscle was denser than fat and weighed more. He had lost it because he had stopped his football training and eating his mum's nourishing lunches would not help him put the weight back on.

He said, 'You've told Dad, haven't you?'

'Yes, I have,' she said. She stood upright and closed the door of the dishwasher with a slam that rattled its contents. She said, 'I promised you I would. I promised me I would, too. I told him the evening he got back from his trip.'

'Was he upset?'

'What do you think, Jack?'

'Did he cry?'

'Yes. We both cried.'

'It's weird,' Jack said. 'You seem happier than you were before.'

'I'm just relieved. I'm relieved that I have ended something I should never have begun and I'm relieved that your father seems to have forgiven me for my stupidity.'

'I mean, you both seem happier. He seems happier too. You're much more cheerful around one another. You're laughing. You're touching one another.'

'Had we stopped touching one another?'

'Pretty much,' Jack said. 'That family hug in the hospital was the first time for ages I'd seen you and Dad holding each other.'

'Maybe we weren't as locked on as we ought to have been.'

'But we are now,' Jack said, 'all of us. That's the important thing.'

She paused and looked at the backs of her hands. She had rested them on the granite surface of the kitchen counter. 'I want you to try to find it in your heart to forgive me too, Jack.'

'I have,' he said.

And he believed this to be true. He had seen his mother's misery on the towpath at Hampton Court. He had seen that complicated expression of guilt and regret and shame and his heart had lurched for her. She was his mum. He would have forgiven her out of love at that moment, even if she had not always been, to him, the best mum imaginable. But she had been. And his father's happiness made forgiving her okay.

He felt less forgiving towards Robert O'Brien. He thought O'Brien a preening tosser who had jeopardised his family when he had no right to. There were plenty of unattached women in the world. Someone as good-looking and successful as O'Brien was could probably have his pick. What was wrong with going out with a woman of his own age? O'Brien was only thirty years old. Why had he thought it all right to hit on a married woman, someone with a husband and kids?

Jack was not a violent boy by nature. He was strong and fit and had defended himself when attacked on the bus until the tyre iron had intervened. Football was a contact sport and he was a centre back and therefore no stranger to the physical side of the game. But he had never committed a deliberate foul and had never retaliated to one. There was no malice in his one booking, which had been a borderline dangerous play decision when he'd been judged by a fussy referee to have raised a foot too high.

He did not generally harbour ill-will towards anyone. But he wanted the three thugs who had beaten him senseless for his mobile and wallet punished. That's why he was happy to go to court. And it occurred to him, there in the kitchen of his family's Bermondsey home, that he would very much like Robert O'Brien taught a painful lesson for involving himself with his mum. He deserved to be brought down a peg. He deserved to pay a price for the awful damage to other people's lives his mischief had come so close to causing.

He wouldn't be punished, though. People like O'Brien were born lucky, weren't they? They got away with things. They came through it all unscathed. He would just carry on writing his bestselling books and wearing his ponytail and parading his muscles on his windsurf board. Still, there was always the chance that he might windsurf somewhere hot. If he did, a shark might get him.

'What are you grinning about?'

'I don't know, Mum. Nothing much, really.'

'You okay with the plan for the weekend?'

'Fine, I like Uncle Mark. He's cool.'

Jack had been given the choice. He could have a weekend sleepover with a school friend, or he could stay there with Livs and Uncle Mark, his dad's brother, while his mum and dad checked out Brodmaw Bay together. He'd chosen home because he really did like his Uncle Mark, could just about tolerate his sister and did not want to re-live the attack on the bus, which he thought a sleepover with any of his mates from school would make inevitable. They would be curious about what had happened to him and he would end up having to tell them.

What he really wanted to do, obviously, was go to Brodmaw with his mum and dad and have Livs stay behind in London with Uncle Mark. That wasn't on the cards, though. His mum and dad had to make a grown-up decision and the kids were a distraction. It was a big decision. Distractions were something they could probably do without.

Uncle Mark would be fun. He was totally unlike his dad. He was a fanatical Man U fan and they would wind each other up about football. He was an engineer and had done work on the construction of football stadia throughout

Europe. He'd been involved with something called cantilevering that Jack didn't really understand. He had a pilot's licence and had nearly killed himself flying too low over a forest in a helicopter he'd had to crash-land.

He was not married but had lived with Auntie Lucy for ever. Jack had asked his dad why Uncle Mark did not have any children of his own. His dad had raised an eyebrow and said, 'Too much responsibility.'

'You mean looking after them?'

'I mean for them, looking after him.'

Jack's mum had been in the room when he had asked the question and had snorted with laughter into the drink she was sipping from and gone into a coughing fit. Adult humour was sometimes a bit lost on Jack. But he kind of knew what his dad had meant. It was very easy to imagine what Uncle Mark had been like when he'd been a child. With some adults, particularly teachers, this was impossible. Not with his Uncle Mark.

Maybe they would play tennis if Livs could be bribed to sit at the courtside without moaning for a couple of sets. Like most gifted footballers – and he knew he was a gifted player – Jack was good at every ball game he had ever tried from squash to snooker. He thought it would be interesting to play tennis against someone like Uncle Mark, who could handle a racket.

It would be slightly scary, too. He would learn whether the beating on the bus had done anything to damage his hand-eye coordination and hamper his balance. His eyes seemed to be working perfectly okay. But he wouldn't know whether he could accurately sight and respond to a moving ball, in three-dimensional space, until he actually tried to do it.

Uncle Mark played from the baseline and hit heavily top-spun shots on both flanks. Jack wondered if there wasn't some way he could persuade Livs that it was really fun to act as ball girl. He thought probably not. They would have to bribe her to get her to do it. His parents were strictly against bribery with kids. It was, they always said, the slippery slope. But Jack felt confident that Uncle Mark would be all for it.

James booked the room for them at the Leeward Arms he insisted on calling the Byron Suite. It wasn't called that, of course. There would have been no point. It would have been a tourist ploy and the bay was beyond the geographic reach of weekenders and perhaps just too insular and self-contained to attract people for longer stays. It made James wonder why Charlie Abraham bothered to maintain a bed and breakfast facility at all. There didn't seem to be the demand to justify the effort. And if his previous experience had been an accurate indication, the pub was a goldmine just on indigenous trade, without the hassle of renting the rooms upstairs.

'Is that what you call Brodmaw now?'

'What?'

'You just referred to it as "the bay". It's like people from Wight always calling it "the island". It's how you spot a native.'

'I'm not a native. My dialect lacks the burr. There's no hay in my hair or mackerel scales on my boots.'

'You're a fraudulent fisherman, James Anthony Greer. You're a dishonest son of the soil.'

'Guilty as charged,' he said.

They were in the stone circle, on the plateau above the village, having yet to descend down the road and arrive properly. Wonderful how a dash of infidelity can rejuvenate a marriage, James thought. But the thought did not insist on lingering in his mind. What resentment he felt was inconsiderable compared to the almost overwhelming feeling of relief. In his long descent over recent months into despondency, he had been unaware of quite how close his marriage had come to disintegration. That would have been infinitely worse than what he was currently being obliged to endure.

He had texted Richard to tell the Penmarricks he was returning with Lillian to look at Topper's Reach with a view to buying. Richard had responded almost immediately with an offer to put the two of them up for the duration of their stay at their palatial Tudor pile. James had been inclined to accept, so much had he taken to the bay's pre-eminent couple on his first visit.

Then he had thought better of it and politely declined. It would be awkward if Lillian did not respond positively to the village and particularly to the property that Richard, through the Trust, represented. More than that, there was an element of second honeymoon about their westward trip that James did not want inhibited. A certain formality would be required of them as house guests.

Richard's daughter, Megan, was a fan of Lillian's. But there were things the Penmarricks did not know about her. The recent dalliance with Robert O'Brien was one of them. James was keen for the sake of his wife's reputation and his own self-respect to keep it that way. Lillian was anything but a tramp. No man liked to be thought of as a cuckold. They would stay in the Byron Suite and their lost intimacy would be restored and their romance resurrected tenderly, to no one's timetable but their own.

'This is a fascinating place.'

'Is it provoking memories?'

'Not at all, it isn't, no. I can put my hand on my heart and swear I've never been here before. I recognise the view of the bay from my illustrations. But I do not feel as though I have ever seen it before in life.'

'You're doing it now, Lily. You're calling it the bay.'

'Fate,' she said, smiling at him. 'One simply cannot escape it.'

He was glad that they had the plateau to themselves. He somehow felt that the little apparition in the purple school uniform would have seemed twice as sinister had they both seen her. Sinister was not what was required at all. It was his intention for his wife to see the bay in the best light possible. He had already decided that there would be no visit to the derelict church. He would not have stopped at the standing stones had Lillian not spotted the Neolithic monument from the road and insisted upon it.

Lillian nodded down towards the settlement at the edge of the sea. It was a clear day. There was a slight haze on the horizon, but the water was blue and placid and the buildings clustered in their semicircle on the shore bright and sharp with detail. 'It could be 1940 down there,' she said. 'It could almost be 1840.'

'They didn't have cars in 1840.'

'There are precious few cars. I take your point. A car would be pretty anachronistic in 1840. But this is the twenty-first century and I've only counted about ten.'

'There are actually only seven cars in the bay,' James said. 'The other three vehicles are vans.'

'Oh.'

'Yes. They belong to the butcher, the baker and the candlestick maker.'

'You're very witty, Mr Greer. Is Topper's Reach visible from here?'

'Not in its best aspect. Let's go down and sneak a look before we ask for the keys.'

They walked back to the car. They had come in the Jag. There was no point in false modesty when the price of Topper's Reach had been openly stated and Megan Penmarrick knew exactly who Lillian Greer was and her astute parents pretty much what someone with Lillian Greer's artistic output would likely be worth.

On the short walk, James mused on his own phrase, on the subject of the bay's best light. One of its brightest features, to his mind, was an unlikely primary school teacher called Angela Heart. He wondered what his wife would make of her. He was really intrigued to know what Lily would think of Angela.

To him, for all her potent allure, Angela was a character who did not quite add up. She had gone from here and then come back, she had told him. She had implied the story was a complicated one. He assumed she had left because someone as exotic as she was belonged naturally in a more exotic habitat; he would have put his money on somewhere like Paris or Barcelona. He could not help but speculate on the reason for her return.

He thought the bay the perfect place to build a home for a family with growing children. It was a clean and beautiful environment. It was prosperous and crime was not just low but uncommon and it had a stable population with a strong sense of tradition and civic pride. It was the ideal location for married parents who were able to earn a living without being tied to a specific region by their employer.

It obviously suited the likes of the chandler Martin Sharp and the builder Ben Tamworth. He imagined the bay provided their identity as much as their livelihood. And he suspected that was equally true of the headmaster Philip Teal and others he had met more briefly like the poet Michael

Carney, the boatbuilder Billy Jasper, the pharmacist Rachel Flood and Bella Worth, who edited the local rag. They were what were always described in the photo captions of free-sheets like Bella's as pillars of the community.

Angela struck him as fundamentally different from them. She had admitted herself that her job was more employment than vocation. According to the Schools Inspectorate, she excelled in the role. But it wasn't the suspicion of half-heartedness or mediocrity. It was that she was a comically poor fit for the spinster schoolmistress of popular stereotype. There was a sense in which, despite her being a native, her occupation and the bay itself were far too parochial not just for her femme fatale image but for her personality too.

He smiled to himself. He did not know for certain that Angela was a native of the bay. That was his assumption. Was he developing a taste for gossip? Surely that was an essential requirement in any resident of anywhere so small and isolated. He was really going to fit in.

'What?' Lillian asked.

'Nothing,' he said.

Isolated was not a bad word to describe Angela on the night of the singing, outside the pub, when she had made that enigmatic remark of hers about the storm having only just begun. She had been smoking, for which a kind of voluntary exile was always necessary nowadays. But he sensed her isolation had to do with more than just the answering of the craving for a cigarette.

They arrived at the Leeward just before six o'clock in the evening. Mark had appeared punctually as promised at noon on their Bermondsey doorstep. Saying goodbye to Jack had been relatively fuss-free. His father got the distinct impression that he was happy and perhaps even relieved to see his parents going off to do something together. The journey west had been somewhat beset by Friday traffic. They had dawdled at the stone plateau and then Lillian had been given her first look at Topper's Reach. She had gasped and said a single word when the house came into view. The word was 'Perfect.'

Charlie Abraham greeted James with a hearty slap on the back and Lillian with a handshake and a short bow. It was a fine early evening by now and when they were shown up to the Byron Suite, the twin south-facing windows were open to sunlight and salt air and a view of the glittering sea. Gulls cried in the sky. The room smelled of brine and the fresh bouquet of cut lilies in a crystal vase placed on the night table. James did not generally like puns but thought this one a charming jest on the part of their thoughtful and welcoming landlord.

Lillian took a shower. She did this habitually after a journey of any length. It was simple good hygiene in dealing with the dirt that could accrue on the body and hair and clothing during air or train travel. James did not think the interior of the Jag would have soiled her very substantially during their drive. Still, she had her ways and they were, some of them, very endearing. Perhaps she just wanted to get rid of the leather smell of the seats.

She left open the bathroom door. He could smell the heady, familiar lime and basil scents of her soap and shampoo stirred and liberated by hot water and steam. He wondered, for perhaps the hundredth time, whether the sex Robert O'Brien had enjoyed with his wife had been unprotected. He suspected it had been. Passion and precaution did not go hand in glove.

Lillian emerged from the bathroom wrapped in towels. She had fastened one in a turban around her head and had tucked the second above her breasts. The flesh of her shoulders was smooth and pink with heat. A single damp strand of hair had escaped and snaked along her neck and coiled above her collarbone. The towel worn around her body was not as long as those they used at home. It revealed her legs to the thigh. O'Brien had been exorcised from Lillian's emotions. There could be nothing of him left inside her, no adulterous residue. He had been thoroughly sluiced from her body and soul in the days before this expedition to the bay.

James was lying on the bed, reading an Adam Gleason sonnet from a volume of his poetry picked from a short row of books lined up on the bedside table. As Lillian passed him he reached for the towel concealing her nakedness, snagging it between finger and thumb and she smiled at him and allowed it to unravel, revealing her.

The stir of arousal was very strong in him. She seemed to him both familiar and new. He had not known everything about her. What she had recently done had shocked and surprised him. It was a long time since he had enjoyed or even contemplated sex with a stranger. But the attraction of that unknown adventure was still compelling. And making love to his wife now would to some extent be that, because she was really quite different from the person he had assumed she was. And there was something else, because they were naked to one another now as he could not remember them having been for years.

She smiled and raised both hands and her breasts rose and she released the towel wrapping her head and her hair fell unconfined around her face. The damp ends of it brushed his face as, climbing on to the bed, she stooped to kiss him.

'Charlie Abraham will have heard us,' Lillian said afterwards.

James linked his fingers with hers, on the bed beside her, where they lay on their backs together. 'We'll be the talk of the bay.'

'If we're not already,' Lillian said.

She took a second shower. This one, he took with her. They were dressing when the landlord knocked softly on the door and said through it that someone was waiting downstairs to see them.

Richard Penmarrick leaned with his back against the bar. Both elbows rested on it, hands hung loose at the wrist. He was facing the view out of the picture window over the sea. The pose was pure gunslinger, but, with his long ripple of wavy hair and shirt open halfway down his torso and the various pendants and charms hung from their chains and strings of leather adorning his chest, he actually looked like someone who might have hung out with the Rolling Stones at their most imperious and debauched.

He could have been the pusher, James thought, the main man, the fallen aristocrat who supplied the drugs fuelling the band in their *Exile on Main Street* period. He had that louche, relaxed, devil-may-care quality about him. He had a reckless, insouciant sort of style. He would have impressed their Satanic Majesties. He would have fitted right in with them.

He pushed himself away from the bar with a thrust of his hips and nodded and smiled at James as someone not quite respectable might at an old friend who shared some compromising secrets. He looked at Lillian and almost pulled himself formally to attention. He bowed and reached for her hand and raised and kissed it. 'Welcome home,' he said.

O'Brien thought there were any number of ways it would be preferable to spend a late Friday afternoon than being observed through the steepled fingers of his therapist, while her sharp mind dissected his words and she formulated a strategy for overcoming his problems.

Dr Eleanor Deacon was beautiful. It was generally Robert's habit to subsume inconvenient truths about himself in trying to impress beautiful women. However at two hundred pounds an hour, even by Harley Street standards, she was expensive. To lie just to impress her because she was so easy on the eye would be both futile and extravagant. There was also the fact that he was there because he needed to be. He was desperate and, in his desperation, prepared to be brutally honest about his predicament.

She had seen him at short notice as a favour. She had helped him out a couple of years earlier, when grief over the quite sudden death of his mother had resulted in a barren interval when nothing he wrote seemed to be any good. She had correctly deduced that the writing he was doing in this period was therapeutic, a way of dealing with the grief by distracting himself, rather than an authentic effort at structured creativity.

She had suggested to him he try to write something in tribute to his mother's memory rather than as a means of diverting him from his loss. This tactic had eventually resulted in one of the novels of which he had been proudest. In gratitude he had taken Dr Eleanor's daughter, a fan, to tea at Fortnum and Mason. Alice Deacon had been thirteen then and had brought along her collection of his books, each of which he had duly signed for her.

Dr Deacon had not owed him any sort of preferential treatment. If anything, he considered himself in her debt. But when he had called, she had taken the call personally and she had shifted things around in her appointments diary to see him at very short notice. She said that her daughter remembered fondly her formal tea with the distinguished author and, even at fifteen, still treasured the books he had signed for her.

Now she said, 'Let's talk about the cocaine. Are you quite certain that you regard it wholly as a recreational drug?'

'Yes,' he said. 'No. There have been occasions when I have used it to kick-start my mind.'

'You mean at the outset of a period of writing?'

'Yes.'

'I see. Have the incidences of use in those circumstances recently increased?'

'Yes, they have. I'll be honest with you, Dr—'

'Eleanor, please, Robert.'

'I'll be honest with you, Eleanor. I am terrified of the page remaining blank. Every day it seems more difficult to begin. I'm not sleeping. I'm exhausted most of the time. I don't have the energy for exercise.'

'This apparition, the little girl you see: she wakes you?'

'She wakes me, yes.'

'How does she accomplish that?'

'She sings to me.'

Dr Deacon rose from her chair and walked behind it to her desk. Robert had brought with him some of the draft illustrations Lillian had done for the series of books about his telekinetic heroine from County Clare. They were spread out on the polished wood, curling slightly in the June sunshine slanting through the big Georgian window of her consulting room.

'She looks like this?'

'No. She looks nothing like that. That's the confusing thing.'

Robert had not always pictured his heroine in the way that Lillian had. He had always imagined her waif-like; but Lillian had given her an almost elfin quality, as though the capacity for potent and practical magic lay behind the drab reality of a young life in servitude. It was there in the translucent skin and the halo of blonde curls and the green sparkle of her eyes. It was Lillian's talent of course to communicate such things visually; the mischief concealed by the apparently mundane, each child studying the images would assume a secret only they had spotted.

'If she does not look like this, what does she look like?'

'Like a ghost.'

'You need to be more specific.'

'Why? Why do I need to be more specific about a hallucination triggered by cocaine psychosis? I need some help in getting off the coke, Eleanor. I need to believe I can carry on working without the inspiration provided by a line snorted before I even sit down to begin. It's as much a part of my morning ritual now as brushing my teeth and brewing my coffee and I haven't the strength or the courage or the self-belief to stop.'

Dr Deacon looked up from the pictures on her desk and walked back to her chair. She sat down and crossed her long legs and pulled the hem of her skirt to the knee. 'Describe the little girl who wakes you with her singing,' she said.

Robert did not really want to think about the little girl. One had to face one's demons – it was the reason why he was in that august and imposing wood-panelled consulting room – but it was an unnerving ordeal to have to do so. It should not have been, really, in such eminent company and in the sober light of day. But somehow the sober light of day and the therapist's cold professionalism made his night visitor even scarier to recall.

'I called her a ghost. By that I mean that she is quite real and not at all human.'

'Like a memory, you mean?'

'No. I don't mean that at all. There is nothing vague or diaphanous about her. She is not your stereotypical ghost. She is not vague and insubstantial. She is solid and detailed and occupies three-dimensional space. She is dead, though. She is emphatically dead.'

'And yet she speaks, which corpses do not, in my experience.'

Robert smiled. 'You can be as sarcastic as you like, Eleanor. I do not have that luxury. Seeing a child, one who died a long time ago, at the foot of your bed, having her communicate with you, is not an experience that provokes much mirth in me.'

'Your Irish accent is much stronger when you are upset. That's quite interesting. Is your apparition Irish?'

'No, she is not. She speaks the English of a native. She is refined in her speech. There might be a hint of the West Country about it, but only a hint. She does not use contractions. She is from another time. She sounds Edwardian. She is attired in a school uniform. It is purple and grey, this livery. Close to, it is as threadbare as she is. She is not imagined. She is resurrected. She has not been dragged reluctantly back.'

'What precisely does that last sentence mean?'

'It means I think that she enjoys teasing me. Precisely, there is a sense in which she cavorts.'

'I see.'

'What do you think?'

Dr Deacon pondered for a long time before replying. Then she said, 'There are two possibilities. You are right that cocaine psychosis is the most obvious cause and, trust me, we can deal with that. It's a much more common problem than you might suppose and there are tried and tested therapies with which I have enjoyed encouraging success. Only a tiny percentage of my own patients relapse and that is because they are deliberately self-destructive, which, with your strong streak of narcissism, you are not.'

'What's the second possible cause?'

'You have recently suffered the trauma of sudden and unexpected separation from someone to whom you have developed a strong emotional attachment. You need to resolve that situation yourself.' She glanced behind her to where the illustrations were laid out on the desk. 'She is a very talented woman.'

'She is also quite captivating.'

'My advice would be to take her at her word and accept that the affair is over. That said, you are not paying me to function as an agony aunt.'

'No. You are much too expensive.'

'And I'm far better qualified, Robert.'

'Who do you think she is, the little girl?'

'You want me to establish the identity of your ghost? That is quite straightforward. I think she is simply a character from a story you have not yet written.' Dr Deacon glanced at her watch. Their session had concluded on the stroke of the hour. She was very professional. 'What does she say to you, by the way? What does she talk about?'

Robert laughed. The consultation had left him feeling unexpectedly much better. It would have been cheap, he thought, at twice what he was being charged. Eleanor's expertise would wean him off his destructive narcotic habit. He would woo and win Lillian with the stout heart and unwavering will a woman so lovely deserved.

'What does she talk about? She tells me rather gleefully that I am going to die.'

'We all owe God a death,' Dr Deacon said.

'So you believe in God?'

'It's a quote, Robert. It's from Shakespeare.'

Robert grinned. 'I knew that,' he said. He really did feel much better than he had an hour earlier on walking into the room. Dr Deacon gathered the Lillian Greer illustrations up and put them back in the folder he had brought along and he put it into his bag.

He was her last appointment of the day. As he wrote his cheque or more likely paid with his debit card at the reception area two floors below, Dr Deacon considered the treatment Robert O'Brien would require from her to restore his mental equilibrium by conquering his cocaine addiction. She sat at her desk and wrote some notes on a pad. The first word she wrote was *confidentiality*.

A coke habit was not that serious a slur on the reputation of a writer of adult fiction. In some of the more hard-boiled genres, it was probably viewed as a necessary qualification, she thought, a badge of credibility. But in a writer of fiction for children it would spell disaster, should it ever become public knowledge. Children's writers were not so much expected to live blameless lives as lives that in personal terms were invisible.

If the press found out about his habit, the consequences would be dire. Libraries would stop stocking and lending his books. School libraries would come under pressure from governors and local authorities and perhaps even parents to ban them. Bookshops would be reluctant to stock them for fear of public indignation. A man who derived a living from children's pocket money could not squander that money on narcotics without encouraging widespread disapproval.

He was a role model, whether he liked it or not. And she suspected that he did like it. He revelled in his status. He was narcissistic and was proud of the position his success had earned him in the world. He liked the attention, the wide-eyed adulation he got from young readers like her daughter. That was why he did the school visits.

The first time she had treated him, in the aftermath of his mother's death, she had thought him a very attractive man. He was physically beautiful, talented and so sensitive his sensitivity was almost as tender as an unhealed wound. She had identified two characteristics in him back then that she would have termed flaws. One, of course, was the narcissism. The other was stubbornness. He could be almost childishly petulant and this immaturity, allied to a strong will, caused him to be stubborn.

On this second consultation, she had not found him attractive. She had actually found him repellent. The flaws were more apparent and accompanied by rather too much self-pity. She did not think the stubbornness would hamper the cocaine habit treatment. He would not cling to that. She thought, however, that it would likely pose a problem for Lillian Greer. She was fairly sure that he would ignore her advice concerning the affair. It was obviously a lost cause. Or rather, it was obviously so to anyone but him.

Dr Deacon thought the flaws in O'Brien's character very probably the consequence of a spoiled upbringing. She suspected that his Spanish mother had indulged him totally. He had been an only child. Prematurely born, he had almost died in the incubator on the maternity ward before his mother had got the opportunity to hold her son in her arms.

Analysing the reasons for his personality weaknesses was child's play. Treating them was impossible because he refused to recognise their existence.

She went over to her window, long experience having taught her to time the moment to perfection. And she saw him exit her premises and take the crash helmet from the case bolted to the back of the Harley Davidson motorcycle gleaming in the sunshine at the side of the kerb.

He zipped himself into his leather jacket. He pulled on his helmet. And across the road, against the railings of the far pavement, movement caught her eye as just for a moment she thought she saw a small, slight figure in purple and grey, the face pale and serious under a straw hat, gazing up at her.

Robert O'Brien kick-started his bike into an abrupt blat of loud engine noise. At her window, Dr Deacon blinked and recoiled. Straddling the machine, her patient opened the throttle and roared away. And when she looked again at the far pavement, it was entirely empty of life.

Richard Penmarrick showed them around Topper's Reach. Lillian thought the inside of the house every bit as impressive as the exterior had earlier suggested it would be. It was light and spacious and stood in the sort of isolation that gave its occupants privacy. The views out over the bay were breathtaking in their scope and scale. It was a potential home for them more ideal than any they had coveted together poring over the pages of *Coast* magazine in the evening back in their Bermondsey sitting room. The contrast with their terraced townhouse, with its views of harried pedestrians and gridlocked rat-run traffic, could not have been more acute or pleasing.

The early history of the house was poignant, even tragic.

Adam Gleason had been killed by a German sniper bullet at the front in 1916. His wife and daughter had not long survived him.

'How did they die?' Lillian asked Richard.

'They perished within hours of each other, victims of the Spanish flu epidemic of 1919,' he told her. 'Sarah had not recovered at all from Adam's death and was not physically or emotionally strong. Little Madeleine was only eight years old. Not that strength or maturity provided any meaningful protection against the epidemic. It was incredibly virulent.'

'I'm surprised it reached this far,' James said. 'The bay is pretty remote now. It must have been even more remote in those days.'

Lillian looked at her husband. She could still feel the faint throb inside her of their earlier lovemaking. It had been as passionate and raw as when they had met. He was the reason they were here, in this beautiful place. His vision and resolve had delivered them there. His forgiveness had overcome the infidelity she had allowed to jeopardise her family's future. She looked at him in the vibrant light reflected upward through the windows from the sea and knew without doubt that she loved him.

'Adam Gleason wasn't the bay's only volunteer,' Richard said. 'Others answered Kitchener's call. A handful more were conscripted. Some of them perished as he did. But some returned and they brought the infection back with them.'

'Of course,' James said, nodding.

'It was very virulent, as I said. Thank God it resulted here in only a few fatalities. But it hit this house hard, I'm afraid.'

Lillian looked around her. They were in the kitchen. She did not think there was anything sinister about the house, nor any lingering sadness. It was too brightly and lambently lit. Its proportions were far too generous. Many people had lived there very contentedly in the ninety years since the sad events Richard Penmarrick recounted. Devoid of a stick of furniture or a scrap of carpeting, the house did not even look empty in the hollow, negative sense. It looked instead like its exciting potential; like a vibrant domestic project waiting to begin.

She thought Richard quite extraordinary. He was picturesque, with his mane of hair, in his baubles and bangles, with the tattoo of his snakeskin boots on the bare floors of Topper's Reach. But he had an impact well beyond the calculation of his dandified accessories.

His physical presence seemed a rude affront to space. She supposed that the word to describe him would be charismatic, but did not think it adequate. He actually possessed something she had always derided in her mind as an exhibitionist's cliché. Richard Penmarrick had star quality. He has even more of it than Robert O'Brien has, she thought guiltily. Then a thought came into her mind that made her laugh out loud.

Both men looked at her, bemused.

'I was just thinking,' she said, 'that you, Richard, must be the least likely person to be taken for an estate agent in the entire history of property sales.'

James frowned. Richard appeared to process what he had just heard. Lillian feared that she had just made a terribly tactless mistake. And then Richard threw back his head and laughed a generous, genuine laugh of pure amusement.

'The question is,' he said when he stopped laughing, 'do I have a sale, madam?'

They agreed the deal verbally there and then. They shook hands on it. Richard embraced James in a manly hug and then kissed Lillian on the cheek. She recognised his after-shave as one her father had worn back in the late 1970s when she had been a very young child. It was Eau Sauvage. She hadn't thought it was manufactured any longer.

He asked if they had arranged to eat that evening at the Leeward and they told him they had not. He said that should they wish to celebrate deciding on their new home with a decent dinner, he could recommend the very place, 'Assuming you are both of you carnivores.'

'We are,' Lillian said. She could not remember having felt more excited. All her happiest personal memories were connected to the children. This was different. The children were fundamental to what they were planning, but for the moment it was a grown-up adventure and she was savouring every moment of it.

'Good. The place I'd like to recommend is the Lodestone. I'd advise only against the crustacean element of the menu.'

He led the way. They twisted and turned down several cobbled lanes before arriving outside a whitewashed building embellished with a row of painted wheels from old horse-drawn wagons. They paused and James looked the place over and said, 'Surely the crab and lobster will be good here, won't they?'

Richard said, 'There's an event tomorrow night on the east beach. It is a custom here going back centuries. If you can attend, I suggest you stay away from the crab and lobster at the Lodestone. I won't tell you any more because it will spoil the surprise.'

'We'll be there,' Lillian said.

'Fantastic,' Richard said. He clapped his hands together and rocked slightly on his heels and the trinkets hung against his bare chest glimmered and chinked in the descending sunlight. 'I'd recommend the lamb. The beef is equally good and the rabbit casserole simply to die for.'

'We can't thank you enough,' James said.

Music was playing from inside the restaurant. It was Sandy Denny. The song was 'The Sea'.

'We can't,' Lillian said. 'We can't thank you adequately for what you have done for us.'

'Nonsense,' Richard said. He turned and began to walk away. 'See you tomorrow night, people,' he said, with a backward wave of his hand.

Uncle Mark had gone to fetch them a late supper of fish and chips. Their regular dinner time had come and gone. He was not as domesticated or as health-conscious as their dad was. The idea of him cooking was actually pretty ridiculous, Jack thought. Jack's money would have been on pizza, since the pizzeria was closer than the fish and chip shop and Uncle Mark was on foot. The kebab shop was even closer than the pizzeria but even Uncle Mark wouldn't have dared flout their mum's well-known food fascism with kebabs. Jack could keep a secret. Olivia could not. Treated to something as exotic as a large doner with all the trimmings, come Monday, Olivia would have split on him.

They were in their dad's study. Jack was there because the study computer was the most powerful and therefore the quickest in the house. Olivia was there because something had spooked her and she would be pretty much glued to him until Uncle Mark returned. He didn't mind, really. He was in a very good mood. He had played tennis with Uncle Mark in the afternoon before his uncle had to go and fetch Livs from school. And all his fears about his sight and balance and hand-eye generally had proven to be worries over nothing.

He had actually taken a set off Uncle Mark, which he had never done before. They had played on the public courts around the corner from the house on Tanner Street. His footwork had been nimble, his volleying solid and he'd seen the ball as early as he'd ever done. Uncle Mark did not take prisoners on the court and there was no way he tanked in the set Jack took. Jack earned it and Uncle Mark said afterwards the difference was the six inches Jack had grown since the last time they had played. It had given his serve more penetration and it had a lot more kick.

'What's spooking you this time, Livs?'

'Huh, like you've never been spooked.'

'I have occasionally, I admit it. But not like you. You're the spookmeister.'

'What are you doing? It looks really boring. Can I go on Facebook?'

'In a minute, you can.'

'What are you doing?'

'I'm rating Robert O'Brien's books on review sites. I'm giving them all one star.'

'One star isn't very much. I thought you liked him. You read all those Casey Shoals books.'

'Well, I don't like him any more. I'd give him no stars if I could. But one is the lowest rating they have.'

'If I was the spookmeister, that would mean I was the one doing the spooking, wouldn't it?'

'Nobody likes a smartarse, Livs.'

'I'll tell Mum you called me that.'

'The only thing worse is a smartarse snitch.'

'I'll tell Dad you looked at girls' boobies on his computer.'

Jack wondered what story he could make up about Olivia

that was worse. He couldn't think of one. So he said, 'What are you scared of?'

'The spookmeister,' she said slowly, looking out of the window as dusk gathered shadows in the tiny garden beyond.

She raised her arm slowly from her side and pointed a finger towards the glass.

Jack frowned and looked up from the screen to where she was pointing. He could see nothing buts shadows and leaves. He shrugged. 'You're weird, Livs,' he said.

'It's not my fault,' Olivia said. 'I can't help it. I'd like it all to stop.'

'Now you're freaking me out.'

Olivia dropped her arm. 'I'm sorry,' she said. But she did not shift an inch from her brother's side.

Uncle Mark returned with a bundle of fried and battered food wrapped in rolls of cream paper. He was slightly breathless and he smelled, when he exhaled, sweetly of fresh beer. He had stopped on the way to the fish and chip shop for what Jack remembered his dad termed a swift one. Maybe he had enjoyed a swift two. His cheeks were pink and his eyes slightly moist, but that might have been smarting from the vinegar in which his own portion of chips had been drenched.

They ate in the kitchen. Uncle Mark took off his pullover but was still sweating slightly at the hairline when they had finished their food. He said, 'I'm going to open a few windows.'

'Please don't,' Olivia said.

He looked at her. Jack looked at her, too.

'It's okay to open the windows upstairs,' she said.

'But we're boiling alive down here, Livs,' Uncle Mark said.

'You can open the windows at the front, then. But you can't open the windows at the back of the house. It might get in.'

Uncle Mark said, 'What might?'

'The spookmeister,' Jack said. He felt pretty jolly. The tennis had gone brilliantly. Dinner had been a carba-tastic treat. Uncle Mark had brought back cans of Fanta to wash it down with. He would definitely let his nephew stay up much later than was usually the case. Now his little sister was making a spectacle of herself in front of their dad's only brother. Did life get any better?

Olivia turned to her uncle. 'I'm frightened of the thing watching us from the garden,' she said. 'If we open one of the back windows, it might be tempted to come into the house. It hides itself really well. But when you catch sight of it, it looks very angry that you've spotted it. I think it is bad-tempered and easy to annoy. I think it would be very dangerous if it got into the house.'

Uncle Mark said, 'What have you been reading, Livs? What have you seen on the television that has scared you so? Do Mummy and Daddy let you watch *Doctor Who*?'

'I'm not scared of *Doctor Who*,' she said.

He smiled. 'I don't believe that, darling. Sometimes *I'm* scared of *Doctor Who*.'

'I'm scared of the thing in the garden,' Olivia persisted. 'I'm scared of the crouching thing without a proper face. It moves so fast. It moves the way an insect does.'

Jack said nothing. He wasn't feeling quite as buoyant as he had been a moment earlier. He knew his sister; knew when she was lying and when she was telling the truth. She wasn't even exaggerating now. She was truly afraid and you had to wonder if something real rather than imaginary had done this excellent job of spooking her.

'Wait here,' said their Uncle Mark.

No two more redundant words had ever been spoken to

the Greer children. They were going nowhere. Certainly they were not about to follow their uncle into the study where they suspected he intended to unbolt the door that led to their garden.

Mark Greer had a duty of care to his nephew and niece beyond the responsibilities with which his brother and sister-in-law had charged him. He no more believed in crepuscular demons than he believed in little green men from Mars. But something in Olivia's tone and facial expression had raised in him the possibility of genuine danger. She was afraid of something she really believed she had seen. It moved with a spider's prancing speed and possessed a face contorted by fury. Could a child of eight make up such a thing?

There was a lot of burglary in this area. It wasn't the random break-ins of desperate crackheads, either. There was a degree of professionalism involved. Intruders often did covert surveillance before breaking in. His brother had several thousand pounds worth of easily sellable computer hardware installed in the house. The pictures and the high-end stereo system were also pretty valuable.

Mark had no intention of being a hero. He had enjoyed a single pint of bitter shandy on the way to the chippie and so was somewhat short of the Dutch courage required for that role. But he could not ignore Olivia's fears if doing so meant leaving two children in his care vulnerable to the possibility of attack in an aggravated burglary. He would take a look. That was all he would do. He had an obligation to his charges to do that.

He walked into the study without switching on the light and closed the door firmly behind him. He would be able to see nothing beyond his own reflection if he illuminated the room with either the overheads or the desk lamp. He walked towards the glass-panelled door that gave on to the garden. Outside he could see foliage and the bright dabs of flower petals stirring slightly in the evening breeze.

It was a tiny garden and at first casual glance, concealment seemed impossible. There were two trees right at the rear but their trunks were too slender to hide a man. The foliage was thick, though, the leaves dense and fleshy on the bushes against the rear wall, and the spaces between them were cast into deep gloom.

The study was very quiet. There was no sound but for the regular tick of a quartz clock on the wall every second. If anything the ticking of the clock emphasised the silence. Mark could not hear the children. They must be trying to be very quiet in the kitchen to help him, he thought. He looked outside, the detail of the garden clarifying as his eyes adjusted to the absence of light. And he listened intently. It was a good three minutes of this vigilant inspection before he finally turned and put his hand on the door knob.

It was then that he heard the snicker of laughter. It was mordant, mocking, cruel and addressing him. He turned back. There was a face outside, pressed up against the glass. It looked to Mark Greer like the face of someone who had lost their features to a fire. The eyes were lidless and the mouth a lipless maw under the space where the nose had been burned away. The skin had been coarsened by heat into something resembling burlap sacking more than flesh. It was capable of expression, this face. It appeared to leer emptily at him.

Confronted by this sight Mark's first thought was that Livs had been right. There was after all a spookmeister in the garden. And it had ambitions beyond merely lurking there. He forced himself to walk towards the door. His instinct was to flee. But he needed for his own sake and the sakes of the children in his care to try to rationalise the threat. As he approached the glass, the crude features of the thing he was looking at seemed to slide into refraction and disappear entirely and he realised with a surge of almighty relief that it must have been a mere trick of moonlight and leaf shadow.

This did not explain the laughter Mark had heard. That, he put down to imagination. He must have heard it inside his head because he knew that the windows of the house were double-glazed. They had been insulated, at some expense, by his brother and sister-in-law against traffic and aircraft flight-path noise.

For him to have heard laughter from the garden would have defied the laws of physics. He could be a bit frayed around the edges; a bit ramshackle and disorganised in his private life. He would have been the first to admit that. But he was a qualified and practising engineer and, as such, believed the laws of physics immutable.

He had heard it, though. He could hear it still in his mind. It had come from somewhere; from something. It had been the audible expression of mockery, a gleeful cackle of utter contempt that had been inspired by him and that had not sounded even remotely human. Hearing it had made his scalp tingle and his heart thud and his arms crawl with goose flesh. He turned away from the glass and very slowly and deliberately walked out of the room, aware as he did so that the eight steps required to reach the door were the longest he had ever taken and that his back felt not so much exposed as flayed of its skin.

Chapter Eight

Charlie Abraham guided them to the east beach after closing and shuttering the pub. The Greers were a bit incredulous that he was doing this on a Saturday night, but as he explained to them, the entire village would likely be attending the celebration on the shore and there was no point in keeping a pub open unless it had some customers to serve.

The harbour was to the right of the pub as you faced the seafront, the boats bobbing at anchor beyond the breakwater. In front of the pub, the sickle shape of the bay itself stretched leftwards in a shallow curve. The sea wall ran parallel with the bay and it was this they took to reach their destination, the area beyond the far point of the bay where the strewn boulders lay to which women suspected of witchcraft had once been shackled.

On the sea wall they joined a procession of people, some of them carrying pitch-topped torches that provided a ragged, ruby and orange light in the gathering darkness. Many of the people they walked among, Lillian saw, were wearing a sort of costume of white britches and hooped sweaters and baggy cloth hats that to her resembled the headqear worn by commoners during the French Revolution.

There was a buzz of conversation and anticipation and an excitement that was contagious. People hurried in their progress. The torches bobbed. Leather boots rang and clattered on the cobbles of the sea wall and the surf boomed in the night to their right and sent salt vapour into the air they breathed and the spray touched and caressed them and tingled on their exposed skin.

They saw the glow from the fires above the headland dividing the bay from the east shore. They saw sparks ascending and the shimmer of escaping flames. The sea wall ended and there was the climb and rough descent to the shore itself and as Lillian topped the rise, hand in hand with James, she saw the scene on the shore below her and gasped slightly at the scale of it.

The whole of the bay seemed to be gathering. There were everywhere on the packed shingle griddles over heaps of burning driftwood and dug pits of glowing embers and sea coal in iron troughs white-hot under rows of skewers. The light cast by all this fire flung shadows from the strewn boulders that gave the landscape a strange aspect, as though it was some almost alien place at the furthest border of the world. The black sea beyond, with its roiling lines of white spume, strengthened the impression.

Lillian descended with her husband to the shore. She saw among the crowd Richard Penmarrick, attired in the hooped shirt and britches worn by most of the rest, but without the hat, bareheaded, his rock-star mane wild and damp with wind and wave drench and a tall and willowy woman at his side she knew from the description James had given her was his wife, Elizabeth.

Elizabeth was not in costume. She wore a clingy pale diaphanous dress and, over it, a shawl of ivory silk. There was a turquoise choker around her throat that drew attention to the length of her neck. To Lillian she looked like one of the gorgeous singer/song-writers of the early 1970s; she had that ethereal beauty and hint of another age about her.

It was easy to imagine her appearing before an audience between sets by the youthful Emmylou Harris and a shy and callow Joni Mitchell. Looking at her provoked an odd feeling in Lillian. She would have described it as nostalgia for a time she had never known.

There was another woman among the crowd who naturally claimed attention. She was pale and dressed in black and smoking a cigarette and when the torchlight caught her full in the face her eyes had a green glitter and she looked captivating and beautiful. There was glamour in the bay, Lillian realised. It was a slight shock but a pleasure too, an exciting realisation.

James had told her about Elizabeth, of course. He had neglected to mention the black-clad woman who paced the shingle in suede pixie boots that set off her slender calves. Her hair was pulled back from her face and her cheekbones were high and her shapely mouth picked out in crimson lipstick. It was the eyes, though. It was those green eyes she suspected would mesmerise and captivate her husband. She smiled to herself. If they had met, she did not think James would have been able to describe this woman with anything like neutrality.

As if aware of her thoughts, James coughed and introduced her first to Elizabeth and then to the femme fatale, whose name was Angela Heart.

Elizabeth smiled and shook her hand. Richard embraced her warmly.

'Welcome to the cabaret,' Angela said.

Smell was a strong feature of the east shore. Seaweed drying on the beached boulders was a rank bass note competing with salt crystallising in the still warm pebbles and the smart of pitch from the torches and beech and oak smoke and burning tar from the pits of washed-up and gathered coal glowing with searing heat under the skewers.

'Where is the food?' Lillian asked the general company.

'Wait,' Angela Heart said with a smile. In the capricious wind, Lillian caught her scent, then. She wore the Guerlain fragrance, Shalimar. Lillian somehow doubted it was bought locally.

People were drifting down to the waterline. Lillian noticed for the first time that many of them carried barbed hooks or baskets with them. They formed a line just above where the waves tumbled and broke. The torch carriers broke free of the rest of the crowd and formed a circle behind this line, before the biggest of the boulders. In the light of their flames, a set of ancient chains was visible hanging from iron pinions in the stone. Shackles were attached to them and these glimmered rustily. She saw that Elizabeth Penmarrick stood at the centre of the torch circle. She had taken off her shawl and the bodice of the dress she wore underneath was transparent. Her breasts were high and smallish and firm and the nipples proud.

The line of people at the edge of the sea set off a percussive crunching on the shingle. They were stamping on the spot in unison. They were murmuring something that sounded ancient and tribal in a language Lillian had never heard before but thought was probably the old Cornish tongue. Then Elizabeth Penmarrick began to sing and the air seemed to ripple as a voice more ethereal and strange than any she had heard before began to ululate out of the woman.

The singing was unaccompanied. The language sounded a little like Gaelic and the words and phrases as old as time as they shuddered and reverberated through the night air. The tune was discernible because Elizabeth possessed the gift of perfect pitch and the slow tempo at which she sang was sustained seemingly without effort. Her voice was not summoned, Lillian thought. It was released like some powerful and dormant force created simply to soar.

Lillian looked at James who looked back and merely shrugged. There was no expression she had ever seen on her husband's face adequate to reflect the sheer strangeness of the moment. Beside them, Angela Heart's features were unreadable. Richard Penmarrick gazed down at the pebbles beneath his feet with his arms folded across his chest and a hint of secret amusement about his pursed mouth.

Lillian felt the ground shake. There was no mistaking it. A seismic shock rippled subtly under her weight. She saw pebbles shift and topple and squirm. At the edge of the sea, the water began to boil. She walked forward, hand in hand with James, curious. Elizabeth had stopped singing. The line of people at the brink of the water had stopped their rhythmic stamping. They took a step back as the surf in front of them seemed to writhe blackly and she heard a skittering sound as claws and mandibles emerged and crabs and lobsters crawled ashore all along its length.

Mandibles twitched and segmented limbs skittered and brine escaped dribbling from the armoured bodies of the creatures summoned from the sea bed as they scrabbled on to the beach.

There was a cry of triumph as the first barbed spear skewered the first crab shell and raised high the twitching beast. Lillian thought it was the biggest crab she had ever seen. Its claws were monstrous. Everywhere the line broke as the men and women and boys and girls composing it brought back their catches to be broken up and cooked or dropped alive into the simmering iron pots amid the coals.

Lillian realised that Angela Heart stood flanking her. She turned and smiled and under the green allure of those remarkable eyes the smile was friendly. 'Works every time,' she said, lighting a cigarette from a brass Zippo lighter.

'Does the earth tremor bring them ashore?'

Angela exhaled at the sky. The smell of cooking flesh was growing strong already, stirring Lillian's appetite. She remembered she had not eaten dinner. She remembered Richard's culinary advice of the night before. She looked up. The stars were infinite.

'The tremor is more effect than cause,' Angela said.

'Then what brings the shellfish ashore?'

'The singing,' Angela said. 'The singing delivers our feast.'

Bread was lowered in baskets on a pulley and line strung from somewhere above the shore and as it swung down, Lillian knew from the smell that it was freshly baked. Wooden cases of beer were hauled across the shingle on a hand-drawn cart, their bottles rattling. The ceremonial aspect of the evening was obviously at an end. People chatted and laughed and cooked and ate and drank without formality. It was just a big barbecue, a beach party. If she had not seen the ritual enacted at the edge of the sea, she would not have believed it had ever taken place.

She was introduced to the chandler Martin Sharp and Ben Tamworth the contractor and the boatbuilder Billy Jasper and Bella Worth, who edited the local newspaper. She was served fresh lobster on a paper plate by a polite boy in a Scout uniform. She found herself in conversation with Angela, discussing Olivia's capacity to adapt to a new home and educational environment.

'Better change all at once than piecemeal disruption,' Angela said. 'Children are adaptable to change and so long as the consistency of her nuclear family is sustained, she should be absolutely fine. I'm assuming her parents have endowed her with good communication skills?'

'She's a bit precocious for an eight-year-old,' Lillian said. 'She can be a self-possessed little madam, quite insular, actually, when she wants to be. But she is not naturally timid or shy. She does not lack confidence.'

'I'm sure she'll be fine,' Angela said. 'But I promise you I will keep a very close eye on her for the first few weeks of her settling in.'

'Thank you.'

Angela excused herself and wandered away.

Richard came over and offered some wine, apologising for the plastic cup. As she took it gratefully, stressing that no apology was necessary, she saw men carrying an array of musical instruments crunching over the shingle to his rear. She noticed that a small stage was being built from empty beer cases. This work was being supervised, in humorous fashion, by Ben Tamworth, being verbally abused by his impromptu workforce variously as a cowboy and a slave-driver.

'You must come to lunch tomorrow,' Richard said, moving on through the crowd. 'Our daughter Megan is a huge fan and absolutely dying to meet you.'

'Elizabeth is going to sing,' James said, returning to her from a conversation with an elderly man with rather long hair she guessed might be the local scholar Michael Carney. Carney was an authority on the soldier-poet who had originally owned the house they were in the process of buying. She resolved to ask him about Adam Gleason, if it was indeed him and not just some other elderly and picturesque resident of the bay. James seemed to know all of them. She felt that she was quickly making new friends herself.

'We're about to witness a miracle,' James said. 'Just wait till you hear Elizabeth Penmarrick sing something in English. Better than that, wait until you hear her sing a song you think you know.'

Lillian nodded at her plate. 'We've already witnessed a miracle,' she said. 'How would you explain what we saw half an hour ago? Do you think it was the vibration of their feet, stamping?'

James shrugged and smiled and brushed a stray fragment of lobster meat from the corner of her lips with his thumb and kissed her on the mouth. 'I don't know,' he said. 'I don't care, frankly. The real miracle is our finding this place. We're going to be happy here, Lily. We're going to be happy and at home and from now on, everything in our lives is going to be wonderful.'

'Do you really believe that?'

'I do. This place makes it easy to believe.'

'Then perhaps this place found us, James. That might be the real miracle.'

'We'll be happy,' James said again. 'All four of us will be. And we will be safe.'

She is simply a character from a story you have not yet written. Well then, he would write her, he had decided. And then he would write her out. He could put her at the centre of a story and then, if he so chose, he could write that threadbare little apparition into some fate she could never return to him from. He could send her sailing off into the sunset or have her grow into a beautiful woman or a wizened old crone. He could condemn her to the tedium of a really boring occupation or he could kill her young by having her contract something tragic and fatal at a heartbreakingly tender age.

He would write a story about her that would preclude very firmly the possibility of a sequel. Killing her would be the best way, rather than having her mature or emigrate or disappear mysteriously. Death was unequivocal. It was final. She could not come back from the grave. Unless, of course, he brought her back as a ghost. But he would not. He would leave her to lie undisturbed in the lonely graveyard of his imagination, the arid badlands where his fictive creativity never roamed.

All he needed, really, was an opening sentence.

He had already done a couple of lines. There was no point wasting the stuff. He would not buy any more after the gram on his writing desk was gone. He was confident that the treatment planned by Eleanor Deacon would work. Her prognosis had been so matter-of-factly optimistic he'd felt totally reassured by it. But he had not yet begun that treatment. What he was doing now therefore did not qualify as a relapse. It was just a final evening of indulgence before the hard and sober remedial work began in earnest.

Robert lifted his credit card off the desk and chopped out more coke. It was flaky, crystalline, with the slightly damp character and almost bluish hue under his desk lamp of the really pure stuff; not dried out by being cut with any of the crap the street dealers used. It was the cocaine equivalent of a Cuban Cohiba cigar or the twenty-five-year-old Glenmorangie single malt. He snorted it as he always did, through a pen barrel.

He closed his eyes and waited the seven seconds or so the hit took to get to the synapses of the brain. His heart was thudding along at about seventy beats a minute. That was no cause for concern. All his aerobic gym and roadwork had given him a resting heartbeat of under fifty. He reckoned it could go as high as a hundred and twenty stimulated by coke before he had to start thinking seriously about taking the edge off with a Valium. The only really unpleasant side effect was that for some reason the stuff made his feet sweat. He wasn't entertaining anyone tonight. It was a price he was prepared to pay.

The drug hit his mind with a thrill of exhilaration and clarity. It did not deliver the first line of the story he intended to write to exorcise his imagination of that girlish little phantom. All at once, instead, he knew what had gone wrong with his relationship with Lillian Greer. All at once, he knew how to alter the balance to put it right.

She was a woman who liked to take care of the people she was involved with. She took fantastic care of her children. She was the main breadwinner, after all, in her household. Before finally running out of patience and straying, she had taken good care of her morose loser of a husband for years. She was one of those people who felt vindicated only if they could reach out and care for the people they loved.

He had denied her that opportunity. He was successful and confident and to her must have seemed invulnerable. His very perfection prevented her from establishing the empathetic bond she needed to cement with people. His flawlessness impeded her from becoming really intimate with him. He did not need her compassion and generosity, her strong instinct for giving without the expectation of getting any return.

Except that he wasn't flawless and invulnerable. He was a long way short of perfect and his confidence had long been shot to shit. He was actually the perfect candidate for her compassion and generosity. All he had to do was provide a convincing demonstration of the fact.

He would get Eleanor Deacon to petition her on his behalf.

He would sanction Eleanor's approach to Lillian and in so doing wave his right to patient confidentiality. Eleanor could tell Lillian that he was addicted to a narcotic drug and that her help and support would be hugely beneficial in helping wean him off it. She could even hint that Lillian's recent rejection of him had deepened his dependence on the drug. It would not be that much of an exaggeration. It was actually pretty close to the truth.

Robert opened a new Word document on his computer and composed a few notes as the basis for this new strategy for wooing and winning back the woman with whom he was besotted. He would still be besotted in the morning; but if he did not write this stuff down, by the morning he would have forgotten what all the excitement had been about. That was the trouble with coke. That was why it was so bloody addictive. The highs were ephemeral and you were forever trying to recreate them and the thrill and intellectual decisiveness they so briefly provided.

His hands stopped on the keyboard. He had experienced another flash of pure inspiration. He chopped out another line and snorted it and kicked off his shoes because his feet were unpleasantly moist now and he guessed that his heart rate had climbed into the mid-nineties. No cause for alarm. Nothing he could not handle.

He would write a suicide note. It was what he did; he was a writer, for fuck's sake. He would write it to Lillian and engineer a way of her seeing it. Eleanor could present it as tangible proof of the fact that in losing Lillian, Robert O'Brien was losing the will to live. Never mind the penthouse dockside flat and the motorcycle in the garage and the list of bestsellers and the Hollywood studio retainer and the toned torso and the handsome face and the Rolex embellishing his right wrist. The note would stand as eloquent proof that none of it mattered without Lillian in his life. Without her love and, vitally, her care of him, his life was worthless.

Robert wrote, inspired. In his new mood of uncompromising honesty, sustained since his session the previous day in Harley Street, he was prepared to admit to himself that the inspiration owed itself to three separate influences. The first, of course, was the drug thudding expensively through his bloodstream and brain. The second was that the subject he was writing about, his own emotional suffering, was one with which he was endlessly absorbed.

The third impulse fuelling his words had a measure of nobility about it. It was not sordid like the first or selfish like the second. It was, simply, his love of Lillian Greer. That was true and profound and he knew in his heart that he would never now give up on it. Clever woman that she was, Eleanor Deacon had been wrong about that. Lillian was everything that was best about him and he would not rest until he had won her back.

He could not have said at what moment he became aware that he was not alone in the room. He had the mad thought that he was the subject of a drugs raid. He glanced at the now empty wrap and the powdery residue that was all that was left of the coke, lying under the pen barrel beside his keyboard. The police broke in, didn't they? They used a steel battering ram. He looked swiftly behind him, aware of just how high he now was. And he saw the girl standing about ten feet behind him in her purple and grey, careworn and frayed, blonde and dead and staring curiously.

Fuck it, he thought, turning back to his keyboard and the words making their self-pitying way across the screen of his monitor. You were supposed to write a story killing her off. You were supposed to do that and you got sidetracked by the coke into composing something else. And now it's too late because she's here.

'Hello, Mr O'Brien,' her voice said.

He pressed 'save' and closed the file he'd been working on. 'You're not real,' he said. He switched off his computer. And he saw her reflection in his darkened screen.

She did not reply. She just stood there, her reflection contradicting him, the room growing colder and the lights seeming to dim and a rank smell festering like something dead washed up by a tide.

It must be something in the charlie, he thought. That bastard has cut it with something slightly hallucinogenic. I'll really have to have a fucking word. I don't pay a ton a time to have the shit cut with anything.

Her reflection in the monitor was growing larger. She was approaching him. He saw that her eyes did not seem to have any pupils and that she did not blink. Real children blinked all the time, much more frequently than adults did. It was one of the observations he had made about children on his school visits.

On his school visits they were deferential because he was famous and they were his fans. This ghost he kept seeing was not deferential. Her body language was hostile, even threatening. But that was just the gear, surely. He was jittery and a bit paranoid and it was exactly like Eleanor Deacon had said in his two-hundred-pound appointment. He was overwrought. She was just a character from his imagination he had not yet found a story for.

'You are impertinent to think of writing about me, Mr O'Brien,' she said. 'You do not know me. You do not know my story. You are a writer of made-up stories and mine happens to be true. You are not qualified.'

There was something not right about her voice. It was like a disembodied sound, something not quite human that rattled, soughing, through her. He thought that if he did write a ghost, this would be exactly how she would speak; not with the use of her atrophied larynx; not with a voice powered by lungs full of air because ghosts were dead people and therefore had no need of the mechanics of respiration. They did not breathe, did they? Her voice was not really that of a little girl. It was thoughts made audible in diction remembered from life, pitched in that shrill voice only because she had died at the age she was now.

He turned. He saw immediately that her reflection flattered her. She could communicate after her fashion and she could deliver herself from place to place and she had summoned to his flat that rotten stench of tidal corruption. She seemed real enough, but she was not really alive. He thought that if she walked into a room of real children they would cower and scream at the dead, shambolic sight of her. Her skin had a greyish tinge. Her hair was coarse and dried out under the fraying hat. The ribbons tying her plaits were faded. Her mouth wasn't right. It was just a black maw beyond the pretty cupid's bow of her lips.

'Am I making you up?'

'I made myself up, Mr O'Brien. I tried and tried to remember what I used to be like and to put myself back together again. It was very hard to accomplish. I had to do it for my friend Olivia.'

'Am I going to make up Olivia too? Is she like you? Are there more of you in my imagination?'

'Your imagination is not needed.'

'Except that you're a figment of it.'

'You think the world begins and ends with you.'

'Doesn't everyone think that?'

'It would be truer to say your world is coming to an end.'

He was frightened, now. The stench in the room was overpowering, despite how cold it had become. And there was something about the tone of the apparition's voice that sounded threatening. When it spoke, its voice sugested more than confidence. It suggested finality. 'I made you up,' he heard himself say. He had meant the words to sound defiant, but even to his own ears they sounded less like a boast than a plea.

'You did not make me up, Mr O'Brien. I made myself up. Shall I show you who I am really? Would you like to see what I am really like?' The lips drew back in a leering grin from the little black abyss, narrowing as it did so under her nose.

'No,' he said.

'I think I shall show you anyway. You interference has to stop. I have to stop it. So I shall show you who I am. You will see what has become of me.'

Megan Penmarrick took after her mother. She was tall and quite serious in her demeanour and on her graceful and unhurried way to becoming a beautiful woman. Lillian spoke to her for an hour about her ambition to become an illustrator. They conversed in the garden, at a circular stone table so old it looked medieval to Lillian, in weathered rustic chairs hewn from the wood of an ash tree.

They drank homemade lemonade and ate water biscuits and Megan had to be coaxed into bringing her own portfolio from the studio her father had converted for her in a room under the eaves of the house. Lillian looked out over the descending trees and the sea, thinking what an idyllic place the Penmarricks lived in, hoping that the charming girl whose dreams she had just shared had the necessary talent to fulfill them.

Megan sat back down and pushed a folder of artwork across the rough surface of their table. She flicked hair out of her face in a gesture Lillian knew betrayed anxiety, because at the same age it was a gesture she had shared. She opened the file and the first of a pile of pictures was revealed and she experienced a feeling of relief that swiftly transformed itself into delight and then amazement.

This was the work of an eleven-year-old child. Some of the subject matter, the mermaids and unicorns and vapid princesses with ankle-length manes and the trolls and other creatures, were pretty stereotypical of a fanciful eleven-year-old's enthusiasms. They were exquisitely done, though, her draughtsmanship and brushwork really skilled and remarkably mature.

Lillian assumed the work was filed chronologically. It became more sophisticated and original the further through it she explored. Towards the end of the portfolio were some exquisite seascapes and pictures of shells and sea life motifs. A small boat endured the odyssey of an Atlantic storm with a stoical old salt at the rudder. This series was so accomplished it was difficult to credit it as the work of a child at all.

At the very end of the images was a portrait of a girl on a swing hanging from the perpendicular branch of a tree in a garden. The garden was beautifully imagined, discarded tennis rackets in wooden frames and leather-bound books and a wicker picnic basket on the lawn giving it a lost, Edwardian atmosphere. The little girl on the swing was very pretty in purple and grey, almost white-blonde in bunched plaits and blue-eyed under the rim of a straw boater.

'Who is this?'

'Someone I made up. I call her Madeleine. I call her Maddy, for short. I'm going to think up some adventures for her.'

Lillian raised her eyebrows and shook her head and shuffled the illustrations neatly together and replaced them in the folder. She closed it and handed it back to its creator. 'You are really gifted, Megan. It delights me to be able to say it, but I have never come across anyone so young with quite so much pure talent.'

Megan blushed. She brushed hair away from her face again. 'You really think so?'

'I know so. You need luck to succeed at what I do. You need good fortune and to develop contacts and timing is always very important, though you only ever become aware of that after the event. But I have never come across anyone better equipped to succeed at it than you are. And I will help you all I can.'

She surprised herself with this last sentence. She had not meant to say it. It was not necessary or even necessarily wise to make such an extravagant promise to an eleven-year-old. Six months down the road, Megan Penmarrick might decide she hated illustration and that what she really wanted to do with her life involved quantum physics or drama school. She had the kind of wealthy parents who could indulge her attempts to fulfil her ambitions, however unlikely or unrealistic.

Lillian did not think, though, that she would change her mind. The quantity of material in the portfolio suggested a strong and persistent work ethic went along with the precocious skill. She really would help her all she could and she would do it, if for no other reason than *because* she could.

Except that that wasn't the only reason, was it? She felt empathetic towards Megan. She felt a part of something already in this blessed place. She very much wanted to move here and embrace what the bay offered and have that embrace returned. She did not even want to do the necessary going back that moving here would practically involve. They had a house to lease and she had a studio to try to sub-let or sell. But she did not simply want to move here; she wanted to stay. She thought that she belonged, that she had found a missing piece of herself in the bay and that its discovery had made her complete.

She thought briefly about the old complications in her life. She pictured Robert O'Brien and the recollection of that episode made her shudder. Her involvement with him had been symptomatic of everything that had been wrong with her existence over recent months and that the bay would put right. James had been right about that, the previous night. They would be happy here, the four of them. They would be safe.

Richard sauntered across the grass towards where she and Megan sat. He was dressed in a pair of jeans and a faded denim shirt and there was a silk scarf tied loosely around his neck and his feet were shod in wood and leather clogs. His abundant locks had been gathered in a ponytail and he had a pair of secateurs in his right hand. Lillian looked at him and squinted in the sunlight and smiled to herself. If Robert Plant could farm outside Stourbridge, she thought, Richard Penmarrick could prune Cornish roses. Horticulture: obviously it was the new rock 'n' roll.

'What's amusing you, Lillian?'

'Life generally is amusing me, Richard. Your daughter is a very special talent.'

'Well,' he said, 'she is certainly a very precious girl.'

Lillian nodded. She knew exactly what he meant. You did not love them for their accomplishments.

'Lunch is ready,' he said, 'if you are ready for lunch.'

The three of them strolled, through the midday sunlight, the distance to the house. Richard offered Lillian his arm and she took it. Megan asked questions about Jack and Olivia. Lillian was truthful in a fairly sparing account of what had recently happened to her son.

'Is that why you are moving here?'

Lillian hesitated before replying. She thought that the honest answer was that the assault on Jack was more catalyst than cause. But she did not think it was a word an eleven-year-old would be familiar with. She said, 'It was what got us from the daydreaming stage to the actuality of planning a move to the coast.'

'So it was the catalyst,' Megan said.

Richard chuckled. He was obviously proud of his lovely, talented, clever daughter. Why wouldn't he be?

'They'll adore it here,' Megan said. 'There is so much to do. They can join the Club.'

'The Club?'

'Our version of the Scouts and the Girl Guides, kind of rolled into one,' Richard said. 'Phil Teal runs it and it runs like clockwork. All the kids seem to love it. It fosters a sense of community and a strong team ethic.'

'I was served food by a boy in a Scout uniform on the beach last night.'

'The Club members always help out at civic events. They rigged that contraption last night that got the bread to the east shore still warm. They do more serious stuff too: sailing courses and survival skills, rock climbing and abseiling, all sorts of wholesome pursuits.'

'Jack has always had a strong team ethic. It comes from his football. He's an exceptional player, but he won't be allowed to play again before Christmas.'

'He could coach the younger boys, though,' Richard said. 'He could coach Angela Heart's nine- and ten-year-olds.'

'He would enjoy that,' Lillian said. 'But would it be permitted?'

Richard chuckled again and patted her hand. 'This is still England,' he said. 'Everything is allowed here, if we judge it to be right. This is a corner of our green and pleasant land where common sense is still allowed to prevail.'

They were on their way back to London late that afternoon when, about twenty miles east of the bay, James's mobile pinged into life and he was informed by the display that he had eight messages, two of them from Lee Marsden and the remainder from the Colorado people. He had drunk a beer with his lunch and Lillian had stayed on the lemonade. He was not over the limit but never drank and drove so she was driving the car. He told her about the messages.

'When were they left?'

'Late yesterday afternoon.'

'Lee needs a hobby. He should take up golf or something.'

'He thinks he's on to 20 per cent of something big.'

'Maybe he is. Yesterday afternoon was Saturday, even in Colorado. Plus, it was Saturday morning. They're five hours behind us. It must have been a breakfast meeting. They must be awfully keen.'

'Either that or they're fanatically geeky sociopaths.'

Lillian laughed. 'I can just picture them,' she said, 'gathered in a donut shop at the foot of the Rockies, drinking American coffee from outsize paper cups, discussing you and their scheme for your game to dominate the world. It's all very exciting, Jimbo.'

'Jimbo?'

'You'll have to get used to being called that, out there.'

'It's bad enough Lee Marsden calling me Jimmy.'

'We all have to make sacrifices, darling.'

James glanced at his wife, smiling at the wheel. The Jaguar's roof was down and her hair blew behind her in the slipstream so that he could see the finer, paler strands exposed at her temples. She was not wearing her sunglasses and the laugh lines at the corner of her eye were small and faint and an exquisite flaw as if there to emphasise just how perfectly beautiful she looked. He did not know when he had loved her more or felt closer to her. They had found their focus and direction again. There was an expression Jack used; he would have it in a minute.

He leaned over and kissed Lillian on the cheek. 'We're locked on,' he said.

'Yes,' she said, 'we are.'

James thought his brother less ebullient than usual, more reserved than was usually the case with him, when they got back. Given that they had only been away since Friday lunchtime, he also seemed much more relieved at the sight of them at the door than he could have any real justification for being. James knew his children. They were well balanced and well behaved, obedient by inclination as well as training and they doted on their Uncle Mark and revelled in his company. Taking care of them surely could not have been that much of a chore.

It was on the walk back to London Bridge underground station an hour later that James discovered the reason for his brother's unusual demeanour. James was escorting him as a courtesy. Mark and perennial girlfriend Lucy lived in a smart newish apartment block in Kentish Town. He was headed north of the river and home.

'Do you fancy a pint?'

'Not really, Mark. I'm probably in for a longish evening with the kids.'

'Can we stop for a cup of coffee, then?'

James shrugged. There had been plenty of coffee at the house. They went to the Starbucks in the station tunnel that led to the Jubilee and Northern Lines and sat at a zinc table there. Mark ordered them both a latte and remembered at the counter that his brother enjoyed his with an extra shot. James heard him request it.

'Don't tell me, Mark. You caught Jack looking at a porn site on my computer.'

'The only action on the computer that seems to animate Jack is goal highlights on YouTube.'

'Well. I'm sure his time will come.'

Mark was toying with his drink, ladling foam off the top of the mug with the thin wooden paddle designed for stirring it. He was avoiding looking at his brother. He said, 'I think your house is haunted.'

A few weeks earlier, James thought that he would have laughed out loud at the absundity of this claim. Since then, he had experienced the strange and still unexplained intuition that he was being watched by something lurking in the shadows of his garden. There had been the children's dreams. There had been the painting too that Livs had done at school, though that had been more to do with his research into the bay and the way that witchcraft had been dealt with there than with the house.

'You had better explain,' he said.

Mark said, 'Lucy has never been comfortable in your house.'

'That's undeniable.' James thought Lucy very easy on the eye. But he also thought her an attention-seeking pain in the arse. The woman who had been threatening on and off to become his sister-in-law for a decade now claimed a psychic sensitivity. She had heard the story that a slave-trading ship-owner had originally had the Greers' townhouse built. This much was historical fact. But she claimed that the tormented souls of his human cargo sometimes visited the house. At least, she claimed that a couple of them did.

She had aired this theory loudly over lunch one weekend, a couple of years earlier, as their reluctant guest. Olivia had overheard her and the idea that their house was haunted by captive spirits from a slave ship had frightened their daughter for weeks. She had kept imagining she could hear their seasick moans and the iron jingle of their manacles. It had been an ordeal for her and for her parents until they had finally managed to persuade her it wasn't true.

'Lucy has never been comfortable in our house. But you are an agnostic where ghosts are concerned, Mark. Or you were.'

Mark shifted uncomfortably. He had never tried to impress his brother and it was evident to James that he was not attempting to do so now. He did not share the attention-seeking exhibitionism so irritating in his girlfriend. He was a bit rumpled and chaotic, but was actually someone with significantly more impressive achievements to his name than James could honestly boast.

James had written a few clever lines of computer code and provided some neat software solutions for prestigious clients and was the creator of a game about which some geeks in Colorado were becoming excited. Among other professional exploits, Mark had engineered football stadia in some of the major capital cities of the world.

'I think there was something in the garden on Friday evening. When I went to investigate, what I saw resolved itself into a trick of the light against one of the glass study door panes. But I still think there was something there, James. It was malevolent and watching me. All my instinct told me it was cunning and very dangerous. I've never experienced anything like that sensation before and hope I never do again. But I've learned to trust my intuition. It was there, James. It was not human. And it was real.'

A silence elapsed between the brothers. James sipped coffee and looked up, towards the end of the tunnel, where in an oval of light, cars and people moved along the busy thoroughfare beyond through heat ripple. He had spent the morning with his wife in the bay. He had joked with Richard Penmarrick about Elizabeth's reluctance as a singer to bathe in the spotlight. The four of them, five with Megan Penmarrick, had eaten a leisurely lunch on their terrace. He wished he was back there.

'There's more, isn't there?'

'No. Yes. Yes, I'm afraid there's more. I looked in on Livs this morning. I heard talking and so just poked my head surreptitiously around the door. I wanted to make sure she wasn't watching something inappropriate on the TV in her room. But she wasn't watching anything. She was sitting up in bed. She was too engrossed to be aware of me. She was talking to someone. I could only hear one half of the conversation though, James. The person she was conversing with wasn't there.'

'She might have an imaginary friend.'

'Does she?'

'No.'

'I'm sorry to bring this complication into your life.'

'It doesn't really matter, Mark. I appreciate your reasons for doing so. You love your niece and nephew.'

'I happen to love my brother, too.'

'We're moving. We're finally doing it. Lillian was totally entranced by the bay. The house purchase was done on Saturday on a handshake.'

'Good for you, mate.'

The two men stood. Mark cracked a smile that looked to James inspired by pure relief. They embraced. James would walk back from here, out of the tunnel into the light. Mark would journey down into the earth for the tube train taking him home.

'There's something else, isn't there?' James said to Mark's retreating back.

Mark turned. 'Nothing,' he said, 'a dream inspired by too much greasy food eaten much too late.'

'I'm not even going to go there,' James said. 'I'm not even going to think about what you gave the kids to eat over the weekend.'

'I dreamed of the sea at night,' Mark said. 'I dreamed the sea was singing.'

The call from Alec McCabe came the following afternoon. They had told the children that the move was definitely on the previous evening. James was right. It did result in a late night, both Jack and Olivia far too excited at the prospect to want to go to bed before an exhaustive discussion about the likely specifics of their new lives on the coast.

Then in the morning, Livs protested about having to go to school. She said that it was pointless. She was right, Lillian privately conceded, her logic could not be faulted. She would not start year five at her Brodmaw primary until September. They planned to leave London, if they could, well before the end of the current school term. There was no way she would be able to complete her existing year-four coursework so there was no real point in her continuing to attend. But her parents had too much to do to cope with both children in the house while they attempted to get through it all. So, under duress, off she was packed.

Most of the detail about the bay Olivia and Jack heard on the Sunday evening came from their mother. She was slightly less of an authority on the subject than their father was. But he had to spend an hour fielding an exasperated call from Lee Marsden. Lee was adamant that the appearance required of him in the States could not realistically be put off for more than another week.

'A week Monday, you are there,' he said.

'This is a very busy time in my domestic life, Lee. We're involved in a massive upheaval. We're relocating. You can go to Colorado and talk to them. You speak the language of development deals and contracts. Plus it's what I pay you for. And 20 per cent is a fair old slice.'

'What do you think I've been doing, Jimmy? I've been negotiating with them night and day. But they have one or two crucial creative suggestions to make to you and they want to meet you, which given the sort of money they're projecting is only fucking reasonable and fair.'

'Face time.'

'Exactomundo.'

James was using the landline and made a face into the receiver. Lee could be a terrible tosspot. He was good at his job, though, and on this occasion he was absolutely right. 'A week on Monday it is.'

'Hombre,' Lee Marsden said, 'amigo.'

James ended the connection and shook his head. He was fairly sure that Lee Marsden had told him he came originally from Wimbledon.

McCabe called just after 4 p.m. on Monday. He called Lillian, who was at her studio with Olivia and answered on her mobile. She had picked Livs up from school and was spending an hour packing stuff away into removal boxes so that the letting agent could show prospective commercial tenants around. Livs was happily helping in this task.

McCabe got to the point. 'Robert O'Brien is dead,' the detective sergeant said. 'It does not look suspicious. A mate of mine is the senior investigating officer. It will make tomorrow's papers.'

Lillian sat down on the desk she had just cleared. She swallowed. 'How did he die?'

'It won't say so in tomorrow's papers, won't be made public until the results of the autopsy report are made known, but he had been taking cocaine.'

'Cocaine killed him?'

'He died of heart failure. He does not seem to have been a chronic user. His liver and kidneys will tell us more—'

'Jesus.'

'—but a preliminary examination suggests he used the stuff recreationally rather than habitually. There is not the corrosive damage to the septum generally typical of heavy users.'

'It must have been the coke. His heart wouldn't fail,' Lillian said. 'He was fanatical about working out.'

'The SOCOs seem to think he might have had a shock.'

'What kind of shock?'

'Something that caused him to die of fright,' McCabe said. 'He bit through his own tongue.'

'And you are telling me this because of our conversation the other day,' Lillian said, 'when I accused you of being perceptive.'

'The last thing he was working on, retrieved from his hard drive, appears to have been a letter intended for you. It could be interpreted as a suicide note.'

'Please don't tell me that.'

'Unless the death was suspicious, there is every chance it will stay out of the public domain. The tabloids will dig, though, I have to warn you, once the fact of the cocaine use becomes public knowledge. They will do so inevitably because his target market was kids. He wrote for an audience of children.'

'I knew that. I was working on a book with him.'

'Just out of interest, where were you on Saturday night, Mrs Greer?'

'Is that a joke?'

'No. It's a question.'

'I was in Cornwall, Detective Inspector. Lots of people can vouch for my presence in a coastal village there. I attended a beach barbecue.'

'Lucky you,' he said. He suggested a meeting later in the week at the house to bring the Greers up to speed on the legal situation with Jack's trio of alleged assailants. They agreed a day and time. He broke the connection.

When the call ended, Lillian stood up from the desk and

looked at her daughter, busily oblivious, packing items away in careful wraps of tissue paper in boxes brought as flat-packs by the removal men. She studied Olivia for a while. She felt guilty for feeling it, but her strongest identifiable reaction on the news of Robert's death was not shock, it was the sensation of relief. She had been very stupid and completely faithless ever to have become involved with him. But he had been a selfish and destructive man, capable, in his immaturity, of terrible spite.

He felt remote from her. She was almost incredulous when she thought of their affair. He was a part of a history she barely recognised, because it attached to the damaged person she no longer was.

She waited until the children had gone to bed before telling James that Robert O'Brien had died. She told him the source of the information. She told him about the circumstances of the death.

James shrugged. 'I can't say I'm particularly sorry. I didn't know him. And he did something that hurt me very much.'

'It wasn't a capital offence.' They were in the study. Lillian was looking out of the window, at darkness. She said, 'I hurt you more badly than he did, I'm sure.'

'I've forgiven you. It was in my interest to do so. And there was some mitigation.'

'It's odd that he wrote me that letter on the night he died.'

'Not really, Lily. You'd have been on his mind. You would be a very hard act to follow, I should think. I'm glad I will not now be forced to discover just how hard.'

'No,' she said, turning back from the window and facing him. 'You will never be obliged to do that.'

Chapter Nine

She read the Robert O'Brien stories carried in the following day's newspapers at the computer in the study on press internet sites. The consensus, given his success, struck her as somewhat mealy-mouthed and peevish. There was a persistent inference from unattributed 'friends' and 'colleagues' that he had been struggling for most of the second half of the decade with writer's block. He had employed a number of strategies for countering this over recent years. It was hinted at, but of course not said outright, that one of these was cocaine.

There was nothing about the suicide note in the stories. McCabe had suggested the note itself was ambiguous. It could be interpreted as a love letter or a maudlin tribute or an elegy to a lost love. It was only a suicide note if he had deliberately killed himself and she supposed that conclusion would be determined during autopsy by the quantity of the drug he had ingested. Lillian thought dabbling with coke in any quantity about as safe as Russian roulette. But a recreational quantity, a gram or so taken over a whole evening, would not be interpreted as a deliberate attempt at killing himself by an athletic young man.

There was not that much coverage in the newspapers. Mostly it was confined to single columns and almost all the stories carried the same cropped agency picture of O'Brien grinning bareheaded and in sunglasses astride his Harley Davidson. He was only a writer, after all. It was not as though a pop singer or soap star or Premiership footballer had died.

Jack walked in on her. He had just finished his breakfast and there were crumbs in the bumfluff thickening and coarsening on his upper lip. Puberty was in full swing with him. The assault had done nothing to retard that. He was on the way to becoming a man. She took a tissue from the box of them on the desk and stood and wiped his mouth clean, noticing that her son was almost as tall now as she was. He glanced beyond her at the story on the screen.

'Blimey. How did he die?'

'Drugs overdose,' Lillian said.

Jack looked outside to the garden. It was overcast, raining, the fleshy leaves of the shrubs against the far wall glimmering greenly in the wet, matt light. 'Good riddance,' he said.

'You should not speak ill of the dead,' his mother said.

'Nor should you be a hypocrite, Mum.'

They tried to share equally the burden of work involved in the preparation for their move over the following week. Inevitably, though, more of it fell to Lillian than to James. He had the Colorado meeting to prepare for and neither of them underestimated its potential importance and the beneficial impact it could have on their lives.

Lillian also understood, privately, that it was more than a question of prosperity. James had fallen into despondency and depression because he had lacked self-esteem. Colorado could restore his confidence, giving him the professional direction and personal vindication he felt his life lacked. It was vital that he was allowed to prepare properly for a trip upon which so much could depend.

Whatever the outcome in Colorado, she did not think they would ever fall back into the dismal situation together that had triggered her affair. They were too close and too passionately honest with each other now for that to happen. In Jack's phrase, they were locked on. But she wanted the game he had invented to succeed. She wanted the man she loved to earn happiness and satisfaction through achieving success on his own terms. He had certainly worked hard enough and long enough for it.

They did talk about delaying the move until after the Colorado deal was signed and sealed. But relocation to the bay was something they could afford comfortably without supplementing their existing resources. And these things had their own momentum. Summer beckoned far more seductively on the Cornish coast than it did in Bermondsey. Topper's Reach was waiting for them. The children almost literally could not wait.

So it was that Lillian organised the specifics of the move. She liaised with a very helpful land agent called Cooper who worked for Richard Penmarrick. She saw to it that the house was opened up and aired and supplied with its utilities. She ordered new furniture she judged to be of a piece with Topper's Reach; arranged for it to be delivered there. She did not really want physical reminders of their Bermondsey home. Not beyond the four of them. There had been happy times in the house, but she agreed with James that this should be as fresh a start for them as possible. They would rent their townhouse furnished. They would leave almost everything tangible behind them. James drove the Saab to his brother's house and simply parked it up and tossed his brother the keys.

'The documents are in the glove compartment,' he said. Mark had written off his own car the previous month in what he described as a takeaway cappuccino-related incident. The Greers would not be a two-car family in Cornwall. It was unnecessary and ostentatious. James thought Mark touchingly grateful for the gift.

On the Thursday afternoon, DS McCabe arrived promptly at 2 p.m. James and Lillian were both there to see him. Olivia, outraged by the fact, was probably not very much enjoying her penultimate day at school. Jack was in his room, involved in the pain and pleasure of deciding what among his many possessions he could and could not dispense with and see donated to the nearest charity shop.

McCabe told them that the boys accused of assaulting and robbing their son were now unlikely to be brought to trial. Their families had offered to rescind voluntarily their asylum seeker status and return to Somalia as soon as they possibly could. They were begging to return. The nightmares endured by the three alleged assailants had got much worse. They were not sleeping. They were living in terror. They were convinced they were the victims of witchcraft and thought returning home the only way of escaping the curse they had incurred.

'It's an interesting ploy,' James said.

'I've spoken to the family liaison officer assigned under their bail conditions,' McCabe said. 'She said if they're acting, they are the best actors she has ever seen. She says they're genuinely terrified.'

'I wonder if they're as genuinely terrified as an innocent thirteen-year-old being beaten on a bus with a tyre iron by complete strangers in the middle of the afternoon,' Lillian said.

'It might simply come down to cost,' McCabe said. 'We live in straitened times.'

'I thought justice in this country was done partially at least simply so that it could be seen to be done,' James said. 'I thought that was how the criminal justice system functioned.'

McCabe said, 'Think of the cost of bringing this case to trial. Prosecution counsel, expert witnesses, legal aid defence, jury expenses to compensate those jurors whose employers won't and then if the prosecution is successful, the cost of incarceration in a secure youth facility. And then the cost of deportation, if a deportation hearing arrives at that outcome. You've got the involvement of the Borders Agency. After their sentences were served they would be entitled to relocation expenses when they were repatriated.'

'You're kidding,' James said.

'No,' McCabe said, 'I'm not. Much easier and cheaper just to accept their offer to return to their homeland, isn't it?'

'I've said this to you before, but there is such a thing as natural justice,' James said.

McCabe smiled. He sipped the coffee Lillian had brewed him. He looked tautly muscled and immaculate in his uniform. James did not think it remotely funny or ironic that the police officer seated on their sofa took his coffee strong and black.

'Natural justice is not a real world concept,' McCabe said. 'It's as illusory as the village life idyll in that picturesque place by the sea where you and your family are escaping to.'

The Greers were both silent for a moment. James said, 'You don't believe there's such a place as England any more?'

McCabe shrugged. 'It depends on what you mean by England. Maybe in a tourist theme park sort of way, there is. Beefeaters still guard the Tower. Stratford has been dressed up to look fairly Shakespearean. You've always struck me as a pragmatist, Mr Greer. You should go back to trusting your instincts because you can butter crumpets from now till kingdom come. Rupert Brooke isn't coming to tea. It isn't going to happen.'

James said, 'You've changed your tune, Detective Sergeant. You approved of our plan the last time we spoke about it. You told us that you'd moved out yourself, from Brixton to the Kent suburbs. You said you and your family were glad you'd done so, had no regrets at all.'

'The tune where you're going is by Elgar, played at 78rpm under an old-fashioned gramophone needle. It's Elgar or it's Benjamin Britten. He was very partial to the seaside. Do you know there has not been a felony crime recorded in Brodmaw Bay since the summer of 1932?'

'You looked it up?'

'I was curious. It's fifteen years since a new surname was added to the electoral roll. The last census shows everyone there is of the same ethnic origin. No prizes for guessing which. Joblessness is registered officially at 0 per cent. But it's the crime statistic that really stunned me. It seems less like a living community than a bricks and mortar museum. It's not right.'

'Well, thanks for your optimism and encouragement,' Lillian said. 'It's much appreciated, Detective Sergeant.'

'Thanks for the coffee,' McCabe said, climbing to his feet. 'It was excellent.'

'You're welcome,' Lillian said. 'What happens now?'

'Nothing happens, at least for a few weeks. I'll keep you informed. I gather your move is imminent?'

'We leave on Monday.'

He nodded. 'Could I say goodbye to Jack?'

'Of course,' James said. 'He's in his room. Just go up.'

Lillian and James listened to McCabe's light, agile tread receding up the stairs. Lillian said, 'I wouldn't have had him down as an authority on classical music.'

'Maybe his daughter's ballet has made him one. Books and covers, you of all people should know that. I mean, what music do you think Richard Penmarrick enjoys?'

'His wife's singing, if he has any taste.'

'Generally, I mean.'

'Easy,' Lillian said, 'the Doors and a bit of Free and Traffic and the Strolling Bones, obviously.'

'He told me he likes Curtis Mayfield and Marvin Gaye and the Isley Brothers. I think that shows how deceptive appearances can be.'

Upstairs, they talked about Chelsea and their next season prospects for a bit before McCabe steered the conversation in the direction of the assault on Jack and his feelings about it.

'Still want them punished?'

'Yeah, I do.'

'An eye for an eye is it, Jack? Is that how you play your football?'

'No, it isn't. I don't go in for retaliation on the pitch at all. Only muppets play like that.'

'But you want revenge against the boys who hurt you.'

'It isn't about revenge, Alec. I want them to get what's legally coming to them. I want them punished. But mostly I want them off the streets so they can't do it again to someone else.'

'Looking forward to your move?'

'I was and I wasn't. I was looking forward to leaving school. Against that, I thought I was going there damaged goods, like one of those people sent to a convalescent home in an old-fashioned movie. But I played tennis against my uncle at the end of last week and I'm going to be fine, I think. I'll be heading a ball again before Christmas.'

'That's great.'

They shook hands. Jack said, 'Will you keep in touch?'

'Would you like me to?'

'Of course I would.'

'Then I will.'

On the following morning, Lillian received an email forwarded by her agent, from the publisher of the series of books she had been collaborating on with Robert O'Brien. It stated that it would be unlikely now that any but the first of them, the single completed story, would ever be put into print. Nevertheless, in recognition of her commitment to the project and the quantity and quality of material she had already produced, her contract was to be honoured. She would be paid the original sum agreed in full.

She replied saying that she wanted the entire amount minus her agent's percentage donated equally to three charities. They were ChildLine, the NSPCC and Great Ormond Street Hospital for Children. For a moment she thought about adding a fourth. She thought about listing Narcotics Anonymous. But she was actually quite unsympathetic to mature adults with drug habits. She thought the problem largely, if not wholly, self-inflicted.

They left for the bay not on the Monday as originally planned, but on the preceding day, the Sunday. This meant a pre-dawn drive back to Heathrow and his flight to Denver for James less than twenty-four hours later. But Lillian thought it important he go with them. She thought it essential that they all leave their old home and arrive at their new one together and her husband agreed with her. And Richard Penmarrick's man Cooper had assured them that Topper's Reach was ready and Richard had himself made sure the fridge and food cupboards were provisioned as a welcoming courtesy.

They arrived at four in the afternoon. As they crested the rising hills and passed the circle of standing stones to their left and the bay came fully into view, the children in the seats behind them gasped audibly at the panorama revealed by the descent they were about to take. Lillian could understand why. It was a vista full of the promise of adventure and vibrant new life. The sun still hung high in the sky before them. The beach was a vivid orange crescent against the deep blue of the sea. The fishing fleet bobbed picturesquely beyond the granite breakwater to the right of the Leeward Arms and the whitecaps stretched to the horizon almost infinitely before them.

'Blimey, Dad,' Jack said, 'you didn't half come up with the goods.'

James heard air escape Jack's lungs in a rush as his sister elbowed him expertly in the side. 'Mum organised most of it,' she said.

'Dad deserves the credit, Livs,' Lillian said. 'Dad was the decision-maker on this one. On this one you were the big cheese, weren't you, darling?'

'Uurgh, they're going to kiss,' Olivia said.

'Not while Dad's driving,' Jack said. 'Mum's too sensible. He might crash and kill us all.'

'You mean in a ball of fire?'

'Yep, in a raging inferno of flames.'

James smiled, thinking about what his wife had just said. It was odd. He had only found the bay in the first place because her illustrations had led him to it. That was a mystery the accelerating pattern of events had forced him almost to forget. But it was a puzzle, too, wasn't it?

Jack thought the bay pretty cool on first impressions. He thought that living in the sort of place you generally only went on holiday would be great. He couldn't see a downside, other than for the fact that it was all so hilly. The sea was flat, obviously. But the land behind the town rose steeply. The only flat patch was that big circle surrounded by standing stones they had passed on the way down. That was the only place you could realistically have marked out a football pitch. It looked like an ancient monument, though, so the prospect was unlikely. And they weren't going to do it just for him.

As his dad drove down into the village, he still couldn't quite believe that his parents had actually done this. They had been talking about it for as long as he could remember. It had got to the point where he had thought talk was all it was and that it would never really happen. At some point he had come to the conclusion that his parents talked about moving to the coast *instead* of doing it.

When Alec McCabe had shaken his hand and said goodbye, he hadn't really believed they would go. Even when he had taken his old boots and Xbox and jigsaws he'd outgrown and a couple of Airfix kits he'd never got round to building to donate to the Oxfam shop, he hadn't really believed it. But here they were. The car roof was down and the sun was hot in his face and the air smelled fresh and clean and strongly of salt and the sea. Some kids who looked about his own age were wobbling in wetsuits on windsurf boards just off the beach.

He thought then about Robert O'Brien. This was a day O'Brien had not lived to enjoy. He would never enjoy anything ever again; not windsurfing or riding his motorbike or signing autographs for fans. Jack thought for a moment about how rarely he considered death. People of his age didn't, did they? They thought they were never going to die. Even on that bus in Peckham he had not really thought he was going to be killed. And at the time someone had been trying to kill him and making a pretty good attempt at it.

He thought that he should feel sorry about the death of Robert O'Brien. They were always being told in the R.E. lessons no one listened to at school that human life was sacred. Also it was usually quite shocking when someone young died and O'Brien had definitely been younger than his parents and they weren't exactly old.

He didn't feel sorry, though. He didn't feel exactly happy about it, but he did not think it a tragedy or a waste. He would never have read another of his stories. They had been spoiled for him. During a game he would turn the other cheek, as they called it in R.E., because that was the sensible thing to do. Off the pitch, he did not suppose he had a very forgiving nature. Maybe he should work on it. Alec McCabe had hinted at something like that and he liked and admired the big policeman.

The village was so picturesque it was like something out of a film. The shops were all old-fashioned. The streets were narrow and cobbled and there were flowers in hanging baskets above the shop doorways. People nodded and smiled as his dad drove the car slowly along. But there were not many pedestrians. Jack noticed that the shops were all shut, which was odd because it was a Sunday afternoon. He wasn't worried about it. His mum had said there was plenty of stuff already bought for them to eat and drink when they arrived.

When they got into the new house there was a huge bunch of flowers on the kitchen table next to an equally huge bowl of fruit and he just beat his sister to it and they started wrestling over the grapes until their dad told them in his stern voice, which was not actually particularly stern, that they should remember their manners and share. They did share, wolfing grapes while their mum opened an envelope and read the note it contained.

'We're invited to a little gathering being held to welcome us at the Leeward at seven o'clock,' she said; 'seven till eight, totally informal, completely child-friendly, no obligation to go.'

'We can't really refuse,' their dad said. 'Then again it's only an hour, why would we want to?'

Jack explored. Their new house was much bigger than their old one and his new room had an epic view out over the bay. His new bed was bigger than his old one had been. Everything in his room looked more serious and grown-up and he was delighted with it all. It only lacked a few team photos, but he'd wait until the new season for those, when the transfer activity had calmed down and the new Chelsea squad was complete and settled.

Livs was up to something. By now he thought she should have had him by the arm, pulling at him, begging him to go and look at her new room, excited by all her boring, girly new things, thrilled by her new wallpaper, which was probably floral and pink. But wherever she was, she was being very quiet. Having greedily gorged herself on them, maybe she was throwing up her grapes in one of the loos, sending a stream of purple vomit into the toilet bowl.

It was funny, that. It wasn't a funny thought for very long, though. It was actually quite worrying because he suspected that an eight-year-old could easily choke on her vomit. Plus it was unlike her to be so quiet. Sometimes two and two did the obvious thing and made four. What had happened to his little sis? What if she was gagging on a bathroom floor? He went to look for her, calling her name anxiously along the high corridor their bedrooms were off.

He felt a surge of relief when she called down to him from the floor above. It meant she had not drowned in a puddle of her own drool. She was okay. He climbed the stairs up to her.

She was kneeling on the bare boards of a small room with a fireplace and wooden shelves in the alcoves to either side of it. The fireplace was small and had a little engraved hood made of iron he thought was there to stop smoke from the fire getting into the room. It was a cosy sort of room with one window that overlooked the slate roofs of the village to the left of their house. Jack thought that it had probably been a study.

Livs had taken up a piece of floorboard. Jack could partially see into the cavity she had revealed under the floor. She had a package in her hand. The package was yellow, like the oilskins fishermen wore to protect them from the wet. But it was old and faded and cracked and tied up with twine that had turned brown.

'Wow,' Jack said. 'Cool, a secret compartment. Clever old you for finding it, Livs. How did you find it?'

'Madeleine told me where to look.'

'Who's Madeleine?'

'She's my real imaginary friend.'

'She can't be both.'

'She can so.'

'Is she an old friend?'

'Very. She's easily the oldest friend I've got.'

'What's that in your hand?'

'Something Daddy must read.'

'Is it valuable?'

'It isn't treasure. It's a story.'

'Is it a secret?'

'I don't know,' Olivia said. She frowned. 'It won't be when Daddy has read it.'

Jack held out his hand. 'Can I look at it?'

'No. It's only for Daddy. I promised Madeleine.'

Jack decided he would not debate the point. He could hear their mother calling them from downstairs. He thought the whole idea of imaginary friends slightly disturbing. He had the feeling that Olivia was a bit frightened of this Madeleine. He thought that Livs was very brave. She was much less scared of the dark than he remembered being at that age. The house was not sinister. The room they were in was not in itself scary. Madeleine sounded, though, like someone he wouldn't much want to meet. He would let it go.

Obviously Madeleine had not told Livs where to find the package because she had made Madeleine up and even if she was real, she was likely someone in Livs's year at her school in Bermondsey and therefore hardly an expert on secret compartments in a house in Cornwall she had never seen.

There was another explanation, but it involved elements Jack did not want to think about. They would make the house seem eerie and he did not want that. Anyway their mum was calling them and they needed to go down to their parents.

Mum and Dad were drinking coffee in the kitchen. Livs walked straight up to her father and presented him with the package she had discovered. 'Please promise me that you will read this, Daddy,' she said.

Their dad took the package and hefted it in his hand and glanced at their mum and shrugged. He put down his coffee mug and untied the twine and unwrapped a small hardback book. The book was bound in musty-looking fabric and when he opened it and thumbed through the pages, they were covered in neat handwriting that looked as though it had been done with a fountain pen. The letters were small and sloping and the ink black. There was a name and a date on the inside front cover of the book.

'This belonged to Adam Gleason,' he said to their mum. Then to Livs he said, 'Where did you find this, darling?'

'In a secret compartment,' Jack said, 'in a room that looks like it used to be the study.'

Jack had a feeling he thought would best be described as a hunch. It was very strong and it insisted that his dad should read the notebook his sister had found. His interruption had been to try to prevent Livs from mentioning Madeleine. If she mentioned Madeleine their parents would simply stop believing what she said. And it was very important that their dad read what she had uncovered. It was vital. Jack's hunch told him so.

Their dad held the notebook between the thumb and forefinger of his right hand and tapped it against the knuckles of his left. To their mum, he said, 'I should pass this on to that florid old scholar chap, the local archivist.'

'Michael Carney,' their mum said.

Livs burst into tears. She did not just start to cry. Her shoulders heaved once and her face flushed a sudden bright red and tears rolled down her cheeks and then her little body shook and she wailed.

Jack reached out his arms to comfort her but he was not as quick as their dad who sank to his knees and wrapped his daughter in his arms saying, 'I will read it, darling, I promise. I promise you I'll read every last word of it.' He kissed her. He ruffled her hair and dabbed at her wet cheeks with his shirtsleeve. He reached up and handed the notebook to their mum and said, 'Put this in my small bag, darling. It's in the boot of the car. It's the bag I've packed as hand luggage. I'll read it on the plane tomorrow.'

She hesitated. She said, 'And Michael Carney?'

'It's been wherever Livs found it for about ninety years, by the look of it. He can wait a few more days to learn about its contents.'

Their mum frowned. 'Okay,' she said, 'I'll go and put it in the bag. When I get back, I want to see this secret compartment, Olivia. Will you show it to me?'

Livs nodded. 'Yes,' she said.

They left for the pub about fifteen minutes later. Jack had feared they might be forced to dress up for the event. He'd never been to a welcoming party before. But they went as they were, except that their mum put on a bit of lipstick and brushed her hair in the mirror. It had become a tad wild on the journey what with the roof down and all and, in the words she always used, needed taming.

Jack wondered on the way to the pub what Livs could possibly have said upstairs to her about the secret compartment. He was pretty sure she had left Madeleine completely out of it. That was his second hunch. Mention of the real imaginary friend and her instructions regarding the package would have worried and distracted their mum. But she wasn't worried. On the walk to the pub her face was free of the frown that sometimes troubled it.

His sister looked happy too. She looked carefree, he realised, thinking that she had been unusually quiet by her standards in the car on the way down. There had been the one perfectly aimed elbow in the ribs, but that had come after nearly four hours of travelling. She had been subdued, hadn't she? She had been worried about the task Madeleine had given her to carry out. It had been on her mind, nagging away at her on their journey. And now that she had done it she was unconcerned. She was free. Madeleine, Jack thought, imaginary or not, must be a right piece of work.

When they reached the pub the grown-ups of the bay struck him as every bit as picturesque as the place they lived in. The Penmarricks looked like rock stars, pure and simple. The woman who ran the school his sister was supposed to go to in September looked like one of those women James Bond snogged early on in the film and then ended up having to kill near the end. The bloke who ran the pub was the nightclub bouncer from hell. The man his dad had called the local scholar was about a hundred and twenty years old and totally gay in an orange tweed suit and a bright yellow cravat, with white hair so long it touched his shoulders.

Much more interesting to him was Megan Penmarrick, eleven years old which wasn't ideal, but a total babe, all the same. Megan was absolutely gorgeous. She wasn't like the girls at his old school, in that she seemed completely unaware of her sensational looks. He was used to good-looking girls being very conscious of the fact and stand-offish as a consequence. Megan didn't seem to be at all like that. She was really friendly and approachable and interested in what he had to say. Sadly, she was also interested in what Olivia had to say. But nobody was completely perfect.

There were some other kids there. There was a boy about his own age called Andy Jasper and a boy and a girl called Rachel and Simon Tamworth who were ten-year-old twins. They all spoke quite slowly, with accents that curled the words they pronounced. Andy was a Plymouth Argyle supporter. Jack felt that he could only sympathise. Alec

McCabe had told him that unless you had lived in Cornwall for about three hundred years you were an incomer and sometimes given the cold shoulder. That wasn't happening, so far. Everyone there was friendly.

They all belonged to this club. They called it just that, the Club, and it seemed to involve loads of fun activities. Jack was quite anxious to get back into shape after his football lay-off and the Club seemed to be a good route to doing that. Windsurfing would help restore his upper body strength and climbing and trekking would strengthen his legs. They would learn to sail. The Club had a club-house – naturally – based on a small island they usually reached by canoe or dinghy. It all sounded, in a way Jack admitted to himself was obviously a bit Famous Five, actually quite exciting.

'We've got a meeting tomorrow evening,' Megan said. 'Why don't you two come along and see if it's your sort of thing?'

Jack said, 'You mean we can just turn up?'

'Just a second, I'll find out.' Megan went and over and tugged at the sleeve of a bald, sinewy-looking man Jack knew was the headmaster of the Mount, the school he would be attending from September. He was a bit disappointed his school wasn't being run by the headmistress who looked like a sexy Bond villainess, the one just then talking to his mum, but you couldn't have everything and Philip Teal seemed friendly enough. He walked back across the room with Megan. They were both smiling.

He looked from Jack to Olivia and back again. 'Do I sight new recruits?'

'We can't do anything,' Olivia said. 'I mean, we can swim and stuff, obviously. But we can't do sailing and rock climbing.'

'You're more than welcome to learn,' he said. 'The Club exists in large part to teach those skills.'

'It would be up to our parents,' Jack said. 'Personally I'd love to join.'

'Me too,' Livs said.

'I've already mentioned the Club to your mum,' Megan said. 'I did so when your parents came to our house for lunch. So she does know a little bit about it.'

Philip Teal winked at them and said, 'Don't worry, I'll have a word with your folks, I'm quite persuasive.'

In no time at all it was eight o'clock and then suddenly it was almost nine and they were out of there and on their way back to their new house through the gathering dusk. Jack felt really happy. He looked up and saw some remote seabird soaring high through the silvery-blue sky on wings of brilliant white and thought that was how he felt. Then he remembered that his dad was going to America the following day and his heart plunged swiftly to earth. It didn't seem right. It seemed the wrong time altogether for him to be going away from them.

Lillian got up with James the following morning as he prepared before dawn for his departure to America. She thought it only fair. He had travelled to the bay with them at her insistence. He was in for a long drive, a long check-in and a fairly long flight. She thought that the least she could do was send him off with a bacon sandwich and a decent cup of coffee inside him.

He seemed a bit preoccupied, which was understandable. The trip was so important in terms of his self-esteem and he had not really had a very tranquil time in which to prepare for it. That said, she thought that he must have rehearsed the moment to come in Colorado endlessly in his mind over the past few years just as a means of spurring himself on. He would not let himself down.

For one thing, the old anxiety had gone. He had confided that to her. He no longer needed the mental tricks and deflections taught him by the hypnotherapist who had treated him for his panic attacks. He was not prey to them any more. The anxiety of waiting for his son's prognosis, when he did not know whether Jack would live or die, had cured him of it completely. He had fought to retain his composure then and had won the fight. Nothing in business life could flay him in the way his ordeal in the hospital had threatened to do. Everything, by comparison, was a stroll in the park.

Lillian considered, though she had not said as much, that the hospital vigil had made her husband a much stronger man than he had been before it. She believed she had seen the proof of this strength in his reaction to her confession of infidelity. He had lost his composure briefly to shock and the bitter grief of betrayal. Then he had gathered himself and found from somewhere in him the strength to forgive her. The result of this for her had been that she did not just love him more than she had; she had far more respect for him too.

She walked with him to the car, parked at the back of the house. Mist concealed the hills that rose to the rear of the bay. The stone circle would be wrapped and enfolded in it, damp and stubborn in its ancient mystery. The fishing fleet would be miles out, nets trailed through a tranquil sea. James asked her if she would feel stranded and trapped by his taking the car and she said no. The single word sounded more emphatic about that than she actually felt, but it was still not quite yet a lie.

She kissed him. She wished him luck. She said goodbye.

She waved at the retreating car until it turned a corner out of sight and then she went back into the house and closed the door softly behind her and stole up the stairs past the rooms in which her children slept and went to examine the room on the third floor in which Olivia had found that old notebook under a section of floorboard.

She had replaced the board. Lillian's eyesight was excellent, but it was still difficult to make out the section that could be lifted, with the naked eye. It was a foot long and so smoothly fitted to the boards with which it adjoined that though nothing but gravity secured it, it did not move even a fraction of an inch when pushed or trodden on.

It had been cleverly concealed. The hiding place was the result of work painstakingly done. Only by applying thumb pressure at a very precise point at one end of the board could the other end be made to stand proud the fraction of an inch necessary for fingertips to lever it out.

There was no way in the world Olivia could have found it, as she had claimed she had the previous afternoon, by accident. Her account contradicted itself. It provided no compelling reason why James should have to read the hidden book. Olivia sincerely believed in the importance of that. Urgency was not something a little girl manufactured in her head for no reason. Someone had told her daughter precisely where and how to find the package and instructed her very firmly on to whom it must be given.

Why?

The answer to that question would only reveal itself when James had read whatever it was Adam Gleason had committed to paper. Lillian was fairly sure, though, that, whatever it was, it was more than just ideas for poems.

It was very quiet in the house. Lillian had remembered the

imaginary friend with whom her daughter had been seen conversing, by an alert teacher on playground duty, at the railings near the school gate. She shivered. She did not really believe in ghosts. But the mysteries were mounting up, weren't they? She had pictured perfectly a place she had never been to in a book she could not remember having worked on. Something had frightened Robert O'Brien to death. Her brother-in-law had told James he had seen something not really human haunting their Bermondsey garden. Mark Greer ate too much junk but takeaway kebabs, for all their ills, did not provoke demonic hallucinations.

She put her foot on the unsecured board and pressed with all her weight and was not even rewarded with a creak. She had remembered Richard Penmarrick's words of greeting to her when she had first met him and his beautiful wife. 'Welcome home,' he had said.

Her maiden name was Matlock. It was not that common a name. She remembered what McCabe had said about the census and wondered if there was a parish register. She recalled her painting of the church in the book. It was the one anomalous image included there. It was the one illustration that jarred with the idyllic portrait of the village conjured by the rest.

The church might still be derelict. She had seen no cleric at the mass gathering on the beach that Saturday night. That did not mean there wasn't one. He might have been costumed like most of the rest for the event. Or more likely he would not have gone. Essentially that had been a pagan gathering, had it not? She had not understood the chanting and singing and the strange dance at the edge of the water that had summoned the shellfish from the sea. But they had all been too blasphemously pagan for a priest to feel comfortable with.

Even if the church was a ruin and the parish register long disappeared, there were still gravestones. She would go and look at them. O'Brien's death had robbed her of her most pressing work commission. In the absence of her husband, she had a bit of time on her hands. She would go and look at the church and its headstones. She would do it while the kids had fun and learned wholesome new skills at the Club that evening.

She had not lied to James. She had resolved never to deceive him again. In doing so, she only deceived herself and, anyway, he deserved better. She did not feel trapped or stranded without the car. It was only a couple of days, after all. She did not feel isolated or claustrophobic. But she was starting to have thoughts that, however ill-defined, might make her feel differently when they clarified further in her mind.

Welcome home, Penmarrick had said with his charismatic smile. Home now to her family was a place where no one had committed a recorded crime since 1932. You could view that statistic with a smug glow of white-flight relief. Or you could side with the clever police detective who thought it signalled something very wrong.

They weren't canoes. Strictly speaking they were kayaks. And the ones Jack and Livs were in were two-man kayaks because they had to have someone experienced accompanying them. Livs was sharing her kayak with Philip Teal who was now Mr Teal to them. Jack thought that fair enough. He would not have been comfortable calling his future headmaster 'Phil'.

Jack was in his kayak with Megan Penmarrick, which all things considered was not so much cool as totally epic. They were wearing wetsuits and life jackets and the flotilla of five kayaks was keeping a close formation because it was safer that way.

The sea was calm. The tricky bit had been getting the kayaks over the surf at the edge of the beach and then getting in once they were on the calm beyond, but Mr Teal and an older boy called Ricky Sharp steadied the craft so there was no real danger they would capsize. Ricky's dad was the chandler Martin Sharp and Ricky obviously knew boats backwards.

Jack liked him immediately. He looked as strong as a bull but he had no attitude at all. He was totally expert on the water without being at all flash. And once they were off, because his balance and coordination were naturally good and because he had every incentive not to look a complete dickhead in front of Megan, Jack found that he paddled quite competently.

It was fun. The tide was out now and there was no current to fight against. Mr Teal explained that they would return at about eight o'clock on the incoming tide, which would assist them. Before that, they would barbecue a supper on the island. They had sausages and homemade burgers and baps in watertight containers. Two of the kayaks trailed baited lines in the hope of catching fish to grill.

They passed a shoal of basking sharks. Mr Teal had said they might and explained that these monsters of the deep were gentle and timid and lived on krill. Seeing their dorsal fins sticking abruptly out of the water was still quite shocking. They were huge. The sea was a strange and alien element and it was thrilling to be out on it and to think that this was part of their new routine.

The only slightly dodgy bit had been their mum insisting on coming and seeing them into their kit and kayaks before waving them off from the beach. But mums were mums and the sea was awfully deep and it had been their first time. Besides, Megan thought their mum just about the most brilliant woman on the planet. So it hadn't actually been too embarrassing.

Jack glanced at his little sister and felt a sharp stab of pride at how well she was doing. She had got the rhythm of paddling straight away. He looked at the firm set of her pretty little face and loved her despite himself. Of course he loved her; she was the piece of the puzzle that made it whole. In his preferred way of putting it, they were locked on. At least, they would be when their dad got back from his business trip to America.

The island was quite small when they got there, almost circular, rising to a rocky peak in the middle, with heather and gorse bushes and blackberry thorns and quite a lot of bird shit on the exposed bits and a small hut made of split logs painted over with something to weather-proof it.

The hut was fantastic. Inside it there were bunks with blankets and tins of food and hurricane lamps. There was a paraffin heater. There was a really old-fashioned radio set. It was like base camp in a film about Scott of the Antarctic. Outside the weather was gentle and cloudless, with barely a breeze. Jack almost wished it was stormy so that they could light the stove and barricade the door and evenly divide their rations.

He walked back outside. They had taken off their life jackets and wetsuits, were in their normal clothes again. He closed the door of the hut. Its hinges creaked on a harsh lack of lubrication. Something, some kind of carving in wood, had been mounted at its centre. 'What's that?' he asked, out loud, shocked into speech by the sight of the effigy.

'That's the spookmeister,' a voice from behind him said. He turned. It was Livs, of course. It was her word, wasn't it? And it really was the spookmeister. The figure on the carving was evil-looking. It was like a gargoyle or an imp. You couldn't even properly look at it, Jack didn't think. It made you wince and raised goose bumps on your skin to do so. His sister looked very pale and completely unsurprised by the sight of the carving. She looked scared and resigned and he was reminded of her indignant claim that she never told lies.

The others, the proper members of the Club, were a few metres away, surrounding the fire, the hut not a novelty to them as it obviously was to the Greer children. They had hooked five mackerel paddling to the island and everyone seemed to be concerned with fanning the flames and gutting the catch.

Megan looked up and across to them, smiling. The smile disappeared when she saw the concerned, distasteful look on their faces. She was kneeling by the fire. She stood and approached them, wiping fish slime from her hands on the thighs of her jeans. Jack thought the expression on her face a hard one to read. It was not one he had seen her use before.

'What's the matter?'

'The spookmeister is the matter,' Olivia said.

Jack thought that his sister sounded very serious. There was a word, wasn't there? The word for how Livs sounded was grave.

Megan's eyes switched from them to the carving mounted on the hut door. She put her finger to her lips to signal hush and her eyes grew large in her head before she lifted them in a gesture signalling that Jack and Olivia were to follow her. They did. She stopped out of sight of the cooking party, out of sight of the hut, out of the group's earshot in a patch of clearing surrounded by dense foliage. She squatted on the ground and, taking her lead, they did the same.

'What is that thing?' Jack said.

Megan hesitated. He had not seen her do that before, either. She was a confident and fluent speaker. She was clever, not the tongue-tied type of girl from a home without books and conversation that there had been a depressing number of at his old school. 'We're not supposed to say its name,' she said. 'It's bad luck to do so.'

Livs said, 'Why is it on the door, if it's bad luck?'

'It's on the door as a sign of protection. They're sort of like guardians or soldiers or something; warriors from an old myth. They're not unlucky, only naming them is. It's just a superstition. You wouldn't whistle on a ship, would you?'

'I might,' Jack said.

Livs said, 'I might too. If I could whistle, I mean.'

Megan raised her eyes to the sky. 'Incomers,' she said.

Jack said, 'What do they guard?'

'They guard the Singers under the Sea.'

'And what do they do?'

'They do magical things, Jack. They can grant your wishes.'

The smell of grilling mackerel was drifting deliciously around them. It was time to go back to the others and their food.

'Do you not have any wishes?'

The wish that came to Jack closely involved the girl who had just put the question. He wanted to kiss her, confident that she wanted to be kissed. It would very likely not come true for a few years yet. 'I wish for my dad to come back to us safely,' he said.

'Olivia?'

'I'm keeping mine a secret,' Livs said. 'Otherwise it might not come true.'

Lillian Greer did not know much about organised religion but she knew desecration when it stared her in the face. She had opened the church tabernacle because it had been left slightly ajar. Her instinct on ascending to the altar had been to close it. It was the instinct of someone habitually neat. But she had noticed the slightly nauseous whiff of the sea about the large, ornamented box at the centre of the altar-piece. She had opened it. She had almost screamed out loud at what doing so had revealed to her.

The severed head of a conger eel, a huge specimen with rows of vicious teeth visible in its gaping mouth, had been placed inside. The hook used to catch the eel was still there, its barbs stained bloody. They had pierced the roof of its mouth in the struggle to land this monster and torn through the flesh of its upper jaw.

The dead-eyed gaze of the eel returned her own. The head had been severed raggedly, while the creature still lived and struggled for freedom or more likely tried to bite its captor, Lillian thought. The flesh was dull and half a dozen listless flies were buzzing around it but it did not yet stink. It had been put there fairly recently, a day or two ago at most.

The previous day had been a Sunday, hadn't it? That was the traditional Christian day of worship, when the most important service of the week, would be held in a church still consecrated and functioning. This one was not. It was derelict and abandoned. Someone had done this, though. Someone had been here.

Something glistened in the gloom of the tabernacle interior, she noticed, in the dim light she had provided by opening its door, in the mouth of the eel beyond those rows of razor-edged teeth. It looked a bit, she thought, like caviar. Struggling with her own distaste, she leaned closer to take a proper look. She saw that it was the black beads of a rosary, deliberately placed there in a symbolic act of blasphemy.

She took a step back. She closed the tabernacle door on the grotesque joke made at God's expense inside it. She looked around the church interior, at the sagging roof, the smashed stained glass of the windows in their high arches, the burlap sacks slumped as though in mockery of worship on the old wooden pews. She walked back down the aisle, listening to the slightly gritty sound her boots made on the smooth stone of the floor. It was sand. Wet sand had clung to the tread of her boots as she had watched her children paddle off on their Enid Blyton adventure an hour earlier.

She had not expected this. She had not anticipated the heavy dread that had started to subsume her the moment she stooped under the broken door and entered the building. There had been no Matlocks commemorated in granite or marble tribute on any of the gravestones in the churchyard. But her curiosity had not been satisfied. It had driven her into this blighted and damned interior.

Who had done this? She wondered if one of the men who had welcomed her family so warmly in the pub the previous evening had been responsible. She could not imagine it. They seemed such relaxed and friendly people.

It seemed even less likely that one of the women could have done it. She could not see frumpy Bella Worth or mousey Rachel Flood landing the beast whose head decorated the tabernacle. She could not see Elizabeth Penmarrick severing the head of the great, thrashing specimen it must have come from with a gutting knife. *The butcher, the baker and the candlestick maker*, she thought giddily. And Lillian realised that she wasn't alone in the church.

'Hello, Angela.'

'You should not be in here. It isn't safe.'

'Would that be structurally, or spiritually?'

Angela Heart was standing at the foot of the aisle. She looked beyond Lillian to the altar and the tabernacle at its centre. 'This is the west of England,' she said. 'Some of the pagan ways still persist. Nowhere is perfect, Lillian; picturesque maybe, but not perfect.'

'You can say that again.'

Angela glanced around, up at the roof. She looked uneasy. Her usual air of urbane nonchalance was not in evidence at all. She said, 'It's just mischief, Lillian. It is crude and done with spiteful intent but the church is deconsecrated and it is a very long time since a believer in a Christian God came here to worship, or to pray for intercession.'

'Whoever did what I've just seen is very sick and quite seriously deluded,' Lillian said.

'We need to get out of here,' Angela said.

'What happened to this church? Why did it fall into dereliction? What happened to the priest?'

'My home is a two-minute walk away from here,' Angela said. 'Where are your children?'

'They're in the charge of Philip Teal. They're with the Club.'

'If you've time, come back to my house and I'll tell you exactly what happened here.'

Angela's cottage was quaint on the outside and had a pretty back garden visible through the sitting room's French doors, while the interior struck Lillian as a reflection of the woman herself. It was handsome, but austerely so. The décor was stylish, minimalist and largely monochromatic. Where there was colour, it expressed itself in various shades of red. Most vibrant among these was a bunch of roses in a slate vase placed on a table topped with black marble.

Angela made coffee for both of them and then they sat with the late sun slanting through the panes in yellow ingots on the ivory-white carpet. Lillian thought that you would not need the detection skills of Alec McCabe to know straight away that this was the home of a woman without children. And there was evidently no man, either.

Angela Heart was either a widow or she was a spinster. If she was a widow, that was sad. If she was a spinster, it could only be through choice. She wasn't just attractive. She had a very potent sexuality. It had deserted her in the church, along with her composure, but it was returning now. There was something feline about her as she pulled her legs up sideways on the sofa and tilted her head and her eyes caught the light like those of a bold and confident cat. Her hair was glossy and her fingernails wore the same crimson hue as her lips.

She explained that the church had first fallen into dereliction in the first decade of the last century. It had been High Anglican and the Church of England priest incumbent in the parish had become involved in a sex scandal. His paramour had been a boy. He had been only fifteen years of age and skilfully groomed by someone he had been taught to respect and even to revere.

When the priest was exposed, the bishop supervising the diocese had elected to deconsecrate the church. The parish of St Stephen's was abandoned. Feeling had run very high over the paedophile crime committed by a trusted man of the cloth and the bishop did not see how the resentment could be overcome without a properly symbolic mea culpa.

There were other villages with other churches those people from the bay wishing to continue to worship could attend.

'The Church doesn't usually abandon its flock,' Lillian said. 'It contradicts its missionary function. It goes against the direct teachings of Christ, doesn't it?'

The bishop was a pragmatic man, Angela told her. His rise through the hierarchy signified a politician as much as a priest. St Stephen's had never had more than a very meagre congregation. Even in those more devout Edwardian days, the people of the bay preferred their folk superstitions to High Church orthodoxy. They did not like the priestly paraphernalia. They thought that they could differentiate between right and wrong, between good and bad, without having to endure incense and candles and plaster effigies.

'What the fundamentalists call smells and bells,' Lillian said.

'Exactly,' Angela said.

No attempt to revive St Stephen's was made until after the Great War. Then in 1921, a cleric belonging to an independent branch of the Protestant faith arrived and bought the freehold of the site from the diocese and had the building blessed and refurbished and began to try to convert followers.

'He had been an army padre,' Angela said. 'He had known Adam Gleason. He had ministered to the men of Gleason's battalion and they had forged a friendship on the Western Front. Like Gleason, the Reverend Baxter was a poet, though he was not anywhere near so gifted.' She was silent for a moment. She said, 'Can I give you the rest of this account in the garden? I would like a cigarette and I do not smoke in the house.'

Lillian looked at her watch. It was ten past seven.

'Do you have time?'

'Yes. And I'm all ears.'

They went outside. It was still warm and bright. It was

bright, Lillian remembered, because they were on the coast and the sky was lightened by the sun reflected back off the sea. She thought about her children in their wetsuits and orange life jackets smiling as they paddled off in their kayaks. Then she thought of the obscenity, stinking and ferocious in death, in the church tabernacle.

Something gave Baxter a sour demeanour, began Angela. It was as though he bore some grudge against the people of the bay. He would walk the lanes in a black cassock with his hands clasped behind his back and a scowl worn permanently on his long, ascetic face. Some of the villagers began to suspect that Adam Gleason must be responsible for this. They could not think of any other explanation. He must have said something deeply disparaging about the place or its community. Had he accused them of some sin, of some corruption of the soul?

Lillian remembered Richard Penmarrick's remarks about the soldier-poet Gleason; the slight tone of sarcasm, discussing him in the Topper's Reach kitchen, she had not really understood the reason for.

One of Baxter's parishioners most ardent in his Christian belief was a St Ives-born mariner called Thomas Cable. Cable back in those days owned half the bay's fishing fleet. In the spring of 1923 he commissioned Jasper's yard to build him a new boat. The *Carol-Anne* was launched, with much fanfare, in the September of that year. She was blessed on the slipway by the Reverend Baxter before the chocks were hammered from under her and she entered the water. Almost everyone in the bay had gathered to see the launch ceremony and they all witnessed this.

It was a gentle day. The *Carol-Anne*'s newly recruited crew were young lads. But they had been familiar with boats since infancy and the skipper was an experienced man of twenty-eight. They set off on their maiden voyage with much cheering and waving of handkerchiefs and toy flags from the quayside. A fog quickly descended. In those days before sonar, there was a lightship in the bay to warn of the reefs at its southern extremity and its bell began to toll.

'The *Carol-Anne* never returned,' Angela said. 'The fog swallowed her.'

'The sea swallowed her,' Lillian said. 'She must have sunk.'

'It was taken as an omen,' Angela said. 'The church was subsequently vandalised. The porch was burned down in an arson attack carried out at night. Baxter's milk was tainted on his doorstep and the food spoiled in his pantry and people ostracised him. Not the bay's finest hour, I don't suppose, but Brodmaw people in those days were very superstitious. They took against the arrogant incomer in the dog collar and the disdainful frown and when he could take the hostility no more he packed up and left.'

'And the church has been derelict since then?'

'It has.'

'Were there no other boats out that day when the *Carol-Anne* was lost?'

'There were two. They did not see anything. The fog was blanket thick.'

'Did they not hear the cries of the crew when she foundered?'

'I'll tell you what they said they heard. You can make of it what you will. Most of them stayed silent on the subject. Three or four of them swore they heard the sea, singing.'

James Greer sat in the departure lounge at Denver Airport trying to inventory the good things about his life. It was his way of trying to deflect the disappointment threatening to overwhelm him. There would be a point at which disappointment became despair. He knew he was close to it. More accurately, it was close to him. He had to try to force a perspective that diminished what he felt. The Americans had coined that phrase, hadn't they, about keeping it in the day.

The difficulty with keeping it in the day for him was that his disappointment centred on something over which he had been toiling for close to a decade. Even on the flight on the way out there, he had spent the time tinkering on his laptop embellishing, improving, fine-tuning in a last-minute effort to make his game not just good, but perfect.

Americans spoke in a code. In business meetings they did, anyway. He had sat with the beaming reception committee of geeks and they had told him his game was a masterpiece. And then they had spent two hours telling him how he could improve it even further by turning it into something completely different from what he had always intended it to be.

They used this word all the time, which was *terrific*. Except that *terrific* had a completely different meaning in American from what it signified in English. His concept was *terrific*. His execution was *terrific*. The structure of his game, its internal architecture, its levels and avatars and variously realised landscapes and domains were all *terrific*. And what this actually meant was mediocre, lightweight, rankly amateurish and nowhere near achieving the potential as a package the concept deserved.

He peeled the cellophane from a tuna and cucumber sandwich and took a bite and then folded what remained back into its package and rose without appetite and walked over to what the Americans called a trash can and dropped it inside. He chewed, unable to taste anything, the swallow reflex reluctant to come, a physical symptom of the malaise afflicting his soul.

They had wanted two fundamental changes to his medieval survival epic. The first of these was the introduction of a character, a roaming mercenary they even had a name for. He was to be called Krull. He was an assassin, an executioner. He was utterly cruel, totally ruthless and profoundly cold.

The player was supposed not just to root for Krull but to admire and aspire to be him. His let-off, the secret gimmick that enabled him to avoid the moral consequences of all the slaughter he was responsible for – and the Americans were very pleased with this – was that he came from another planet. His planet was very advanced. This made Krull's slaying of medieval humans no worse morally than puffing ant killer on to a troublesome nest.

The second improvement was a mobile torture chamber that trundled through Europe in the charge of a psychotic sect called the Marauders. James had researched the medieval period very punctiliously and he was absolutely bloody sure the Marauders had not trundled through Europe then with their wagon train of portable racks and flays and whips and branding irons. Why would they? What would have been the point? Anyway, someone would have stopped them. The world in the Middle Ages wasn't some anarchic free-for-all.

He had wanted something with the values and sophistication of Risk and Diplomacy wrapped in a software package complex enough to seduce cutting-edge gamers. They had wanted yet another apocalyptic, heavy-metal gore-fest. He had left the meeting after three hours without having signed the proffered contract or even having agreed anything with them in principle.

His son and his daughter, he thought. His children and

their love were the best things in his life. And the love of his beautiful and adulterous wife, that was important to him too. Three people elevated his existence. Emotional pain had figured rather too much in his recent family experience, but it was Lily and Jack and Livs on whom he relied for happiness and fulfilment. The game was not important compared to them and the Colorado experience was a setback he could and would live with and overcome.

Krull had his nemesis in their version of his game, of course. But it wasn't some veteran of Crécy or Agincourt schooled since the age of seven to be invincible in martial conflict. A knight on a warhorse, a noble-blooded European warrior of the period was too mundane for them. Krull's nemesis was a mythic winged creature, a dragon, for fuck's sake. He was quite surprised they hadn't dragged Merlin into the mix.

He was in his seat aboard the plane and the seatbelt sign had been switched off before he remembered the notebook Lillian had packed for him and his promise to his daughter that he would read it. He would do so now, he decided. He had to keep his children's faith. The contents of the notebook might divert him for the duration of the flight, or at least for some of it.

Chapter Ten

June 21 1916

The house is very empty without my beloved wife and cherished daughter. They haunt it. They do not do so in the spectral sense. They do so through the abundant and joyful memories I have of them. They filled these rooms with their energetic and playful spirits as they filled my heart with love. It is not possible to continue to live without them. I do not know whether we meet those to whom we were closest in some afterlife. I have never possessed the zealous certainty of religious faith. I pray it is true, to a God I only half believe in, because it is the only hope left to me now.

These are the last words I shall write. I am certain at least of that. I shall return to France and seek the bullet that will end my mortal existence. I am impatient enough to provide it myself if the enemy should prove reluctant to do so. My grief is beyond endurance. It has cost me whatever poetic gift I possessed. There are not verses to describe this loss. The language does not possess words freighted with sufficient sorrow.

Might I have saved them, had I returned sooner? The answer is that I would have died with them. They could not have been saved. They had been chosen. There would have been no influencing the likes of Teal and Tamworth, Jasper, Carney, Worth, Sharp and Flood. And I would never have been able to persuade Penmarrick or that cold and beautiful creature he calls his bride. The old ways are sacred to him. The ancient spirits must be appeased. The prosperity of the village depends upon it. More: its very survival. Neglect to honour the Singers under the Sea and the legend says caprice will turn to spite and then destruction.

My mistake was in marrying an incomer. Doing so provoked the thirst for fresh blood which my wife and daughter have paid for with their innocent lives. I see them manacled to the rocks in my mind whenever I close my eyes. They wait for the tide to creep upward and touch and slowly engulf them. They see the Harbingers caper and fret on the night shingle awaiting the sound of the demons they serve. And they hear the music toil from the depths as they struggle against their iron bonds, drowning. Such a desolate death and deliberately so because the spirits the old way serves are strangers to mercy.

Everyone born in the bay grows up knowing its secret. Thus is the ritual made to seem simply a part of the pattern of existence. It is a custom, a tradition and a necessity. I matured into adulthood believing all of that. Then I went away to Cambridge and university and instead of reflecting on the pagan strangeness of the place in which I grew up, I almost forgot about it altogether.

I suppose I thought of it, if I thought about it at all, as a necessary evil. And Penmarrick's glib reasoning has a certain objective logic to it. He calls it the price only occasionally exacted of the very few for the profit and permanent wellbeing of the many. I accepted this. Only when the price was exacted of those nearest to me did I see it for what it is: which is ritual murder and human sacrifice and not something with any place or justification in a civilised world.

I should start at the beginning, in medieval times, when witchcraft first summoned the sea spirits we call the Singers with an incantation legend insists was composed in druidic times and then secretly taught and remembered through the centuries. The druids believed that the sea spirits were far stronger than those that roamed the land. They would bring you luck and prosperity and could even grant those wishes not based on personal greed. But they were powerful and once summoned could not be dismissed again. And their potency came only at mortal cost.

They were first courted by the Cornish enchantress Ghislane in a ceremony enacted in the stone circle during one particularly bitter winter in the fourteenth century when the sea had frozen and the village was starving for want of fish. The summoning was successful. Lots were drawn to decide the sacrifice. That was duly made and the weather broke and the bounty of the following spring and summer were without precedent.

They gained in power quite by accident. The witchfinder sent west in Cromwell's time unwittingly assisted this. He manacled those suspected of witchcraft to the boulders of the east shore as one of his tests. The sea spirits were nourished by their innocent deaths. Thus did they become stronger than Ghislane ever imagined they would become.

There is no written record of when the Harbingers first came among us. They were so called because their appearance signified the time for fresh sacrifice was becoming due. They are somewhere between emissaries and foot soldiers in nature. Perhaps they are closer to the latter than the former because they are not capable of communication but they can inflict physical harm along with the corrosive sense of dread that just sighting them can provoke.

I now realise that one of them visited me in the days before my leave and this desolate homecoming. I was on night patrol, in the line, at the forward observation post when a private on sentry duty began to shoot rifle rounds from the fire step into no-man's-land late on a clear and moonlit evening. My immediate concern was that our section was the target of a trench raid. But when I reached the sentry and swept the ground beyond the wire before him through a periscope, there was no movement and there were neither the muzzle flashes nor the sound of return fire that would signal enemy approach.

I ordered him to stop firing and to descend the ladder to where we could communicate out of sight and range of German snipers. I was anxious on two counts. He had fired sufficient rounds to give their mortar parties a good indication of the exact position of our forward base, our principal dugout and our forward supply dump. And practically, the noise of his rifle fire would disturb men robbed of decent rest already by the sustained enemy bombardment we had endured there in our part of the line for close to three days.

'I saw something,' the man insisted. 'Sir,' he added, as a stubborn afterthought. It was Davies, a tenant farmer's son from Totnes, a sturdy boy of eighteen cool under fire, not given in the slightest to flights of imaginative fancy.

'What did you see precisely, Davies?'

'I saw a figure, sir.'

'You saw just the one?'

'Aye, sir.'

'They do not attack individually, Private.' I supposed he could have been a scout doing night reconnaissance. It seemed unlikely. I climbed the ladder and risked a look through my field glasses. They were not military issue but ship's binoculars given me by Sharp the chandler as a parting gift when it became known in the bay I had volunteered for the fight. They were of excellent quality and the moon was bright and yet I saw nothing.

'You must have hit him,' I said to Davies. But Davies looked doubtful about this. 'Describe him to me.'

'He moved very quickly, sir. He had a loping gait, rapid, like a hare. And he had on a mask.'

'You mean a gas mask?'

'Burlap, it looked like. Sockets of glass stitched over his eyes, sir. Must have been glass, gave him a look like he had no eyes in his head. Altogether right strange, he looked.'

I told Davies to make his way back to the support trench and to brew himself a can of tea and to return to his post in half an hour. I would occupy his position while he took a short absence from it that I considered he had earned. He was cool and vigilant and the carrot is more useful than the stick the further forward men are ordered to go. War is enervating on the nerves. My conclusion, as the Devon boy went to get his beverage, was that he had killed a scout wearing some sort of camouflage or experimental protection.

I took and, while he was gone, examined his rifle. The weapon was clean and well lubricated; the barrel smooth and his bayonet polished and stropped to the keenest edge. He was a good soldier, disciplined and professional. I did not think he had been shooting at shadows.

Dawn and daylight revealed no body in no-man's-land. This did not mean he had not been there. He might have crawled back unscathed to his own lines once I ordered Davies to stop firing. He might have crawled back wounded. He might have sought cover in a shell hole and drowned in the putrid water that has filled them half full after the recent rain. He might still be there, hungry and thirsty and afraid, waiting for the night, praying for cloud cover and concealment from the bright moon after dusk.

But he was not there, I know now, because he was not a man at all. He was a Harbinger, one of the grotesque apparitions that come to visit us when sacrifice is due. They come to scare and remind and prompt us and I do not think that bullets fired from a Lee Enfield rifle can conveniently eradicate them. Neither can prayer do it. He came that I should see him. I do not think it would have made any difference to the outcome if I had.

The following afternoon I was writing to the mother of a comrade killed in the earlier bombardment. I told her of course that he died bravely. In fact he died oblivious, blown to pieces while he slept in a direct hit from a howitzer shell on the dugout where he slept. The single largest piece of him recovered intact was the thumb of his left hand. I did not tell his mother this.

I felt a chill of malevolence as I wrote so cold it made me shudder. I looked up and saw something grey-faced and unblinking gazing back at me with incurious fury. It was not a human countenance. The features were crude and ragged and somehow unfinished, the mouth a vacant leer under the empty scrutiny of eyes that were little more than holes. It appeared to crouch and lurk, this creature. I blinked and looked up at the dirty sky and back again and all I saw where it had appeared to me were sandbags, shoved together in a damp and wrinkled pile against the corrugated tin wall of the officers' quarters.

I thought that my eyes were playing tricks on me. It was the Harbinger again, of course, come to summon me home; come to remind me that the people of the bay have duties from which war provides no escape.

I find it the deepest irony of my life that I have written verse inspired by human sacrifice. The brave men who have perished on the altar of freedom have pushed my pen across the page, posthumously, in commemoration of their valour and loss.

They were my comrades, my brothers in blood and common cause and I have tried in my way to honour them and their memory and to celebrate their youth and courage and deeds. I have shared their laughter and lived among them and sung our ardent songs marching shoulder to shoulder with them and trod through their gore in the aftermath of battle. I have mourned them.

Now I mourn my sacrificed wife and daughter. Sarah was, simply, the sunlight in my life. We met at Cambridge. Romance overcame all the many and deliberate obstacles to any sort of contact between male and female students. The attraction was instant and obvious to both of us and simply would not be denied. We walked and punted and told one another of our dreams in endless talks. We made forbidden love and it was magical.

We duly married. We lived in London at first. I taught English at a prep school at East Dulwich and we found a small house in Kennington in Lambeth affordable within our means. Sarah worked as a governess, teaching her young charges Latin and Greek and giving them music lessons on the piano. She was a fair pianist, though her real gift was for fine art. She could paint and draw with wonderful accomplishment.

When she fell pregnant with Paul we were overjoyed. He was a robust infant and athletic and graceful. He walked before his first birthday and could ride a bicycle before his third.

That was a milestone he never reached. Our beloved boy was taken from us by a bout of diphtheria. Grief afflicts people in strange ways sometimes and the loss of Paul made us more determined to be parents together to a second child. Sarah duly fell pregnant just a few short months after we buried our son.

This was in the autumn of 1907. At about that time, my cousin Edith Heart wrote to me from the bay. She mentioned in her letter that there was a vacancy for a new head at the Mount School. She inferred that were I to apply for the job, my local connections would of course count in my favour when the selection process took place among what competing candidates there were.

She said she had recently spoken to Penmarrick and that he had asked fondly about me and whether I might one day return to live in the village of my birth. Some of my early poetry had been published in a couple of the literary journals by then and he said he had seen and admired them, as indeed had his wife.

The temptation was made irresistible by my own wife's condition. I knew that no harm would come to our baby as the child was to be born and raised in the bay. That is the way of things, the charm of it, its uncanny freedom from the pestilence and poverty and general misfortune that can befall anywhere that does not exist in a state of enchantment. London, the great metropolis with its turbulence and squalor, felt to us by then like a tainted place. We were almost anxious to escape from it. All we saw in the west was a safe and bountiful life ripe with opportunity.

Madeleine grew into a kind and beautiful child about whom there was always something dreamy and almost ethereal. As she grew up, she developed a fascination for the plateau above the bay and the standing stones that shape its enigmatic circle. Many was the day I would climb the rise to the rear of the bay with my daughter seated on my shoulders, hand in hand with my wife, to enjoy a picnic in the solitude up there.

Madeleine's other-worldly curiosity was perhaps most pleasingly satisfied in that place. She would gambol and play among the stones in games of hide and seek. She played these with her mother or with me for hours, some days, until she was about six years old.

The most precious time I spent with my daughter was when she was put to bed at night. Then I would tell her a story until she drowsed too sleepily to listen any more. I always made up the stories. She would sometimes request favourites among them I would struggle to recall because they had never been written down. When I got a detail wrong or made an error in chronology, she would always correct it, the way a patient schoolmarm might with a dull-brained child.

The stories are all told. I shall fight nor write nor mourn no more. I am done with life. The will is quite gone in me. I died with Sarah and Madeleine. Three of us, not two, were taken. All of us perished.

Penmarrick knows this. He came to see me at the house. He left an hour ago. He sat there, goading me with his sympathy and sadness, all the more provocative because I suspected they were feelings sincerely felt. My service revolver lay on the table between us, eight soft-point shells in their brass jackets in its steel chamber and I thought about picking it up and pointing it at him and pulling the trigger and watching his skull explode and his life extinguished in a squalid mess of bone fragments and brain matter.

And he read my thoughts and smiled, knowing I would not do it. It would be retribution but it would be murder too and I want only one death on my conscience and that is my own. It will not help to have committed the sin of coldly killing a man, if I am to find my family in whatever afterlife I hope for.

I do not believe the legend of Ghislane. Neither do I believe a druidic incantation first summoned the Singers under the Sea. The druids lay fraudulent claim to all the important Neolithic sites. But the constructions at the sites pre-date the druids by thousands of years. It is reasonable to assume that the rituals for which they were erected do then also.

I think the sea demons pre-date man. I think they are creatures from a prehistoric time before magic and rationality became separate and opposed. Stand in the stone circle on the plateau above the bay and you cannot but get some sense of the remote and imponderable strangeness of the ancient past. Man is a usurper on the earth: rude, disruptive, brash. In some places the old gods must be appeased and the village at the edge of the sea from which I come is one of those places and I think has been since men first crawled out of the slime and stood erect.

I have been wondering who to tell about what has taken place.

There is no arbiter of law or justice to whom I can appeal. Penmarrick rules the bay by custom and bloodline and historic right. All of them will follow his lead; even those, like the publican Abraham, who I believe secretly disapprove. My wife and child drowned. Accidents occur at sea. Every coastal community is familiar with those mundane tragedies caused when boats venture on to the water and storms gather and break suddenly and without warning.

Baxter, padre to my company, might be the man to confide in. I do not think he will be able to do anything to undermine or influence the people of the bay and I doubt he could be made to possess the inclination to travel to the place and try. But I do not want to go to my death without sharing the truth with someone.

We have become good friends. He can be as dour and pious a Scot as any clergyman Edinburgh ever gave birth and education to. But he is principled and strong-minded and a brave man and kind and has the virtue, rare I have discovered in the extremes of martial conflict, of consistency.

He might not believe me. Then again he might. The trenches have acquainted him with some brutal truths about the darkness of men's souls. His theology has schooled him to accept the forces of darkness as real and tangible entities. If he believes in Satan, and I believe he does, he can be persuaded to believe in other demons too.

If he does venture to the west, in Nicholas Penmarrick, Baxter will meet the devil in human guise. Penmarrick has the glamour Milton's Lucifer possessed. He has charm in abundance and an easy aspect on the eye. There is a careless elegance about him that prevents people from glimpsing his true character. I saw it though this afternoon, when he came to the house. In my grief I saw him stripped of his affectation and his finery; of the aristocratic air he wears like a dab behind the ear of expensive cologne.

I poured myself a cognac from the cabinet sited between the sitting room's tall west-facing windows. It has a mirrored back and I glanced at his reflection there and the mask had slipped and he sat slumped and debauched-looking. Worse, he looked depraved. I observed as though for the first time the ragged length of his hair and the coarseness of his skin and the fingernails worn talon-length on the crossed hands in his lap and, not at all for the first time, I wondered at what mockery of the calendar his true age would represent.

The sun has slipped in the sky, where it hangs out over the sea. The sea is blue now but will turn orange later and then later still will reflect that dipping orb with the crimson richness of blood.

I am reminded of Madeleine and my last leave, back in the spring, when all she wanted of her father was for me to show her a sunset. She sat in the pretty purple and grey of her St Anselm's school uniform and implored me to let her be with me to look at the western sky on the beach as day declined into darkness. I hesitated, saying that this phenomenon of nature would only occur at that time of the year, past her bedtime. But in my heart I had relented straight away.

In the event, we watched our sunset from the stone circle, the perfect vantage point, its familiarity made strange and even portentous by the stretching shadows of the monoliths and the ripple of the darkling grass. As gloaming turned to dusk, the heavens shone gloriously, the descending sun touching the water beneath cumulus shaped like some vaulted cathedral of fire. Madeleine gasped at the wonder of it and put her arms around my neck where we sat and hugged and kissed me on the cheek in gratitude.

There are persistent rumours that Haig and his French counterpart have planned a huge assault for the end of the month. I have not been blind to the recent toil of the sappers: tunnelling, laying mines, building underground routes along which our strike troops can approach the German line in cover. Nor, coming back through the support system of trenches on the way to the boat, and my leave, was I blind to the endless convoys of wagons at the railheads with their deadly cargo of shells for the bombardment that will precede the attack.

Any experienced soldier would draw the same conclusion from the scale of the preparations. It is giving nothing away to write about it here. By the time these words are discovered, it will all be history. Will the assault succeed? Personally, I do not think so. There is no want of courage or morale among the men. They are trained and disciplined and committed. When the moment comes, they will go into the fight without a hesitant thought, most of them.

This war is a stalemate, a conflict of attrition. Two years of fighting it has taught me that. It will only end when one side or the other loses hope. Only when hope is extinguished in the fighting hearts of men do they capitulate.

The fight in me is extinguished. My loved ones have perished and with them, my hope. I will be dead soon and pray there is an afterlife. If there is not, I will be grateful for oblivion.

In God's truth,

Adam Frederick Gleason

Chapter Eleven

It was eight o'clock in the evening and bedtime when the phone began to ring and Olivia saw her mum through the open door pick up the kitchen extension and answer it. Livs was in the sitting room, watching a Little Princess DVD on their epic new wall-mounted flat-screen television. It was so big, watching it was almost like being at the cinema. Kind Mr Cooper, who did jobs for nice Richard Penmarrick, had fitted it.

Jack was upstairs. She thought that he was probably chatting on Facebook to Megan Penmarrick. Livs had enjoyed their Club adventure of the previous evening and she thought that Megan was kind and friendly as well as very pretty and she could quite understand why Jack was so taken with her. After their barbecue on the island they had gathered in a circle around the fire and sung 'Row, Row, Row Your Boat', and 'The Wheels on the Bus' and a couple of other, more grown-up songs everyone but Livs and Jack had known by heart and Megan's voice when she sang was simply the most beautiful sound Livs had ever heard.

Their mum was on the phone for quite a time. Livs thought this a good thing because it meant she got to watch more of the DVD than she would have otherwise. Their mum was strict about bedtime. Dad was slightly less strict, but still strict-ish. She wondered if it was her daddy on the phone but thought that it couldn't be because he would still be in

America or he would be up in the sky on his return flight. He was not coming home tonight, she knew that. He was going to land in England very late and stay at their house in London which had not yet been rented out. He wasn't coming back until tomorrow.

She missed her daddy. He had only been gone for one night and they had really had fun with the Club, but Livs still missed him. She missed him when she woke up and he wasn't there in the morning. And she feared for him too. The spookmeister was there at their old house in London, lurking in the garden, hiding and watching through the absent eyes in its spade-shaped, sacking face. It was frightening and though it was crafty about hiding itself it was real and fierce and angry-looking when you did spot it. It was there for something. Everything had a purpose. They had been taught that in R.E. at school. She hoped the purpose of the spookmeister was not to hurt her daddy.

Their mum said goodbye to the person she had been speaking to on the phone and came into the sitting room. It would have been very bright in there because of the angle of the sun in the sky outside, but Olivia had closed the curtains so that she could see the television screen better. She thought that their mum looked very pale. She thought she looked so pale that something must be wrong and she thought that Daddy's aeroplane had crashed and thought, It can't have, please, it just can't have crashed.

Their mum picked up the remote and switched the Little Princess DVD off. Then she glanced around and opened the curtains and the room became light with sunshine. 'Please go and fetch your brother, Livs.'

'Has something happened to Daddy?'

'No, of course it hasn't. Please go and fetch your brother.'

In the sunlight through the big windows their mum's face was so pale there were tiny blue veins underneath it visible at her temples that Livs had never seen before. Her lips were pale and her eyes were wide and had no expression in them at all.

She came back down the stairs with Jack. He had been on Facebook and he had been talking to Megan. He was nice and not grumpy when she knocked and entered his new room and gave him the message. She thought this might be because of the look on her own face, still shocked at the horrible thought that something awful had happened to their dad.

They sat on the sofa together and their mum knelt in front of them. She looked at them both for a moment before speaking. Then she said, 'There will not be a trial at court now as a consequence of the attack on you, Jack. You will not have to go through that. The case is closed.'

'You mean they've got away with it.'

'I don't mean that at all. They cannot now get away with it. They are dead.'

Jack frowned. 'How did they die?'

Livs, who felt suddenly cold, thought it best to say nothing. What she wanted to do was to run away and hide or, better still, simply disappear.

'They died in accidents.'

'How?'

Livs thought that she knew. Actually, she did not think there was any doubt.

'They died accidentally,' their mum repeated. 'I am not going to go into the details. You need to know, but that's all you need to know. There will be no trial, but they have not got away with anything. They have lost everything. They have lost their lives.'

'I wanted them to be punished,' Jack said. 'I never wanted them dead.' He stood. 'I was angry at first. Once I realised I was going to get completely better, the anger sort of went. Mostly I wanted them locked up so they couldn't hurt anyone else. I think they had done bad things before and would likely do them again if they weren't locked up. That's all.' He turned and went back to the stairs and his room and Livs assumed the chat he was having on the internet with Megan Penmarrick.

'It's my fault, Mum.'

'Don't be ridiculous.'

'I know how they died.'

'Hush.'

'They burned, didn't they?'

Lillian Greer had been pale already. After her daughter had spoken those words, her facial skin turned translucent; waxy and blue-hued with the blood beating coldly under its surface.

'How can you possibly know that?'

'I made a wish on the island last night, Mum. A fire had been lit by Mr Teal. I smelled the fish grilling over the fire on their skewers as I was making it. I wished harm to come to the nasty boys who had hurt Jack.'

James dozed fitfully after finishing what Adam Gleason had written and then concealed and left for providence. They called it shell shock, didn't they? Or they called it neurasthenia. That was his first thought. Battle trauma had tilted the balance of the valiant infantry captain's mind, made him paranoid and delusional. He would have to show this last testament to the Gleason scholar Michael Carney. It would add greatly to the store of knowledge about the soldier-poet, because as an insight into his state of mind it was nothing less than revelatory.

He had suffered the delusion that his wife and child had been deliberately killed in a pagan ritual. He had returned to the front suicidal as a consequence. He had certainly died only days after committing what he had to paper. He had kept his threat or promise never to write another poem. Had a German bullet killed him? Or had it been one from the handgun he so vividly described being tempted to use on an ancestor of Richard Penmarrick, over cognac in the sitting room on a sunny afternoon at Topper's Reach?

There was more than one problem with this theory. But the most obvious was Gleason's rationality. He had described his routine inspection of the weapon Davies had discharged in the manner of a practical man who remained a punctilious soldier. People did not generally act with such conscientiousness and professionalism when their minds were damaged. Sending the private for an unscheduled tea break and standing in for him while he did so signalled more than compassion and good leadership. It was the act, wasn't it, of an officer who was coldly and completely sane.

James was in the Jaguar, driving on the route from Heathrow to Bermondsey, when his mobile, on the passenger seat next to him, began to ring. He took his eyes off the road and glanced at the display thinking that it was after 11 p.m. and surely too late for Lee Marsden, whom he did not feel like talking to at all. At first he did not recognise the number. Then he realised that the first five digits were the area code for West Cornwall. The unfamiliar number must be his own, their own, the number of the landline at the house into which they had recently moved. He had not yet had time to learn it by heart. Seeing it made him feel more anxious, he felt, than he should have.

The caller did not leave a message. He pulled into the

first lay-by he came to and rang back. Lillian answered immediately.

'How did it go?'

'Badly. It could not have gone worse, I don't think. It was actually a disaster.'

'It doesn't matter. In the scheme of things, it doesn't matter.'

James was silent. If it mattered so little, why had she called?

'Alec McCabe rang me earlier. The boys who attacked Jack died last night, James. They burned to death in their beds.'

'Some sort of gang retribution?'

'Their families are blaming witchcraft. The forensic people could find no reason for the cause or timing of the fires. They burned ferociously but were self-contained.'

'An accelerant must have been used. It's murder, gang crime.'

'Olivia thinks that she is responsible. She was given a wish to make at her Club meet on Monday evening. Something she calls the spookmeister granted her wish, she says. She is quite insistent. There was a carving of this spookmeister on the door of the hut on the island. She says she saw one in the garden of the London house. She says that your brother saw it too and it spooked him.

'After she had gone to bed I asked Jack about the carving. Megan Penmarrick told him that they should not be named. It is bad luck to name them. But they do have a name, she said. They are called Harbingers.'

'How is Olivia now?'

'She is sleeping. Things are happening here I don't like, James. I think we have made a mistake in coming here.'

'You don't believe it, do you, about Olivia's wish?'

'I know my daughter and she is not telling lies. Last night I went to the church, James. I saw an act of desecration there. Then I saw Angela Heart. She took me back to her lovely home and in her pretty garden gave me an explanation for why there is no organised religion practised in the bay and not a word of it rang true.'

'I'll see you tomorrow, darling.'

'You remember what we saw on the beach, James?'

'Of course I do, vividly.'

'It was magic, wasn't it?'

'I don't know what it was.'

'It was magic,' Lillian said. 'And magic exacts a price.'

'Lock the doors and windows tonight.'

'I'm sorry it didn't go well, darling, in Colorado.'

'Remember to lock the doors and windows, Lily, before you turn in.' He ended the call and stored the number in his phone's memory.

He did not feel like staying in the Bermondsey house. He was disappointed by his reception in America. He was slightly jet-lagged from two transatlantic flights in as many days. He had been more affected by what he had read in Adam Gleason's testimony than he had been prepared to admit to himself. He was shaken by what his wife had just told him over the phone.

In some significant ways, James Greer was quite a stubborn man. This stubbornness did not just manifest itself in concerns about the integrity of the computer game he had devised. He was not the man be intimidated by folkloric myth or ghoulish coincidence into booking into a fucking Novotel when he had a perfectly good house in central London where the power was still switched on and where he remembered there still reposed a perfectly comfortable bed.

The trouble was, he thought as he put his key in the lock, that he had seen the thing lurking in the garden with his own eyes. He had rationalised it, of course. But he had seen it. And then his daughter Olivia had seen it. And his brother had seen it and felt disturbed enough by the experience of doing so to warn him about it. Gleason had called it a Harbinger. Megan Penmarrick had called it that too. It was somewhere in function between an emissary and a foot-soldier loyal in the service of the Singers under the Sea.

It was ridiculous, he thought, switching on the sitting room light and dumping his bag on the sofa, aware of the weight of the laptop inside with his game prototype stored there, redundant now, just a broken dream expressed in lines of code encrypted on the hard drive.

They signalled the need for sacrifice. They demanded fresh blood. They could hurt you physically. They could not be killed by the bullet from a Lee Enfield rifle coolly aimed by a vigilant teenage veteran of the conflict on the Western Front. They could grant a child's vindictive, murderous wish.

He poured himself a consolatory whisky and walked through to the study and stared out of the window at foliage stirring on fleshy-leaved shrubs against its rear wall in darkness. It was ridiculous, wasn't it? He took a sip of Scotch. He remembered that Alec McCabe had told Lillian that Robert O'Brien had probably been frightened to death.

He resolved then to do something the following morning. He knew that it might be a total waste of his time and he was anxious to get back to the bay and his family as soon as possible. Even a few weeks earlier, his failure in America might have shaken his marriage. His bond with his wife then had been weak. He had not known how weak. It was much stronger now, though. It was honest and crucial to both of them. He wanted to return to the bay and the wife and children he loved and found he missed even after only a couple of nights away.

First, though, it was necessary to try to find something out. Either attempting to do so would be an exercise in futility, or it would provide the reassurance he hoped it would, or it would confirm suspicions he could not help his mind engendering since his reading of the Gleason testament and his bleak lay-by conversation on his mobile with Lillian of an hour earlier.

He stood there in the darkness and silence of his study and watched carefully through the windows for any sign of furtive movement in the bushes and undergrowth outside.

There were things James was afraid of. He was afraid of professional failure. Less so now than before, he was still afraid that his wife might one day stop loving him. He was afraid of harm coming to one or both of his beloved children. At that moment, he was afraid also of a spade-shaped face with a gaze of empty fury and grey skin as rough as burlap resolving itself over a squatting body in the gloom of the garden he stared into.

He watched and waited for it. He sipped occasionally from his drink of Scotch. Then when his glass was empty and it had not come, he went back and turned off the sitting room light and climbed the stairs wearily to bed.

The rest home to which Lillian's mother had been taken occupied a handsome, sandstone building in Surbiton. Lillian had chosen it because it was near to the area in which her mother had lived for most of her life. She hoped that the familiarity of the streets, on those occasions when her mother was taken out, might stimulate her mind.

It had not worked. Her dementia did not respond to stimulation. What was strange only intimidated and confused her as her mind retreated further and further into what was familiar and comfortable because she recognised it and regarded it with fondness.

Lillian had taken in her mother when the first symptoms had made it impractical and then dangerous for her to live alone any longer. She had been their house guest for a year. Then, when her condition worsened, when she failed to recognise her grandchildren any longer and the incontinence became a daily aspect of her life, the decision was taken to have her cared for somewhere the job could be accomplished by compassionate professionals. They were thankful they could afford it. Lillian thought it the least her mother deserved.

In truth, she did not visit much. It distressed her too greatly. The blank stranger who greeted her with polite bewilderment was not the woman she knew and remembered and loved as her mum. It was weak of her and selfish, she knew, but the visits declined until they were no more frequent than once or twice a month. That was why Cornwall had posed no practical difficulties. The visits could be fitted in when she came up to town to talk to clients or authors or her agent. Living in the bay, despite the distance, she would see her mother no less.

James arrived at the reception desk of the home at 8 a.m. The elderly had a habit of rising early. It was true of those even with dementia, as though they were impatient for the opportunity to experience another confused and fragmented day. He knew most of the staff there by sight and three or four well enough to enjoy a conversation with. The girl behind the desk was called Magdalena and she was originally from Gdansk. She spoke flawless English and she possessed alert blue eyes and she seemed able to remember the name of everyone she had ever met.

She smiled. 'Mr Greer.'

'James, please, Magdalena.'

'James, then, charmed, I'm sure.'

It was their little ritual of spoken greeting. Magdalena told him that his mother-in-law was taking tea in the music room. He would find her alone there. Most of the other residents were still at breakfast. She did not need to show him where to go. He knew the location of the music room. She did not ask him what the bag he carried with him contained.

April Matlock sat by the window, looking out of it, seeing, James supposed, whatever tableau from the past was unfurling through the remnants of her mind. Her hands were clasped in her lap. There was a slight tremor to them, or to one of them, which the other could not successfully still. Her long grey hair had been brushed and pinned and the trouser suit she wore was clean and recently pressed. The only wrinkles were the ones on her neck and cheeks, under the bright and vacant gaze her eyes wore, reflecting the sunshine through the glass.

He pulled over a straight-backed chair and sat in it next to her, leaning forward with his hands on his knees to bring their heads to the same height. He was not so tactless as literally to look down on her. He did not think that she would remember or recognise him. She had not done so for more than eighteen months. He wanted her to think of them as equals, though, if she was capable of coherent thought at all.

Without a glance at him she said, 'I expect you have come about the drains. They have needed attention for weeks, you know. The lavatory has backed up most unpleasantly and the kitchen sink smells of sewage. It is neither hygienic nor acceptable.'

'I have not come about the drains, April,' he said.

Now she did look at him. She said, 'My Lily is very gifted at drawing, you know. She has a quite astonishing gift for a six-year-old. Mr Davenport at the school says that she is most precocious. He does not mean cheeky, when he calls her that. He means that she possesses a talent mature beyond her years.'

'I'm sure she does. I am quite certain of it.'

'Who are you?'

'My name is James.'

'A good English name, James. What is your surname?'

'Greer.'

She frowned. 'Are you doing a survey, Mr Greer? Will there be a questionnaire to complete?'

James bent down to where he had put his bag, between his feet. He took from it the book about Brodmaw Bay published by Chubbly & Cruff and illustrated by his wife, whose memory of having done so was as blank as the woman's in front of him seemed on everything that had happened since her life as a young mother. He placed the book gently in her lap. She looked down at its cover and then began to turn the pages. Her eyes were no longer on the view through the window. But the expression on her face had not changed at all.

April Matlock turned the pages. When she came to the spread on which her daughter had depicted the church, she stopped. She placed the flat of a hand on the image with her fingers splayed and expelled a sound that James thought might have been a sigh.

'We had never thought about adoption,' she said. 'But by then we knew that I could not carry a child of my own to full term. I think my husband craved fatherhood. In fact, I know he did. He was friendly with Father Reid, who ran the refuge. The girl was only fourteen. She could not have looked after the child. She had fled Brodmaw to escape the scandal and had no means of supporting herself. She was too young for work, never mind motherhood.'

'Do you remember the girl's name, April?'

'Of course I do. She was a beautiful child. I was quite jealous of two attributes she possessed. She had the loveliest eyes. I was jealous of her fecundity, of course. And I quite envied Angela Heart those striking green eyes.'

'And the father?'

'Penmarrick. She said he was important. He was sort of the squire, but more important than that. More like the lord of the manor, my husband said.'

'Why did you not tell Lillian she was adopted?'

'She never was, legally. Angela gave us her baby. It had to be a secret.'

'Did Lillian ever visit the bay?'

'Once, when she was five, we took her. We thought that she should see where she came from. It was a pretty place, very picturesque. She drank it all in, as a child will. There was an excursion to an island. The local Scouts had organised a jamboree. The bay possessed its own old-fashioned charm. I expect it is all quite spoiled now.'

'Yes,' James said, 'yes, April. You are quite right. It is completely spoiled.' He eased the book off her lap and put it back into his bag and rose to go.

She raised her head to him and blinked once and said, 'If you could fix the drains, we'd be ever so grateful.'

Chapter Twelve

Richard Penmarrick was charm itself when he called Topper's Reach about ten minutes after Lillian had concluded her conversation with her husband on his instruction to lock their windows and doors. He explained that the following day was an inset day at the Mount. He apologised for the short notice, but asked if Lillian would consider helping escort the members of the Club to their island for a day's activity and adventure.

Lillian assented for two reasons. The first was that Richard had done so much for them that she did not think she could in all conscience refuse. The second reason was the simple human impulse of curiosity. She wanted to see the carving of the spoookmeister on the hut door for herself. She wanted to see the Harbinger it was considered unlucky to name and that apparently granted vindictive wishes. Olivia's wish had been a ghastly coincidence. But she still wanted to see the thing that her daughter claimed to have seen in life in their old garden.

She did not for a moment consider they would come to any harm. There were some pretty strange people living in the bay. She had had that fact demonstrated to her by the desecration in the church. The community was more insular than she had first supposed and the paganism of the shell-fish ritual on the beach was stranger and more shocking, paradoxically, the more she thought about it. She did not think, however, that they would have been so warmly received if anyone thought ill about them. Their reception had been, in some ways, little short of rapturous.

There were mysteries in the village she wanted solving. She did not think Angela Heart had told her the whole truth about the Reverend Baxter. But Baxter's ordeal had taken place in the aftermath of the Great War and uncovering what had really happened almost a century ago, whatever it was, was hardly an urgent priority.

The shock of her daughter's confession wore off somewhat as she listened to Richard on the phone, outlining the Baden-Powell-ish nature of the following day's programme. In his tone and language, he managed to be enthusiastic and ironic about it all at the same time. He was gently sending up both himself and the tent-peg and bugle, jamboree nature of what they had planned for the kids.

'We're expecting a swell, so we'll probably go over in a small flotilla of sturdy boats. We need some cargo space, you see, for the instruments the band will play if the weather is fine at the picnic in the afternoon. And we will have to ship the raffle prizes too.'

You can butter crumpets from now until kingdom come. Rupert Brooke isn't coming to tea.

She thought that the island trip, with its mundane and cheery timetable, would help Olivia put her wish concerning Jack's attackers into a perspective where it could only be an unfortunate coincidence. The next time she confronted that carving on the hut door, it would be with the comfort of her mother's arm around her shoulder and it would seem like exactly what it was: a good luck symbol, no more than a rather crudely executed image of a figure from local mythology.

Lillian had found the bay a bit claustrophobic since James's departure. She was aware of it as she locked the doors and windows. Topper's Reach was a spacious house, it had large rooms with high ceilings and in the daytime it was gloriously bright. But it was still hemming them in. The absence of the car was probably, she thought, the main cause of this feeling of being slightly trapped.

Angela's arrival at the church had made the feeling worse because it had almost suggested she was under some kind of surveillance. The boundless expanse of the sea, the exposure of the island itself, would be an antidote to how she felt and pass the day pleasantly and when they returned here, her husband would have arrived back.

She did not really care that the trip to America had gone badly. She was confident that James, this new and tougher and more resilient James, would have given a good account of himself. He was no longer the type of man to go to pieces in front of an audience under the pressure of delivering a presentation.

She cared, for him, because she wanted him to succeed on his own terms and the game was something on which he had spent a lot of time and creative energy and in which he had invested a significant amount of hope. She thought that he would be disappointed. His tone and language in their brief phone conversation had suggested that. But she knew that career disappointment was no threat now to their relationship. They were locked on. They had never been closer. They had survived the ordeal of her adultery and emerged as though tempered by fire.

She suspected that the Americans had suggested some sort of compromise that James felt threatened the integrity of what he had created. Projects like that were collaborative and the finished article seldom very much resembled its original concept. James had been open to compromise once. It had been a feature of his character. Jack's accident had changed him in that regard.

It could have been argued that he had compromised his principles on the matter of her betrayal, but he hadn't, really. His defining imperative in that matter had been his love for her.

Lillian thought that in the long term, James would be better off if she was right and he had refused to capitulate to the demands of the Colorado software outfit. His strength, the new strength and confidence he possessed, enabled a measure of self-respect in him that had not been there before. He was a better man for it. He was not just better, he was much happier too.

James climbed into the Jaguar in the rest home car park, tossing the bag with the book inside it over onto the rear seat. He sat and glanced at the clock on the dashboard. It was still only eight forty in the morning. He took out his mobile and called Topper's Reach. There was no reply. He called Lillian's mobile, but there was no signal.

He wondered where they could be. The children did not have to be up for school. Neither of them would be enrolled at their new schools before the start of the new academic year in September. Jack was not habitually an early riser if he wasn't getting up for school or for a football training session. He was like every thirteen-year-old: pretty much comatose until he was physically roused. They must have gone out. But without the car, where would they go so early in the day?

There was a phrase in his head. He could not get it out of

his mind. It was the words Richard Penmarrick had used in greeting Lillian on her arrival in the bay. They had come down from their room with the glow of their recent love-making still on them to the saloon bar of the Leeward where he had been standing, waiting for them. 'Welcome home,' he had said.

James called Alec McCabe. 'Can we talk?'

'Only if it's life and death, I'm not on duty until noon.'

'It's life and death.'

'I was joking, James. I recognised the number. If I wasn't prepared to talk to you, I wouldn't have accepted the call. I assume you're joking too, by the way.'

'No. I don't think I am, Alec.'

'I told your wife as much as we know last night. The circumstances are pretty gruesome and, so far, totally inexplicable. We've got some very experienced people. None of them has ever seen anything like it.'

'I'm not calling you about that. I'm calling you about Robert O'Brien.'

'Not my case.'

'I remember you said a mate of yours was the investigating officer. Totally off the record. Just between us, as a favour, Alec. It really could be life and death.'

'I like you, James. You are an honest man, no bullshit, and in a world mired in bullshit, I respect that. And that lad of yours is an absolute gem. If you are in some sort of trouble, tell me. Tell me truthfully and I promise I will do everything I can to help you.'

'You said that Robert O'Brien was scared to death. I want to know what it was that scared him.'

'Cocaine killed Robert O'Brien,' McCabe said. 'You'll be reading as much over your breakfast cornflakes, if you're one of those quaint people who still buys a newspaper. You probably do, since you now live in so quaint a place. He only took a gram, but it wasn't street stuff. It was top Bolivian product, 98 per cent pure and it caused a valve in his heart to rupture.'

'The scene of crime people thought he might have died of fright. Could anything have scared him?'

There was a pause. James could hear his own heart hammer in his chest. Then the detective sergeant said, 'This is privileged information because there is some ethical concern over whether the source should ever have revealed it. I will therefore not name the source. But O'Brien saw a psychiatrist in the afternoon on the day of his death. He told her that he had been plagued by an apparition. He thought he was being haunted, James.'

'Did he describe this apparition?'

There was another long silence. Then McCabe said, 'The reason the shrink breached patient confidentiality by telling us about it is that after O'Brien's departure, she thought she herself saw someone who strongly resembled the person he had described, looking up at her from the street.'

'It was a little girl, wasn't it?'

'She was dressed in the grey pinafore and purple of what appears to have been a school uniform of the more traditional sort. She was blonde and pigtailed and wore a straw hat. Best guess as to age is around eight. Don't tell me you've seen her too.'

'I can do better than that. I can tell you her name, Alec,' James said. His mouth felt dry. 'She died more than ninety years ago and I do not think that she died willingly or well. In life, she was called Madeleine Gleason.'

He started the engine, put the car into gear. If he put his foot down, if the Wednesday traffic cooperated, he could be in the bay by one. It would not seem a sinister place on a sunny, early July afternoon, would it? It would look charming and picturesque and in the detective sergeant's slightly contemptuous word, the bay would look quaint.

Lillian had been lured back exactly as Adam Gleason had been. Both had returned with the fresh blood of their respective families. Gleason had followed the lure of a job after diphtheria had killed his son and poisoned his mind against London, a city he subsequently saw as tainted and sought to escape.

London was not afflicted with diphtheria in the early twenty-first century. It did, though, have plenty of other potentially fatal hazards. The white-flight impulse James had first felt in the hospital had been triggered by the attack on his son. The mentally unstable ringleader of the gang that had carried it out had been responding, he said, to instructions he heard in his head. He had been ordered to carry out the attack on Jack. There had been nothing random or even really feral about it. The voice in his head had commanded and he and his acolytes had obeyed, too terrified to consider doing otherwise.

How far back did all of this go? How much careful magic had been employed to impel them west to the place his wife had been conceived in a tryst between Richard Penmarrick and an underage Angela Heart? The book he had found about Brodmaw Bay on a hospital shelf had been deliberately planted there. The seed had been deliberately sown. And after that it had all been made very easy for them, hadn't it? They had been welcomed as incomers surely never were in the far reaches of a county notorious for its insularity. Except that Lillian had not been an incomer. Not really, she hadn't. Lily had been coming home.

* * *

They embarked from the small harbour sheltered by the breakwater to the right of the Leeward Tavern. The water was quite calm there, the anchored boats rolling gently on a modest swell. Beyond the harbour the sea looked much rougher than Lillian had so far seen at the bay. There was a keen offshore breeze that felt chilly for July. The air was damp. The morning sky was grey and the sea dull and greenish and vast under flecks of white foam on its turbulent surface.

Richard approached and put an arm around her and gave her shoulder a comforting squeeze. He was wearing jeans tucked into canvas boots and a blue wool sweater. A red and white bandana was knotted around his neck and he had on a seaman's blue cap. He smelled of Eau Sauvage aftershave and looked strong and handsome and capable. 'It'll clear up,' he said, blinking at the sky. 'Don't worry, Lillian.' He grinned and winked. 'This is just the storm before the calm.'

She thought his witty wordplay amusing enough but was not really comforted by his prediction concerning the weather. The quayside was busy with children and supervising adults going up and down the gangplank of a large, turbine-driven craft, loading the day's provisions and the band's instruments and various items of equipment to be used for outdoor games. They were not attired in wetsuits for the voyage aboard this larger vessel. They were wearing dun-coloured attire, like Scouts. Hers were the only children dressed as civilians.

When in Rome, she thought. But Rome was sited on seven hills on dry land under a southern Italian sun. So the saying did not really apply. She had a sort of presentiment, imprecise but uneasy, about the day to come. She thought it must have been provoked by the sea and the stiff wind scouring off it and the pervading greyness of the light. The conditions were raw and slightly gloomy. She was aware for the first time since moving there of the elemental force of the sea, of its capricious moods and potential for violence. They were intent on recreation but the sea was a place of peril, to those upon it, much of the time.

She thought of the fate of the boat built for Thomas Cable and blessed by the Reverend Baxter. She had been called the *Carol-Anne*. She had foundered in the fog and lost all hands in these waters. They had been expert mariners but had died helplessly, catching the sea in a vindictive mood.

Lillian sighed. She knew that she had to shake this despondent perspective she really did not have sufficient justification for. She looked at Olivia bouncing back down the gangplank intent on another load and all she saw was excitement and anticipation in the sparkle of her eyes. The day was a treat, not an ordeal or some looming tragedy. It had been devised purely for enjoyment. There was no sinister subtext for her to be concerned about.

As the children laboured and jostled, as the adults ordered and joked, she could not help remembering what she had said on the phone to James the previous night, prior to the reassurance of Richard's buoyant call. She had described the event they had witnessed that evening on the east shore as magic. She had said to her husband that magic exacts a price. The trouble was that she really was well on the way to believing that and, in a way becoming less vague all the time, growing in the conviction that they had made a terrible mistake.

Megan stood in front of her. She had on a flat-brimmed hat with a chinstrap like the one Baden-Powell habitually wore in archive photographs. There was a kerchief secured with a leather toggle around her neck. She smiled and saluted and Lillian wondered suddenly what the future held for this girl with her luminous beauty and promising gift.

'Time to get aboard, Mrs Greer.'

'I'm Lillian to you, young lady.'

'I know. And I can't quite believe you're here.' Megan smiled and her cheeks flushed and Lillian remembered that she was still in the throes of hero-worship. She picked up her bag off the quayside next to her and followed her worshipper up the gangplank on to the boat.

She was reassured when she got aboard. The smell of diesel fuel and the deep chug of the engines were mundane and secure realities and the deck felt immensely solid, riveted steel vibrating with the power of the turbines beneath it under her feet. She looked out over the bow for a pilot boat, but there wasn't one. Then she looked back along the length of the vessel and saw that Billy Jasper was at the wheel. He could probably get them safely beyond the hazards of the harbour wearing a blindfold.

Richard was suddenly next to her. 'We're brewing coffee below,' he said.

'I don't deserve it,' she said. 'I was daydreaming just now while everyone toiled to load up.'

'You were daydreaming very decoratively,' he said. 'Sometimes it's enough on a grey morning just to stand there looking beautiful.'

Was he flirting with her? She didn't think he was, really. It was just a gracious compliment, coming from a naturally gracious man. If anyone could charm her out of her mood of pessimism and uneasiness, it was him.

'I'd love a cup of coffee,' she said. She followed him down the companionway.

Below decks, the boat seethed with youthful chatter and

activity. Lillian had not supposed, before they set off, that there would be the leisure time for coffee in their crossing. Her children, novices both, had paddled to the island in kayaks. She had imagined it would be no distance at all in a vessel like this. It wasn't as if a detour was necessary, was it? Didn't ships sail as the crow flew?

She mentioned this to Richard. He smiled and said, 'Reefs, Lillian, sandbanks too. A kayak has a draught of about four inches. Our keel runs rather lower in the water than that.'

He said it in a diplomatic tone, but it made her realise just what an idiot she was concerning matters nautical. She was a seafaring ignoramus. She was quite literally out of her depth. She nodded and smiled what she hoped was a warm smile and climbed back up to the deck. She had felt queasy and bilious in the humid confinement of the ship's bowels. She was a practical woman who tended towards a degree of forward planning and should she need to puke, she thought she was better off within heaving range of the gunwale.

Waves slapped and shuddered off the hull. Spray broke on to the deck in salty droplets and mist. She thought that, if anything, the weather was getting rougher. The swell looked high to her and the wind out in the exposure of the open sea had risen from brisk to strong. The cloud was just a gunmetal shroud stretching to an uncertain horizon. It was too heavy for her to be able to guess at the position of the sun it concealed.

Her coffee rose in her throat and she emptied her mouth over the side. She stayed like that, bowed and feeling a bit defeated, while her breakfast followed, welling sourly out of her. Her nose stung with the sharp trickle of vomit and she wiped flecks of something sticky off her chin. Down below, the children were singing. They had begun 'Ten Green

Bottles'. It was a long and monotonous vocal trek, that one. Lillian wondered blackly, with a nauseous churn of her stomach, if she would live to hear the end of it. Then she felt warmth on her back and turned and saw that the sun had broken through.

It beamed through a patch in the cloud and the sea glittered and danced in a bright blue dazzle under it. There were several ragged spots of blue, she saw, in the sky. The clouds were thinning, moving slowly because the wind had all at once almost died down completely. The surface of the water was calming, azure in broad brushstrokes now competing with the green.

'You were right,' she said to Richard, who was approaching her along the deck. In his fist, he held a packet of wet wipes. He plucked a couple free and handed them to her. The wood fittings of the boat were warming. She could smell beeswax and tar and metal polish and hemp. From through the hatch, they were down to seven green bottles.

'I'm usually right about some things. It's a question of experience.'

'But not everything.'

'Not everything, no.'

'How old are you, Richard? Do you mind me asking?'

He grinned. 'I don't mind you asking. And the colour is returning to your quite lovely face. But I think if I answered that question truthfully, you might faint dead away.'

She laughed. She balled up the used wet wipe and went to find a bin for it. She felt much better with the hull shifting less underneath her, warmed by the sun and with her stomach empty of food. She would get a drink of water. She was thirsty and needed to get the sour taste out of her mouth. Vomit was acidic and corroded the tooth enamel. She could not remember having been sick since the early part of being pregnant with her daughter. She was healthy and her constitution was, thankfully, strong.

The island had come into view. In this light, seen from the deck of a boat, it really did look as Jack said it did, like somewhere out of a Famous Five adventure. It was sandy and then verdant where it rose beyond its shoreline and then craggy at its quite high summit. Seabirds wheeled in the sky above it.

It was a beautiful little place, the perfect spot for a childhood adventure. The kids below must have sighted it through the starboard portholes. She heard a huge cheer from down there and the clatter of excited feet up the companionway. Then they were all on the deck, cheering and whooping.

She saw Jack put his fingers in his mouth and gather a big breath to let out a celebratory whistle and she saw Megan Penmarrick give him a sharp look and he froze. He took his hand from his face. Lillian remembered that of course it was considered unlucky to whistle aboard a boat. Megan's expression towards her landlubber son had been quite severe. It occurred to her for the first time that there might be a bit more than sweetness and light to this particular girl.

Getting everyone and everything ashore took a while. They dropped anchor and then lowered two rowing boats from davits fixed to either side of the vessel. They lowered a rigid inflatable from the stern, Billy Jasper shouting precise commands all the kids seemed schooled to obey. Phil Teal was in nominal charge of the Club, she remembered, but obviously his area of expertise was dry land and he deferred to others on the water.

The sense of community shared among the people of the bay was so strong it seemed almost tribal to Lillian. When an urban school had an inset day the kids attending it would mostly mooch about the local shopping centre or drag themselves off to the skate park on their skateboards or astride their BMX bikes. The boat they had come here aboard was probably thirty years old. But she was a large and therefore fuel-thirsty vessel and she required a crew and considerable maintenance. Did she have a day job? How did she finance herself?

Phil Teal had the day off because he was the Mount's headmaster. Richard Penmarrick seemed a good fit for the old-fashioned gentleman of leisure role. He possessed independent wealth, James had told her. But Billy Jasper had a boatyard to run and Martin Sharp a chandlery and Ben Tamworth a building firm. Nevertheless, they were all present for the jamboree. She wondered how the economics of the bay quite added up. Did Penmarrick simply subsidise things with a bottomless coffer of regal largesse?

The butcher, the baker and the candlestick maker. That sensation of gloomy presentiment dispelled by the sunshine came upon her again despite it. There were things about the bay, mysteries and contradictions and anachronisms, weren't there? And all this should have occurred to her much sooner than it was doing, shouldn't it?

It was her turn to disembark. She climbed down a metal ladder hung over the gunwale to where the rigid inflatable waited with its outboard idling to take her ashore. Martin Sharp's son Ricky, who had inherited his father's stocky physique, was sitting at the tiller. He grinned at her from under his flat-brimmed hat. His neck was so thick that there wasn't much of the kerchief wrapping it left to toggle beneath his throat. Jack had spoken highly of this boy, calling him modest and approachable. But Lillian did not really care for the way in which his eyes roamed across her body before his expression glazed into a smirk.

On the shore they were unpacking griddles and piling food and unlatching cases to check on the instruments inside. A bugle was experimentally blown and there was the rat-tat of a drum tattooed with sticks. All the children seemed excited. Lillian wanted to go and look at the carving on the hut door but did not want to be obvious about it. She did not really know the reason for her caution over this. She put it down to instinct, which she generally trusted.

She felt that she was being observed. It was done in a fairly sly and subtle way, but she was self-conscious, which she wasn't usually, and she thought that the feeling was a consequence of being under scrutiny. It was not just Richard and Martin Sharp and Billy Jasper, now that he was no longer engaged with steering a large seagoing vessel. It was Ricky Sharp and Megan Penmarrick too. She did not think it was her imagination. She was imaginative, but the fanciful part of her nature restricted itself to her refined visual sense.

Olivia approached her. She looked subdued. She trailed a stick in the sand, leaving a damp line wavering behind her. In a whisper, she said, 'It isn't there, Mum.'

'What isn't there?'

'The spookmeister, the Harbinger thing. It's no longer on the door, it's disappeared.'

'That's strange,' Lillian said. 'I wonder where it has disappeared to, Livs.'

'I don't think it's strange at all,' Olivia said. 'It's gone because it's done its job, Mum.' She sounded very forlorn. 'It's gone because it granted my wish and did away with those boys.'

* * *

James was on the A30, the traffic light, Dartmoor a brownish, barren wilderness to his left, having just passed the Meldon Viaduct. The needle was hovering between seventy and eighty on his speedometer and Stevie Nicks was hectoring her way through 'Sarah' on the radio, the Fleetwood Mac song putting him in mind of Charlie Abraham and the warmth, improbable in retrospect, of his initial greeting on his first visit to the bay. Pub landlords were a suspicious breed. Their experiences did not encourage them to take anyone at face value.

If the Leeward publican had been any more welcoming, he could only practically have done so by going down on one knee and presenting him with a bouquet. And yet he had seen nothing suspicious in it. It was vanity, James thought. Vanity deluded people into believing they deserved to be liked. He had been as prey to it as anyone.

If anything that thought made him accelerate slightly in the moment just before the front nearside tyre blew and the car slewed left in a screech of ribboning rubber and rim steel and he braked and then thudded from tarmac on to earth and through the tearing wire and plucked wooden posts of a fence and into the ditch beyond. There, a hundred and twenty metres from where he had punctured, the car abruptly jiggered to a halt.

James revived knowing two things. The first was that the impact had knocked him unconscious. The second was that he'd been a victim of deliberate sabotage. He knew this because his air bag had not deployed. That was why his head had hit the door pillar unimpeded with the impact of the crash. He felt his right temple and it was sticky with blood.

He had not been out long. The blood had not yet congealed. He looked at his watch and it told him, after a short struggle to bring the dial into focus, that the time was just after midday. Then he heard the wail of a siren and saw a police car approaching on the road behind through the few reflecting fragments that were left of his smashed right wing mirror.

He unlocked his seatbelt and struggled out of the car. He felt slightly numb and confused and wanted to see whether a change of wheel would be enough to get him back on the road and his journey. He staggered when he got to his feet and steadied himself with a hand on the car roof. Then he threw up. That was normal, he thought. People with concussion did tend to vomit sometimes and he knew he was lightly concussed. He wasn't seeing double, but everything he looked at had a bit of ghosting, like a faulty television picture, when he tried to clarify it. He felt nauseous and he had a thumping headache.

Two police officers, a male sergeant and a woman constable, left their patrol car on the hard shoulder and approached him on foot. He felt grateful that they had turned off their siren. But the light bar was still flashing on the roof of the car and in the overcast light was almost painfully bright.

One of the officers, the woman, sat him down on the Jag's back seat while her colleague walked around the car to see what had caused him to crash.

'Strange your air bag didn't deploy,' the constable said, when they had checked his licence and breathalysed him. She was slender inside her stab-proof vest and blonde and barely looked old enough to vote. 'Have you owned the vehicle from new?'

'Yes.'

'You could probably sue.'

He did not think he could. He would not share his sabotage theory. It would only cloud the issue and consume more time than he felt he had. It was only half past twelve but he had lost his only means of transportation and he wanted to get to his destination as soon as he could. 'Are you local to this area?'

'We're based in Okehampton,' the sergeant said. He was dark-haired and looked slightly older than the constable, but not much.

'Could you give me a lift there? Is there a car hire place?'

'You're going to the hospital in Okehampton, sir. You need a medical examination. At best, you have suffered a mild concussion. At worst, you could have sustained a skull fracture. With respect, you're not driving anywhere.'

James nodded. The important thing was to act rationally and remain calm. He had plenty of time before darkness fell. He had the best part of eight hours. He thought that it was very important to get to the bay before dark and was sure that someone had done something to his car to prevent him from succeeding in that, but panic would be counter-productive. He said, 'How long before the ambulance arrives?'

The constable answered him. She said, 'It should be here within half an hour. We'd take you there ourselves, but we're instructed not to risk conveying accident victims who have suffered a head injury. Do you have breakdown cover, sir?'

James nodded. He could do that. He could call the AA and arrange for a recovery vehicle for the Jag. Or he could pretend to do it and come back for the car himself once he got away from the ambulance crew. There was a spare wheel in the boot and the only damage seemed to be to the wheel and the front bumper and one side mirror. And to him, of course; there was some slight damage to him. He could get a minicab to bring him back. Failing that, he could steal a bicycle.

A paramedic strapped him to a stretcher in the ambulance

and then carried out a preliminary examination of his head wound. James pondered, for the first time really, on his daughter having found the last testament of the poet-soldier Adam Gleason at Topper's Reach. The young policewoman, who wore her hair in plaits, had reminded him of Gleason's daughter, O'Brien's ghost, Madeleine.

She was his ghost too, though he had seen her only once, at the standing stones, and then but fleetingly. Her appearance had been a warning, hadn't it? He had not known to heed it. He had not seriously considered the anomaly of the uniform she had worn, even when the Penmarricks had told him it was the livery of a school that had closed fifty years ago. He should have thought that ominous but had chosen to ignore it.

She was Olivia's ghost possibly more than she was anyone's, he thought. She must have told Livs where to find what her father had written. It meant that she was on their side. She was their ally but she had returned with the black and white perception of an eight-year-old child, ruthless and without compunction. She had scared O'Brien to death.

That part of it he did not understand. He could not see why the ghost of a murdered eight-year-old would seek the death of a man born sixty years after the crime that ended her own life. O'Brien had been guilty of something, but it had not been an offence that had impinged upon Madeleine in the slightest. Adultery was a very grown-up sin. O'Brien's philandering had not affected her at all. If she had deliberately frightened the writer to death, her reason for doing so remained a mystery.

He spent two frustrating hours in the A&E department at Okehampton General waiting for his skull to be X-rayed. He did not feel that he could do what he was tempted to do and simply flee the hospital before his examination. If he did that, the local constabulary would be informed and his intentions guessed and he would return to a slightly damaged Jaguar sitting in a field with a police guard and going absolutely nowhere any time soon.

The wait was anxious as well as frustrating. Despite the throb of pain from the blow to his head, he did not feel that badly knocked about. But there was always the possibility of a hairline fracture. The temple was a vulnerable spot. If he had sustained a fracture they would detain and admit him and he would not reach the bay for several days and by then he felt sure it would be too late.

A gloomy certainty had settled in James Greer. It sat like something dark and heavy and unwelcome in his heart and soul. It occupied him completely and it was the conviction that if he did not get back that day, he would not see his family in this lifetime again.

Their deaths would be accidental. They would be mundane and barely worthy of attention. It would be a cautionary tale of sorts; a warning that inexperienced people should not go out in boats in unpredictable weather without someone knowledgeable to accompany them. It would be a small tragedy of the domestic sort. It might make a story in the middle-brow tabloids on the strength of Lillian's professional profile and glamour in the accompanying publicity shot. What it would not do was raise any suspicions that it was anything other than a slightly pathetic mishap.

The irony was not lost on him that he was sitting in a hospital and his concern was once again a head injury. You could crudely regard what the Greer family had done, he supposed, as white flight. It had been a bit more complex and contingent than that though, hadn't it? They had required a fresh start really after his wife's adulterous affair. They had needed to do something pretty drastic about their son's disillusionment with school. When they had seen the bay, it had seemed far less like flight of any hue than fate.

There was an old saying, that the road to hell was paved with good intentions. James thought that their intentions as a couple and as parents had basically been good. Their relocation to the bay had been less about escape than transformation, though he was prepared to admit to himself that a fair bit of wishful thinking had probably played a part in their decision to move. He remembered what McCabe had said about Rupert Brooke not coming to tea no matter how many crumpets he buttered. He had thought the detective was being a killjoy at the time in pointing it out. The expression on Lillian's face had told him that his wife had, too.

He thought glass embedded in the tyre the probable cause of his own automotive mishap of a couple of hours earlier. A small, sharp fragment of glass, slyly pressed into the tread, would gradually pierce even the highest grade of rubber compound and cause a blow out.

Disabling the air bags was a bit more grown-up than provoking a puncture. But both acts had been deliberate and malicious and intended to incapacitate him. Everyone in the bay had known he was soon to undertake some serious road mileage at the wheel of the Jaguar. His trip to the States, via Heathrow, had been one of the dominant subjects discussed on Sunday evening at the party held to welcome them in the Leeward Tavern.

It could easily have been a fragment of Leeward glass. There was no shortage of the stuff in the vicinity of Charlie Abraham's bar. The landlord probably swept broken glass with a brush and pan from the pub floor every day of his working life. He did not think, though, that Charlie had been responsible. When he pictured someone in his mind, tinkering with his car, it was not a man but a woman doing it. And she wore the beguiling face of Angela Heart.

When the doctor came and told him his X-rays were clear and that he was free to resume his life, James quickly walked to the bank of payphones he had seen earlier in the entrance lobby. He would make the call on his mobile. But where there were payphones there were usually cards left by minicab firms touting for trade. He was relieved at what the doctor told him. But so dark were his premonitions of death by then that he could not raise a smile at the news.

There was a game of hide and seek being played in woods on one side of the island by the younger children. It was restricted to years seven and eight among the Mount pupils, the eleven- and twelve-year-olds, but Olivia was allowed to play because it seemed a bit mean to leave her out. The other children were very friendly to her despite the age difference. Hiding was harder for her, though. Their dun-coloured outfits meant that they could blend into the trees really easily. She had on blue jeans and a bright red sweater and as far as she was concerned, she stuck out like a flag waving on a flagpole.

Megan Penmarrick did not play. She qualified age-wise. But some of the kids had been chosen to collect driftwood for a large bonfire they were going to build. Olivia had tried to discover the reason for the bonfire, but everyone, Megan included, was a bit vague as to its exact purpose. She ended up thinking that it might not actually have one. Big fires were exciting and spectacular. Grown-ups thought so too. You didn't really need an excuse to build one, just permission.

Mr Teal was the permission-giver on the island and therefore could do whatever he liked.

The wood was quite dense. It was a mixture of trees and ferns and vicious-looking thorn bushes that it would be best to avoid. It was cool and surprisingly dark after the brilliance of the sunshine, when you took a few steps into it. The ground was sandy and there were pine cones everywhere on the sand under the trees. It was very quiet. You could strain and hear the waves breaking on the shore a few hundred feet away because the breeze carried the sound. But apart from that, the wood was silent.

It came to be Olivia's go to hide. She felt a bit nervous about taking her turn. Some of the other kids had managed, in their blending-in clothes and by staying perfectly still, to hide for a surprisingly long time. One of the Tamworth twins, the boy, had managed not to be found at all. They had given up and called him eventually and he had swung down from the branches of a high tree looking very pleased with himself, if a bit scratched around the face and neck and arms and legs.

She had their count of one hundred in which to conceal herself. She could hide behind a tree, but that was pathetic and they would find her straight away. She could climb a tree, but that had been done. They'd be looking out for that and anyway, it seemed too painful to be worthwhile. Hide and seek was only a game. The same argument applied to hiding in the thorn bushes. She might get in, but the thorns were great vicious curved things and she was not confident she would ever get out again.

She looked around. They would be down to about thirty in their count. They would be upon her and she was too panicked to move. There was a ridge, she remembered, she thought it lay to her rear. She turned and saw the ridge and saw that a pale figure with a straw hat in a pinafore stood atop it. She looked frail and so wispy she was almost see-through. She curled a finger just the same and as Olivia always did when Madeleine summoned her, she climbed obediently to where her oldest friend stood.

Madeleine looked more frayed than ever. She had become truly scary, now. She was a genuine fright. Olivia was brave. She knew that. She was less afraid of the dark than her wuss of a big brother, Jack. But Madeleine was in decline and the decline was not a comforting sight. Her oldest friend was looking her age. 'Can you hide me?'

'They will find you, Livs. They are going to take you.'

This sounded ominous to Olivia. It was not just the words themselves. Madeleine's voice was the low shriek of the wind over something vast. It was a sound you might hear on the sea at night, she thought. It was a lonely and gloomy sound and not remotely human. It was the creak of rigging, the distant moan of a whale. Her imaginary friend's face was cracked like old brick mortar and her eyes could no longer keep up the pretence of being alive at all.

Madeleine turned and walked and Olivia followed her. Beyond the ridge there was a sort of dip or hollow. The hollow was filled with gorse and thorn bushes and ferns all jumbled densely together. Madeleine, the frail and disturbing thing that had once been Madeleine, wound a path through all this undergrowth. She stopped when she reached a thick tree trunk lying on its side. The tree had shallow roots that looked to Olivia like a great circle of writhing snakes. They formed this shape because the trunk itself was hollow.

'We'll be safe here, for a while at least,' Madeleine said. She bent and walked into the tunnel of the hollow tree trunk, a dank den of bark and decayed wood with toadstools growing palely in the thin loam on its floor.

It was a chilly little refuge, Olivia thought, kneeling rather than sitting down inside. It was quite dark, which was a blessing, given how dead Madeleine looked in daylight with her straw plaits and clothes now mouldering into rags.

'Is it lonely, being a ghost?'

'I'm a poor sort of ghost, Livs. It would be different had I been buried on land. I'd have more substance and wouldn't be fading like this. The memory of life is far stronger on the land. But the sea claimed me. It is a struggle. I cannot do it for much longer. And in what little time I have left, I will be confined.'

'Confined?'

'To the bay, Livs. I cannot roam beyond the bay. I am now confined to a few favourite places from my life.'

'Was this a favourite place?'

'It was. I played hide and seek here just as you are doing. My life was very happy right up until my death. I missed my daddy, away a lot at the fighting at the front in the war. But I loved my mummy very much and we were happy when we moved here.'

'You were not born in the bay?'

The thing that had been Madeleine Gleason laughed. It was an awful sound, to Olivia. It was an emptying drain of a sound. She had not known that a ghost could perish, but she thought she had just heard the laughter of someone undergoing a sort of second death.

'We were fresh blood,' Madeleine said. 'That is what they told us, at the finish.'

'I'm afraid, Maddy,' Olivia said. She had not known she was going to say it until it was said and it was not Maddy she was afraid of and she knew it was true. Something was wrong and her dad was not around and she was frightened. She began to cry.

'Hush,' Madeleine said. 'You must try to be brave, Livs. Your father is coming back and he might be in time.'

Outside their makeshift den, she could hear gleeful cries as they crashed through the glade. She turned her head to the noise. They had discovered her. They had found the trail of bruised and trampled undergrowth that must lead to this spot, left by her boots as she followed her imaginary friend.

She turned back again, but Madeleine had gone and she was alone now and felt it, felt alone and isolated and not a part of a game at all but prey, coldly pursued, hunted down like a timid woodland creature by hunters with only hunger and murder in their hearts.

Chapter Thirteen

Jack Greer was worried about his mum. She did not look happy to him at all. He thought that her distracted mood might have to do with his dad and what had happened in America. His dad had been working on that bloody game for ever. Jack had played a few prototype levels and thought it probably in his top three games of all time in terms of excitement and difficulty and the way the hours flew by when you were involved in it.

But the grown-up world was a ruthless place and his experience of football had taught him that his dad was not really a very ruthless man. Jack had played at the elite level for as long as he could remember. All his coaches had tried to instil in him the winning mentality. To a man they had been winners and they had possessed an edge he had never been aware of in his dad. He feared his dad might have been humiliated or given the run-around or just the bum's rush in the States and his mum had got word of it. He hoped he was wrong.

Being a winner wasn't everything. Robert O'Brien had been a winner and he had been a tosser too, messing about with a married woman, reliant on drugs to stimulate his imagination so that he could keep on writing his stories. The was the rumour, anyway. Alec McCabe had been a winner. But he had deliberately turned his back on a life of competition because he thought other things were more important.

It did not matter in the slightest to Jack whether his dad

was a winner or not. He just wanted him to be happy. He wanted his mum to be happy too and she did not look it at the moment on the island, staring at the high, steep hill of driftwood they had constructed to burn as a bonfire later. They had draped it in fronds of kelp. Jack did not know why they had done this. Apparently it was a custom. He actually thought it was somewhat weird. It made the whole haphazard wooden construction look somehow alive. Perhaps it was just the way the kelp glistened and flapped in the breeze.

Jack dusted his hands together to get the sand off them and went over to his mum. He put an arm around her, surprised, as he always found himself these days, that he had reached her height and would soon be taller than she was even when she wore heels. He hugged and kissed her on the cheek and she smiled, returning his embrace.

'What's the matter, Mum?'

'I've remembered something, that's all. I've remembered something I should never have allowed myself to forget.'

'Are you going to tell me what it is?'

She looked past him, her eyes flicking this way and that, uneasy to Jack, now, as well as unhappy. This was worrying. For the first time, he had the hollow feeling in the pit of his stomach prompted by the realisation that they were among strangers and a long way from the place he had always thought of as home.

When his mum spoke, her voice was not much more than a whisper. 'When I made my mistake with Robert O'Brien, I resolved that I would never lie to my son, Jack. And I won't. But I don't know if this is something I should tell you because I don't yet really know what it means.'

'Just tell me, Mum. We'll worry afterwards about what it means.'

She gestured with a tilt of her head at the flapping, glistening hill of seaweed-draped wood that now towered above the beach. 'That thing brought it back. I remember painting it. I painted it among the other images that ended up illustrating that children's book your dad found in the hospital. That kelp and driftwood pyre brought it back to me.'

'They didn't use that one?'

'No. They did not. I'd assumed I'd done the illustrations from photographs. Evidently they were done from memory.'

'You mean you think you've been here before?'

She smiled. 'When I came here with your dad? When Uncle Mark looked after you?'

'Uncle Mark, the toxic avenger,' Jack said. But the joke did not put the smile he had expected it to on his mum's face.

'The first words Richard Penmarrick said to me were welcome home.'

'Jesus. Sorry, I mean heck.'

She looked at him. The look was serious. 'We had an illustration tutor at St Martin's that term, at the time I've isolated as the one when I must have completed that project. She was only there for the one term. She was very glamorous and always wore black clothes and red lipstick. I'd forgotten about her, too. Maybe I'd been encouraged in some way to forget. But I'm fairly sure now that she was Angela Heart.'

Jack could not reply to this remark. He would have done, but he saw that Richard Penmarrick was strolling along the beach towards them and Richard would have heard whatever Jack said and his instinct told him that would not be at all wise.

He had not worked out the implications of what his mum had just told him and did not know whether he was really capable of doing so. But it seemed ominous and wrong. It suggested the decision to go to Brodmaw Bay had not actually been theirs at all. They had not really chosen it. It was more as though it had chosen them. If that was the case, an awful lot of trouble had been gone to. You couldn't help but wonder why. He felt an urgent need just to do something positive and useful. He said, 'I'm going to find Olivia.'

Jack passed Richard Penmarrick with a curt nod and started to walk towards the centre of the island, but had covered only a few metres of sand when his sister emerged with a group of Mount year sevens from the bushes beyond. She looked much smaller than them, which she was. She was at the centre of the group, but to her brother looked separate and apart. It wasn't just that she didn't share the uniform. She was pale and apparently lost in her own thoughts, twisting a plait of grass between her fingers.

Livs did not look like she was having a very good time and it occurred to him that, actually, none of them was. He heard the band behind him strike up a tune, gathered near the edge of the water when he twisted and looked, facing it in a neat, three-tier formation, as though performing for the sea itself, which he thought bloody odd. Everything was odd, wasn't it? It wasn't even a question. It was a statement of fact.

He saw Megan Penmarrick over to his right, by the driftwood and seaweed monstrosity they had built, standing next to Ricky Sharp. They both had their arms folded across their chests and were openly staring at him with expressions that were neither friendly nor cheerful. He shrugged to himself and went and gave his sister a hug and she said, 'We're not locked on, Jack. We're just not. I think we really, really need our dad.'

He took Livs by the hand and led her back to where their mum stood. Richard Penmarrick was standing next to her, smiling, looking at the band, listening to the shrill music pouring forth from their shiny brass horns and clashing cymbals and the discordant triangle someone kept striking out of time with the rhythm of the rest.

Their mum said, 'In whose honour is the band performing?'

The smile did not leave Penmarrick's lips. He spoke through it. Jack thought that he looked very smug. He said, 'We honour the old gods.'

'You mean the Singers under the Sea.'

'If you know, Lillian, then why do you ask?'

'My husband researched the legend before we came here. I did not realise that the old religion was still practised.'

'This is a venerable part of the country. Our traditions go back even to ancient times and we value them.'

'Who are the Singers?'

'Spirits, evoked originally to protect us and help us prosper.'

'Have you ever seen one?'

He laughed at that. 'I don't think seeing the Singers a very practical ambition, my dear. I have heard them and that is quite enough.'

'You can see the Harbingers, though, can't you?' Olivia said. 'I've seen them myself.'

Penmarrick frowned. He rocked in his boots. 'You can,' he said, 'though it is not considered particularly desirable to do so. Seeing them does not bring good luck.'

'Do we need good luck, me and my family?' Lillian said.

He looked at her, she thought, frankly, for the first time since they had met. She suspected that the time for transparency had come. It was why she had posed the question. He glanced at her children, flanking her. He said, 'My dear, I think you need a miracle.'

Jack looked back to the glistening bonfire. There was an effigy now at its peak. The figure of a man in a grey suit and a clerical collar had been tied up there to a plank of wood protruding at a slight angle. The angle undermined the figure, giving it a slightly comical aspect. It was as though he leaned drunk and about to fall. The head above the white collar was a mockery of a person, made of a stuffed pillowcase with crudely painted features and its hair a bunched crop of greying straw.

James was finally picked up by a minicab outside the hospital at 3.30 p.m. He was back with his car in less than thirty minutes and it took him less than twenty minutes to change the wheel using the spare and the hand-jack from the Jaguar's boot. His tank was almost full, but he was gratified to see the four- gallon can of petrol he always kept there. He was good with mechanical things, precise and efficient. He found himself tightening the final wheel nut wishing everything in life was as straightforward and simply dealt with as machinery.

The traffic had increased in his absence from the road. It was always heavier as late afternoon stretched into evening. He crested the rise that brought the bay into sight at 6.30 p.m. There was still plenty of light. He braked sharply as he passed the stone circle on its plateau to his left only because he saw a small and ragged apparition there attired in purple and grey.

There was a reason she was there. She did not appear at random, did she? He switched off the engine and got out of the car. He could smell the salt of the sea so strongly it was almost like sluicing his throat and nostrils with brine. The scent of it assaulted him. He thought this probably the effect of the concussion. He felt febrile, vulnerable in the high, buffeting breeze. The grass seemed impossibly green under his feet when he gained the plateau and the looming stones screamed dumb questions about themselves to which time had forgotten the answer.

Little Madeleine Gleason was nowhere to be seen. She had vanished. He walked to the spot where he had sighted her, next to one of the stones. And he saw that the ground beneath its interior facet had been scuffed. He smiled at the smudge of disturbed earth. He did not think Madeleine possessed the weight on her feet to inflict it. He walked the circle, inside the stones but close to the perimeter, so that he could look at the base of each. All had been marked in the same curious, subtle manner.

He looked around. There was no one on the plateau with him. When he looked downwards to the village, there were no cars moving in the streets, no people visible. The bay was otherwise engaged. He got down on his knees before one of the disturbances and probed it with his fingers. He felt metal and pulled from the earth a key. It was brass and long-shafted with large, old-fashioned teeth.

He dug three times before successive stones and came up with a key at each. They had been ceremonially buried, he concluded, one before each of the stones in the circle. They were all identical. And he thought he knew what it was they would lock. He put all but one of them back. That, he put in his pocket. Silently, he thanked the dead girl for detaining him. He did not think he would catch sight of her again. She had done what she could.

He thought he knew now why she had killed Robert O'Brien. It had been to stop him hampering their move to the bay. Lillian had described him as a spoiled and immature man and he had not given up willingly on his romantic ambition. Saving the Greers had not been Madeleine's first consideration. The little girl's ghost had led them to what and to where she had because she wanted revenge.

James was minded to give it to her. He drove the car into a

copse of trees by the side of the descending road where he thought it would have a good chance of remaining concealed. He took the petrol can from its boot and put it on the ground beside him. For perhaps the twentieth time during the course of the day, he rang his wife's mobile number and for the twentieth time her mobile failed to ring. Wherever she was, she was out of range of a signal.

He looked down the hill, getting his bearings. He saw that he could approach the place he wanted to, concealed for most of the route by a dry-stone wall. He would have to crouch, but that was all right. When he got closer to his destination, the building itself would conceal him. He would get to the rear of it without its vigilant sentinel seeing him from her cottage window.

The church looked no more inviting from the back than it had from the front. He ducked under the broken door into the gloom within, unscrewing the cap from his petrol can, and began to slosh the contents over the sacks slumped against the pews. He glanced at the tabernacle, wondering what fresh abomination lay inside. He had the feeling that the desecration here was a frequent duty industriously and enthusiastically accomplished.

One of the sacks rippled. James only caught the movement out of the corner of his right eye and the eye was still bloodshot and slightly blurred from the blow to his temple in the crash. He did not imagine it, though. The things kept in the sacks, the stored and sleeping Harbingers, were stirring under the assault of the accelerant he had soaked them with.

There was another ripple and a mewling sound and one of the sacks fell from its pew as the thing confined inside it sensed the danger and struggled to unfold its limbs and escape. But the sacks were tightly sewn, weren't they? The Harbingers, whatever their function in the rituals here, were not allowed to roam free. This blasphemous congregation left the church only on special occasions. That was his intuition. Angela Heart had been telling the truth. This was a dangerous place. More than the decrepit state of the building fabric made it so.

As if to prove the point, a mandible, something more like the sectioned limb of an insect than a human finger, pushed through the thick burlap confining its owner and scrabbled about, seeking greater purchase. James walked backwards away from the spreading puddle of fuel under his feet and took out the book of matches he had bought at the newsagent's concession back at the hospital.

'No.'

'Angela,' he said, without turning. 'You're just in time.' He struck a match, used it to ignite the tips of the rest of them and, as the book flared intensely into orange and yellow life, dropped it on to the church floor.

He walked out of the church, ducking carefully under the canted door in its arch, already able to feel the blossoming heat from the fire he had set in the nave, aware of the screeching sounds coming from the burning sacks as the things within them rattled and perished.

It would sober them, this act of destruction, he thought. It would rob them of their power to menace. It would show the people of the bay that they were not invulnerable to harm. The conflagration would alert the county fire brigade. He would tell Penmarrick that the police were already on their way. Then he would flee with his family back to London and safety and forget about the insanity that reigned in this blighted place.

Ben Tamworth and Martin Sharp were standing in the churchyard. He could hear heat shatter diamonds of stained glass in the windows behind where he stood. There was a taste of burning, bitter and loathsome in the throat. He was obliged to spit on the ground. Angela Heart brushed past him, their shoulders touching, and he smelled smoke on her clothing mingled with the sweet, expensive perfume on her skin. The concussion had really heightened his senses.

Another man, more flamboyant, older, was walking down the path from the gate towards Tamworth and Sharp. It was the scholar, Michael Carney. James thought, giddily, that he had something in his jacket pocket Carney would probably find very interesting to read. Then an intuition told him that Carney knew it all already, that none of it would be a revelation to him. He helped sustain the convenient fiction that the Gleason women had died years later than they had, as victims of the Spanish flu.

Angela Heart leaned forward and whispered something to Ben Tamworth. He separated himself from the group and approached James.

'Nasty blow you've taken to the head.'

'Not quite as nasty as it could have been.'

'You were lucky.'

'You think so?'

'You can come with us voluntarily, under your own steam, Mr Greer. Or I can drag you. I really don't give a fuck either way.'

He walked. They walked together. They were a cluster of people out for a stroll, he thought, unless you looked closely. Do that and you would see the scorch marks on his own clothing and notice that Angela Heart's disdainful features were slightly blackened by soot and that there was blood seeping from under a dressing on the side of his own head and that the faces of Sharp and Tamworth, flanking him, contained a dark sort of fury.

People passed them, going the other way. It seemed that the whole village was climbing out of the bay up towards the hills. They straggled in ones and twos and bigger groups, in packs and snaking single-file but all going more or less in the same direction. James thought that they were headed for the plateau and its stone circle. He saw that few if any of them spared a glance for the blazing church. The pillar of smoke would be seen for miles. And people elsewhere would take it for a farmer clearing a field of its hedgerows or simply burning deadfall.

None of the people passing him engaged him with their eyes. Even those who passed quite close did not look directly at him. They gazed upwards. Mostly their expressions were neutral. He saw something akin to rapture, though, on the faces of a few. He looked for his wife and his children, of course. But he did so in vain. They were nowhere to be seen on his short route through the streets.

They rounded a corner and he was confronted by two lines of masked pallbearers carrying a sort of throne on their shoulders. The masks worn by the men were carved from wood and studded with shells. The shells erupted from the flat surface of the masks in whorls and swellings like the protrusions of some disfiguring nautical disease.

Richard Penmarrick slouched on the throne. He wore rings on his fingers and a crab-shaped pendant cast in bronze around his neck. He was dressed in a priestly cassock of black and some white substance daubed on his face gave him the pallor of death. He grinned. His teeth were large and yellow in his head against his painted complexion.

'The children have had a lovely time of it today,' he said. 'But it is time to put childish things away, Mr Greer. The party is very much over, now. The ceremony begins. We experience a grave and serious moment.' The bearers gripped the rails of their burden and shuffled past James and his party, on up the hill to the stones.

They took him to the Leeward Tavern. When they got him inside Ben Tamworth clubbed him without warning on the injured side of his head with the heel of his right palm before they tied him to a straight-backed chair. His temple had started to bleed fairly freely again under its sodden dressing but he did not feel likely to lose consciousness when Tamworth hit him and neither did the impact make him feel sick. He was better, he thought. He was on the mend. He had a fighting chance.

It was only a few minutes later, after they had left him, that he was overwhelmed by a feeling of hopelessness. He had spent too long groping amid the standing stones and too long subsequently creeping down to the church intent on remaining unseen. He had assumed the church central to whatever they did because Angela Heart had guarded it so alertly. He had been taken in by his own reaction to Lily's sinister representation of it in the book. He had made a misjudgement. It had cost him time. It was now after eight o'clock. And his failed strategy had cost him his liberty too.

They had put him in the saloon. He had a view through the picture window of the sea with the descending sun above it in a sky filling from the horizon up with tumbling mountains of cumulus cloud. They were colossal, dizzying even at this distance in their scale.

'There's going to be a storm,' a voice from behind him

said. He recognised it. It was the first voice James had ever heard in the bay and it belonged to Charlie Abraham.

'All the people up at the plateau are going to get soaked.'

'Very likely, but they'd consider that a tolerable state of affairs.'

'Where are my wife and children?'

Behind him, he heard Abraham lift the bar partition and squeeze himself something potent into a glass from one of the optics. 'I think you know where they are.'

'And is that a tolerable state of affairs?'

But Charlie Abraham chose not to answer him.

James had remembered something. He had remembered what Adam Gleason had written in his last testament about the Abraham who must have been Charlie's great-grandfather, if James had got his chronology right.

The landlord of the Leeward in those days had been unenthusiastic about the bay's grisly rituals. James thought that antipathy might be generational. If it was, it was something he could work on. There was nothing else he could work on. The bonds tying him had been too tightly secured. Perhaps Abraham had been left here guarding him because he wasn't one of those who climbed to the plateau rapturous. He wouldn't be too disappointed to miss their gathering amid the stones. He might, like his ancestor, be a reluctant believer. It was just possible he might actually not believe at all.

Someone breezed into the bar. There was no other word for it. They opened the door and the breeze followed them and James, with his heightened senses, smelled on it the metallic, electric smell of the storm swelling the sky, with cloud becoming bruise-coloured now in his view out over the sea.

It was Megan Penmarrick. Well, he thought, the pub was child-friendly, as had been so warmly demonstrated to them on the evening of their welcoming party. The Leeward was a place that catered to the whole community. Nobody was excluded. She walked around and in front of where he sat, partially silhouetted by the violent colour of the sky behind her, still beautiful and poised, with her arms folded across her chest and her slender weight rested on one hip.

'I want you to know something,' she said.

To Charlie Abraham, James said, 'How can a child be complicit in this?'

Abraham did not reply.

James heard again the squeak of pressure against the optic spring as a glass was pushed up beneath it. 'Easy on the anaesthetic, Charlie,' he said.

Megan Penmarrick approached him and unfolded her arms and slapped him surprisingly hard across the face. 'Listen to me,' she said.

James was too shocked to reply.

'I'll be a worthy successor to your wife. Lillian Greer inspired me and I'm grateful. I will always be grateful. But I know that I am worthy. I will shine as she did. My father says I will eclipse her.'

'What does your mother say, Megan?'

'My mother tends to say what my father tells her to.'

'I see.'

'You don't. You never would have.'

'Your choice of tense seems ominous, Megan.'

'I don't understand what you mean. I will always be grateful for Lillian Greer's inspiration. That's all. I'm sorry I hit you.'

Megan left. Abraham drank. James watched the gathering storm and listened to him do it, biding what very little time he thought he still possessed to save the lives of his family. 'When does the tide turn?'

'In another twenty minutes. How much do you know?'

'I know that the girl who just slapped me and my wife are half sisters.'

'You chose not to tell her that.'

James laughed despite himself. 'She's eleven years old for Christ's sake, Charlie. If she's corrupt, it's only because she's been corrupted.'

'Very Christian of you to see it that way,' Abraham said. 'But Christ does not have a great deal to do with what goes on in the bay.'

Outside, the first flash of lightning forked from the sky into the sea, followed a few seconds later by a hollow boom of thunder.

'It's a question of belief,' Abraham said.

'No, it isn't. It's a question of morality. I believe that what goes on here is corrupt. I suspect you believe that too.'

'It works.'

'But is it worth the price, Charlie?'

Abraham did not answer him.

'I burned those things in the church, Charlie.'

'I heard.'

'Why were they kept there?'

Abraham was silent. Outside, the rain had started to fall. It was heavy in a downpour that sounded already relentless. 'There are too many of them,' he said. 'They're predatory, Mr Greer, in the sexual sense. They can't be culled. It would anger the Singers. They can be subdued, like hooding a hawk. They're largely content to rest like that.'

'Angela was their jailer.'

'A sacred duty, Penmarrick would say. Though there was the odd escape.'

'Then I've done you all a favour.' Had there been just a

hint of sarcasm in that reference to Angela's sacred duty? James thought there had.

'You'd never make it to the rocks, you know, not on the full tide. The current is too strong and the water will be too rough. You'd drown.'

'I'd try.'

'Byron tried it once. At full tide it's better than a thousand yards to the boulders and back.'

'Did he make it?'

'No.'

'He did not have the incentive I would.'

Byron had been a very strong swimmer. He had famously swum the Hellespont. He had written a poem about it. James thought that Charlie Abraham would be familiar with the verses.

'You'd drown, Mr Greer.'

'I'd take the chance.'

Behind him, the optic squeaked. Out of the window, the sky was darkening. The sea was almost black under odd, staccato lightning strikes. They lit the turmoil of the storm in brief flashes.

'I read something Adam Gleason wrote after coming back here and finding his family had gone. He mourned his daughter very bitterly, Charlie Abraham.'

'She was a sweet child. She was altogether delightful.'

'You sound as though you knew her.'

Silence from behind him in the bar.

'Her father went back to the front and killed himself. He invited the bullet. He wrote that if that ruse didn't work, he would supply the bullet himself. He was as good as his final word on the subject.'

Silence.

James cleared his throat. He could not maintain his composure for much longer, he knew. He would rant and weep and squirm in the futile effort to free himself and attempt to save his family. He would curse his captor through grinding teeth as his mind skittered and panicked and betrayed him. He said, 'My children too are sweet and delightful, Charlie.'

Booted feet thumped across the floor. Abraham's breath was an open whisky cask. Its odour made James's bloodshot eye smart as the landlord bent over him and cut through the rope binding him with the blade of a pocket knife. 'I'm killing you, doing this,' he said.

James stood. His limbs were stiff. The sprint along the sea wall to the east shore would leave him supple enough. He looked the landlord in the face. 'Then why are you doing it?'

'I'm trying to save my soul, God help me,' Abraham said.

James was out, through the battening door, into the venting fury of the night, soaked before he'd taken half a dozen steps, the sea to his right lit like a panoramic photograph each time the lightning struck, the thunder booming so colossally above it made the teeth vibrate in his aching head.

He could see nothing when he got to the east shore. He could not see the boulders to which his loved ones had been chained. The churning swell was too high and he thought them submerged and drowned and lost to him already but he still had to try. The wind was a gale, a persistent roar in the beating deluge. The sea was alive with writhing peaks of white spume. He had no plan beyond the key to their shackles in the pocket of his jeans. He stripped to the waist and kicked off his shoes and went into the water.

He heard the singing straight away. It was as real to him as the cold and the salt as he struggled first to find and then impose some rhythm with his strokes. He was a strong swimmer. He had swum all his life and had no fear of the void deepening under him as he kicked away from the shore. The singing was an ardent, angelic chorus, vibrant and so painful to listen to he thought his ears might bleed at the shrill loudness of it.

He had to ignore the sound. He had to ignore the way the water seemed to pluck at him from beneath. When he looked up he could see the humpback boulders glimmering under lightning in the distance. They seemed very far away from him. He could not allow himself to think about what his wife and children, manacled there, were suffering. He simply had to reach them. It meant executing each measured stroke. He had to swim deliberately. If he clawed his way through the water, he would get there exhausted and would be too weak to help them.

He reached Olivia first. She was draped over her rock with the waves lapping at her pale head. They had clothed her in some sort of costume. It was black and voluminous and coarsely sewn and, of course, soaking wet. James unbuttoned and removed it. He did not want to swim against the weight of any handicap and was furious at the indignity they had done to her.

She was secured to the rock by a single manacle on her right wrist. It was very hard for James not to lift his head and check on the condition of the other two. He had to steel himself not to do it. There was no order to it, no favour; but he could only free them and get them out of the water one at a time. Even if his wife and son were conscious, they would be too weakened and numbed by exposure to get back to the shore without help. They were not strong enough swimmers.

Olivia felt insubstantial in his arms. He feared that she

was probably dead. Hope fought in him with the cold facts of her icy skin and unconsciousness as he kicked strongly back towards the shore. When he staggered to his feet, his daughter in his arms and the shingle under his soles, Abraham was there, waist deep in the surf, a rope around his middle anchoring him to the beach.

He took the child. No words were spoken between the men. None was necessary. James turned and went back into the water.

He went for Jack, next. He did not want to dwell on the reason for the choice. He was entitled to the love he felt for his son. He was intent on saving them all. Lillian would be the more buoyant burden than his tall and sinewy boy. He should ration his strength. If he went for Jack last, he might not possess by then the stamina to get both or either of them back. That was the logic supporting his choice, if not the truth of why he made it. He did not have the time or energy to argue with himself.

The singing seemed louder. The water had the density of some gravid element. Struggling through it inflicted a sort of torpor on his limbs. He held Jack's precious head on his chest between his hands and kicked with his own strong legs and babbled beseeching prayers between gasping the huge breaths of air sustaining him. Above them, the sky roiled and was shaken by lightning flashes. James kicked and swam and prayed.

Abraham had put a coat over Olivia, pulled up to a spot beyond the reach of the waves. He took Jack in his burly arms as though the boy weighed nothing. 'I'd go myself,' he said, shouted. 'I can't swim.'

James nodded. He was beyond words.

'Your ears are bleeding,' Abraham said. 'I fear your girl has gone, Mr Greer.'

He swam for his wife, weeping for his daughter. He swam with the crazed strength of a man defying fate. He reached Lillian entirely spent and strangely energised. What little thought he was capable of suggested to him dimly that this was what it might be like to be possessed.

Lillian's head was beneath the water and he knew that she was dead. But he was not ready to surrender her to the sea. He would get her back to land. She would be buried, dry, in a box fashioned for the purpose. He released her limp hand from the killing restriction of its manacle. He hugged his wife to him on the boulder's top as the waves heaved around them. Lightning bolted across the sky in a ragged infliction of brightness and the water, bathed in it, became for a shutter flash of time, translucent.

He saw them, then. He saw on the seabed the ragged maws of the Singers under the Sea, mouthing their ancient song, hungry for sacrifice.

Holding his wife tenderly, his arms under hers, hands linked for what he knew would be the last time across her chest, James kicked with strengthless legs back for the shore. The water seemed calmer. He thought the storm might be abating. Lillian felt cold and soft-skinned in his embrace and her hair washed loosely against his face, sticking and then freed in a teasing, intimate rhythm as they bobbed together shoreward.

Jack lay on his back on the beach. His breathing was very shallow, inaudible against the crash of the surf and the wind's persistent howl. But his chest was moving. He was alive. Abraham, who had gone, had put a blanket over him before departing. He had left his coat too. It draped Olivia. It covered her face.

James laid Lillian on the pebbles beside her daughter. Jack jerked up abruptly from the waist and brine spewed out of him and he coughed and retched and said, 'You left Mum till last, Dad. You left her till last because of what she did to you and she's dead because of it. You could have saved her. You could.' A sob heaved out of him.

James looked at his wife and daughter lying dead together on the shore. He turned back to his son and staggered over the pebbles to where he sat and knelt before him. 'It isn't true, Jack,' he said. He shook. The grief shuddered through him and he moaned with the pain his heart cradled and could not endure his loss. He could not endure it.

Jack raised his arms and wrapped his father in an embrace and they hugged one another in the wind and fret from the sea. 'Look,' Jack said.

James turned his head. Lillian and Olivia, their limbs limp and their faces slack in death, were moving. They were jerking and sliding like marionettes strung from invisible strings towards the sea. There was a crunch on the shingle and James looked up and saw that Abraham was there, had returned. There was a rope between his hands. James saw that it was still attached higher up the shore to the pulley contraption that had delivered them the baskets of fresh bread at the feast of a fortnight earlier.

'We'll have to tie them,' Abraham said. 'The sea still wants them, Mr Greer. Help me secure your loved ones. If we do not moor them firmly, they will be taken.'

The bodies of Lillian and Olivia were slithering and writhing, jerked seaward incrementally over the pebbles, in this last indignity inflicted upon them. James got numbly to his feet and did as the bay's publican had asked him to. For Lillian and Olivia, their ordeal was not at an end. Death had not concluded it.

The struggle would continue until day came, James resolved.

The sacrifice would remain incomplete, whatever else he felt, whatever sorrow he endured, he was determined about that. The Singers under the Sea would hunger. Their appetite would not be satisfied by dawn. Then they would exact their retribution on those with whom their ancient bargain had been struck. Madeleine Gleason would have her vengeance.

When the knots were tight and the rope taut James stood at Abraham's side and turned back to look at his son. Jack sat with the sodden blanket he'd been given wrapped around his slight frame, wide-eyed and shivering. He had surrendered to the refuge of shock and his father felt grateful for that. His mind had put Jack beyond seeing what he could not make sense of and feeling what he could not tolerate. The respite would help. It would not heal him. It was natural though. It was a beginning.

'Why did you help us?'

'I knew them,' Abraham said. 'I knew Adam Gleason and his family. I endured the self-loathing of that hypocritical day we held the memorial tribute to our soldier hero who would not return. What was done to that family was a terrible wrong and I've lived with it on my conscience since.'

'You've had a long life.'

'Too long,' Abraham said. He looked out over the water. 'I'm reconciled to paying what it will cost.' He smiled and raised a hand and squeezed James's shoulder. 'I'm sorrier than I can say, Mr Greer, for your loss.' He turned and walked away.

Epilogue

The bay did not prosper in the aftermath of that night. A number of its leading citizens were lost, believed drowned, only the following day, when the boat they had chartered to take them to a small island for some folkloric celebration foundered in fog. After that the community, what was left of it, seemed to lose its spirit and impetus. Within a few years the population had halved. The fishing fleet had dwindled to three or four boats as fish stocks inexplicably decreased.

What happened was a familiar story of rural economic decline. Too remote for tourism, once its principal resource was exhausted the village could not sustain the size to which it had grown in prosperous times. It shrank and dwindled. It could no longer boast a butcher, a baker or a candlestick maker. Almost nobody lives there now.

James Greer sold the house in Bermondsey. He moved eventually to a flat in Camden Town. He says that he enjoys the cosmopolitan flavour of the area. He finds its frenetic bustle a comfort in what had become, considering his recent personal history, a fairly solitary life compared to the one he once enjoyed.

He does not see a great deal of his son. They remain close emotionally. Perhaps the problem is that they are too close. When they meet, they are reminded, inevitably, of those they loved and cherished and lost. Jack no longer believes his mother was left deliberately to be the last to be saved by his father. Or more accurately, he no longer believes it consciously. He had some counselling sessions with a Harley Street psychiatrist called Eleanor Deacon. They were a help to him. He even developed a bit of a crush on Dr Deacon in the end.

He plays as a professional footballer now. He has a very successful career. He plays for Liverpool, instrumental in the club's recent renaissance. He has earned wealth and success and a deserved measure of fame. He never really doubted that he would make the grade. He had trials at Chelsea. And they signed him. But childhood dreams can sometimes perish and his did, farmed out to other clubs for loan spells that frustrated him.

Liverpool brought Jack Greer as cover when their first team centre backs were both injured. His performances were so consistently strong that he had become a regular first-choice player by the end of his first full season with the club. He has trained with the international squad. He is only eighteen but maturing quickly and there are those who speculate already in the press that one day he will captain his country.

Towards the end of that first Liverpool season he grabbed the winner against Chelsea at Stamford Bridge when he rose to meet a corner with a towering header in the final seconds of injury time. He thought it quite ironic that he should score that particular goal at that ground against the club he revered in his boyhood. But irony is something Jack Greer has had to learn to live with.

His father was not in the stand that day to see his son score. On his rare visits north to Anfield, despite feeling no greater fondness for the game than he ever did, James does feel very proud when Jack makes a crucial tackle, or brings the ball out of defence in a counter-attack that has the home crowd chanting his name. The fans call him Jacky G. Football has its own language. James makes a point of always watching his son's performances when Liverpool games feature on the television.

Jack sees quite a lot of Detective Inspector Alec McCabe. McCabe was faced with redundancy or transfer as a consequence of Metropolitan Police budget cuts and opted for the latter. He relocated with his family to Merseyside after applying for and getting a transfer-cum-promotion and he meets Jack for lunch or dinner more or less weekly. These occasions are very important to Jack. McCabe says that his colleagues on the Liverpool force are inclined to rib him about what they call his cockney accent. He has to tolerate their legendary Merseyside wit, he says, daily. He's happy there.

Jack has never told McCabe about the night his mother and sister died and the policeman is far too tactful and intuitive to ask. There are just the two secrets kept between these friends. The other concerns his own lovely daughter's ardour for her Anfield hero.

McCabe has resolved one day to tell Jack about that, because having seen them in conversation at one of his family barbecues, he suspects the feeling might be mutual. He is jealous of his daughter's virtue. But he thinks they might in the future make a really good and happy couple. He does not honestly think he could have anyone finer for a son-in-law.

James Greer spends a lot of time walking or just sitting on benches on Hampstead Heath. He has developed a reputation for eccentricity. No one would go so far as to call him mad. He is far too rich to be derided as a madman.

He sacked Lee Marsden. He represented himself when he courted potential backers. He raised boutique finance to fund the development and marketing of the computer game he created. The interest on his loans averaged out at almost

40 per cent. He took a real chance in doing it and it could have been ruinous. But work was the only successful way to distract him from the grief he thought might consume him otherwise. He needed to survive in those first months following the tragedy for the sake of his son. And his industry proved to be very profitable.

An adaptation of the game is used in schools in Europe and the United States as a history teaching aid. In the Far East and in China, it has been customised to help businessmen learn the English language in a relatively painless way. The adult consumer version, a huge hit with gamers globally, inspired a film franchise still going strong at the box office after the fifth movie in the series.

There is a reason for his eccentric reputation. It is that James can often be seen on the Heath, talking animatedly in broad daylight to someone who isn't there. Quite often he laughs at something no one but he can hear said and most of the time he is smiling. He is very successful in business. He gives a lot of his money to good causes. Anyone with a heart would surely forgive him the indulgence of the person he refers to, when he refers to her at all, simply as his imaginary friend.

Do you wish this wasn't the end?

Join us at www.hodder.co.uk, or follow us on Twitter @hodderbooks to be a part of our community of people who love the very best in books and reading.

Whether you want to discover more about a book or an author, watch trailers and interviews, have the chance to win early limited editions, or simply browse our expert readers' selection of the very best books, we think you'll find what you're looking for.

And if you don't,
that's the place to tell us what's missing.

We love what we do, and we'd love you to be part of it.

www.hodder.co.uk

@hodderbooks

HodderBooks

HodderBooks